"A must-read for every stuc
their vocation. It should be
schoolteacher, for the Texas l.   ..., ... psychologist.
Finally, for the tender of heart, it is a dreamer's sad love story that
truly ends like love, without an ending."

S. Elton Hamill, Jr. P.E.
Retired Professional Engineer
Texas Department of Transportation

"Carol Vinzant has written a beautiful and candid story of her
grandmother. It is a book that carries you into the early 1900s that
you cannot put down until you have read the last page!"

Nancy Stansberry, Vice Chair, The GTD Group

"Carol tells her grandmother's history in an intimate and entertaining
way. She is good at tying it all together with historical events
happening in the world."

Phyllis McConnell
English Teacher

"After reading Carol's book, for the first time in my life I felt like I
had been present for the birth of a baby."

Dr. James Crowder
Historian
Tinker Air Force Base, OKC

"The extreme poverty of the Depression Years came home to me
as never before while reading Carol's book. Also, I loved the word
pictures of the bluebonnet hills and the romance of the Texas hill
country, for I am Texan!"

Carolyn Mickey
English Teacher
Abilene, Texas

"This book gives me a feeling for the events of that time period. I like the fact that these people are real, and one even became well known in Texas. And he goes from a buckboard wagon to an airplane!"

James McConnell
U.S. Postal System
Edmond, Oklahoma

"I found Carol's book to be authentic, humorous, spiritual, and insightful into this period of Texas history."

Jane Norton.
College language teacher
Searcy, Arkansas

MEET ME IN
THE GLOAMING

MEET ME IN
THE GLOAMING

Out of the twilight of the Great Depression dawns
an unforgettable story of love

CAROL MITCHELL VINZANT

TATE PUBLISHING & *Enterprises*

Published by Tate Publishing & Enterprises, LLC
127 E. Trade Center Terrace | Mustang, Oklahoma 73064 USA
1.888.361.9473 | www.tatepublishing.com

Tate Publishing is committed to excellence in the publishing industry. The company reflects the philosophy established by the founders, based on Psalm 68:11,
"The Lord gave the word and great was the company of those who published it."

Book design copyright © 2009 by Tate Publishing, LLC. All rights reserved.
Cover design by Jonathan Lindsey
Interior design by Stephanie Woloszyn

Published in the United States of America

ISBN: 978-1-60696-974-8
1. Fiction / Christian / Romance
2. Fiction / Romance / Historical
08.11.21

DEDICATION

First and foremost, I dedicate this book to my grandmother Clementine Wilmeth Briley, who told her own story to her diary every night for most of her adult life; secondly, to my grandfather John Robert Briley, whom I loved deeply; thirdly, to the two daughters of this union, my mother, Ruth Briley Mitchell, and my aunt Grace Briley Belich; and last but not least, to my husband, Don Eugene Vinzant, who has lovingly supported and encouraged me in every way, including taking his shirts out and bringing dinner in, creating time for me to complete this project.

ACKNOWLEDGMENT

I want to thank many people who took a sincere interest in this book and improved it greatly.

Many donated countless hours to reading the manuscript and suggesting improvements.

My editors, Carol Hartzog, Tamie Ross, and Barbara Campbell

My aunt Grace Belich, who let me keep the diaries for many years

My cousin Martha Carroll, our family historian and graphic artist

My cousins Lucille McClung, Opal Cawyer, Beth Everett, John Belich, and Bill and Charlotte Belich

My niece Brenda Stephens

My siblings, Marilyn Sheffield, Dr. Robert Mitchell, Jill Faulkner, and Jan Terrell

My children, Caroline John, Gene, Danny, and Larry Vinzant, who even supplied me with personality traits

My friends, Dr. Ron Durham, Carolyn Mickey, Elwyn Partin, and many others

My publisher, Tate Publishing Enterprises, including Janey Hays, Rachael Sweeden, and Kylie Lyons, Associate Executive Editor, Extraordinaire

My husband, Dr. Don Vinzant, my main man

"IN THE GLOAMING"

by Meta Orred
Annie F. Harrison
1877

In the gloaming, oh, my darling!
When the lights are dim and low,
And the quiet shadows falling,
Softly come and softly go.

When the winds are sobbing faintly
With a gentle unknown woe,
Will you think of me and love me,
As you did once long ago?

In the gloaming, oh, my darling!
Think not bitterly of me!
Though I passed away in silence,
Left you lonely, set you free.

For my heart was crushed with longing,
What had been could never be;
It was best to leave you thus, dear,
Best for you and best for me.

*In the gloaming, oh, my darling!
When the night meets gold of day,
And they say God shows His face, Love,
Walks with us in cool of day.

Through the winter hard and cruel,
We were beaten down and blue,
In the morning when the doves coo,
We'll find love when spring breaks through.

(*Last two stanzas written by the author)

TABLE OF CONTENTS

PART ONE

PART TWO

PART THREE

FOREWORD

My wife, Carol Mitchell Vinzant, has had a deep yearning for six decades to make her grandmother's life story rise out of the yellowed pages of diaries and become known to a wide audience. Her grandmother Clementine was a lovely lady with a heart full of dreams and idealism and a will of iron. She longed to help others and to glorify God. She longed to see her West Texas prosper economically and educationally.

The book lays Clemmie's dreams and aspirations against the centerpiece of the Great Depression and the cruel toll it took on good people: people who loved God and each other, but found themselves on an impossibly unequal playing field. Yet, Clemmie never gave up.

Do not pity Clemmie, but rather let your heart beat with hers as you enter her world of a hundred years ago. Carol brings the sixty-two diaries to life. We see Clemmie dream and plan for a better life with her dear husband. John was her mate, God her Resource, her diary her best friend, and Carol her champion.

This is a typical farm couple's struggle against the hardscrabble circumstances of Texas's rural folk, as well as poor city dwellers in Dallas from 1909–1937. This is poor folks' history at its truest. It is an authentic chronicle recast as a thrilling, heartwarming novel. Carol's masterpiece, *Meet Me in the Gloaming*, defines the genre of historical novel of the first third of the twentieth century in the U.S. Southwest. This story culminates in the Texas Centennial Year of 1936, the year Carol and I were born.

Don E. Vinzant

INTRODUCTION

Meet Me in the Gloaming begins exactly one hundred years ago with Clemmie Wilmeth writing in her diary every night. A single teacher in an obscure place in Texas, she dreams of changing the world. She wants to marry her childhood sweetheart, an educated, somewhat driven man who shares her ideals. She envisions them building a fine home on the farmland she adores, hosting people from all over the world. She wants to publish a great book that will inspire generations to come. Her confidante is her "Big Hill," and her best friend is her diary.

Then reality sets in.

Her sweetheart marries a younger woman in 1909, the year the book begins. Clemmie later marries a childhood friend—handsome, but uneducated and poor, previously married and divorced. The marriage suffers with the economy in the twenties. John's inability to hold a job and his fear of loss of love make him an unlikely companion for Clemmie. She is an idealist in pursuit of intellectual excellence, a dreamer with a tendency toward self-pity and depression when life doesn't go as planned.

This romance is based solidly on facts, with historical references and other perspective added by the author. It carries within its pages the hope of helping readers see themselves in the common disputes of married life. Hopefully, you'll feel like you've stepped into a time machine and feel yourself living in their world of one hundred years ago. Clemmie and John Briley, unable to get along with each other, resolve to rekindle that first love when all of life was happy and carefree.

Clemmie was my maternal grandmother, and I thought I knew her well until I read her diaries and discovered a girl with altruistic dreams and a will of iron. I feel that I was able to get inside her head and to understand her heart.

I am Carol Mitchell Vinzant, the daughter of Ruth in this story. All my life I wanted to get Clemmie's diaries into a book and make them come to life again. Finally, through the grace of God, the book will get out to you, and I pray it will lift you above the cares and troubles of your life. May you know the love of God and the great sacrifice of His Son and understand that this life is only a vapor that appears and then vanishes, but we can live forever. And the very Spirit of God can reside in us and guide us.

Don and I met at Abilene Christian University in 1954, and this year we celebrated our Golden Anniversary of our college class. Don preaches in Edmond, Oklahoma. We have four grown children and even our grandchildren are grown, and our first great-grandchild is due in February of 2009! I think you will find similarities in my family and yours and know that your grandparents and great-grandparents walked these same pathways. After all, human nature, nature, and God's natural plan for our lives are the same yesterday, today, and forever. "In the world ye shall have tribulation, but be of good cheer; I have overcome the world," said Jesus in John 16:33.

PART ONE

IN THE GLOAMING

A rooster crowed, and Clemmie sat straight up in bed. The tiny room was pitch-dark, and the silence of the country was broken only by the far-off, sad howl of a coyote. The narrow Murphy bed was not comfortable, and Clemmie had slept on her stomach, which always made her back hurt. Suddenly, she remembered it was going to be the most important day of her life so far—the day she would see Raleigh Ely, the man of her dreams! A delicious feeling of sheer delight coursed through her body, and she jumped out of bed.

It was early Saturday morning in Ebony, Texas, April 17, 1909. Julia Clementine Wilmeth had come home from teaching school in Locker, Texas.

Clemmie had graduated with honors from Daniel Baker College in Brownwood, Texas, in 1903, obtaining a degree in English. She was twenty-eight, single, and loved teaching.

She was a small woman with gray-blue eyes and brown hair,

which she pulled up in a chignon with a stylish pompadour. She was attractive and intelligent, if not sensual, a dreamer more than a practitioner. She had a wonderful laugh that lit up her whole face. The man who was coming today had been her childhood playmate, and she dreamed of his declaration of his love for her.

As dawn's first light filled the small house, Clemmie folded up the bed. Her eyes scanned the floor, making sure there were no scorpions, for she *was* in the country.

The night before she had laid out her blue-checked gingham dress from the small trunk and pressed it with the heavy kerosene iron. She dressed very quietly and crossed the modest living room to the kitchen, only a few steps away.

As she turned the back doorknob, she prayed, "Please, Lord, don't let it squeak and wake up Mamma." The door made its persistent squeak as it swung on rusty hinges, but Mamma did not stir.

The beauty of the countryside in the early dawn never failed to awaken Clemmie's soul, usually inspiring her to utter a prayer of thankfulness to God. The sky was showing the pink and gold of the imminent sunrise. Clemmie knew it must be about six.

Back behind the house and sheltered by bushes was the old chair, the cane bottom worn out and removed, that the women used as a toilet. Carefully watching her step back to the house, she was acutely aware that the rattlesnakes were beginning to crawl. She jumped when something moved, then saw it was a harmless horned toad.

She returned to the house and dipped water from a crock to wash her hands, pouring it over an enameled pan. In the bread tin she found a biscuit left from last night's supper; she carefully buttered it and added a spoonful of molasses. She ate while standing, then quietly stepped out on the little porch and lifted a pitcher of last evening's milk from a cloth-covered trough filled with water. She poured herself a small glassful and drank it in two swallows.

Quickly brushing her teeth with a homemade twig brush and baking soda, Clemmie then put the kitchen back in perfect order, carefully replacing everything she had moved. Mamma was German and strict about housekeeping and protocol, so Clemmie had decided not to tell her about today's agenda. Not only would Mamma have disapproved, but she would have refused to let Clemmie leave the house.

Clemmie could not believe that she had the audacity to initiate a meeting with Raleigh. It made the color rise in her cheeks when she thought about how bold she had been. But she had waited a long time for *him* to take some action.

Nellie Murphree and Clemmie had roomed together during college in Brownwood, and Clemmie had confided to Nellie that she hoped to marry Raleigh one day. Then there was that weekend in 1902 when Raleigh came to visit Clemmie on the train. Nellie was very impressed with Raleigh and decided to encourage the rather lukewarm romance. She spent quite a bit of time making a scrapbook for Clemmie.

Being a writer herself, Nellie weaved together the facts of Clemmie's life with an imagined ardent courtship with Raleigh, culminating in a gorgeous garden wedding. The scrapbook was decorated with pictures cut from a popular magazine. Nellie proudly presented her creation to Clemmie for Christmas of 1902, and it had been Clemmie's most prized possession since. Clemmie believed that Raleigh really cared for her and that women were made to wait.

Finally, at age twenty-eight, Clemmie was tired of waiting. Nearly all her girlfriends and her cousins were married. Edna, Clemmie's sister, had eloped when she was only seventeen and had a little daughter who was four. Clemmie's brother, Jim, had married last summer, and Jim's wife, Callie, was in the family way. Clemmie was afraid she was going to end up a spinster, living with relatives the rest of her life.

So she had decided to take things into her own hands and set up a rendezvous with Raleigh. If she had not received the two postcards, one in February and one the first part of April, she would not have believed he desired a more serious relationship. But the cards were so romantic!

The first one had a picture of a river, and underneath the river, on a scroll, Raleigh had written: "The Silvery Colorado." Underneath that was a verse by Edgar Allen Poe.

Fair River! In thy bright, clear flow
Of crystal, wandering water,
Thou art an emblem of thy glory
Of beauty…the unhidden heart—
The playful maziness of art.

On the other side there was a personal note:

2/12/09

Dear Clemmie,

I saw this card and it brought back old memories of the river. Wish I could see you all. I think I shall come down this summer, sure. How are you and what are you doing?

Raleigh

The second card had arrived on April 9, only a week ago. It was even more romantic. Clemmie was thrilled the day she received it in Locker. It seemed to be a definite desire for the two of them to get together. On the front, there was a picture of Cupid, the symbol of love, and the caption read, "When shall we three meet again?"

4/6/09

Dear Clemmie,

I really and truly expect to see you this year if possible. And I want to see the old river, the hills, and everything so bad. It would be sweeter music to me than the grandest orchestra to hear the water running and purling over the shoals and draw another lesson from its tireless, ceaseless energy. Things will be changed, however—except you, my dear friend, and I feel that I can call you that forever.

Raleigh

Oh, he has the most wonderful way with words! And he really wants to see me! thought Clemmie. And so she wrote back immediately and set up a meeting. They would meet on Saturday, April 17, at nine a.m. on Big Hill. And that day was today!

The night before Clemmie had packed a cloth bag with a few items. She put in a small green coverlet to sit on, *Song of the River*, the book that Raleigh had given her, and the two postcards. Grabbing her little looking glass, Clemmie checked her face and decided to apply just a touch of the lip rouge she had bought in Brownwood last Christmas. Afraid she would look like a "painted woman," she wiped most of it off.

Quietly, she let herself out into the early-morning sun, pleased that neither her little sister, Grace, nor Mamma had awakened. Her papa, a preacher, was away for the night.

Clemmie knew she had plenty of time before Raleigh arrived from Baird. She wanted to be there early to think and have some time alone with God.

— — — — — — — —

Her mind traveled back to that first spring the family had arrived in Ebony. Her father, J.R. Wilmeth, had traded fifty acres of black land in Collin County for 1,500 acres in Mills County, sight unseen. The J.R. Wilmeth family packed all earthly belongings in their wagon and traveled over the dry, narrow roads through north central Texas until they finally found what would be their home.

Clemmie's mother, Clara, looked over her new land and later said there was no feeling of optimism in her bosom. The preceding years had brought the worst droughts in the history of Mills County. The land was rough and unsettled, and there were ruins of old chimneys. Mamma felt like the country had been too hard for those who had come before them. It looked like Papa had made a poor trade, but no one spoke those discouraging words aloud.

Papa found the closest schoolhouse and was soon preaching there on Sundays. He hauled lumber from Brownwood, twenty-five miles away, and hired a man to help him build a small box house for his family. Several years later, a second floor was added that served as a bedroom for the children.

Clemmie felt lonely in Ebony. She missed the big white house of her grandparents in McKinney and all the Wilmeth cousins she used to play with there. Besides that, Mills County was ugly compared to Collin County. But with the coming of spring in 1889, the quiet and pensive little girl was given two life-changing surprises. The drab, dry hills of Mills County turned royal blue with bluebonnets, and a family named Ely moved onto the Wilmeth land. Clemmie went with her papa to welcome the Elys and immediately befriended the youngest of the big family, Raleigh, who was two years older than Clemmie. And now, twenty years later, Clemmie had high hopes.

– – – – – – – – –

The sun was out in all its glory, and grasshoppers tried wildly to get out of her way. Clemmie brushed through the tall grass, trying to miss the rocks in her path. The climb was not hard, and her feet, in black-laced shoe-boots, were as sure-footed as a mountain goat's.

Reaching the top of the hill, Clemmie ran to the south side. There it was—the beautiful river. Clemmie's arms pricked in goose bumps as she looked down on the ambling, slightly muddy river.

"Oh, here are the very rocks where Raleigh and I sat that evening, and he explained to me about the *gloaming*. He said it was a Scottish word that means *twilight* in English, and that it is the time between sundown and dark. Some people in the old country said that God would come and walk with you in the gloaming, that you could almost see God's face.

"This is exactly the place to spread out the green coverlet, and maybe Raleigh will remember about the rocks and our conversation so long ago," Clemmie said aloud.

There were patches of bluebonnets, lots of grass burrs and rocks, and one live oak tree nearby. Choosing the best shade under the tree, Clemmie tossed open the blanket and let it float to the ground. Then she straightened it just perfectly and removed little twigs and rocks from underneath that made it puff up.

She sat down, spreading her blue-checked skirt in a circle around her. She brushed her bodice with her hand to be sure it was clean, with no strand of hair.

She lay down on her back and looked up through the live oak leaves. She traveled back in time, to that first spring after her family had arrived here. It was April of 1889, and she was eight years old. She sat with crossed legs, staring at eleven-year-old Raleigh, who was wearing overalls and a white shirt.

Clemmie saw potential in the skinny boy with dark hair and beautiful blue eyes. And now, so many years later, he was educated and had become a lawyer, the county attorney of Callahan County. She liked to think that she had a small part in his success. She remembered telling him that he could become something fine one day if he wanted to.

At that moment in her reverie, Clemmie heard the noisy, unfamiliar sound of an approaching automobile. A shiver ran up her spine, and her heart pounded. She jumped to her feet, straining to see Raleigh's head.

There he was, wearing his collegiate cap with the popular knickers and high boots and a white linen shirt.

He looks like a thousand dollars!

OH, MY DARLING

"Hello, girl! Have you been waiting long?"

"Hello, Raleigh! Not long at all. You're right on time!"

Clemmie squelched her desire to rush into his arms. He was taller and more handsome than she remembered. Her knees were weak, and she thought she might fall. Raleigh held out both hands, grabbed hers, and spun her around.

"Remember the games we used to play on this hill? I feel like I'm twelve years old again! And look at you, Miss Clementine Wilmeth. What a beautiful, stylish young lady, my Clemmie!" He put his arm around her small waist, and they walked to the edge of the hilltop.

"Clemmie, how many times have I seen this in my mind's eye? This view of the Colorado River, and you, my best friend and little sister!"

"Oh, Raleigh, this place is the happiest of all my childhood memories. Thank you so much for meeting me here today! I know you are busy, and I know the trip from Baird was hard."

"It wasn't so bad in the automobile. A friend of the family insisted that I drive his Oldsmobile Model S. I've heard that car costs over two thousand dollars! It made these terrible roads seem like they were glass, much faster than my buggy. Clemmie, it may not be too long until all families have a horseless carriage. I'd take you for a ride, but I'll need to start back to Brownwood by ten."

Clemmie could feel the perspiration under her arms. "I thought we might read a poem together...in memory of old times," she said. "Remember this book about the river that you gave me back in 1902 when you came to visit me at college in Brownwood? I've nearly worn it out, Raleigh, bringing it up here on Big Hill to read. And your picture—it was inside the book. These cards you sent me meant a lot."

"I can't believe you've kept that book so long, Clemmie. Yes, I remember that trip on the train to Brownwood, and how you looked as we met at the station."

The two settled down on the blanket, and Raleigh began to read in his melodious voice. Clemmie stole sideway glances at him and felt drawn to his lips. His mouth was well shaped, she thought, and he was clean-shaven. She tried to bring her mind back to the river poem, but she could think only of what she had dreamed about for a long time—from girlhood till now, at age twenty-eight—a loving embrace and one kiss.

Finishing the river poem, Raleigh slowly closed the book and commented on the soothing sound of the water as it tumbled over the rocks. They talked a little about their lives, hers in the classroom and his in the courtroom, and future plans. When he extracted a pocket watch from his vest, Clemmie knew he was nervous about the time.

"Clemmie, I can hardly stand to leave this beautiful spot and such wonderful company, but I have an appointment in the early afternoon in Brownwood." He uncrossed his long legs and stood up, helping lift Clemmie.

Pulling her close to his chest, Raleigh placed his hands on Clemmie's sides, his fingers spread on her ribcage. She could feel the warmth of his hands through her dress and his warm, sweet breath on her face. Gazing directly into her gray-blue eyes, he knew he needed to ask permission.

"May I?" inquired Raleigh.

Clemmie could not find her voice, but the slight motion of her head and the look from her expressive eyes gave him her answer. Turning his head slightly to the side, he pressed his mouth firmly on hers and slightly parted his lips. For Clemmie the whole world stood still, then began to spin. Something like liquid fire raced from below her stomach and seemed to circle out, encompassing and infiltrating her whole body, even her fingers and toes.

"Thank you, my dear." Raleigh broke her daze. "And thank you for inviting me here today. If the Lord's willing, it will not be too long until we meet again. Clemmie, if you won't be disappointed, I need to get into town. The ride will have to wait for another time. As I said before, it has been a beautiful morning."

"Raleigh, do write me soon. We can arrange an outing. Perhaps you can come to see me at Locker before school is out."

"That would be very pleasant indeed," Raleigh replied, already on his way down the hill. He was propelled by an anxiety of accomplishment, the curse of city men. He turned and looked up at Clemmie, shading his eyes from the sun with his cap pulled low.

"Could I walk you partway home, Clemmie?"

"No. I want to spend a little more time here before I go back to the house. Good-bye, Raleigh. I'll remember this always."

Clemmie lay prostrate, face buried in the green coverlet. She listened as Raleigh cranked the Oldsmobile and turned it around on the narrow trail. She kept listening until the last sounds of the motor faded and then let the extreme joy she felt flow out of her body and upward to her Father in heaven.

"Oh, God, Thou hast answered for me today my most precious dream, and I know Thou wilt give me this man to be mine. Father, although he's a Methodist, I believe he can be taught the Way more perfectly. He's going to make a fine living and such a wonderful husband and father of our children. Now I know why I haven't met anyone else who would love me, dear Lord. Thou planned this union all along. Thank you, my wonderful Father. I want to serve and love Thee all the days of my life. Father, help Mamma not to be too mad at me for being gone so long. Give her some kind of understanding. I'm offering this prayer in Jesus' name, amen."

The sun was scorching by now, and Clemmie caught her first whiff of dreaded body odor. She got up, folded the blanket, and replaced everything in the cloth bag. She replayed the entire time with Raleigh in her mind, recalling every word, gesture, and facial expression in sequence.

I feel convinced that Raleigh's friendship of all these years has been converted to true love, she thought. Then she extended her arms straight out and shouted aloud, "Oh, Hill, and oh, River, you two are witnesses of the love born here today...and may it last until this world comes to its final end and we rise to meet our Lord in the air!"

Clemmie's thoughts were consumed by their kiss. Her first real kiss, although she had had a few little pecks before, it was the outstanding sensual event of her life. Simply recalling that moment reproduced the same sensations—the pressure of his lips, his large hands gripping her upper body, their lower bodies slightly touching, the lingering of his lips, and the gradual opening of his mouth. Clemmie became light-headed and her knees trembled as she descended the hill.

As she approached the little house, her mother fairly screeched: "Where have you been, young lady? You are the one who invited all those people to come over here for dessert tonight, and not *one thing* has been done toward preparations."

"Good morning, Mamma! I'm sorry I was gone, but I had to go up on Big Hill and talk with the Lord. I'll take care of the preparations that must be done for the evening."

"Well, you know how slow you are, and you should have begun baking things early."

What torment, thought Clemmie, *to have such a strict, unfeeling mother. But I will not let anything spoil this day for me. This is the best day of my whole life.*

Nearly every Saturday night, weather permitting, the neighbors in the Ebony community got together to visit and have music, taking turns in different homes. The Wilmeths were the hosts for the evening, which delighted Clemmie and distressed Mamma.

By suppertime, Clemmie and Grace, her fifteen-year-old sister, had made two syrup pies, a white cake with lemon jelly filling, and a plate of tea cakes. Clemmie straightened the front room's meager furnishings and pasted magazine pictures of gardens and flowers on the wall.

In the gloaming, a group of neighbors and a few young people from several miles away arrived in horse-drawn hacks. Everyone seemed merry and ready to forget their hard lives and rocky farms and enter the world of friendship and music. Because the house was small, Clemmie spread quilts and placed the few chairs under the mesquite tree in the side yard, allowing for a beautiful view of the rising moon and the river valley.

There was flirtation and banter among the single folk, and the farmers shared predictions of the drought, while the women traded quilt patterns and children chased each other around the house. Clemmie's brother, Jim, and wife, Callie, whose home was just a few hundred feet away, were in attendance. Callie was six months pregnant with their first baby and seldom went out. Clemmie's other sister, Edna, her husband, Oll, and their pretty little daughter, Opal, had walked over from their place, just over a mile away. When Edna had eloped at age seventeen, Papa Wilmeth had been so angry that he cut her name out of the family Bible. Not too long afterward, he apologized to Edna for his indignation and gave her some choice land right on the river. Papa dreamed that each of his children would one day live on the one hundred acres that would be his or her inheritance. To Papa, that would vindicate what some thought was a poor land trade he had made so many years ago.

As the full moon rose high over the river, and the katydids began their loud, sizzling chorus, the time came for the main event, the singing. A well-known, oft-sung repertoire existed, including "Wait Till the Sun Shines, Nellie," "When You and I Were Young," "My Bonnie Lies Over the Ocean," and Clemmie's favorite, "In the Gloaming," which often haunted her. Since Raleigh had first explained what the "gloaming" meant to Clemmie, she had latched onto the word.

> *In the gloaming, oh, my darling!*
> *When the lights are dim and low,*
> *And the quiet shadows falling,*
> *Softly come and softly go.*
>
> *When the winds are sobbing faintly*
> *With a gentle unknown woe,*
> *Will you think of me and love me,*
> *As you did once long ago?*
>
> *In the gloaming, oh, my darling!*
> *Think not bitterly of me!*
> *Though I passed away in silence,*
> *Left you lonely, set you free,*
> *For my heart was crushed with longing;*
> *What had been could never be.*
> *It was best to leave you thus, dear,*
> *Best for you and best for me.*

How sad, thought Clemmie, sitting on the hard-packed earth, full skirt encircling her legs. *I'd like to find out more about that song. It sounds like death from a broken heart. Well, at least that is not to be my fate!* Clemmie thought of Raleigh once more and the short time they had spent together that morning. *Oh, Raleigh, finally you are truly "my darling!"* thought Clemmie.

— — — — — — — —

As Raleigh left Ebony at ten that morning, he reminisced about his first trip to Texas as a boy of eleven. He could remember sitting on the front seat of a buckboard wagon by his father. He had observed the narrow trail winding down into a small canyon, ascending into a hill of bluebonnets. The little trail was full of ruts, and sometimes a dead tree lay across it. Raleigh had begun to dream a dream: "One day there will be a highway over these hills and through the plains— a highway wide and smooth, and some quicker way to travel the highway than a swaying buckboard pulled by a team of horses."

His father had laughed at the dreams of his son, and the wagon rolled on. But the boy said to himself, *Somehow, I'll find a way.*[1]

Now Raleigh smiled as the sun shone on the hood of his friend's automobile. "Well, the buckboard has been replaced. I still hope to have a hand in doing something about these poor roads in Texas," he remarked aloud.

Dark had settled over Brownwood by the time Raleigh finished his business there, so he decided to spend the night at the Crown Hotel and return to Baird by morning light. He sat alone in the simple room and mused over his day.

I hope my friendship with Clemmie meant no more than that to her. I really felt like I owed her a kiss for all her caring, and it was enjoyable… and really gratifying to see the river and my childhood home…but that kiss didn't hold a candle to the kisses my Lucy gives me. I'm afraid it was wrong of me not to have told Clemmie that I am acquainted with someone special who lives in Baird and has finally had her eighteenth birthday. Yes, I must write Clemmie and tell her about Miss Lucy McCoy.

WHEN THE LIGHTS

Sunday morning, the first and best day of the week! Clemmie had always been her papa's daughter, and Sundays meant one thing: going to church to worship God. Hurriedly, before Mamma called, she pulled off the old white nightdress, catching her hair on a button. Looking down at her small, funnel-shaped breasts, she determined to eat more to improve her figure.

She put on a day dress, brushed her hair back, and quickly folded up her bed, stashing it in the corner behind a chair. Never had she felt as good—at least not that she could remember. Thoughts of Raleigh and their encounter on Big Hill bombarded her mind. She thought about the years of writing letters to Raleigh and waiting days and weeks for replies.

She remembered in detail the rare occasions when she and Raleigh had seen each other briefly—at reunions or funerals. She thought of all her daydreams and night dreams of Raleigh, her obsession for nearly eighteen years. She had given him a name from Greek mythology—Apollo, the most handsome of the gods.

At last he is going to be mine! My waiting and praying has paid off in the grand culmination of that hour on top of Big Hill.

Clemmie rolled her eyes up to the shabby ceiling and prayed again. "Oh, I thank Thee, Lord, for attending my prayers. I will be eternally grateful to Thee, Lord!"

Opening the kitchen door, Clemmie felt the fresh morning air, like sweet perfume. It reminded her of a favorite church hymn. She ran quickly down the path humming "Beulah Land."

> *I've reached the land of corn and wine,*
> *And all its blessings freely mine;*
> *There shines undimmed one blissful day,*
> *For all my night has passed away.*
> *Oh, Beulah Land, sweet Beulah Land;*
> *As on the highest mount I stand;*
> *I look away, across the sea,*
> *Where mansions are prepared for me;*
> *And view the shining glory shore;*
> *My heav'n, my home forevermore.*

She was in full voice by the time she returned. Mamma opened the door, shaking a warning finger, and her voice went shrill: "Clementine, you are waking the dead! I don't know what you've got to be so happy about. What time did you ever get to bed last night?" Mamma spoke crisply but had learned to pronounce English correctly.

"Why, I'm not sure, Mamma. I think it was close to two."

"Land o' Goshen! You know that is not enough sleep! And just what were you doing up so late, pray tell?"

"Um, well, I read my Bible, and uh...wrote some in my diary, and uh...went outside to pray in the moonlight."

"Clementine, you are a strange child. I cannot begin to fathom you."

Clemmie stooped and opened the bottom door of the wooden pantry. She got out a bowl, a cup, and a wooden spoon. On the other side she found the lard, salt, soda, baking powder, and flour from the bin. She dipped a cup into the milk crock and started the biscuits.

"I know I'm a disappointment to you, Mamma, and that makes me sad. Maybe I took more after Papa, or even his mother. Did Grandma Wilmeth really bring silk worms to Texas with her and make silk underdrawers for her daughters?"

"Hush, daughter! It is not proper to speak about such things." Mamma had a fire started in the oven. She buttered a pie pan for the biscuits, floured her board, and got out the rolling pin that had been made in Germany and belonged to her mother.

Serving meals on time was uppermost in Mamma's mind. Clemmie thought it would be good not to even have breakfast on Sundays, instead focusing on "the bread of life" that Papa would deliver later in the morning.

"Mamma," Clemmie asked, using her sweetest voice, "do you mind if I go on in the hack with Papa? Jim can bring you and all the others in the wagon." Mamma was usually happy to ride with her only son over the bumpy road to the church building, five miles away.

Clemmie got her Bible and tied her sunbonnet under her chin. She had hurriedly changed into the blue-checked gingham she'd worn yesterday with Raleigh. She planned to keep that dress forever.

— — — — — — — —

Clemmie adored her father. James Ransom (J.R.) Wilmeth was the fifth child in a family of thirteen children. His immediate family came to Texas from Tennessee when he was only ten and settled first near what was to become downtown Dallas. At that time—Christmas of 1845, there were only three cabins. However, by the time the first corn appeared, the family decided to move north to present-day McKinney. Indians were frightening them and more than once had taken the baby of the family away for a day.

J.R.'s father, Joseph Brice Wilmeth, had been a pioneer preacher, and two of his sons, J.R. and C.M. (Mac), followed his example. J.R. went all the way to Virginia as a young man, wearing a homespun suit his mother had made, to study theology at the feet of Alexander Campbell, the man who helped restore the Church of Christ.

Eventually, J.R. missed his sweetheart back in McKinney so much that he returned to marry Maria Lowry when he was twenty-three. The babies began arriving, and eventually there were five children: Charlie, Campbell, Clara Jane, Nell, and Joe. J.R. supported the family by farming. His parents and several siblings lived close by.

When the Civil War broke out, J.R. enlisted as a chaplain for the Confederate forces under General Robert E. Lee. The diary he kept with his sage opinions about the war (he was completely opposed to the "bloody conflict") became a family heirloom.

Maria and her sixth child died in childbirth. She was only twenty-seven years old. J.R. was heartbroken. Overcome with grief and unable to carry on without his wife, he placed the children, ages one to nine, with his relatives and went to Lexington, Kentucky. He wanted to be a minister, and he wanted to be well prepared. He found himself hungry for knowledge, and so he drank deeply from the fount for two years. At one point, he and Mac, his brother, walked a good bit of the way to Niagara Falls, preaching along the way.

Having mastered the languages of Hebrew, Greek, Latin, and Spanish, J.R. and Mac developed an intense interest in the souls of Mexican people. They walked all the way to Mexico with the idea of becoming missionaries.

Seven years after Maria's death, J.R. found himself in Bryan,

Texas, falling in love with a young German immigrant, Clara Antonia Schulz. She was different from any woman J.R. had ever known.

Precise, orderly, and punctual, Clara Schulz wore her long hair with a braid wrapped on top of her head, and long curls cascaded across her shoulders. She was short, only five feet two inches, but she held herself erect. Her students of German and French had nicknamed her "the Duchess." Raised as a Lutheran, Clara was baptized into the Church of Christ by J.R. before their marriage. For a whole year J.R. courted Clara by means of romantic letters. She later told her daughters that it was the letters that had won her heart.

Together, they had produced an interesting daughter, Clemmie, who seemed more intellectual than their three younger children. Like her father, Clemmie was hungry for knowledge, but relationships were even more important to her. And on this fair spring Sunday morning in Texas, Clemmie wanted to deepen the bond with her beloved papa.

Clemmie thought he was handsome. His white beard and his lined and weathered face attested to his wisdom. If he had lived in Old Testament times, Clemmie just knew God would have chosen him for a prophet. He always polished his shoes on Saturday night and carefully cut cardboard insoles to cover the worn-out leather. He smelled of Bay Rum cologne, and his white shirt was starched and ironed.

It had been hard for J.R. to fit into Mills County, with the farmers chewing their tobacco, spitting, and talking about de-worming their cattle. They would even refer to the new schoolteacher as a "filly." "Uncouthness" was a word that Clemmie often used in her diary to describe the low way of talking and viewing life so common in the Texas countryside in 1909.

But this certain Sunday morning was close to true happiness for Clemmie. Riding to church, which was held in the one-room schoolhouse, and having the full attention of her father, who would bring the sermon that morning, she tried to think of a very intellectual question to engage Papa's quick mind.

"Papa, do you think the Methodists and the Baptists will go to heaven?"

"Daughter, many things are for God's final decision. However, I would not want to be in their shoes. I believe they have found much of the truth, but they have stopped short of the pure doctrine we find in God's Word."

Unable to think of another deep question, Clemmie rode in silence with Papa along the rocky, narrow road to the schoolhouse. Pulling up alongside the other hacks and buggies, Papa began to greet the gathering group in his congenial way. He shook each hand and looked deeply into their eyes with his sincere blue eyes. They could feel his genuine caring, and they did not forget that he had been there to visit when they were ill during the winter.

The schoolhouse, like so many in Texas, had a tall ceiling, a pot-bellied stove in the center, a copy of the unfinished portrait of George Washington on the west wall, and windows on the east wall. There were five rows of desks bolted to the floor, seven in each row. The gathering churchgoers slid into a favorite place.

Clemmie sat right behind John Robert Briley on this Sunday, April 18, 1909. John was the thirty-two-year-old son of the Baptist preacher. The Brileys had come to Texas from Kentucky about the same time the Elys arrived. In small communities it was common for Baptist, Methodist, and Church of Christ preachers to take turns in the pulpit.

Clemmie felt a lot of sympathy for John's father, Harris Briley, "Brother Briley." She knew he had suffered a great deal. His first wife, Molly, had died in Kentucky; his second wife, Fannie, and two young sons were buried not far away in Elkins Cemetery. Clemmie studied John's wavy dark hair and his slender neck. He looked a little like Raleigh, she thought, especially from behind.

This particular Sunday morning, J.R. Wilmeth had chosen "Send the Light" for his text. He had three points: The world is in darkness; God sent Jesus to be the Light of the world; and followers of Christ should take the Light to the world.

Clemmie tried hard to follow the wonderful abstract thoughts. When her papa said "darkness," it reminded her of the gloaming, which reminded her of Raleigh's explanation of walking with God in the gloaming. Then she thought of just walking with Raleigh.

She revisited Big Hill with Raleigh in her mind's eye. After he'd kissed her, in her imagination they both wanted more kisses. Finally, he blurted, as a raging sea that could hold back no longer: "Clemmie, I cannot live another day without you. Will you marry me, my darling? Oh, please say you will be the light of my life." Just at that moment, J.R. Wilmeth reached the climax of his sermon and extended the invitation. "And so, my friends, if there is anyone here who has not confessed that Jesus is the Christ, who has not repented of his sins, or who has not put on his Lord in baptism, please come forward right now as we sing Hymn number 36, 'Send the Light.'"

The song leader stepped to the front, book held high.

> *There's a call comes ringin' o'er the restless waves,*
> *Send the Light, send the Light;*
> *There are souls to rescue, there are souls to save;*
> *Send the Light, send the Light.*

Clemmie bounded out of her reverie, struggled out of the desk, and tried to enter fully into the words of the song. She felt guilty that her thoughts had wandered so far from Papa's words. All through the Lord's Supper that followed, Clemmie punished herself for letting her mind wander. *Forgive me, Father. And thank you for sending the light directly to me this day.*

Finally, the dismissal prayer came. As Clemmie smoothed her skirt and gathered her Bible and purse, one of the men, a friend of her father's, Mr. Reeves, handed her a long white envelope. She glanced down and saw her name and recognized the handwriting as Raleigh's.

"Clemmie," explained Mr. Reeves, "I spent the night in Brownwood and happened to see Raleigh Ely at the Crown Hotel. He asked if I would deliver this letter to you this morning."

"Why, thank you, Mr. Reeves," replied Clemmie, her heart racing. *How sweet of Raleigh to write me so soon after our meeting yesterday,* she thought. Her hopes for a serious courtship with Raleigh were confirmed in her own mind. She wanted to rip open the letter and read it on the spot, but decided to wait until after lunch and take it with her up on Big Hill.

Yes, better to wait and enjoy each beautiful word Raleigh has penned. She fairly skipped to the hack and was impatient for her father to drive them home. She barely noticed when John Briley sauntered by her hack, smiling and nodding, hands in his pockets.

ARE DIM AND LOW

Never had it taken so long to get Sunday dinner on the table. Finally, the remains of fried chicken, corn, and biscuits were cleared away. Each family member had something urgent to do, so Clemmie was free to escape to Big Hill with her treasured letter.

"Mamma, I'm going to Big Hill to review my lessons. I'll be back in an hour or two."

Grabbing up the cloth bag from yesterday, Clemmie was out the back door when Mamma called, "Okay, daughter. Don't forget the time."

"Don't worry, Mamma. I won't forget that Will is coming around four."

Clemmie, still wearing the blue gingham dress she had worn yesterday, felt like she would be closer to Raleigh and the precious memory of the day before.

Her hair was loose, falling below the yoke of her dress, tendrils blowing slightly in the spring wind. She felt light and nearly giddy, anticipating the contents of the letter from her beloved.

Following the well-worn path to the east of the house, she was on the hill in less than ten minutes. Looking up to the sky, she praised God for the beauty of her hill.

Glancing down to the rock-strewn ground, Clemmie gasped and stifled a scream. There, right beneath her, was the longest snake she had ever seen, stretched out in the sun, as still as could be. She looked first at its tail and saw there were no rattlers.

It may be a water moccasin, Clemmie surmised, noticing the nearly black color and discernable pattern. She knew the cottonmouth was as deadly as the rattler.

I wonder if I should try to kill it. It began to glide forward with a wonderful liquid motion and disappeared into a bush.

"That won't spoil my hour," Clemmie stated aloud.

Quickly, but somewhat cautiously, she ran to the south edge of the hill where the view of the river never failed to amaze and thrill her—the sounds of the water flowing, the absolute beauty of the shades of green of the trees, the way the river bent westward, then back to the south. Looking across the hill, she noticed the white crocus appearing to spring from the rocks.

That reminds me of the resurrection of Jesus, she thought. *The hopelessness of the huge rock in front of the tomb, and then the glory of the lilies representing the risen Lord and new hope for the whole world.*

A mockingbird chanted its repertoire. There were several vultures circling an area of trees near the water.

"Oh, God, I love Thee. I thank Thee for the preciousness of this scene and of this hour."

Quickly returning to her spot, Clemmie extracted Raleigh's letter.

What beautiful handwriting. He must have written this very late last night, she thought. She pressed it to her lips, anticipating the contents.

Finally, she carefully slid her index finger under the flap and opened it, taking out the one sheet of hotel stationery.

My Dear Clementine,

The memory of today, April 17, 1909, will ever be part of me. Clemmie, I feel compelled to let you know some information which I had not the courage to reveal to you earlier in the day.

Clemmie's heart leaped to her throat.

As you know, Baird has become my home. Several years ago, I began to notice a certain young woman, prominent in the city from an outstanding family, whose name you may recognize. The family name is "McCoy," and the young woman is "Lucy." She is quite a bit younger than you and I, having celebrated her eighteenth birthday this year. She seems older than she is, being one with a level and wise head.

Clemmie, until yesterday, I hardly realized that you were holding me in such hope, with romantic intentions, and perhaps dreaming that we might share our futures as man and wife. Although we have exchanged letters for nearly a decade, I have always thought of you as my dear friend, and even as a dear sister. I know you have had many beaus, as you have told me about some of them in the past. I know the one who is meant to be your spouse will soon make himself known to you.

Your life and mine are interwoven with our childhood fantasies, our youthful dreams and ambitions, and now we continue with the realities of romantic involvements. I trust we will remain friends throughout our lives and will always be available to each other for advice, for counsel, and for encouragement.

Clemmie, I feel that I should apologize for the liberty I took with you yesterday. The fact that I held you in my arms and even pressed my lips with yours was my way of telling you that I have loved you as a wonderful friend, that I truly appreciate you and what you have meant to me in my past life. It was you who first encouraged me to go after higher education and to become a person who could be in leadership of our dear country.

Clemmie, please find it in your heart to forgive me, and please know deep within your soul that this is best for you and best for me.

I remain your true and dear friend, for time and for eternity,

Raleigh

Clemmie could barely see to read the final words on the page. Tears flowed like the Colorado River, and she began to moan loudly. She threw herself on the coverlet and cried as though her heart was breaking, and indeed it was. She pounded the earth with both fists and bombarded the very throne of God with her pathetic questions.

Why, God, did Thou take him away? Why, Lord, right after Thou gavest him to me? I don't understand, Lord. But I know Thou hast another plan for my life. Thou sent me light, and now the light is so dim I feel that my life is ebbing away. But Thou wilt restore joy to my soul, I know.

Clemmie sobbed until she felt as weak as a newborn kitten, a baby who was helpless and unable to take care of herself. Then the waves of nausea began, and Clemmie knew it would be impossible to avoid the inevitable. She got to her feet and bent over as far as she could, hoping the disgusting vomit would not get on the coverlet or her gingham dress. A small amount blew onto her now-hated dress, and she considered taking it off and throwing it into the river. But she knew she could not afford to let her feelings of rage win out over her strong German upbringing. After all, a new dress was a luxury she knew she could not afford.

She walked as fast as she could toward the river, stumbling over a large rock in the process. It took her about ten minutes to reach the rock formation the family had named the "sidewalk." She sat down on the warm stone and removed her shoes and stockings. Then she jumped into the muddy river, nearly enjoying the sensation of the cold, murky water enveloping her. Stretching out on her back, she stared at the gorgeous blue sky and wondered how the world could seem so unaffected by her personal tragedy. How could the sun keep shining? How could the willow trees tower in their lacy spring-green leaves? How could the "Silvery Colorado," of which Raleigh had spoken so poetically yesterday, keep on flowing? Rowing on her back, she stared into the cloudless sky.

"Dear God, I will not let the loss of Raleigh ruin me. I cannot understand why he does not care for me, but since he has chosen this Lucy girl, I can do nothing about it. I will survive, and I will show him one day what a real man looks like." Tears ran off Clemmie's cheeks and became part of the river as she made her solemn promise to the Holy One.

She floated on her back for about ten minutes, then wondered how she could get home in her wet condition without having to explain why she had jumped into the river fully clothed, nor her mother knowing what she had suffered.

The sun disappeared, and the sky darkened suddenly. Strong gusts of wind bowed the willow trees low toward the river. Quick lightning made its jagged statement across the Ebony sky, followed nearly immediately by a loud clap of thunder.

Huge drops of rain fell on Clemmie like tears from a host of angels. She was paddling toward the bank when the full impact of the storm hit her.

"God, my dear Father, Thou hast heard my prayer and Thou hast given me a sign!" Struggling to get her leg onto the rock bank, she caught her foot in the heavy, wet dress and petticoat, causing her head to go under the water. Bobbing up, she grasped the rocky ledge and heaved herself up on the bank with tiger-like strength. She laid her head on the hot sidewalk, enjoying the warmth in spite of the stinging in her nose.

Looking up into the dark, stormy sky, Clemmie uttered her prayer of thankfulness. "Oh, Lord, how like Thee. Just when life has become too sad, too overwhelming for me to bear, Thou hast come to me in ways I never dreamed possible. Now Mamma cannot question my looking like a drowned puppy, nor ever know how impulsively I have acted. Dear God, Thou art my rock and my fortress, my strong place in the time of storm.

"God, Thy sweet mercy is comforting after the sharp and terrible blow dealt by Raleigh. I know it will be a real challenge to ever be free of this deep love I feel for him. In fact, I wonder if it will haunt me forever."

Soaked and drained of energy, Clementine neared home, holding her head and shoulders high. Then she heard a sweet sound—her mother's voice calling out her name.

"Clementine! Julia Clementine! Oh, my child!"

Just as a bolt of lightning came very near, her mamma's arms encircled her in gratitude.

"Oh, daughter, I was so worried about you, out in this storm. We still have time to get you all dried out before four o'clock. I have your dry clothes laid out, and water is boiling in the kettle for tea. Just leave these wet clothes in the kitchen. I'll wash them out later."

Clemmie looked up at the clearing sky and thought, *So Mamma is not mad and did not scold me! Another mercy straight from Thee, Lord.* She would never tell Mamma, but she would never put on that blue gingham dress again! It had brought her the opposite of luck.

Clemmie got herself out of the drenched clothing and dressed in a white blouse and long black skirt. She brushed her hair and pulled it back on her head in a French twist, securing it with hairpins.

Gathering her school papers and books together, she placed them in the top drawer of her small trunk and carried it to the front door. She felt numb and strange. It seemed as though she were falling down a bottomless well, losing contact with reality. In a way, her life had lost its meaning. She knew she had lost all hope of a happy family life and had not realized how much she wanted that.

There had been times when she thought a career of teaching and devoting herself to her students would be enough. Now she knew she must have something more. By the grace of God she would have her own home one day. She would have a handsome husband who loved her and her own children to teach and to love.

Although the light is dim and low, Thou wilt lift up mine eyes and fill me with light again.

"Oh, Raleigh, I'll never understand why you've discarded the very thing that could've made your life a heaven on earth. But I must accept the fact that you now have Lucy, and I must seek another."

AND THE QUIET
SHADOWS FALLING

School in Locker had finally ended. Clemmie didn't know how she had managed to get through the last three weeks. She felt as though she were in a dream—a horrible nightmare. It was all she could do to get out of bed each morning at Mrs. Parks' house, where she boarded. It took every ounce of energy to put on her clothes and force herself to eat the cold biscuit and drink the cup of coffee Mrs. Parks brought to her room on a tray.

She had no strength and no interest in her pupils, nor in anything else. Once, when she was conducting a reading exercise, all the students stared at her with wide eyes. Then she saw the schoolroom grow small, as if it were being sucked away into space. She thought she would faint. As she walked home to her room at Mrs. Parks,' only five minutes away, she collapsed onto the bed and fell into a restless sleep. Every night she would fall asleep, awake around two, and be unable to go back to sleep. She felt full of fears and very, very lonely.

Her sister, Grace, who shared her room at Mrs. Parks' house, was puzzled and scared that Clemmie was acting so strangely. Clemmie was thirteen years older than Grace and had always been the strong one, nearly more a mother than a sister. Tears would stream down Clemmie's cheeks at the most inappropriate times for no apparent reason.

"Is it something I said, sister? Please don't be sad. We'll be home in just a few days," Grace comforted. "Is it because those naughty boys talked back to you at school today? If I were their father, I should give them some hard licks with a razor strap."

"No, Grace, dear. I don't know what is wrong with me. My body and my mind are very weak. I feel so sad and lonely, and very hopeless. I know this will go away, and maybe I can go for some spring water treatments in Glen Rose this summer. Please try not to worry, little Grace. You are such a dear. *It's as if I am walking through shadows now, but God will let sunshine come into my soul once more.*

Grace was usually very fun loving, but she could become quite serious and sincere. She adored her older sister and felt privileged to go along with her to different teaching locations. She had grown quite tall, and it was strange to them both that she was the taller of the two. Grace was the most vivacious of the Wilmeth girls and promised to be the most rebellious, especially in the area of religion. She thought it was unfair that she wasn't allowed to attend the country dances, since dancing was considered to be a sensual, worldly activity by religious folk, including Papa Wilmeth. Grace vowed that when she had a daughter, she would be the belle of the ball!

Finally, the sisters were back at Riverside Farm, as Clemmie had named the Wilmeth acreage, but the "illness" did not vanish as Clemmie had hoped. She wanted to be left alone and would have liked to stay in bed all day.

"Clemmie, you must talk to me." Mamma had climbed the narrow stairway to the upstairs room. There were two hammock-type beds hung from the rafters. It was very hot during the day, unbearable in the summers, but, with open windows, it cooled down wonderfully at night.

"Mamma, I don't know what is wrong with me. It is some type of melancholy that has come on me. You know I have had some spells before when I just didn't feel normal. But this time it's worse."

"Clemmie, did anything happen that made you sad? Did you get a letter from a beau that disappointed you? Did someone in Locker treat you badly?"

"Mamma, something very disappointing has happened. I have heard that Raleigh Ely is engaged to be married. He and I have exchanged letters for a long time, about ten years." Clemmie's voice broke, and she sobbed loudly.

"There, there, daughter. I know what it is like to be disappointed in love." She bent over and patted her eldest on the shoulder. "There are many fish in the sea, my child. Everything happens for a reason. He was not the one for you. There will be one more worthy of you, Clementine. Now, I want you to wash up, put on your clothes, and help me prepare lunch."

"Mamma, I do not have the strength. I will help you with dinner this evening." Clemmie wished everyone would leave her alone. *Here I am going on twenty-nine years old and am practically an old maid. I know I am never going to find anyone suitable who loves me enough to marry me. I will probably live out my life dependent on my sisters and brother and my mother and father in this small, awful, hot house in this God-forsaken country.*

Besides all this, I may lose my soul for being so hateful to Mother, so disobedient to God, and so selfish and evil for wishing that Miss Lucy McCoy would come to some horrible end.

Clemmie continued to think in her downward spiral. *Why was I ever so stupid to think that a handsome county attorney would want to marry someone like me? I am not beautiful, and do not have the hourglass figure that attracts men. My hair is straight as a board, and our family is as poor as church mice. My future is about as bright as this dry farm on a moonless night. I just wish I had never been born.*

▄ ▄ ▄ ▄ ▄ ▄ ▄ ▄ ▄

On July 10, Clemmie's brother, Jim, and sister-in-law, Callie, had their first baby. The child was a little girl, and they named her Clara Marie. The birth of a baby was always a big event, and several families from the community gathered around the porch at Jim's house, just a few hundred yards from Clemmie's parents' home.

Clemmie had forced herself to go to her brother's house that evening and make potato soup for the family group awaiting the birth. It really helped Clemmie feel better to get her mind off herself for a little while. That night, she slept better than she had in many weeks.

The menfolk gathered on the porch and talked until after midnight.

"I wager no farmer in this county will make a dime this year," Jim volunteered.

"The drought is bad...that's fer sure," agreed Oll, Clemmie's brother-in-law.

It was the driest and the hardest summer in many years for Mills County. There was no rainfall from May until September, and the cattle and the farmers were suffering. The corn, cotton, and maize were burning up in the fields. It had turned into one of the hottest, driest summers on record.

"Jest today I seen two heifers lying dead in the Smiths' field," Oll said, spitting his tobacco through his teeth and over the edge of the porch.

"Well, now, you boys need to learn to trust in the Lord," Papa put in. "You know it says in Psalms 37:25, 'I have been young, and now am old; yet have I not seen the righteous forsaken, nor his seed begging bread.'"

"Well, King David weren't in Mills County in the summer of

ought nine or he woulda seen plenty-a folks a-starvin,'" Oll couldn't resist commenting.

— — — — — — — — —

The Locker school did not renew Clemmie's contract for the fall. It was always in the hands of the trustees to keep the teacher or send her on her way and hire another. Although Clemmie was a good teacher, she had no idea how to handle disciplinary problems, and the overgrown adolescent boys were always her nemeses. It would be a challenge to find a new school, especially near home.

Then, like answered prayer, Clemmie got word that Bowser, Texas, only twelve miles from her home, had lost its teacher, so she wasted no time in applying there. By mid-September she and Grace were installed as boarders at Mrs. Hanna's home. Mr. L.C. Smith was the principal, and Clemmie liked him really well.

Near the end of October, Clemmie saw an article about Raleigh's wedding in the paper. As Clemmie read it, she had the sensation of glass shattering and covering her completely.

One of the prettiest weddings ever solemnized in Baird took place Wednesday night at the Methodist Church when Hon. Walter Raleigh Ely and Miss Lucy McCoy, two of Baird's most popular young people, were united in marriage, Rev. W.J. Lee officiating. The church was beautifully decorated for the occasion. The bride was becomingly gowned in white Swiss satin, made en train. She carried a beautiful bouquet of Bride's roses. Her attendants were gowned in white. Miss Mabel Daniel of Fort Worth, escorted to the altar by Tom McClure, sang, "All for Thee." Miss Daniel played the wedding march...Next came the flower girls, little Laura and Clara Boyles, who were followed by the bride and her maid of honor, Miss Nannie Bell, and the groom and his best man, Charles G. Hadley. After the ceremony, the bridal party left in autos for the residence of Mr. and Mrs. W.P. Cochrane in West Baird. The bride and groom left on the midnight train for a few days at the Dallas Fair.[2]

A shiver ran through Clemmie's body as she absorbed the reality that she had lost Raleigh forever.

At this very moment, he and Miss Lucy are perhaps in a hotel in Dallas eating a five-course meal.

"Well, I hope he will be truly happy," Clemmie said aloud. "I know that I shall be."

She prayed, and then she cried herself to sleep.

SOFTLY COME
AND SOFTLY GO

All through the summer and fall Clemmie had begun thinking about a new plan for her life. Sometimes she shed tears, thinking about the loss of Raleigh, and was afraid she would not marry in her twenties. But she liked to think of herself as realistic, and she knew that God wanted her to have a home like other women. Now that Raleigh had married, she resolved to take action.

The one man she knew who was good-looking and had shown interest in her was John Robert Briley. They had been writing to each other off and on and saw each other once in a while, although he lived in Dallas. The negative side of having John as her beau was that he had had a short marriage that ended in divorce in 1902. Clemmie's understanding of the Bible, along with help from her father, was that the only way sure to get to heaven was to steer clear of a divorced person.

However, Jesus Himself had said in Matthew 5:32: "Whosoever shall put away his wife, saving for the cause of *fornication*, causeth her to commit adultery: and whosoever shall marry her that is divorced committeth adultery."

Clemmie decided she would write to John and find out if his former wife had committed adultery, and that was why he had to get a divorce. If that *was* the case, then he would be justified in God's eyes and free to marry again, according to her new understanding of the passage.

Bowser, Texas

November 3, 1909

Dear John,

I am sure you will be surprised to get this from me, but I am in hopes that it will be a pleasant surprise.

I have thought of you so much since you left, for it was lonesome for me when you were gone, and I wondered if it was lonesome for you in Dallas.

I have thought deep of what you said when you were with me, and my heart aches for your happiness as well as my own. I know that you have suffered, and I think that the suffering has made your soul beautiful. And since you were with me last, it seems that there might be in store for us a beautiful happiness. But before we can think of that, I must ask you one question.

Someday when this life shall end, I expect to go up to meet my God in judgment and there render an account of the deeds done in the body. For so does the book of Revelation tell us. And it also tells us that we shall be judged according to the things written in the book of life, and I believe the New Testament is the book of life. And though it might make me beautifully happy to know that we should know each other in the sacred relationship of marriage, yet, "What doth it profit a man though he gain the whole world and lose his own soul?"

So this is what I must ask you. I want you to read the ninth verse of the nineteenth chapter of Matthew, then answer me this: Have you the *right* to ask me to be your wife? Do you believe that it would be right in the sight of God? Though we might love each other dearly, it would be better for both of us to suffer intensely rather than to do something that might bar us from the gates of heaven. However, John, I will say that I believe that in the sight of God you have the right, but I do not know. Write to me soon, John, and be frank with me.

With love,
Clemmie

No one could have been more surprised than John when he received Clemmie's letter in Dallas. He had gone by the car barn to get his check for the week, and someone who knew him shouted to him that his sweetheart must have written to him.

He put the letter in his pocket and waited till he was back at his rented room to open it.

What a turnaround in Clemmie's thinkin', he thought. The last time he saw her, having taken her to a church meeting in Ebony, she seemed to have no interest in beginning a full-fledged courtship.

In fact, she even got out of the buggy and ran on to her house alone while I was opening the gate! Maybe it had something to do with that Riley fella, but it made me feel mighty peculiar.

He had known for a long time that she could be a woman

who would make him a good wife, but since she showed so little enthusiasm, he had about decided to give up on her. And now this!

He looked up the Scripture she wanted him to read.

"And I say unto you, Whosoever shall put away his wife, except it be for fornication, and shall marry another, committeth adultery: and whoso marrieth her which is put away doth commit adultery."

Matthew 19:9

Although John's father was a Baptist preacher, John had never really become familiar with everything in the Bible. He daydreamed through many a sermon.

When he read this, it caused him to begin a journey of reverie…

▬ ▬ ▬ ▬ ▬ ▬ ▬ ▬

It was a beautiful day in May of 1899. John and his brother, Burt, had left the Ebony farm some time before and gone to Dallas to try to make their way in life. They had finally landed jobs with the transit system of Dallas, namely the streetcar line. John was twenty-two, and Burt was eighteen. They were good boys but not immune to having a good time.

It was at the annual picnic at City Park when John first saw Nancy Elizabeth Harris. She was about the most beautiful woman he had ever seen. Generously endowed in the bosom, but with a tiny waist and hips that were narrow, she was wearing a white waist, and the neck was cut low and had a wide ruffle of lace, unlike the high necks that most women wore during the daytime. She had on a black satin skirt with a small bustle, and it was very tight at the waist. Her feet looked small in the high-buttoned boots. Her dark hair was in an upsweep, and her eyes were dark with full lashes. She had a small bow-shaped mouth with lips that were slightly red and full. There were tendrils of hair around her face. When her eyes met John's, he felt a surge of "the male force."

It was already hot in Dallas, and Nancy carried a parasol in one hand with a basket over the other arm.

"Are you with a gentleman, Miss..."

"Harris. Nancy Harris. And my gentleman friend and I have broken it off."

"Miss Harris, I'm John Briley, and happy to make your acquaintance."

It seemed to John that they made an immediate connection. He felt like he was walking in a dream when Nancy suggested that they find a private place to sit and talk and get to know each other. They found a far-off tree and spread Nancy's blanket under it. Nancy sat close to John and began to touch his face and hands. It crossed John's mind that this was unusual behavior for a woman, but he was too captivated to remove himself from the scene.

Nancy told him that she was an orphan, her parents having both died at early ages. She and her brother had lived for a few years in Orphan's House, which was located not far from the downtown area, then they had gotten jobs and worked and shared an apartment. She had been the cook for several cowboys on the outskirts of Dallas, but had left that job after a few years and now worked as a clerk at a downtown dress shop. They talked on for two or more hours, taking down the barrier to intimacy. John tried not to look at Nancy's low neckline and the beginning of her gorgeous breasts. She had olive skin, practically without a blemish. She was what some people would have called flirtatious, but John could tell that she just wanted to be friendly. Just at that moment Nancy reached for her picnic basket, bending so low that John could see even more than before. It was a moment that imprinted on John's mind and was to last the rest of his life.

He thought he now understood what "love at first sight" was.

The sun was nearly gone when Nancy stood very close to John and took his hands in hers. Then she spoke.

"John, I feel like I have searched all my life for you. I just need so much for you to hold me close in your arms."

John was all too happy to oblige her and caught her up in such a tight squeeze that she let out a little gasp. She tilted her full lips up and whispered that John's eyes were the bluest she had ever seen. Planting his lips firmly on hers, he was surprised when she opened her mouth slightly. John felt like he had touched high voltage. As dark enveloped them like a soft garment, John asked if he could see Nancy home.

They rode the streetcar about a mile to her apartment. John asked if he could see her the next day, and she said yes. After that, they arranged to meet in various places: the city park, certain cheap restaurants, they even visited the zoo once. The kissing became more intense, and Nancy seemed to offer no resistance.

He had to get up early and get to the yards where the streetcars were. He found himself obsessed with thoughts of Nancy...her beauty, her sweetness, the admiration she had for him, her desire to be with him, and, most of all, her gorgeous, voluptuous bosom. He had begun to feel like he was living in the Garden of Eden.

John began to walk many blocks in downtown Dallas, looking for places to take Nancy. There was no money to take her to the theater. One day he discovered a cemetery that he thought was very pretty. There were trees and even a little creek running through it. He asked Nancy if she would make them a picnic supper, and they walked to the cemetery. It was the nineteenth of May, 1899.

Nancy was dressed in a gingham dress, pink with white lace ties and a wide sash. She had pearl earbobs in her little ears. They ate the egg salad sandwiches and drank the lemonade John had purchased from a street vendor. Nancy had brownies with fudge icing, and she began to feed one to John. They were both seized with desire so strong that they were swept up as in a tornado. John tried to reason with himself about what was happening, but he was too far gone and hoped God could overlook one transgression.

A few minutes later it was all over, and Nancy cried a little. She admitted that she had had one or two other relationships, but those had been over long ago. John wanted so much to ask Nancy to marry him, but knew there was no money to begin a home. Any extra he managed to save, he and his brother would send home to their dad. John told Nancy he had not meant to take advantage of her in any way and suggested they try to refrain from making love until they could be married.

In late June, Nancy told John she thought she was pregnant. They began to plan immediately to get married. John knew that Nancy was quite a bit older than he was, but age just didn't seem to matter with such a love as theirs. He didn't want to ask her age, since it really didn't matter to him.

On July 9, 1899, at four o'clock in the afternoon, John Briley and Nancy Harris became man and wife in the parlor of Orphan's House. The chaplain, P.M. Murfley, used his shortest ceremony.

John and Nancy started their married life in a small rented room. Nancy had a new job selling cosmetics at a five-and-dime store. The weeks passed, and it became apparent that Nancy was not pregnant. John never knew if she had tricked him, or if she had actually thought she was, or if she had lost the baby. Things did not go right for the couple. After a few months, Nancy began to wish John would not bother her in bed. In her own mind she began to abhor his fingernails with the grease stains from the streetcar repairs. There was very little money, and they could not even afford a buggy. They began to argue over trivial things. Nancy seemed to have no religious beliefs. She liked to go out at night and frequented the dancehalls. One day John's brother, Burt, saw her with another man. He didn't know whether or not to tell John about it, fearing John's temper. Finally, he decided that if it were his wife, he would want to know, so he told John.

John was so angry the veins stood out on his forehead and neck.

He began to imagine just what all might have happened behind his back. That night he waited until Nancy came home at about three a.m. and confronted her. She denied everything. Finally, he told her that his brother had seen her with another man.

"Why, you're a woman of the night! You are a married woman who promised to be faithful to me until death. And here you are running all over Dallas in the night and making a fool outta me. Why, I ought to wring your pretty li'l neck. But you're not worth it. I would have to rot in a jail cell the rest of my life. I want a divorce from you, Miss Nancy Elizabeth Harris, and I don't care what darn reason you give to the court. God in heaven knows the truth, and that's all that matters."

Nancy wasn't one to just stand and take abuse, so she retaliated in kind.

"You think you are so fine and so respectable. You are the one who practically raped me before you even knew me and were so dumb about what to do that I had to teach you everything. You cannot even make enough money to support a wife, and since you didn't go to school very long, you will always be as poor as a mouse in church. You think you are so religious and you treat your own wife like she is some kind of a criminal. I hate you, John Briley. I wish you had never come into my life."

The next day, John moved back with his brother, and Nancy climbed the steps of the red brick Dallas County Courthouse to file for divorce.

Later, John saw the court records, which read:

Nancy E. Briley vs. John R. Briley: Entered as of September 9th, 1902

The above entitled cause being this day called, came the plaintiff, but the defendant came not, whereupon the law and facts being submitted to the court, and it appearing that the plaintiff is entitled to the relief prayed for, therefore, it is ordered, adjudged and decreed by the court that the Matrimonial Connection heretofore made and entered into between the parties, Nancy E. Briley and John R. Briley, be and the same is hereby declared Null and Void, Set aside and dissolved, by a Separation from the bonds of Matrimony as fully and effectually as if no such contract had ever been made and entered into between them, and the said Nancy E. Briley and John R. Briley, in future behold and considered as separate and distinct persons altogether, unconnected by any Nuptial union or civil.

Cause listed for the divorce was cruelty, battery, and slander. The final decree date was 9 September, 1902. The marriage had lasted three years and two months.

John was devastated afterwards and thought his life was over, and that probably, all hope of spending eternity with God had ended—unless God could forgive him and he could find a really spiritual girl the next time.

— — — — — — — —

So in reply to Clemmie's letter written seven years later, John chose to word it this way:

Dallas, Texas
Nov. 5, 1909
Miss Clemmie Wilmeth
Ebony Texas
Esteemed Friend,

Though I must admit I was surprised to hear from you, and I was so delighted when my eyes traced those lines, words fail to express the gratitude of my heart. You have taken more interest in me than I thought you would when I left you last.

Now listen, you have asked me to be honest, and I will promise that I will. Still I didn't think you had given me any consideration a' tall for you didn't ask me to write to you and didn't encourage any thing I Said. I told you I didn't care to cultivate my tender feeling if it was not returned. So I had almost desided to never approach you on that subject again. I still had the same feeling for you and my heart has been longing for Somethin.

Clemmie I feel happy today and I hope and pray it will last. Seems like you and me both have had one sweetheart come and go, and we know the good Lord wants us to stay with the one we choose.

And in regard to the question you ask me I have just read the verse to which you referd and I believe I can truthfuly answer in the Affirmative...an' that means yes, I do have the Bible reason for a divorce.

> Good bye be good
> John

Ebony, Texas,
Nov. 7, 1909

Dear John,

Your letter came today. It was given into my hands just before dinner but I dared not open it then. So much depended on that letter that I could not trust myself to read it until I was entirely alone. I was sewing, so I worked on until it was almost sundown and Mamma and Grace had gone to the tank after the clothes. Then I stole out, went up Big Hill, and read it. I almost trembled with fear when I began, but when I had finished I walked out into the beautiful autumn evening with joy in my heart, walked over to see the river, and praised God for His love and goodness.

You asked me to tell you what has brought about this change in me since you left. Well now I don't call it such a change, neither would you if you had understood my heart. I have always been a conscientious little goose…at least a goose is what I remind myself of sometimes. So I am going to explain my actions. But I do not want it to hurt you. I'll just tell it so you can understand, then I shall not mention it again.

I read a book in my early girlhood that put the idea into my head that it was *never* right for divorced people to marry again. But a friend of mine once made me think a little differently about it. So when you were gone, I could not put you out of my thoughts. My heart needed someone to love as well as yours did. So I read the Bible and studied it until I was convinced that for one thing a man *did have* divine authority to marry again.

But as to the tender feeling, John, it has been in my heart a long time when I dared let it be there. I can't forget the time when you put your head on the gate and cried when dear little Homer lay a corpse, and your heart was so heavy it seemed it would break. I wanted to comfort you then and I want you to hold me in your arms now. Please write back to me soon, for I can think of nothing else. Send the letters to Bowser. I am only in Ebony because today is my birthday. Your letter was the best present of my life!

Bye Bye
Clemmie

WHEN THE WINDS

Clemmie opened her eyes and tried to remember what day it was: *Saturday, November 13, at Mrs. Hanna's house in Bowser, and I have the whole day to myself!* Mrs. Hanna had gone to Locker to visit her sister. Lettie Mae, Mrs. Hanna's sixteen-year-old daughter, was at home, but she liked to go around with girlfriends on Saturdays. The weekends were like treasures to Clemmie. She didn't mind one bit to have some time to herself. At that moment, Clemmie heard strong gusts of wind blowing, then rain began to pelt the tin roof of the house. *Ah, delicious blessing from God after the long, hot summer months,* she thought.

Clemmie heard the back door squeak, and she decided to look out the window. She could barely see the form of a young man in overalls, running his hand through disheveled hair, letting himself out the front gate and disappearing down the muddy road. Clemmie was shocked. *So Lettie Mae allowed her young man to visit her during the night,* surmised Clemmie. Recently, Clemmie had noticed that Lettie was really taken with Samuel Smith and observed that the couple often sat off to themselves during recess at school.

Lettie Mae was a pretty girl and very well endowed. She was an average student, and lately she had been careless about getting her homework done. Samuel was Clemmie's best male student… very courteous, smart, yet never arrogant. Of all the boys, he was Clemmie's favorite.

Now Clemmie wondered whether or not she should tell Lettie Mae's mother. She could just pretend not to know anything, or she could try to talk to Lettie Mae about the seriousness of sleeping with a boy and the possible consequences. She knew it would be the end of her friendship with the girl, and possibly the end of being able to board with Mrs. Hanna.

"Well, I'll just pray that God will lead me to do the right thing about this," Clemmie stated aloud.

It was so early, and the rain made such a cozy and secure feeling for Clemmie that she fell asleep again. The next thing she heard was knocking at the front door. Pulling on her robe, Clemmie tried to smooth her hair and padded to the front door with bare feet. She lifted the chain lock. There stood Mamma, holding a vase of mums. There was Papa in the hack, on his way to Zephyr, where he would preach in the morning. He smiled and waved at Clemmie.

"Good Morning, daughter! Your mother decided to pay you a visit!"

"Hello, Papa. Won't you come in and warm up for a spell?"

"No, I best be on my way. Do you think you can borrow a buggy and get your mother back home by nightfall?"

"I feel sure Mrs. McAtee will loan us hers, Papa. Maybe Mr. Smith will be our driver. Be careful, Papa, and preach the Word!" Clemmie used the favorite Wilmeth expression, taken from the Bible. She wished that Papa wasn't always in such a rush.

Clemmie turned to face her mother and gave her a welcoming hug. Mamma always seemed slightly stiff when it came to hugging. Clemmie wondered if Mamma ever gave Papa a real, tight hug.

Probably not, and I guess it is the German in her, Clemmie reasoned to herself.

Clemmie took the vase of flowers and expressed her sincere appreciation to her mother.

"Mamma, I would much rather receive flowers than food. It just lifts my spirits. Let's go in the kitchen and make a little breakfast. Mrs. Hanna is away, but her daughter is here, and I need to feed her, too."

In the kitchen Clemmie found some of yesterday's biscuits in the breadbox and started heating a little pan of water for coffee. She got out butter, peach jelly, some honey, and a little piece of cheese. She set out three plates and three cups, then knocked lightly on Lettie Mae's door. Returning to the kitchen, Clemmie measured three spoons of ground coffee into the boiling water, let it sit briefly, and then strained it with a cloth strainer into the coffeepot. She heated some fresh milk for the coffee.

When Lettie Mae appeared, she looked like her eyes were swollen from crying and avoided looking directly at Clemmie. Lettie Mae looked guilty as she toyed with her biscuit, leaving it crumbled on her plate. Then she drank a few sips of coffee with milk.

"Miss Clemmie, I don't feel very good, so I'm going back to bed. Nice to see you, Mrs. Wilmeth. Please excuse me." Lettie Mae made her exit.

It occurred to Clemmie that Mamma would have much rather stayed at home and done her own work but had probably been encouraged by Papa to show her eldest daughter that she cared. That thought made her smile again.

"Mamma, would you like to help me sew a new blouse?"

Mamma had been taught the art of tatting and darning as a girl in the Old Country. She could mend a hole in the toe of a sock so that the sock looked like new, and there were no rough or bulky places. Clemmie preferred to throw the sock away but knew there was precious little money to replace it.

Suddenly, a knock was heard at the door. Clemmie jumped up, remembering that she had told the traveling photographer that he could come over to their house today to get a picture of herself, her principal, Mr. Smith, and Sister Grace. Mrs. Hanna had loaned Clemmie some plants of hers the previous day to help decorate the room for the special event. The photographer had said he would arrive at ten a.m., and it was exactly that time. The picture would become part of a simple yearbook and could be bought by interested students and teachers.

Clemmie welcomed Mr. Theo in, then hurriedly dismissed herself to dress and get the room straight for a picture. Mamma helped her put away the sewing. Clemmie fluffed up the pillows and arranged the plants the best she could. Mamma was quiet about offering suggestions, since decorating was not her strong point. The flowers Mamma had brought were placed strategically on the little wooden table that had been Mr. Hanna's last project before he died of consumption the year before.

Mr. Theo was shown to the bedroom and began setting up his equipment. About five minutes later, Mr. Smith showed up. He inquired about Grace, and Clemmie explained that she was sleeping at a friend's house but should soon be home for the picture-taking. By 10:30, Grace arrived and fixed her hair and repaired Clemmie's. She had a few ideas for making the room look better. Mr. Theo wanted the three of them to sit at the little wooden table, as if they were doing lessons or grading papers.

Although Mr. Theo was a rather pompous gentleman, he did seem to know his business and took several poses. The resulting pictures, mailed to Clemmie about three weeks later, were ones that all three would treasure the rest of their lives.

That night, Clemmie's friend, Mrs. McAtee, loaned Clemmie, Grace, and Mr. Smith her buggy to take Mamma home. The moonlit ride to the river and back with Mr. Smith filled Clemmie's romantic heart with so much pleasure. Clemmie began to wonder if Mr. Smith were starting to like her in a special way, even though he was six years younger than she.

Mr. Smith was one to notice the ladies, and he seemed to be concentrating more on little sister Grace that evening. At fifteen, Grace had developed a very nice figure. She was about three inches taller than Clemmie, and much less serious, which was attractive to Mr. Smith. Fifteen was considered too young for courting, so Mr. Smith was biding his time until Grace had her next birthday. Grace was quick to catch on to his glances but would not hurt her older sister's feelings for the world, as she perceived that Clemmie was feeling that she was the favored one.

The next morning was Sunday, so Clemmie and Grace walked the block to the small church building, trying to avoid the main puddles of muddy water.

Settled on the homemade wooden pews, Clemmie thoroughly enjoyed the singing, even if the voices were untrained and off-key. They sang one of her favorite songs that morning, "Shall We Gather at the River."

Shall we gather at the river, where bright angel feet have trod,
With its crystal tide forever, flowing by the throne of God.
Yes, we'll gather at the river; the beautiful, the beautiful river;
Gather with the saints at the river, that flows by the throne of God.

Sundays were even better than Saturdays to Clemmie. In fact, a major doubt she had about John was the extent of his interest in God and Jesus, the Bible, and church. Both of their dads were preachers, but Clemmie's dad had been much more a man of books and study, and

John's dad was a Kentucky boy who never had the opportunity to go to school beyond the fourth grade.

Was it John's lack of education and polish, or perhaps his lack of ambition that worried Clemmie about marrying him and spending the rest of her life at his side?

But then, he was so good-looking, so tall and lean, had such beautiful hair, and he was so sincere. His love for her seemed so genuine and deep, and he needed her, and she didn't see a more eligible person on the horizon. His eyes were so blue, crystal blue.

And he had suffered so much. And here he was thirty-three years old, looking for a good Christian wife who would never leave him, and God must have brought the two of them together, Clemmie reasoned. *And here I am about to become an old maid.*

"Yes!" Everyone in the little church was suddenly staring at Clemmie and smiling. She realized that her "yes" had been audible. She wanted to sink through the wooden floor. She tried to make a little coughing sound, so perhaps everyone would think they had misjudged the noise. Then she had to finish her thoughts.

I will marry John Briley after a decent length of courtship! I'll become the happiest housewife in the United States of America after one more year of teaching school.

Yes, I shall make my dream of home and family come true, with God as my witness, and my strength. Lord, thank you for your soft wind that is bringing change and blessing to me.

ARE SOBBING FAINTLY

Every afternoon, as soon as school was out, Clemmie walked down the road to the little store where the post office was. By Friday there was still no letter from John, and Clemmie felt the old sadness coming on. But maybe the fact that she sat up until three a.m. making white curtains was another reason she felt so tired. For Clemmie, *sad* and *tired* were like twin feelings—she never had one without the other. Samuel was going to help her put up the curtains at four p.m., so she headed back toward school. Maybe she would get a letter tomorrow.

She had mailed hers to John only a week ago, and she only hoped he really wanted to begin a courtship that would turn into real love. Back in August, right before he had left for Dallas, he had taken her to a church meeting, and she knew she had not been very warm to him, much less "lovey." The truth was that she was still in a depression from the loss of Raleigh, so she showed no interest in John. But she could recall every word that he said that night.

— — — — — — — — —

"Clemmie, I have never told any other girl this much, I swear." John was holding the reins of the horses as he spoke. He stopped the buggy in the moonlight and cleared his throat.

"I love you, Clemmie, and I know that you are the only girl that God would want me to marry, since I have nearly ruined my life with that other marriage. And besides, I wouldn't never of gone to Dallas or met that woman if you'd wanted me when we was young."

"Oh, John, you are a sweet boy, and I know you are going to meet someone else who will be a good Christian wife for you. I just don't know if I'll ever marry anyone or not, John. I think that I am just too different from everyone."

— — — — — — — — —

In retrospect, Clemmie knew that it was her depression talking, and not the girl who so wanted a home and a family. So she could imagine the shock John had felt when he read that letter she wrote him about her tender feelings and everything, and how she had changed her viewpoint about divorce for the right reason.

Back in her classroom, musing on these things, Clemmie was startled when the schoolhouse door opened.

"Hello, Miss Clemmie." Samuel was all smiles as he greeted her.

Just like he promised, Samuel returned at exactly four p.m. He was always happy, and just seeing him come in lifted Clemmie's spirits. She had done a lot of thinking ever since she had discovered the secret love that Samuel and Lettie Mae had. She wanted to talk to Samuel, but it was a very delicate subject, and she didn't know how to approach it.

Maybe in the same way I encouraged Raleigh to go on to school and make something of himself, I can help Samuel do the same thing. In fact Raleigh himself, being a county attorney now, might be able to encourage the boy. But if he is really in love and already into serious courtship, or even more, he will want to get married. Then the babies'll come and he'll end up as a poor country farmer, just like his dad and so many other men in this part of Texas, ran Clemmie's thoughts.

"Miss Clemmie, I'm ready to help you. I brought a hammer and some nails from home."

"Fine, Samuel. I bought these two curtain rods the last time I was in town, and I think they are the right size for the windows." Clemmie felt that she had to think of a way to talk to Samuel.

He pulled one of the student desks over to the window and climbed up on it. By stretching he could barely reach the top of the window. He deftly hammered in the brackets. Clemmie handed him another nail, and he held an extra one in his mouth.

"Samuel, you really do like Lettie Mae, don't you?" Clemmie decided to jump into the subject, praying that God would give her courage and the right words to say.

Sam's eyes opened wide. "Yes, ma'am. I like her a lot."

"You are very smart, Samuel, and schoolwork comes easy for you. You can do math and read like an adult. I was thinking it would be so nice if you could go on to college and get training for a city job. Maybe you could be an attorney, and some day you and your family would live in a fine house in Brownwood. And you could buy fine clothes, and even have your own automobile. Why, you could help take care of your folks when they are old.

"But if you get married real young, then you'll have to start working to make a living, and you couldn't go to school anymore."

Samuel didn't answer immediately. He needed to think about what to say. There was no way to explain to his teacher the situation he was already in. There was truth in what Miss Clemmie was trying to tell him, he knew. Still, she could never understand the overwhelming feelings he had for Lettie Mae. That would just be silly to Miss Clemmie…what grown-ups called "puppy love."

Samuel finished the first window, and Clemmie put the curtain on the rod. Sam quickly placed it in the brackets.

"That sure does look fine, Sam. You got that rod perfectly even. Thank you so much."

"Shucks, it was easy, Miss Clemmie." Samuel wasn't sure where their conversation was going and didn't feel at ease with his teacher asking him about personal stuff. He wondered how much she knew about him and Lettie Mae.

For the past two months he could think of nothing else but her, as hard as he tried. He would think of holding her in his arms down by the creek, of how sweet her kisses were, and how it all made something inside of him start to go kind of crazy. He knew sixteen was too young to get married, and he knew it was a sin to do what married folks did *before* you were married. But it was like he couldn't help himself, and Lettie Mae seemed to feel the same way.

The curtain looked good, Clemmie thought. Even if she had stayed up half the night, it was worth it. The soft white fabric was quite a contrast to the six-inch, crude dark planks of the schoolroom walls. It was so gratifying to Clemmie to improve the ambiance. She also had some pictures from home to hang over the blackboard, between the windows. They were pictures of rivers that never failed to soothe her.

Clemmie stared at Samuel's clean-cut good looks. *What a fine boy,* she thought, but more than that, she was amazed at his sweet attitude. He was always willing to help anyone, from Paul Brown, who didn't even own any shoes, to Jewel Mitchell, who was definitely the best dressed girl in two counties. Samuel and Lettie Mae had been paired at school because they were the only high school students. No one, least of all Clemmie, had imagined the end result of those two sixteen-year-olds being together so much. The other students of high-school age had either dropped out of school or had gone into Brownwood.

Of course, reasoned Clemmie, *everyone knows that boys and men like to court and get "lovey-dovey," and it's always up to the women to make them behave.* Clemmie wondered if Mrs. Hanna had neglected her duty in not teaching Lettie Mae the way to conduct herself with a boy. But perhaps when she had seen him leaving the other night, they had just been talking and hugging and kissing. After all, she hadn't actually seen anything happen. Perhaps it wasn't too late to help Samuel aim for more education.

Yes, Clemmie decided. *I will see to it that Samuel Smith gets his education. This is one boy who is worthy of being helped. When it is the right time, I will talk to his parents about this,* she resolved. Samuel's dad, William Thomas Smith, was one of the three trustees appointed by the county superintendent for the school year. The trustees were the governing body for the school, although the county superintendent was technically the one responsible. Due to bad roads, poor transportation, and low pay, the superintendents never visited the schools, leaving everything up to the trustees—especially the hiring and firing of teachers. Clemmie had no desire to be fired, either. She wondered if she should just keep quiet about Samuel's schooling.

The next day, Saturday, dawned bright and clear, and Clemmie could hardly wait for the mail to arrive. Right before ten a.m., she headed for the store on foot. Bowser was so small that anyone could walk nearly anywhere in five or ten minutes.

"Why, yes, Miss Clemmie, you do have a letter today." Mrs. McAtee smiled, handing her an envelope. "How are things going at school? You and I need to talk real soon. Maybe you could visit me tomorrow afternoon?"

"Very well, Mrs. McAtee. I believe this is my best school yet in all the years I have taught. I would love to come calling on you tomorrow. Would three o'clock be a good time?" Clemmie couldn't wait to leave and find a good place to read John's letter.

"Yes, I will expect you at three p.m. Bring Grace, too, if she would like to come."

With a quick wave, Clemmie headed straight for the little cemetery on the hill, just five minutes away. This was her substitute for Big Hill while she was at Bowser. She didn't even notice the grass burrs as she settled on her favorite rock. She opened the envelope carefully, noticing the Dallas postmark and the familiar handwriting.

My dear Clementine,

I've been wantin t' get a letter to you for a couple of days and seems like things went against me. My good friend got sick and needed me to help him so I've been at his house a lot o' the time helping him.

Clemmie, I'm starting t' plan on coming to see you by Christmas. I went an missed your birthday an i'm sorry. But it was some thing that my letter came on november 7. I love you, Clemmie

John

PS Their are roses in my room an they remind me of you.

Nov. 20, 1909

Dear John,

Your letter came today, and I was indeed glad to get it, for I had expected it for several days. I wondered why you did not write, but I understand it all now, and I am glad you were able to be of service and a comfort to your friend who needed you so much.

Although I wrote to you so recently, I didn't tell you anything about how it is here, and I want you to know everything about me and my life. I have found school teaching at Bowser very pleasant indeed so far. Brother brought Grace and me over here in mid-September.

My principal is as fine as I ever knew for his experience. He is trying to take all the work off me that he can. I only have the first, second and third grades in my room, except for music class, as of last week. We think now that we will get the new room and another teacher.

I am glad you told me about the roses in your room. I wish I could see them too. I feel most beautifully complimented that they should remind you of me.

Write to me again soon,

I love you.

Clemmie

Thanksgiving came, and Clemmie and Grace spent the day at Mrs. McAtee's. Mrs. Hanna and Lettie Mae were also invited. The dinner was a feast of turkey, dressing, cranberry sauce, canned corn, tomatoes, sweet potatoes, homemade rolls with real butter, big glasses of tea, and four kinds of pies with whipped cream. Clemmie thought she might burst, she ate so much.

Not too long after lunch, Lettie Mae began to look pale. She excused herself and walked back home. On the way she lost all of her dinner by the side of the road. The week before she had read in a medical book of her mama's about the signs of pregnancy. Lettie Mae began to sob faintly as she threw herself down on her bed at home.

WITH A GENTLE
UNKNOWN WOE

On Friday morning, November 29, parents crowded into Clemmie's classroom to watch their children in the Thanksgiving play. The parents all seemed pleased.

Little Tommy Hall brought down the house with his rendition of Chief Squanto: "Me want-um big fowl to eat. All womans go cook-um, and put on wampum."

Everyone joined in the singing of "Over the River and through the Woods," and Clemmie played the piano. The activities were over before noon, and school was dismissed until Monday.

That night Mr. Smith and Clemmie went to San Saba in the buggy for a one-day "Institute," or teacher training session, on Saturday. Clemmie sat well over on the right side of the buggy. Suddenly, she felt his fingers come to rest on top of her left hand. Chills ran up her arm. She was thrown into a whirlwind of mental activity.

So Mr. Smith is thinking of me as a possible sweetheart! Oh! What should I say now? ran her thoughts.

"Why, Mr. Smith, I'm flattered that you care for me."

"Please, Clementine, call me Luther."

"Thank you, Luther. You know that I'm several years older than you, and I do have a gentleman friend?"

"Yes, Clemmie, I'm aware of that. However, you know the saying, 'All's fair in love and war!'"

"I'm not sure what to say, Luther. I admire you very much—especially the fact that you are educated and responsible and polished."

"Clemmie, let's just not worry about anything, and we'll see where the road of destiny leads us. I believe in a few months, or by the time school is out, we'll know what is meant to be. Now, tell me something about your family."

"Well, there's not a lot to tell. You've met my parents and probably noticed that my papa is about twenty years older than Mamma. Papa's first wife died fairly early, then several years later my parents met and married. My mother is different because she's really German but was born in Brazil. It's a long and unusual story. Anyway, her mother ended up in Texas. Papa's a preacher, and I'm the oldest of four kids, and you know Grace. My other sister's married and has a little girl, and my brother's married and also has a daughter. They both live near my parents on our farm." Clemmie's nervousness made her say too much, she feared.

"So you are the only one who went to college?" questioned the educated Luther.

"Of us kids, yes. I believe Grace will complete her education. Edna and Jim were never real excited about school, and Papa needed them to help him work the farm. Then both Edna and Jim fell in love while they were young, before they could come back to school." Clemmie continued the family facts.

"Clemmie, just look at the view from here in the moonlight. Do you mind if we get out of the buggy and walk toward the river?" Luther's thoughts seemed to turn toward romance and moonlight.

"Why, that's fine with me," replied romantic Clementine.

Luther halted the horse and tied the reins. Then he jumped down and hurried around to help Clemmie out of the buggy. As he helped lift her from the seat, he decided to risk being a little fresh. Drawing her close, he planted a firm kiss on her lips.

Clemmie was so startled, yet so flattered that she did not know how to react.

"Forgive me, Clemmie. I don't know what overcame me to take such liberty."

"Well, Luther, I don't know what to say. I feel very disloyal to Mr. Briley. You know I try to be a person of high moral values. I'll admit I still have a few doubts to overcome before I become officially engaged to John." Clemmie wanted to be honest.

"Well, perhaps you can see me as a friend who's helping you as you contemplate such an important decision as with whom you'll spend your life," Luther made his point.

"I suppose that could be a reason to continue our friendship, Luther."

That night when they arrived in San Saba, they went to Mrs. Hendrick's house, where Luther had stayed in the past. Mrs. Hendrick was a widow, and her late husband had left her well situated. She was so hospitable and kind to her guests. To Clemmie it was like being at the Waldorf Astoria in New York City.

She went into the bathroom and marveled at the indoor facilities. She pulled the chain to flush the toilet. Nothing happened. Then she tried it again, holding onto the chain longer. Water flowed into the toilet, replacing the contents. *Incredible!* she thought. It was the first home she had ever been in with bathroom plumbing. *How wonderful, not to need to go out-of-doors, nor use the slop jar. How lovely it would be if all homes had such accommodations,* Clemmie thought to herself, doubting if things could ever be that modern.

The next day was filled with lectures at the schoolhouse. The purpose of the short session was to instruct the rural teachers how to teach and deal with the high school students. Most rural teachers were certified only through the eighth grade.

Toward the end of the day, there was an opportunity to write down any question concerning students, and Clemmie decided to formulate a question pertaining to Samuel Smith. Questions were extracted from a wide-mouthed fruit jar and read by the emcee, who happened to be Mr. Jones from Indian Creek School. He began to read in a deep, resounding voice: "'Is there anything we can do as teachers to discourage marriage among these young people? So often I see a very bright young man who falls in love and willingly gives up all hopes of going on to complete his education.' This question is signed by Miss Clementine Wilmeth of Bowser."

Clemmie's question was fielded by Mr. Laurence Taylor, the county superintendent for San Saba County. "This is a very good and pertinent question, Miss Wilmeth. I will attempt an answer.

"I doubt if there is anything we can do as educators to put an end to activities taking place after school is dismissed and at night, or in the summer, which is the forerunner of the early marriage.

"Perhaps we can talk to our students about the availability of scholarships and the great advantages of pursuing higher education, as opposed to the strong pull of the lower nature, of spooning and picnics, which often leave a young woman…uh…in the…uh…family way, and, if the young man is honorable, results in a very young marriage. We could hope that parents and churches would help the situation by giving more teaching about the aftermath of such actions and the inevitable consequences."

The trip home was dedicated to plans for the school for December. Luther played the part of the perfect gentlemen and did not try to get fresh with Clemmie.

It was decided that the class would reenact the birth of Jesus for the Christmas play. Sam Smith was chosen to play the part of Joseph, and Lettie Mae was Mary. One corner of the room was fixed like the stable. During dress rehearsal, as Lettie Mae cradled the doll that represented Baby Jesus, she began to cry.

As her body convulsed with sobs, she threw down the doll and ran from the room. Clemmie sent the students in with Mr. Smith's class, then ran out into the schoolyard after Lettie Mae. She found her sitting on a log near the fence, her head buried in her hands, shoulders shaking, crying like her heart was breaking.

"Lettie Mae, please tell me what is the matter," begged Miss Clemmie. "Did someone say something ugly to you?"

"Oh, Miss Clemmie," stammered Lettie Mae. "Oh, I feel such a strange feeling. It is like a gentle, unknown woe. I don't know what I am going to do…I think I am going to have a baby!"

"Why, Lettie Mae, whatever are you saying? You're not even married!" Then the startled teacher remembered the night Samuel had visited Lettie Mae when Mrs. Hanna was gone. She wrapped her arms around the young girl and held her close.

When the night of the play arrived, Lettie Mae came through beautifully, as did Sam and all the other kids involved. No one even suspected that a current, real-life drama was being portrayed on stage, along with the old, sweet story of Jesus' birth. In fact, Samuel Smith knew exactly how Joseph must have felt when he first knew that Mary would have a baby. Except Joseph knew Mary's baby was *not* his, whereas Samuel knew it was *his* very own child. He concluded that Joseph must have felt even more worried than he did, and that would be *very* worried.

Not long after school was dismissed, Clemmie hurried home and packed a small trunk. A weeklong institute for teachers was to be held in the exact same place as the Thanksgiving one, San Saba, Texas. All teachers were required to go.

Luther Smith told Clemmie he would like to take her in his

buggy. They were invited to sleep with a good family, the Harkeys. Luther was the perfect gentleman during the trip, and they arrived at the cozy cottage outside of San Saba in the gloaming. There was a delicious supper, then the adults sat in front of the fire and talked until late.

After Clemmie got into bed in the children's room, she lay still a long time, listening to the wind as it whistled fearfully around the house. She made herself think about her life and try to figure things out. The year of 1909 was all but gone, and it had been a year of many decisions, Clemmie felt. She had decided for sure that she would marry John, now that all possibilities of Raleigh were gone for good. It shamed her to think she was entertaining thoughts of another man. She had trained herself to pray when a conflict assailed her mind.

"Oh, Lord, please be with me in this coming new year and guide me into the pathway that Thou knowest is best. And Father, I thank Thee for this family, so generous and hospitable and deserving of rich blessings. Please guard John tonight in Dallas, and keep him, and me, in your watchcare. And be with Mr. Smith. I ask all this in Jesus' name, amen."

Saturday, December 18, dawned bright with sleet covering the ground. It was an unusual sight for that part of Texas, and the children were delighted and wanted to get out and play in it. Clemmie and Luther went on to San Saba. Clemmie was chilled to the bone. When they arrived at Mrs. Hendrick's, they thawed out around her fire. She was so jolly and told Clemmie she wanted her to bake a pineapple cake. Clemmie was flattered to be asked, and since she had done that for Mamma so many times, she knew the recipe by heart.

On Sunday morning, as Clemmie opened her eyes, she sensed a brightness through the windows. Sliding out of bed, she pulled the curtain to the side and saw a world white with snow.

Oh, thank you, Father, for this gift of snow! It reminds me of that Scripture in Isaiah: "Though your sins be as scarlet, they shall be as white as snow."

After lunch, Luther asked Clemmie if she wanted to go for a walk in the snow. Her face lit up. She bundled up in her cloth coat, her laced boots, and a wool knit hat and mittens. They rode far out of town on the road to Lampasas and left the buggy to walk under some beautiful cedar trees with their branches loaded with snow. As they walked, Luther seemed to enjoy being close to Clemmie and took her hand in both of his.

"Can you believe that in less than two weeks, we will enter the year of our Lord, 1910, Clementine? I read in the *Dallas News* last night a summary of the year's events. It looks like women will begin voting before long in England. We won't be too far behind. That Mrs. Pankhurst, who has led the women's fight to vote, is really something. Pretty old, too, to be so active. I think she is around fifty. She even spent six weeks in jail and then wrote about how unpleasant it was. Another big news story is about Peary making it to the North Pole after all those years of trying. You remember it took him eight tries to do that and around twenty-seven years."

"I'm glad that Cook was exposed as a fraud. The Eskimos said he turned back twenty miles short of reaching the Pole," Clemmie added, wanting to show that she was among the informed, too. She certainly did admire the fact that Luther kept abreast of current events. She wondered if John's world was not smaller, with most of his attention being within a few miles of wherever he was.

"Here's a little quiz for you, Clementine. What famous Indian Chief died this year?"

"Well, that would have to be Geronimo! He was eighty years old, I believe."

"Absolutely correct, Clemmie! And what are the names of two men from Europe who are traveling around in the United States and teaching their theories about the mind?"

"That would be Sigmund Freud and Carl Jung. I believe they have helped a lot of people, but in my opinion, they put too much emphasis on…um…the physical urges." It was important to Clemmie not to be coarse or vulgar in her speech.

"I agree totally, Clemmie," Luther said a little nervously. "And here is your last question: Who is the newest screen star, whose real name is 'Gladys Smith?'"

"I know this one! That would be Miss Mary Pickford."

"You made a perfect score, and I'm impressed. For that you'll get a reward! Oh, and I forgot to ask this one: Which song has been the most popular one for 1909?"

"Let's see, I can think of two or three. 'By the Light of the Silvery Moon,' 'Put on Your Old Grey Bonnet,' and, 'I Wonder Who's Kissing Her Now.'"

"You get top score," Luther said.

Just then they reached the waterfalls where the San Saba River tumbled down to lower ground. Luther pulled Clemmie close in an embrace. He lifted her head up with his index finger curved under her chin. Then he planted his lips fully on hers and made the kiss last fully ten seconds. Clemmie had the sensation that she might swoon but managed to bring herself back under control, holding onto Luther's forearms as he released his hold on her.

"Luther, you have set my mind to work like a churn. I hardly know my own heart. I need more time to know what I should do. Please be patient with me."

"I can be very patient, my darling Clementine! Very patient indeed. You just don't worry your pretty head, and in time you will realize the type of man who is yearning to belong to you."

On Monday the Institute began. That night the teachers entertained each other at the opera house. Clemmie read a poem she had written about the Institute. She had worked several hours on it, usually late at night, and was rather pleased with her delivery. She didn't feel as nervous as she sometimes felt, standing in front of all those teachers. Then there was coffee and cake for refreshments.

Friday was the last day, and they adjourned at noon. It was

Christmas Eve Day. Luther took Clemmie all the way to Lometa to catch her train. He gave Clemmie a peck on the cheek and told her he would see her at SMU the next week. She rode the train to McKinney and had a delightful Christmas visit with her father's family.

Mary Straughn, Clemmie's cousin, took her to catch the train to Dallas for another short Institute. Once at the big building on the campus of SMU, Clemmie's eyes searched the crowd for Luther, and she spotted him just as the group was moving out into the hall from the big auditorium.

That night Luther and Clemmie went together in Luther's buggy to the Southland Hotel. Each one paid fifty cents for a nice room. The next day, they left for home. They arrived back in Bowser on New Year's Eve. It seemed awfully good to Clemmie to be back at home. On the porch in the moonlight, Clemmie looked toward the heavens and said: "Good night, old Year, thou didst bring us drought and hard times. Thou didst bring me many tears and heartaches in thy first part, but in thy latter part thou didst bring the life-giving rain and thou didst bring to me peace and joy and happiness. Welcome, Glad New Year! What dost thou bring? Oh, I pray thee, bring us hearts so strong we shall not faint. Good night."

"The following original poem was written by Miss Clementine Wilmeth and read at the close of the Teacher's Institute held here in December. It is the policy of the *San Saba News* not to print poetry of any kind, but at the request of the teachers as a body and quite a number of individuals, an exception is made to the rule and this one is given space."

THE INSTITUTE

Now what does it mean,
Now what can it be?
That wherever we look
The teachers we see.
They've come from the hills,
The plain and the wood,
From creeks and hollows
Where school houses stood.
For we are informed,
The law hath decreed,
That each must now come
And labor indeed;
In every known way
Endeavor to find,
The very best way
To train up the mind.
And now to San Saba
We bid adieu,
To friends and teachers,
To all of you,
We cannot forget,
The kindness you've shown;
We promise to bring
From seed you have sown
The kindness and noblest
And best of fruit,
And remember with joy,
The Institute.

Clementine Wilmeth
Published by the *San Saba News*, January of 1910

WILL YOU THINK OF ME?

It was New Year's Day of 1910 when Clemmie first noticed that Lettie Mae was thicker around her abdomen. *Yes, she is definitely pregnant. So what is going to happen now?* Clemmie wondered to herself.

That afternoon, Clemmie and Luther went to clean up the schoolhouse. Sam and Lettie Mae appeared after about an hour. For a few minutes they tried to help with the sweeping and dusting. Then Sam blurted out, "We need someone to help us. I think we need to get married."

Mr. Smith pulled four desks around in a group and motioned for each to sit down.

"Sam, do you and Lettie really love each other?" Mr. Smith asked.

"More than anybody knows, Mr. Smith," Sam quickly answered.

"How old are you, Sam?" Mr. Smith seemed to have planned his questions.

"Well, I'll be eighteen in May." Samuel knew eighteen was a lot older than seventeen.

"And don't you think that is a little young to be getting married?" Mr. Smith continued.

"Yes, sir, I do. But Lettie Mae is…well, we think she's…having a baby. And I want to say that this is all my fault. I just love her so much, and once when Mrs. Hanna was gone, we got kinda carried away, and it was like I had never felt this way before, and I just loved Lettie Mae so much, and it seemed like it was…I mean, I just couldn't help myself. It was just one time that we were…together like that."

By this time Lettie Mae had started to cry. The tears were running down her face and dropping on the desk, and she was making little tear circles with her index finger. Clemmie felt so sorry for both of them that she started to cry, too. Luther felt like he should somehow solve the problem and help the young couple cope with this.

"Now, Lettie Mae and Sam, let's make a plan. Lettie Mae, this is not the end of the world. Sure, you and Sam have 'jumped the gun,' so to speak, but your lives are not ruined, and they are not over! Some day we will look back and smile, just thinking about how awful everything seemed, and then how good it turned out."

"Yes, Sam, I have wanted to help you for a long time," Clemmie said. "You're such a good student, and it will be a real shame if you can't go on to college. I want to give you money each month, and I believe there are others who would like to help you."

Suddenly, Lettie Mae started to cry aloud. "Mama will send me away and make me give the baby away." Lettie Mae's tears were copious.

"Lettie Mae, your mother loves you very much and, in the end, will want to do the best thing for you, Sam, and the baby. After all, this is her flesh and blood, and she won't want a stranger to have your baby. Why, she was probably about your age when she married your father," Clemmie said to reassure Lettie Mae.

"Miss Clemmie and Mr. Smith, would both of you go with us to talk to my parents and to Mrs. Hanna?" questioned Sam, sincere brown eyes pleading with them.

"Of course we will, Sam," Clemmie assured him.

All four went and got in Mr. Smith's buggy, since Samuel's home was a mile out of town. The Smith family was upright and hardworking. Sam had two younger brothers.

Finding both parents at home, they all sat down at the kitchen table.

"Mother and Father, Lettie Mae and I want to get married. We know we're too young, but we're gonna have a baby, and it's all my fault." Sam had decided to just blurt it out. His mother began to cry, and his dad turned very red with anger.

"Son, I thought I had taught you to always keep your pants buttoned up. Now just look at the mess you're in, and bringing shame on your mother and me, and Mrs. Hanna."

They agreed that marriage was the best solution and thought it should be the next week in Brownwood at the county courthouse. Then the six of them went to see Mrs. Hanna, where Clemmie boarded. As soon as they arrived and Mrs. Hanna opened the door, she gasped, correctly guessing the meaning of the unexpected visit.

"Oh no! Are you going to tell me that you've gone and ruined yourself, Lettie Mae? Oh, how could you do this to me when I've worked so hard to give you a good life? Wasn't it enough that your father died when he was only forty-nine years old and left me with no means to support myself?" Mrs. Hanna's voice went shrill, nearly into a shriek.

Lettie Mae fled to her room, unable to stand the pressure of her mother's barrage of guilty questions. She lay down on her bed and buried her head under her pillow. Then she remembered that it was exactly on this bed that such unspeakable pleasure had developed into such a horrible nightmare.

"Oh, Lord, just let me die. Let Sam and me and my baby all die like Romeo and Juliet," Lettie Mae implored the Almighty.

The next weekend the nervous young couple was married in the Brown County Courthouse by Judge Jones, and they went home to live with Lettie Mae's mother. This meant Clemmie had to move, so she made arrangements with Mrs. Phillips, who lived only half a mile away, and she and Grace got settled in.

In January a third teacher, Miss Tommie Browning, joined Clemmie and Mr. Smith at the Bowser school, and the new room was completed and given to Clemmie. Toward the end of January, Haley's Comet began appearing, and the whole town would go outdoors and stare at the phenomenon in the sky right after sundown, in the gloaming, in the west.

Although Luther was still friendly, he had dropped Clemmie as a girlfriend and just couldn't get enough of Miss Tommie. Clemmie thought the feeling of jealousy was the lowest of human emotions and resolved that she was *not* going to let that monster get her. But she would catch herself staring at Tommie and trying to see why she had been jilted by Luther Smith for this girl. Tommie was vivacious, funny, pretty, with red curly hair, and had a figure like an hourglass. She had a rounded bust and very pretty clothes.

Now that Luther seemed taken with Miss Tommie, Clemmie could see how foolish she had been to allow herself to think he might be a better catch than John Briley. She felt ashamed of herself for being untrue, but at least she felt more certainty about her future with John.

Grace needed to go to San Saba to appear before the Board of Examiners. At sixteen years a student could receive a teaching certificate if they scored well on the test. It looked like Clemmie's contract would not be renewed at Bowser, so this might be her last time to be with Luther Smith. Luther had agreed to go with the Wilmeth girls in Clemmie's buggy. Clemmie and Luther bid farewell to Bowser and left for San Saba with Grace. Although they felt a little sad as they left, they tried to be jolly and even sang a little bit.

"Wait till the Sun Shines, Nellie" was a favorite of theirs. Luther had a good voice and could harmonize with Clemmie's soprano, and Grace sang alto.

"Wait till the sun shines, Nellie...When the clouds go drifting by...
"We will be happy, Nellie...Don't you sigh...
"Down lover's lane we'll wander...
"Sweethearts, you and I...
"Wait till the sun shines, Nellie...Bye and bye!"

The trip was pleasant, and they arrived just as dark was settling over San Saba. They stayed at the hotel. It cost seventy-five cents for two rooms. The next morning, Clemmie and Grace were up early and went to the courthouse. Luther went for a little while and told Grace and Clemmie good-bye. Clemmie walked back outside with him and couldn't keep back the tears, knowing it was the end of another chapter of her life. He gave her a quick hug and a peck on the cheek, told her he would probably see her in Austin, since both were going for the six-week Normal required of teachers.

Grace scored eighty-eight and qualified for a five-year teaching certificate. Clemmie felt very proud of her little sister. They slept at Mrs. Browning's that night and started for home the next morning.

Jogging along in the buggy, Clemmie noticed that the world had lost its glow—in fact, although the sun was shining on the countryside, clouds had settled over her soul. The river was up, but they were able to ford it at the Reeves' crossing by sitting on the back of the buggy seat. After they got home, Clemmie felt the last vestige of energy leak out and wanted to take to her bed. However, she forced herself to do the things that had to be done—washing, ironing, cooking.

Dear Lord, It is coming back over me, that old feeling of being blue. It must have something to do with loss. A few months ago it was the loss of Raleigh, and now it must be the loss of Luther. I have so little energy and such a lonesome feeling that I can hardly live. Lord, fill me up with Thyself—keep me from being dependent on a man's attention for my happiness.

Please, God, don't let Mamma sit me down for a little talk, she implored silently.

Meanwhile in Dallas, John was eagerly packing for a move back to Ebony. His father needed him desperately to help with the farm, and besides, he could be near his darling Clementine. How he had anticipated this reunion and had daydreamed that he might already have the money to buy a brand new buggy and two fine horses to pull it. He would drive up to Clemmie's home and be so proud to hold her in his arms and take her away in the new buggy.

The reality turned out quite differently for John, nearly dashing all his dreams. There was no money for the new carriage, nor horses, and he first saw Clemmie at church on Sunday morning.

To John, Clemmie didn't seem nearly as happy to see him as he had expected. He gave her a slight half hug, not wanting to embarrass her in front of the gathering churchgoers. Maybe it was the wrong time of the month, John reasoned. He knew he would never understand women. After all, she was the one who had gotten their romance going last fall, and now she had been the center of his world for more than eight months.

John Briley and Press Reeves, a cousin of John's, both went home with Clemmie and Grace for lunch and stayed until nearly dark. After sunset the sisters took them over on Big Hill for their favorite view of the river. John took Clemmie off by themselves and asked her if anything was wrong.

"Clemmie, I've looked for'd to seeing you for a long time. It was all that kept me a-going through the rough kind of life I've had in

Dallas. You don't seem to be happy like I thought you'd be. Tell me what's happened that changed ever'thing."

"Oh, John, please forgive me. About once a year I just seem to go down in spirit and body, and I don't understand it at all. Many times it has been just when school is out, and I realize that I may never see those children again. I become filled with sadness.

"Please don't take this personally. I am truly glad you've come back home to Ebony, and I know this dark shadow will be gone in a few weeks. Please know that this is *not* the Clemmie that I really am, and within the month I will be like the girl you fell in love with."

She knew there was no way she could tell him about Luther and the feelings she had for him, and how he had jilted her for Miss Tommie, and now he was gone from her life, probably for good. How could she expect him to understand that kind of treason? No, he should never know about Luther Smith.

"Oh, John, please…for…give…me," she sputtered between sobs. "I just feel so sad, right when I should feel so glad. It's like all my emotions are all mixed up."

John looked around for a rock to sit on; he sat down, then pulled Clemmie into his lap. "Let me just hold you and comfort you, sweetheart. I understand that our minds can get a little sick and tired, just like our bodies do. You just need me to look after you and protect you from the hard things in life."

Grace and Press had walked on down toward the river, and Clemmie could hear happy voices growing distant. She allowed herself to be coddled and soothed like a baby and didn't mind when John began to stroke her face and hair. It felt good, and she felt safe with him. She knew she owed him a good kiss at least, for all he had anticipated and the way she had been a disappointment to him.

— — — — — — — —

Soon it was time for Clemmie to attend the Normal in Austin, so on a Thursday, in mid-June, Clemmie returned to her hill to say her good-byes. She prayed a long prayer, asking God to help her get things in perspective, to get over her sadness, to forget about Luther, and to love John more deeply. Then she resolutely headed for home, turning once to see her hill in the gloaming.

"May God watch between me and thee, Big Hill, while we are absent one from another. Good-bye."

Early Friday morning Papa Wilmeth hitched his two big-footed, slow horses to the wagon, hoisted Clemmie's trunk in, and they and sister Grace left for Brownwood, twenty-four miles to the north. Clemmie would catch the train for Austin at 7:30 p.m. They pulled into the train station twelve hours after they had started the journey. That was an average of only two miles an hour. Clemmie ran to the ticket counter, kissed her father and her sister on the cheek, and barely got aboard when the train sounded its whistle and pulled out.

The transition to Austin and her new boardinghouse was not easy, but there were a few new friends. There were trips to church and sightseeing tours to see the Capitol, the Confederate Home, the State Cemetery, and the insane asylum, where there were 1,425 inmates. Clemmie wondered if any of them could be cured and go back home, or if they would die there without friends or family.

Clemmie saw Luther several times in Austin. Although he talked to her the first Saturday of registration, he seemed to avoid her or else had nothing to say after that day. He often ate at the boardinghouse where Clemmie lived, yet treated her coldly if she approached him.

On Wednesday, July 20, Clemmie received a letter from Luther, with a partial explanation for his cold behavior. He said since she had Mr. Briley, and he had Tommie, he thought it best that they not be seen together. However, would she meet him on top of the tower on the last day of the Normal at one p.m.?

Clemmie dressed very carefully that day, wearing her prettiest blouse tucked into her nicest black skirt. Her heartbeat accelerated as she approached the tower and began the climb to the top. Sure enough, there was Luther Smith, hands outstretched to assist her with the final step.

High above the scurrying students, Clemmie was transported in time and place. They were the only ones up there, and they took a minute or two to walk around and catch the view. Then Luther took Clemmie into his arms and drew her tightly to his chest. She closed her eyes, head tilted upward. She felt his lips brush hers quickly, then his lips returned, pressed hard and warmly. Then she opened her gray-blue eyes wide, remembered how cold he had been and how much John loved her, and pulled away from his embrace.

"I'm sorry if I have taken advantage of you, my dear. I only wanted you to know how much I care. Please remember I will always admire you, Clemmie."

Tears blurred her eyes as Clemmie found her way back to her boardinghouse. She threw herself across her bed and cried for fifteen minutes. Then she got up, washed her face, and wrote a poem about the tower to give herself some kind of closure.

Good-bye, Mr. Smith...*forever!*

HEIGHT OF JOY

By Clementine Wilmeth

I climbed up the famous tower, to catch a final view;
Out of breath, I saw the Mister…who made my dreams come true.
Above the rushing people, above the busy mill;
Two lovers gently shared a kiss; it seemed the world stood still.
Within those fleeting seconds, my world forgot its care,
Then down we went to earth again with memory of our dare.

AND LOVE ME

As the train began to leave the station in Austin, Clemmie settled into her seat by a window, leaned back, closed her eyes, and relived the events of the day.

Today brought me ecstasy and agony...the meeting high above, the ending of a secret love, she thought. She had put two letters in her purse to reread on the train. Remembering that, she took out the first one. It was from John Briley.

July 13, 1910
Ebony Texas

Miss Clemmie Wilmeth
Austin Tex

Esteemed Friend,

I will write again this morning and no doubt you will be surprised to hear from me again.

Clemmie I guess I will have to disappoint you and my self in regard to meeting you when you return. Now I hope you will not think I have willfully tried to decive you though it may seam so to you as this was my own proposition. The dry weather has held on so long looks like we are not going to make any thing at all and so I am without a buggy yet. Hope this will find you well and injoying life. which I presume you will. Well I will close as I haven't any thing of interest at this writing hoping to See you a gain in the near future Goodbye

John

Clemmie's eyes smarted with tears as she thought about John and how much he had wanted to come to Brownwood in a new buggy with fine horses and fetch her. What a good man, and he cared so much for her. It still bothered Clemmie that he was not very educated and made so many grammatical mistakes in his letters…even forgetting the period, or not capitalizing the first word of every sentence. Perhaps she could teach him some of the rules of writing.

The second letter was from the school trustees at Bowser.

We are sorry to inform you of this, but we have employed Miss Tommie Rogers to replace you for the coming school year.

The letter was signed by the three trustees.

Clemmie had been very surprised, and very hurt, and felt that the way they had treated her was very unfair.

I poured my heart and soul into my teaching all year, and I know that I did my job well, and I did nothing wrong that I know of. So why don't they want me to come back?

The only school she had heard of that was of interest to her was in Ochiltree County in the Texas Panhandle, and that would be so far from home that she could not even visit at Christmas. She wondered what that would mean for her courtship with John if she were that far away. After all, he was back in Ebony partly to be near her. She would have to have more information on the situation in Ochiltree before she could decide to go there for the coming school year.

The train chugged on through the night, stopping at each little town along the way. Clemmie began to feel terribly sleepy and fell into a rather miserable sleep. Just about the time she would fall asleep, the conductor would call out the name of one of the little towns, waking Clemmie up.

"Rogers!"

"Temple!"

"Belton!"

"Nolanville!"

"Kileen!"

"Lampasas!"

"Lometa!"

"Goldthwaite!"

"Mullen!"

"Zephyr!"

When she heard Zephyr, she knew Brownwood was next. She gathered up her things, then looked out the window, anxious to see who had come to meet her.

It was 9:30 a.m. when the train pulled into the Brownwood station, making thirteen hours of travel to cover the 180 miles.

There was Grace in the buggy, waiting to meet Clemmie. She stood and waved excitedly as Clemmie appeared in the door of the car. *She looks so cute with her hair braided and pulled to the top of her head,* Clemmie thought. *And that yellow blouse and the brown riding pants look so modern. She could pass for one of the rich girls.*

"Hi, sis! Welcome back to the Brown County Desert!" Grace had jumped down from the wagon and greeted her big sister with a carefree air and a warm hug and a kiss on the cheek.

"I am *so* glad to see you! You must've slept in Brownwood last night? Thank you so much for doing this for me, Grace. I thought maybe it would work out for John to come, but he probably doesn't have his buggy yet."

The sisters had a lot to talk about. Clemmie told Grace about the happenings at the Normal, including the kiss on the tower. Grace confided that Mr. Smith had also kissed her once in Bowser, and that she thought he fell for whoever was around, till the next one came along. In a way this helped lessen Clemmie's pain over losing Luther and his type of love. At lunchtime, Grace produced the little box of food that Mamma had sent along. They sat under a live oak tree by the side of the road and had a picnic.

"Oh, Clemmie, guess what I heard! Lettie Mae and Sam Smith had their baby about three days ago. A great big boy, and they named him Luther after Mr. Smith, of course. They say that Mrs. Hanna is about to bust, she is so proud. We'll have to go see them soon."

"Oh, I'm so happy to hear that! I really believe that this is going to be one of those stories that started off bad and ends up good. Some of us want to see Sam go on to college, and I intend to help him with the money part. Yes, let's plan to go over for a visit before I leave for the Panhandle, if that job works out. I dread to go so far away, but it is the only thing I have heard about."

It was Saturday night before Clemmie saw John. He came to take her to the Methodist meeting. He looked so proud as he drove up to the little house in a brand new buggy pulled by two pretty, matched horses. Clemmie let him put his arm around her, and she sat close to him in the buggy. He smelled good, like Bay Rum lotion, and was wearing a blue shirt and black trousers and shoes that looked new.

Late that night, underneath a bright moon, John took Clemmie in his arms and gave her a real kiss, firm and long.

"Clemmie, I love you so much, and I've felt this-a-way for a long, long time."

"John, I know I love you, too. I am sorry it has taken me so long to realize that you are the only one for me."

"I have waited many years to hear you say that you love me, Clemmie. I can't tell you the happiness I'm feelin' right now. I don't know how I kin let you go away, since we've finally found each other, but I know it's important that you teach one more year. That'll help us have a good start when we git married.

John and Clemmie sat together in church the next morning, and most of the little congregation noticed that the "die was cast" by the sparkle in their eyes. The last song they sang was "The Lily of the Valley." John squeezed Clemmie's hand and bent his head over and whispered, "This is my favorite song!"

To himself, John thought that God must be saying he approved of John's choice this time.

I have found a friend in Jesus, He's everything to me,
He's the fairest of ten thousand to my soul;
The Lily of the Valley, in Him alone I see,
All I need to cleanse and make me fully whole.
He will never, never leave me, nor yet forsake me here,
While I live by faith and do His blessed will;
A wall of fire about me, I've nothing now to fear,
With His manna He my hungry soul shall fill.
He's the Lily of the Valley, the Bright and Morning Star,
He's the fairest of ten thousand to my soul.

John's favorite phrase was "He will *never, never leave me.*" After all, he had been left, in a sense, by his real mother, his stepmother, his older siblings, his little brothers, Runt, then Homer, and by his ex-wife, Nancy. But Jesus would never leave. And if Clemmie would be his wife one day, she would never leave him. He felt sure of that.

That Sunday, John went home with the Wilmeths for Sunday dinner. It took a good while, nearly two hours, for the women to get the meal to the table. Papa and John walked down to the river bottom to inspect the newly grafted pecan trees. The two men seemed to genuinely like each other.

"Son, I am happy that you and Clemmie seem to be courting. Your papa once told me about your first marriage several years ago, and I regretted that you had such an unpleasant experience. However, I believe you're free and clear to find another wife."

"I'm glad you know about what all happened, Mr. Wilmeth. I wanted you to know 'cause I'm not trying to trick anyone. Clemmie wants to follow the Bible in ever'thing, and we've studied together a lot."

Papa decided to bring all his children together for a reunion that August. After all, he was nearly seventy-five, and although his dad had lived to be eighty-four, one could never be certain of when death might come. He knew Clemmie would enjoy seeing all the family before she had to leave for the Panhandle.

Of Papa and his first wife's five children, Charlie was dead and Campbell was in California, too far away to come. Papa went in the wagon and fetched his daughters from his first marriage, Clara and Nellie. Their brother, Jo, and his wife, Lou, and two sons came in their car. All four of Papa and Mamma's children were there: Clemmie, Jim, Edna, and Grace.

The family visitors stayed two nights, and everyone had a good time. The second evening, they took their supper as a picnic to the river bottom. Papa had arranged for a good friend to come and make their picture under the big pecan tree. Then they decided to walk on down to the sidewalk on the river.

They sat and sang and talked until the moon was high. Someone started singing *In the Gloaming*, and Clemmie thought how that song fit her very well at this point in her life. Tears welled up and spilled down her cheeks.

Then Grace, seeing her sister's tears, decided they needed to sing a happier song, and she began one: "Oh My Darling Clementine." Then they sang some favorite hymns, including "Shall We Gather At the River" and "Amazing Grace."

As Clemmie walked back toward the house with her family, she felt that this reunion was a beautiful "hello and good-bye" present for her, from her papa and her God. She fell exhausted into her bed and dreamed that she was running up Big Hill, into the arms of a man whose face she could not quite make out! Was he Raleigh, or Luther, or John?

Oh, who do I love? And who will think of me and love me?

AS YOU DID
ONCE LONG AGO

The drought of August had wreaked havoc on the farmers of Mills
County. As Clemmie climbed up Big Hill and looked down, she saw
that everything in the field was burned to a brown crisp. The fruit
trees in the orchard were nearly dead and had dropped most of their
leaves. The tanks were dried up, and water had to be carried from the
river for the cattle to drink.

Clemmie decided to pray that God would send an abundant rain.
She opened her well-worn Bible at random, and her eyes fell on
Jeremiah.

She could hardly believe her eyes! She felt that God was speaking
to her and to the people of Mills County.

The word of the Lord which came to Jeremiah concerning the drought; and the cry of Jerusalem goes up. Her nobles send their servants for water; they come to the cisterns, they find no water, they return with their vessels empty; since there is no rain on the land, the farmers are ashamed, they cover their heads.

Jeremiah 14:1

The people had sinned against God, and they were being punished. Clemmie wondered aloud, "Maybe that is why no rain fell in Mills County in Texas. There's a lot of sinning going on around here, too."

Getting out the thick, informative letter sent by Brother Battenfield, who was a citizen of Ochiltree and a preacher for the Christian Church, Clemmie memorized the facts that she found in the brochure. Ochiltree had begun as a trading post about 1880. By 1889, Ochiltree was named the county seat of the thirty-square-mile county of Ochiltree. The population by 1910 was more than five hundred people, and the town now had a wonderful, two-story school which had cost all of $3,500. Education was the most desirable commodity, and best of all, each teacher was paid fifty dollars per month.

Yes, I will make this the best year of all my teaching career, especially since it might be the last. Hopefully, after the school year is over, I'll marry John and become a good housewife back here in Mills County.

Gathering up her papers and Bible, Clemmie walked over to see the beautiful view of her beloved river for one last look.

"Oh, River, you know all my secrets and all my longings. And knowing you are here, calmly flowing along and minding your own business, while I am having this adventure, will be a steadying place in my mind, a silver ribbon that ties long ago with my present and with my future."

John came over that night. He wished he could take Clemmie

somewhere really nice, like one of those fine restaurants he had seen in Dallas. But that was not possible. He did take her in the new buggy with the two fine horses to San Saba.

They both had chicken and dumplings in the only café in town. Afterward they drove down toward the waterfall. Clemmie was reminded of the last time she had walked under the snow-laden cedars with Luther Smith.

John found a good place to stop the buggy, and he turned it so they could see the full moon. One thing he had learned about women was that if you would talk to them first, they would tend to be warmer in a physical way.

"Clemmie, I don't know how I can get along out here without you. It's not a very exciting life over there on our farm with Pa, and he's not feeling good a lot o' the time. You're what keeps me going, all through these hot days. I think about you all the time, Clemmie. I hope I can just get by till you're back here again.

"'Course, I really want to try and have some money ahead for when you get back from up north, and we can get married. Clemmie, that's the one thing that'll be like steam for my engine. Oh, girl, I'll miss you so much!"

With all that said, John tightened his arm around Clemmie, and when she saw the glimmer of a tear in his crystal blue eyes, she melted.

"Oh, John, my precious sweetheart." She nestled closer and put both arms tight around him. She liked feeling his chest pressing on her body, and she could feel the vibration of his strong heartbeat.

"Whoa, boy." John gave a slight pull on the reins to steady the horses. He pulled Clemmie over onto his lap. She was wearing a white batiste blouse with a high neck, buttoned all down the front.

"John, I love you very much. You've made me happy in every way. I even want you to love me more tonight, but I want us to do things in the right way. I want you to know that I do desire you, and I never thought that a woman could enjoy love this much. I guess we had better just stick to hugging and kissing until we're married. Do you agree with that?"

"Yes, Clemmie. That's by far the best way. Clemmie, I've loved you since I first laid eyes on you when you were just a girl. I always wanted you for my girl, but you seemed to be taken with the Riley fella, and I tried to stay back. Then I ended up in Dallas, and as you know, I was sorely tempted.

"I owe you some explanation about how it was with Nancy. It was like the devil took hold o' me. I'd never been with a woman...you know, like that, and uh...and she just knew how to make me really want her. I couldn't stop myself, and I've been sorry ever since. We got married, but things went bad pretty quick.

"There never was no baby a'tall, so either she lost it or she went an' lied to me. She started going out a lot at night, and finally my brother saw her with another man and told me. So when I asked her about it, I discovered it was the truth. I told her I was through for good, and she could take care of all the papers for a divorce. I moved back with my brother and never saw her again. It's a sorry story, but I wanted you to know the straight of it, Clemmie. I never told anybody else, 'cept Pa and your papa."

"Thank you, John, for telling me how it was. That is about what I'd imagined had happened. Knowing you, I just knew it wasn't your fault that things went wrong. We'll try not to talk about this anymore, since I know you have asked God for forgiveness and that you want that part of your life to be over and forgiven."

"Clemmie, you're my ideal of a woman. You're beautiful inside and out, and I don't want you to ever feel like you lack anything that a man could want.

"I've gotcha a present." John pulled a small box from his pocket. It was wrapped in gold paper and tied with a blue ribbon. Clemmie opened it. There was a tiny diamond on a gold ring.

"Oh, John! What a beautiful ring! It's a diamond! How did you ever have the money for such a lovely ring? Please put it on my finger."

Tears rolled down her cheeks as John forced the ring over her knuckle. Just then a huge raindrop fell right on Clemmie's nose. Then a loud roll of thunder clapped and the rain began in earnest.

"Oh, John, it's raining!" squealed Clemmie.

"By Jove, it sure is! This is sure our lucky night, Clemmie."

"John, earlier this evening, I begged God to send rain to save our cattle and our crops. I believe God has answered that prayer. Just like He did for Elijah one time."

The thunder and lightning stopped as suddenly as they began. John whispered softly in the ear of both horses, knowing how the storm could leave them skittish. It turned out to be one of the happiest evenings in Clemmie's life. Years later she would remember how God blessed her and John and all the farmers of Mills County on a certain August night.

John insisted that he would take Clemmie to the train station the following Thursday morning. And so he did, in the wagon, since she had two trunks to carry. She carried a small valise with her, containing her diary, her letters of recommendation, various items of food that would not spoil, some cookies in a little box, a large fruit jar full of water, a change of clothing, some paper, a pen, her Bible, and a book, *Little Women*.

The train rolled into the station with the words "Santa Fe" painted in yellow on the front car and the engine. John helped Clemmie get on and find a seat. She much preferred a window seat so she could see the scenery along the way.

"All aboard!" yelled the conductor. John bent low and gave Clemmie a kiss on her lips.

"Sweetheart, I'll be right here, waitin' for you when you come home. Then we'll never be separated a-gin, Lord willin'.' Let's keep our letters goin' back and forth an' pray for each other ever' night, and ever' morning. God bless you, sweet girl o' mine."

"Good-bye, John. You've been so good to me. See, I'm wearing my ring. It'll remind me constantly of the love you have for me, and I for you. Please take care of yourself. Bye-bye."

John reluctantly jumped off the car just as it began moving. Clemmie felt butterflies in her stomach. But this would be good—an experience to remember the rest of her life.

Clemmie looked out of the window as they left Brownwood behind. Traveling northeast, they went through Blanket and Comanche. Clemmie smiled to herself, remembering a little joke: "Why are Brownwood and Comanche so cold? Because there is just one Blanket between them!"

Daylight was fast fading, and Clemmie felt her eyes getting heavy. Her mother had made several little meals and wrapped them in tissue paper. She took out the first one and opened it. Two biscuits spread with syrup. Later on she would eat a piece of fruit and try to sleep some.

The trip back to the bathroom was quite an ordeal, and there were nearly always several people waiting. One had to pass through the connection to the next car, and that was frightening to Clemmie. It was all she could do to keep her balance as the car jostled and swayed. The noise was overpowering. Although it was only 130 miles to Fort Worth, the stops at all the small towns along the way turned the trip into a six-hour journey.

Clemmie was going to have to change trains in Fort Worth and again just east of Amarillo. Both places had layovers. She knew she was on the *Atchison, Topeka,* and *Santa Fe* from Brownwood to Fort Worth. When she left there she would be on the *Fort Worth and Denver City Line.* It went all the way to Colorado, so she would have to change trains at Washburn, near Amarillo. The connecting train would be from the *A.T. & Santa Fe,* headed northeast toward Ochiltree County.

Clemmie tried to get comfortable with the tiny pillow and small blanket given to her. She hated to tilt her seat back for fear it would bother the woman behind her, a young mother jostling a somewhat unhappy baby.

Eventually the train arrived at a big station as the conductor proudly announced "*Fo-ort* Worth, we're in *Fo-ooort* Worth, Texas!"

"Ladies to the right, gents to the left," was the usual explanation for bathroom locations. Clemmie would have a layover of five hours here. During that time, she had some fitful sleep on a hard bench. A man who reminded her of Papa started a conversation with her. He seemed nice, but she felt too miserable to concentrate.

Clemmie decided that she would never spend a night in a train depot again, if she could help it. When the sun was about to rise, she bought a doughnut and a cup of coffee and sat alone with a newspaper at a little table.

Feeling almost like her head was floating, she finally heard her train come in, gathered up her things, and got on. This was the *Fort Worth & Denver City Railroad* that went all the way to Colorado. Clemmie was relieved that she found a seat to herself and would feel freer to sleep or read or just watch the scenery. Once settled in, she opened up another of the little packets of food her mother had fixed. This one had a big slice of lemon jelly cake, a biscuit with jelly, and a pear.

Clemmie took a brochure about the railroad out of her purse and started reading:

> The Fort Worth and Denver City Railway Company was chartered on May 26, 1873, but it was 1881 when construction actually began. Construction began just north of Fort Worth, at Hodge Junction, and within 10 months had completed 110 miles of track to Wichita Falls.

This is the very track we are on now, thought Clemmie. She looked out the window and tried to appreciate those who had gone before and had worked hard laying that track. She knew that the railways had changed people's lives in many ways. They had ended the long cattle drives from Texas to the north, and they had provided fast and safe and economical travel for all classes of people.

Clemmie watched the scenery as they passed through Decatur. She thought it was a shame that you could never see the prettiest part of town from a train window. But once you were through the ugliness of old buildings and deserted rail cars, weeds and shacks, you could again see the beauty of the countryside as the train rolled on toward the west, right into the afternoon sun.

"May I join you for a few moments?" The voice was smooth and deep, a strong male voice.

Clemmie was startled and looked up to see the gentleman who had befriended her back at the station. He looked to be around sixty years old, and Clemmie felt as though he had only good intentions toward her.

"Yes, please do sit down," Clemmie insisted.

"My name is S.J. Allen from Ochiltree, in the Panhandle."

"Oh, Mr. Allen. What a coincidence. I am Clementine Wilmeth, and I will be one of the schoolteachers at Ochiltree." Clemmie extended her hand, and he gave it a firm squeeze.

"I live near Brownwood, Texas, but couldn't find a school that was real close this year, and I was accepted in Ochiltree."

At that moment there was a huge noise as the engineer applied the train's brakes and the whistle simultaneously. With a great lurch, the train stopped. Everyone looked out of the windows to see what the trouble was. A large herd of cattle had settled on the track and were refusing to budge. It took most of the train crew to get them off the rails.

The afternoon wore on, and the conductor kept calling out the names of small towns along the way.

"Harrold!"

"Vernon!"

"Chillicothe!"

"Quana!"

"Childress!"

"Estelline!"

It was in the gloaming now, and Clemmie noticed how the lay of the land had changed. There was a flatness that was new to her. She began seeing fewer and fewer trees and more large rock formations.

Mr. Allen gently shook Clemmie's shoulder, and she woke up. She felt so bad that she could hardly pull herself together enough to gather up her things and get to the back of the car. She felt dizzy and had a headache. It was nice to have the kind, fatherly Mr. Allen with her. The wind was blowing as they walked into the tiny station. They knew it would be two or three hours before the Santa Fe train came through. Clemmie went to the ladies' room, then she curled up on one of the wooden benches and was soon sound asleep.

Dawn was breaking when Mr. Allen gently awakened her again. They boarded the train that would take them another 150 miles to Glazier, which was the nearest station to Ochiltree. In fact, the biggest problem for Ochiltree was that the railroad, the lifeline for a town, was so far away—over forty miles.

Finally, around noon, they passed through Canadian. Crossing the Canadian River, Mr. Allen said they just had a few more miles now.

As Clemmie looked out the rather dingy train window at the terrain, she commented, "Why, I didn't know there was a place where you could see so far—there are no trees and no bushes!"

"There is a saying here, Miss Clemmie, that you can see so far, you can see *tomorrow*."

"Glazier...Glazier, Texas," the conductor announced. Clemmie looked out and saw the station and a lone man in a wagon, with his hat pushed back, shading his eyes with his hand.

"There's Mr. Baumann, Miss Clemmie. He's a good man. Everything will be all right for you here. You'll see. If you need me for anything, just let me know."

Clemmie put on her hat and pinched her cheeks. She felt so bad and needed to brush her teeth and take a bath. Forty-two miles in a wagon...that would take several hours. But then Mr. Baumann had four horses hitched to his wagon...*Maybe it will move twice as fast,* thought Clemmie.

Glancing at the sun high in the sky, Clemmie guessed that the time must be getting close to noon, perhaps 11:30. As she carefully stepped down the little steps provided, the wind caught her hat and it went bobbing across the plains.

"Mr. Baumann, I am Clementine Wilmeth, the new schoolteacher," Clemmie said as she extended her hand.

"Howdy, ma'am. Happy to make your acquaintance. Welcome to the High Plains o' Texas! I'll fetch yer hat."

PART TWO

IN THE GLOAMING

Clemmie felt slightly nauseated and dizzy as she climbed into the passenger seat of the wagon. It was late morning, and the sun was hot. She was so relieved when Mr. Baumann told her she could lie down on the quilts he had fixed in the wagon bed. She had been afraid she might pass out from exhaustion if she had to sit up and talk for several hours over the bumpy dirt road.

After about an hour of painful non-sleep, Clemmie decided she would sit up front after all. Mr. Baumann seemed to be a pleasant man, suntanned with a receding hairline and a chiseled look to his face, like he might have some Indian blood. He wore clean overalls with a white linen shirt. Clemmie soon found out that he liked to talk.

"We'ns, my wife, Rosie, an' me, moved here 'bout three years ago from Boonville, Missouri. I first come out here on one o' them railroad excursions. I reckon I'm the adventuresome type o' man, and I sure liked what I seed here on the plains. Why, a body kin look farther and see mor'n one glance than any other place in the world, I reckon.

"Rosie was 'greeable to move here if'n I thought we'ns could make a go of it. We'ns done had the two li'l uns...Lester was 'bout three, and Mildred jist a li'l tyke. We'ns shipped out in the fall o' aught seven with some stock cows, horses, mules, and my German shepherd dog. Everything come by freight train t' Liberal, Kansas, then by covered wagon to these parts.

"Did Mister Allen tell ya that some people give him as much as five hundred dollars on the school buildin'? These people sure want their chillun' t' be ejucated."

"That's wonderful! It's education, and religion—that's what will make us a really strong nation, I believe. It's the only way to overcome being poor. How do you make your living, Mr. Baumann? Do you farm?" Clemmie had to struggle to understand what seemed to be the Missourian way of speaking.

"Well, I farm a li'l, but my main job's a freightin' goods fer people. With my mule teams an' wagons, I bring goods in from Kansas, and also take goods t' market in Oklehoma and Kansas and Fort Worth. I done spent many a night sleeping out under the stars. Two times I waked up with a snake right by me. Why, last yer, I made forty-seven trips. If we'ns ever git a train here in Ochiltree, I'll be up a crick. The people in town tried real hard to get a railroad here. Called it the E.O. & W. But 'tweren't approved by the I.C.C. So that's why we'ns have t' go to Glazier t' catch the train."

The hours dragged by. It was surely the flattest land Clemmie had ever seen. There were birds sitting on the telephone wires that were named "telephone birds," Mr. Baumann explained. They saw a few jackrabbits. About halfway home they stopped and had biscuits and beans that Mr. Baumann had brought in his food outfit on the side of the wagon. And once they stopped at an outdoor toilet, built to accommodate travelers.

Finally, they arrived in Ochiltree. By then dark had settled over the little town. Clemmie was so dead for sleep that she thought she could sleep on a bed of nails. Rosa was very gracious, but somewhat reserved, and reminded Clemmie a little bit of her mother.

Maybe she is German, thought Clemmie.

The children were already in bed in their parents' bedroom. Clemmie was to have the front bedroom to herself. She would pay Rosa five dollars a month for room and board. After a supper of soup and cornbread, Clemmie excused herself and went to bed. She slept twelve hours without waking.

When Clemmie opened her eyes Saturday morning, she saw an entirely different world from the one she had known before. The sounds were different. There was the "whooshing" sound of wind sweeping across the flat plains, with no trees or shrubs or hills to interfere. It whistled as it seemed to circle around the house.

I'll have to get used to the sound of the wind, Clemmie thought to herself.

She could see nearby houses instead of the loneliness of her Ebony home, yet she did not really know one soul in this place. She would be able to go to a store, or drugstore, which had never been possible at home, not even in the tiny towns where she had taught school. And yet the unfamiliar seemed depressing. She longed for something, *anything,* that she felt some affection for.

Oh, what have I done? she questioned herself. She asked God to please be with her and help her to not be depressed in this, her new home.

Sunday she attended the Christian church and met some very friendly people. She even found one person who had known her father back in McKinney, Texas. The Baumann family was very sweet to her, but Clemmie could not find enjoyment in anything.

School began on Monday morning, and Clemmie liked the big school building, and her pupils treated her very kindly. The little girls would hang onto her at lunch and recess. The boys seemed less mischievous than those back in central Texas. Yet she felt like dying of loneliness. She decided to go ahead and write to John, even before she had received a letter from him.

— — — — — — — —

Ochiltree, Texas

Sept. 7, 1910

Dear John,

Hello, dear sweetheart! I made the trip out here just fine, but I am very lonesome for you. Monday evening I had such a headache that I went down to the drugstore and got some medicine. Dr. Brewer thinks I'll be all right as soon as I get acclimated.

The wind has just blown constantly this week. I can hardly walk against it…it's so strong. During the night, there are such eerie sounds of whooshing and whistling that the wind makes around the roof of the house. This land is so different from Ebony. And one of the worst things here is a kind of flea that is everywhere…even in bed!

Just one week ago I told you good-bye. So many weeks lie between us until I can tell you hello again.

Yours devotedly,
Clemmie

— — — — — — — —

Two days later Clemmie had another siege of doubting, wondering if she should really spend her whole life with John Briley. She felt nearly disgusted with herself since she had traveled this road before. Nevertheless, the doubts became more and more intense, and she knew she had to resolve the problem.

She decided to write her wise friend since childhood, Sallie Reeves Hamilton, and pray that God would give Sallie even more wisdom than normal, and that whatever she advised would be the course she would take. So late one evening, she spent nearly two hours composing the letter. It was over a week later when the answer came.

Ebony Texas

Sept. 19, 1910

My dear friend,

Your most welcome letter came Sat. eve. and I wanted to answer Sun. but could not. Poor little girl—by the time the wind buffets & the fleas feast upon her nine mos. I fear we will not get much Clemmie back.

First I want to tell you my recipe for nervousness. It has never failed to work for me. Lie flat on your back, get a pan of cool water & 3 cloths. Dip the cloths in the water, wring out and wrap one around each wrist & place the other over your eyes & forehead & straighten yourself out and be quiet for half an hour and it has always given me relief.

Clemmie, I have thought of all you wrote all the time since your letter came & am going to tell you just what I think if it takes a week and numbers of tablets. I believe I understand just how you feel and although I think John one of the most perfect of "natures gentlemen" I ever knew, I know he lacks what education & association would have done for him, but when I think of how much more polished he is than when I first knew him, I am not in doubt of what may yet be done.

My husband likes to use this expression: "You can't get all the coons up one tree." And we know we never find a perfect man with all the good qualities we would like. Several times Cicero has said that "John is the straightest boy I nearly ever knew."

The greatest doubt I had was about your and John's different religious belief, but before John began to go with you he told me that he came near joining the Christian Church about 15 years ago. He went on to tell me all about it and said, "I can't see anything wrong, and I just believe they are right, but I don't say anything to Pa, for you know he is old and it would nearly kill him." I did not tell you this for fear it might influence you more than it should & while we can't know, but must trust God for results, I believe if we do our duty our efforts will be blessed.

Your papa talked so nicely to me of John that I do not think he will object & I will find out for sure the first opportunity I have.

Now my dear doubting Thomas, I have written you the longest letter I have written for years. However, I have been in such a hurry I fear I have not conveyed what I have intended but this you must always know, I want you to be happy and would do anything in my power to make you so. Yes, the Bible is always our guide.

I must stop now.

We all send love,
Sallie

Clemmie cried, kissed the simple tablet letter over and over, and thanked God for giving her a clear, sure answer. After she prayed a fervent prayer, she fell across the bed and slept soundly.

Shortly thereafter, Clemmie received a letter from John. Thus began the true romance of Clemmie and John, through the letters they exchanged that school year of 1910–11. Clemmie would write of daily happenings, and John would reply with his sparse news. Both would express desire to be in the arms of the other. The letters gave both Clemmie and John the hope and encouragement they needed to make it through the year.

— — — — — — — — —

Ebony, Texas

Oct. 3, 1910

Miss Clemmie Wilmeth

Dear Clemmie,

I must write you to night for I am a fraid you will be disappointed a gain This week I've been Just run to Death Papa has been Sick and I have been waiting on him and trying to do Some work besides.

Well I am truly glad That one month of School is gon but it is to bad That you have to waite for your money Say I no you had not recived my letter when you wrote I Think you have plenty of money if you ever get it I took the mule and Oll Said they had Sold Some cattle for you And also The horse Say Dearest when you answer this tell me if my part of the trading was Satisfactory with you I mean paying $45 Dollars and putting the rest in the bank for you? I tolde Oll I didn't no what to do he Said he new That would Suit you and I hope it will too for I want to always pleas you.

Yours,

John

— — — — — — — — —

As the holidays approached, Clemmie made plans to visit a good friend who lived near the Oklahoma state line at Thanksgiving. She wrote John about the experience.

— — — — — — — — —

Ochiltree, Texas
Dec. 5, 1910

My own dear sweetheart,

I must tell you about my trip to Texhoma now. It was Saturday around 3 p.m. when Dr. Haverly came into the drugstore and asked me to go. I was ready by four o'clock. The auto came and we started. We reached Texhoma a little before nine o'clock. Flora had supper and a good warm fire for me.

Flora was so glad to see me, and little Hazel had stayed awake to welcome me. Flora has beautiful children. I walked over the state line into Oklahoma the next day, then the auto came for me at two o'clock. It had been such a short little visit but I was so glad I had gotten to go. We left Texhoma at seven minutes till two o'clock and reached Ochiltree by 5:30, a distance of 74 miles.

I love for you to call me "Darling" and tell me you love me, for it makes me so beautifully happy. You have been without fault in your treatment of me. I want to be always worthy of the love you have given me and when I am your wife I want to live so that you shall always be as tender to me as a husband as you have been as a sweetheart.

Dearest, I would like to write you more but there is still no fire in my room and I am so cold that I must go to bed. I am always longing for you, dear, and I am always wanting you to love me and kiss me. So good night, dearest, I love you.

Your devoted,
Clemmie

OH, MY DARLING

Clemmie was glad when the holidays were over, since she couldn't go home for Christmas. The trip was too long and too expensive. Now that it was 1911, it wouldn't seem long until school would end and she would go home and be married.

Clemmie wasn't writing much in her diary, but she did make this entry: *The goods for my wedding dress came! I have the skirt made.*

As more weeks passed slowly by, the letters kept coming, and John got bolder in his declarations. The wedding date was moved up to the last of May.

Oh Clemmie I don't care for any one but you my Darling promised wife and you would have a hard time to get away from me a gain I no I am foolish about you Dear Darling

You are all of this world to me. good night Sweetheart a kiss for you.

I will Start early That morning of the 24—I want to get there in time to meet you at the depot if I can I will have my hair cut and my New Suit on and the lisence. Well I must quit and go to bed. God bless you and keepe you Through This night and Through all coming life is The sincere wish of your Lover. Darling take good care of your self with a kiss from your man.

Good night,
John

At last it was mid-May, and school in Ochiltree ended on a Wednesday. It was bittersweet to Clemmie to tell the children good-bye, knowing she might never see them again. Many of them brought her little gifts—handkerchiefs, small bottles of perfume, combs for her hair, and even a bunch of wildflowers from the field. Clemmie swept out her room for the last time and thought how she would miss the creaking of the overhead rooms and the sound of the wind whistling around the schoolhouse.

Clemmie stayed on at the boardinghouse where she had been for some time. She was able to finish her wedding dress and the veil and felt gratified that it looked very beautiful and professional. Then on May 22, an auto came and took Clemmie east across the plains to Glazier. There she boarded her train and soon was fast asleep.

Twenty-four hours later, Clemmie was back in Fort Worth and got to spend that night with Mamma's little sister, Aunt Mattie. The next morning, Uncle David took Clemmie to the train station in his buggy. She kissed her uncle on the cheek and told him how rested she felt as she boarded the train for the final leg home.

"Today is my wedding day!" she kept saying to herself. Walking through the dining car, Clemmie found herself a window seat in the coach car. She had no more than gotten settled with her small bag under the seat when she felt a gentle hand on her shoulder. Looking up into the sincere face of Luther Smith, Clemmie could have fainted.

"Why, Luther Smith! Whatever are you doing here? Oh, do sit with me and tell me what brought you to Fort Worth."

"Why, Miss Clemen*teen,* the royal *queen!* What a wonderful surprise. Stand up and give me a proper hug!" Clemmie obliged and felt rings of goose bumps run down her spine. "But weren't you at Pflugerville this school year?" Clemmie hoped the question would make things seem casual and hoped he didn't sense her delight in seeing him again. "Yes, but school is out, and I needed to check on a family situation in Fort Worth, so I am on my way home now. And what about you? Was the Texas Panhandle as bad as you were afraid it might be?"

"Oh no. Actually, this was one of my best years in the teaching profession. However, I may be giving up my career in teaching. John Briley and I will be getting married tonight in Brownwood. We carried on a wonderful courtship by correspondence this past school year. It has been nearly nine months since he put me on the train, and he will meet me this evening at the Brownwood station."

"Well, I suppose congratulations are in order, Clemmie. I do hope that you and Mr. Briley will be very happy. I have continued to see Miss Tommie, but we have not become officially engaged yet. She stayed at Bowser this past year, and we saw each other two or three times."

The conductor came through with his, "All Aboard!" warning, making sure the visitors were all off. Then there was the great lurch forward, the loud hissing sound, and the journey was underway.

"Clemmie, after a while I would like to treat you to a fine dinner in the dining car as a type of wedding gift. Will you accept?"

"Why, yes, Luther. I think that will be a lovely wedding gift from a man whom I greatly admire."

It was a wonderful meal of fried steak, mashed potatoes, English peas, a good dinner roll, and the big, heavy glasses full of sweetened iced tea. There was a real red rose in the little vase on the table, and the kerosene lantern was aglow. Clemmie watched the sunlight play on Mr. Smith's strong, handsome face and prayed she had not lost the best of her beaus. But she knew John's love was stronger than Luther's had been, and besides, the die was cast and she had no right to think other thoughts.

The waiter returned to inquire about dessert. Clemmie was about to decline when Mr. Smith spoke up: "I think we need two of the warm apple dumplings, and please add some whipped cream on top. And two cups of coffee, please."

"Luther, that was the best lunch I ever had. Thank you so much."

"I'll always admire you, Clemmie. But let's not look back with regrets, but rather know that the past has brought us to the present, and your marriage to Mr. Briley is meant to be."

"*Comanche!* Next stop, *Comanche, Texas!*" shouted the conductor.

Clemmie knew this was the last town of any size before Blanket, then Brownwood. She tried to picture what John would be doing about now. He probably had gotten their marriage license at the Brown County Courthouse, had bought himself a suit and might even be wearing it, and maybe had made a reservation for them at the Crown Hotel in Brownwood.

Clemmie was slightly regretful that her papa would not be saying the ceremony, but he tried never to take part in a marriage where one partner had a previous marriage. Although he knew that John was the innocent party, he still believed it was best to have no part in the marriage, but he did plan to hold his daughter and John in "full fellowship."

A few weeks before, Clemmie had written her good friend Jennie Manley, who lived in Brownwood, and asked if she and John could be married in her home on May 24. No family was expected for the ceremony, but the next evening there would be a wedding supper at Ebony, at Callie and Jim's home.

"Clemmie," began Mr. Smith, "what do you say to me going into another car for these last few miles and you can meet your bridegroom with nothing to explain."

"Luther, you are indeed a kind friend and a gentleman. I must try to keep everything smooth for tonight."

"Clemmie, I will always remember the kiss atop the tower. You didn't tell anyone about that, did you?"

"Why would I do that, Luther? It was one of the most special moments of my life so far."

No need to say that I told Grace, Clemmie rationalized.

"Clemmie, could I give you a good-bye kiss now?"

"Well, many brides receive kisses on their wedding day."

Luther managed to encircle her in his arms and planted a sweet, warm kiss right on her lips. He lingered a little long. With a parting squeeze he gathered up his things and made his way to the car ahead, turning at the exit to wave and wink at Clemmie.

Clemmie wondered if she would ever see him again. *How coincidental,* she mused, *that he should be on this same train with me. It helps give me closing to one of the brief romances that I will always hold sweet in memory, second only to the long friendship with Raleigh.*

"So, Mr. Ely," Clemmie thought half aloud, "you ended up with only a nineteen-month head start on me in the married life. I do hope you are beautifully happy, because that is what I plan to be."

Clemmie journeyed to the restroom and fixed herself up the best she could. *Oh, I hope John will not feel any disappointment in me today, dear Lord,* she implored. Swaying with the train as she walked back to her seat, the ticket master shouted, *"Brownwood! Brownwood, Texas!"* The train pulled into the station at six p.m. With her eyes glued to the dingy window, Clemmie strained to see John. There he was!

Oh, my, he is looking handsome, thought Clemmie. He was standing as near to the track as possible, wearing a black suit, a white shirt, and pale blue tie. His dark wavy hair looked like it had been cut earlier in the day. He was very slender and stood very erect, crystal blue eyes scanning each window of the train.

Suddenly, his eyes locked in on those smoky-blue eyes of his bride. Clemmie waved excitedly. The train jerked and hissed to a complete stop. The conductor readied the steps, and Clemmie was one of the first ones off, flying into the strong arms of Mr. John Robert Briley. He hugged her very tightly, then held her off at arm's length as if to look her over totally, and then they both began to cry.

"Oh, Clemmie, I was so 'fraid I might never see you again! It has been the longest nine months I ever wanna live through. Oh, my darlin,' you are so beautiful. You're like a dream girl...you *are* the girl o' my dreams."

"Oh, John, I have lived on your letters and your love. I'm *so* glad we decided to go ahead and marry tonight. I could not have borne another day without you. Is everything in order? Do you have the papers?"

"Yes. Ever'thing's ready. I've arranged for the preacher from the Church of Christ t' meet us at 8:30 at Mrs. Manley's. She's excited and wants to help you get ready. We have a reservation at the hotel tonight. I wish I could take you somewhere like Dallas for a honeymoon. But that'll have to wait until the crops come in."

"Oh, John, the last thing I want to do is spend more hours on a train! Just to be in a buggy with you on our way back home to Ebony will be like heaven."

Loading on the two heavy trunks, they went straight to the home of Jennie Manley. She gave Clemmie a big hug and told them she had a light supper for them. She had prepared a warm tub of water for Clemmie in an upstairs room and had a curling iron heating on the kitchen stove. While Clemmie bathed, Jennie pressed the beautiful wedding dress and veil, taken from the top of the trunk.

"Clemmie, there is a surprise for you that came today. Nellie Murphree sent you the most beautiful fresh-cut flowers. I have made up a bouquet for you to carry."

"Oh, Jennie, my dream has come true! Nellie is the sweetest person. But no one is as dear as you, sweet Jennie."

Finally, Clemmie was decked out in her homemade drawers, her store-bought corset, her wedding dress of dainty white organdy with a high collar, an over-bib, a tight blouse, and a tiered, pleated skirt. Her white veil hung to the floor and was fastened on her head with ferns and artificial forget-me-nots. She held in her hand a bouquet of real flowers. She looked in the mirror and felt pleased.

Tomorrow we will need to go by a studio and have pictures made, she thought to herself.

Jennie sat at her small Steinway organ and began playing *The Wedding March.* As Clemmie descended the stairs, she smiled shyly at her handsome groom standing near the preacher, Dr. Taylor (a medical doctor) in the front of the room. There were no guests present. Dr. Taylor used a short ceremony, explaining that marriage was ordained in the beginning by God, and emphasizing the Scripture found in Matthew: "'Wherefore they are no more twain, but one flesh. What therefore God hath joined together, let not man put asunder.' Matthew 19:6."

Then he dwelt awhile on the passage from Ephesians 5 where the Apostle Paul compared the marriage union to Christ and His bride, the church. Finally, the couple repeated their vows, promising to love, honor, and obey, forsaking all others, to cling only unto themselves, in sickness and in health, as long as they both should live.

John placed a wide gold band on Clemmie's ring finger. They were pronounced man and wife, and Dr. Taylor said that Mr. Briley could now kiss his bride. John delivered a quick peck. The wedding was over.

Jennie asked Dr. Taylor to stay for cake and punch. Clemmie felt like she was in a play, like it couldn't really be true that she was Mrs. John R. Briley. All those months of loneliness, anticipation, preparation…and now it was all over! Jennie played "Let Me Call You Sweetheart" on the Steinway, then served the cake and punch.

Clemmie just couldn't thank Jennie enough and tried to pay her for her trouble and expense. She wouldn't even hear of it. John gave a dollar bill to Dr. Taylor.

Finally, the couple was on their way to the hotel, the buggy barely accommodating the big trunks, the happy couple, and all the flowers Nellie had sent.

Neither John nor Clemmie had spent many nights in a hotel. The Crown was clean and nice, but not luxurious. Arriving at their second-floor room, there was a bed with clean sheets turned back, a big armchair, a little table with a lamp, and a small bathroom. Clemmie went in the bathroom and began to undress with the door locked. She took off all but her drawers and put on the long, white satin gown she had made with so many loving thoughts back in Ochiltree. She let her hair down and brushed it back.

Meanwhile, back in the room, John took off his clothes, except for his underwear. Then he got under the sheet, asking the good Lord to be with them. The anticipation of holding Clemmie in his arms, along with his much thwarted sexual desire, gave him all he needed for a successful night with Clemmie. Timidly, Clemmie opened the door and came out.

"John, I'm scared." Clemmie looked like she might cry.

"Oh, my darlin'! Just pretend you died and went to heaven," was John's reply.

Once under the cover with John, Clemmie felt like this couldn't be real. She had not passed through a sexual awakening and had no experience to guide her. She wondered why some young girls, like Lettie Mae, seemed to love the sexual aspect of romance so much, and here she was on her wedding night without one sexual feeling.

I must be a kind of freak, she thought to herself.

John began to stroke her back and arms. She wanted to please him, but fear of the unknown would not let her abandon her inhibitions. She asked him if she could just wait till tomorrow.

"All right, my darling." John blew out the kerosene lantern.

"Oh, John." Clemmie began to sob. "I wanted *so much* for tonight to be good for you, and I'm a failure as a lover." She was bordering on a real crying jag.

"Now, sweetheart," John consoled, "we're gonna have a long time ahead of us t' enjoy married life. You're tired from nine months of teachin' and two days of being on a wretched train. Jus' let me rock you t' sleep like you're m' beautiful baby, and the sexy part kin wait till later."

And that is what they did. John held Clemmie in his arms and rocked her and sang the songs he could remember his mother singing to him before she died. It was nearly one a.m. when Clemmie's breathing was even. John struggled to his feet and tucked his sleeping bride into bed. He lay awake another two hours and finally fell asleep and dreamed that he was having a wonderful honeymoon with Nancy, but he was startled to see that she had Clemmie's smoky-blue eyes.

THINK NOT BITTERLY OF ME

The sun was shining in the room at the Crown Hotel when Clemmie opened her eyes. Her disappointment about the wedding night crept over her like flies over molasses. After all the dreams and anticipation of May 24, she had ruined it!

"Well, it couldn't be helped," she stated aloud. "Tonight will be different. That is, if John hasn't left me for good. Dear Lord, help John to not think bitterly of me. Help me be a true wife to him tonight."

John was definitely not in the room. Clemmie got out of bed and used the facilities in the small bathroom, namely an enameled jar.

There was a small wooden table with a large pitcher full of water and a washbowl. She washed her face and hands and looked at her face and disheveled hair in the little mirror.

Just then John returned, carrying a tray with sweet rolls, juice, and coffee. He had on a blue shirt with the pants to his new suit and looked wonderful, Clemmie thought.

"Oh, dear hubby," Clemmie began to form her apologies, "I am so sorry about last night!"

"Clemmie, 'tis the happiest mornin' o' my life, and we won't spoil it. You were tired from the train ride, and besides, now I know you're a virgin girl, and you've been honest with me! We'll have 'bout fifty years to get ever'thin' right."

"Well, they say that life expectancy is now fifty years, so we may have less than twenty years left. We need to make good use of the time. Tonight is going to be much better, I promise you, John. Even if it kills me." Clemmie and John laughed and embraced.

"I've made an appointment for our weddin' photographs, and the photographer will come here to the hotel in 'bout an hour. Then we'll start for home. Your folks are havin' a weddin' supper for us tonight, you know."

"Oh yes! I'm so eager to see everyone and to be introduced as Mrs. John Briley to all my people. I hope your papa can come, and maybe your brothers, too. John, I hope I can fix myself up decent for our photographs. I may need some help with my hair."

"Well, that's not one o' my talents, Clemmie, fixin' up hair."

The two got themselves ready, with the lady at the desk helping Clemmie comb her hair. The pictures would be mailed to them in Ebony within a month. John insisted that Clemmie have one picture made alone with her bouquet. They ordered several for relatives, even though John knew he shouldn't spend the money. He was sad not to be able to take Clemmie for a real honeymoon, and pictures were the least he should give her, he reasoned.

When they were all loaded into the buggy, Clemmie stated with great satisfaction: "I'm finally going home with my own hubby!"

They were out in the country now on the little dirt road, headed south to Ebony. The countryside was as green as it ever got in Mills County. Clemmie was wearing a pink gingham dress with matching bonnet, and her cheeks were rosy.

"Clemmie, my dream was t' take you to our own farm instead of t' Pa's. Maybe it won't be long till we have our place."

"Oh yes, we will, John. I want to begin my housewifely duties and take care of you and your papa, and I know we can all get along. It's been a long time since he had a woman in his home to cook and wash and clean for him, and I want to gladly do that."

"Clemmie, I heard a new song the other day. It goes like this:

I want a girl, just like the girl that married dear old Dad;
She was a pearl, and the only girl,
that Daddy ever had ;
A good old-fashioned girl with heart so true,
"One who loved nobody else but you—oo—
I want a girl, just like the girl
that married dear old Dad.

"Oh, I really like that John! I didn't realize you had such a good singing voice!"

The hours went by and before sundown they had covered the twenty-five familiar miles. They jostled down into the creek bottom, and John reined in the horses.

"Mrs. Briley, could I hava kiss since we're on your papa's land?"

"You certainly may, Mr. Briley." Clemmie moved very close, and John held her tight and gave her a very passionate kiss. Clemmie really hoped that she could be all she wanted to be in bed that night. She so hated to be a disappointment to John, especially since he had that Nancy who probably knew all about loving a man.

The katydids were sizzling out their mating call, as if to welcome the couple home. Finally, they could see the little house at a distance with several buggies nearby. There was Brother Jim and Callie on their porch, each holding a child and waving. Clemmie began to wave and felt so emotional. There was Papa and Mamma out on the porch, and Grace and little Opal were running toward them. Edna and Oll were in the yard. There was Brother Briley, waving a welcome.

As they pulled up into the yard amid barking dogs, Clemmie jumped down and fell into the arms of her beloved papa, and even Mamma gave her a very good hug. Her sisters and brother and all those present seemed so happy to have her back and were just as glad to welcome John into the family. John's papa spoke very friendly to Clemmie and gave her a nice hug.

The wedding supper was excellent. Mamma had gone all out and fixed a long table out in the yard. There was fried chicken, mashed potatoes, green beans, hot homemade rolls, sliced tomatoes, and fried okra. For dessert there was a beautiful wedding cake that Callie had made, decorated with real roses. Clemmie held out her arms to her new nephew, Jim's little boy, Ralph, born in January. He held out his little arms for her to take him. He seemed to be a contented, happy baby. Little Marie was happy to see her Aunt Clemmie and was talking very plainly for a two-year-old.

Clemmie looked up at Big Hill and thanked her Lord for all the blessings and for letting her come home to her husband and family.

Later that evening, John and Clemmie loaded their presents in the buggy and went over the rocky, dim road to their new home. It was only about five miles away, back toward town. Brother Briley said he would be sleeping at Fowler's that night so the newlyweds could be alone. Clemmie felt very grateful.

Everything was totally dark as they arrived at the Briley place. John hustled in first and began lighting the coal oil lamps. He had worked pretty hard trying to clean the place before he left for Brownwood. It was a simply built four-room house with a porch on two sides. It had never been painted. The bedroom was very simple with a homemade wooden bed and a feather mattress.

There was an outdoor privy with the usual strong smell of ammonia and more. You could tell the house lacked the touch of a woman's hand. It was clean, but there were lots of things stacked in corners, and nothing was very colorful. Clemmie began to plan how she would bring in some wildflowers and maybe a pretty quilt for the front room. Perhaps a rug and some magazine pictures on the wall would cheer it up.

Clemmie started to undress and get ready for bed. *Please, dear Lord, let it happen tonight…Please let me be normal and be able to enjoy this part of my marriage someday, dear Lord, I beg Thee.*

John brought the best lamp into the bedroom. He was waiting for Clemmie in bed and tried to offer some comforting words. Secretly, he wondered if they might need to get an annulment if Clemmie was unable to have relations with him. But he still thought everything would soon be normal.

"Clemmie, you're tremblin'! Now I don't wantcha t' be afraid. If there's any pain, it won't last long," John tried to reassure her.

"I want you to just do whatever you have to, John."

"But I don't wanna hurtcha, Clemmie. Just lay down here and let's talk an' hug an' kiss."

About two hours later, with Clemmie whimpering like a little puppy and finally screaming out in great pain, the two became one flesh. There was quite a bit of blood on the sheet, and both John and Clemmie wondered if she might die of blood loss.

The next morning Clemmie found it hard to walk and needed to rest a lot during the day. Brother Briley arrived home about ten and asked her if she was sick. John explained that she had taken a cold on the train ride home and just needed to rest a lot for a day or two. Slowly, things began to improve behind the door of the "bridal chamber."

Soon it was June, and summer arrived in all its glory in Mills

County. Clemmie tried hard to have good meals ready for John and his pa when they would come in from the field at noon and night. She tried to keep up with the washing, which involved carrying water and heating it in a huge black pot in the yard. John would help her all he could with the heavy chores. Clemmie was slow with food preparation, having never had to cook much before. Many times Brother Briley would be irritated that meals were not ready on time, or that John had to take time out from planting to help with washing.

By the end of July the heat was sweltering, and one morning Clemmie vomited up her breakfast. She began to feel so tired and lethargic, like she could hardly put one foot in front of the other. The nausea didn't go away; in fact, it began to last all day, every day.

Near the first of August, Clemmie announced to John that she could go on no longer. John fixed her a cot on the porch where there was usually a breeze blowing. He tried so hard to take care of the meals, the wash, the cleaning, and his own work in the fields, not to mention the cows and chickens, and most of all to see after Clemmie and her needs.

John had hoped every day that Clemmie would get well. He knew that she was really sick in both her mind and her body. He figured that some of it was the situation with his papa, the huge adjustment of being married, and the horrible heat of Texas in the summer, with the temperature soaring into three figures for most of July and August. John also knew she didn't have a close friend in whom to confide, even though she had a mother and a sister not far away. The way she was throwing up most of her food and losing weight scared John that she might actually die. He just had to get her well, and quick.

On one of those desperately hot days of late August, John found a pamphlet at the post office store in Ebony that touted the excellence of the mineral baths in Marlin, Texas. The little booklet explained that twenty years before, well-drillers had hit a steaming geyser of mineral water.

It seemed that the taste and the temperature of the geyser were a great disappointment for the drillers, who had gone down three thousand feet in an effort to find clear, sweet water. The geyser seemed to pour from a boiling cauldron inside the earth. Finally, it became necessary to dig a ditch to drain off the warm, peculiar-smelling water and carry it out of town.

One day a traveler named Wiley Clark, with no money, whose body was sick and whose skin was all broken out, passed through Marlin. He had no place to bathe and noticed the smelly drainage ditch. He decided to soak his tired, erupted feet in the warm stream. After a few days, his skin cleared up. He began to tell the townspeople his experience, and many of them who had ailments tried the water and also found healing.

A young, ambitious doctor, just out of medical school, heard the stories of the magical water in Marlin. He went to Marlin, secured a sample of the water, and had it tested by the state chemist. Sure enough, the water was found to be rich in medicinal salts: calcium sulphate, sodium chloride, sulphates of potash, soda, iron, aluminum, magnesium, lime, and bicarbonate of soda. The young doctor found an older doctor to join him, and they moved to Marlin and established a bathhouse with ten tubs and began a practice specializing in hydrotherapeutic treatment of disease.

This began a pilgrimage of people, from fifty to one hundred per day, causing Marlin to become one of the world's leading health resorts. Many hotels and bath-houses were built to accommodate the thousands who arrived by train, wagon, and even automobile to be treated for multiple illnesses: rheumatism, arthritis, malaria, stomach trouble, skin and blood diseases, eczema, nephritis, high blood pressure, diabetes, nervousness, indigestion, constipation, and other chronic ailments.

The brochure closed with these words, which helped draw the people to Marlin:

If you have lost your health, if your system is run down, if you suffer from chronic nervous fatigue, or from any of the diseases mentioned that have responded to the effects of Marlin water, visit Marlin and join the multitude of health-seekers who are literally washing their afflictions away in these marvelous waters.

Here was John's answer; here was Clemmie's salvation! On September 10, 1911, John lifted the very frail and pale Clemmie into the wagon, laid her on a quilt, packed in trunks and bags with most of their earthly belongings, and left for Brownwood, where they caught a train to Marlin. John's papa went along to the Brownwood depot in order to drive the wagon back home. Brother Briley hummed "Amazing Grace" all the way back to Ebony.

John found some rooms for them to rent and secured a job hauling water to homes and businesses. Clemmie began her bath treatments, and within six weeks her doctor said she was well, but that they should stay a year in Marlin to be sure there was no relapse. Clemmie didn't seem to notice that at the same time her nausea began to go away, her waistline began to expand.

By November it was obvious to the observant that Clemmie would be giving birth in the spring. In fact, one of the attendants at the hot baths had first brought it to Clemmie's attention back in September. She had suspected that she might be pregnant but had not mentioned it to John yet. Women just didn't talk about such private matters to anyone in 1911.

On the seventh of November, Clemmie had her thirty-first birthday. John told her she could buy some flower bulbs that she wanted. She purchased a paperwhite narcissus, six tulips, three hyacinths, and six jonquils. It rained some that day. That night Clemmie recorded her happiness in her diary, calling it the "best birthday ever."

John and Clemmie paid Mrs. Turek ten dollars a month for rental of the rooms, and she furnished nearly everything. The house was a brown cottage, trimmed in white with shutters on the windows. It faced west, and the two rooms on the north side of the house were the Brileys.'

The furniture pleased Clemmie. Besides the iron bedstead, painted green and white, there was a dresser, washstand, a small table with chairs, and an iron heater. The other room was a kitchen with a square of linoleum on the floor and a small cookstove and a sideboard with lots of pretty dishes. With the new wedding sheets and a few little decorative items of her own, Clemmie thought their first home was very attractive.

During those months Clemmie spent many an hour in those two rooms and found satisfaction in knitting some tiny clothes for the baby. As the year came to a close, Clemmie recorded her thoughts in her diary, as had been her custom for years.

> The old year is almost gone. In less than two hours the New Year will have dawned. Oh, short fleeting, year of 1911. You brought me so much of joy, so much of happiness that I had not known before. You brought to me my wedding day, my hubby. You have brought me so much that is sacred and beautiful. But New Year, I have the hope of the crowning joy of my life—the sacred privilege of motherhood. O God! Prepare me for it, I pray.

A meningitis scare swept through Marlin and other Texas towns in February. Clemmie was so large with child that she didn't go anywhere, not even to church. She tried hard to feel contented with her knitting and sewing and with John's spasmodic short visits home in between his duties and odd jobs he took to help financially.

March arrived, and the jonquils and daffodils brightened up the drab Texas landscape. Seeing a plum tree in full white blossom spoke to Clemmie of things too deep for words. Somehow it related to Jesus coming forth from the damp coolness of a tomb, bursting out into the garden, bringing life eternal to undeserving humanity.

And now the fact that that her first child would come right with the springtime was meaningful to Clemmie. On Sunday, March 25, Clemmie awoke and tried to turn over in bed. Her belly was so huge she had trouble sleeping for more than an hour at a time. John felt terrible with a cold or flu. He murmured that he really wasn't able to go to church, but maybe he could that night. There had been some rain before sunrise, but it had cleared off by dawn. It had rained so much lately that John's job of hauling water was nonexistent. Most homes had rain barrels, and they were overflowing.

For the past day and a half Clemmie had felt erratic pains, and she knew the baby would come soon. She had been knitting some tiny bootees and a little sweater and cap. John had hired a black woman named Mandy to wash the clothes for the past few weeks. Clemmie found great joy in knowing the clothes were all clean and white.

Childbirth was looked on with a certain amount of trepidation. There were plenty of stories the women knew about babies that were turned wrong, that were too large, or pelvic bones that were too close together to give passage to the child. Clemmie's doctor assured her that he could foresee no problem, and arrangements were made for him to come to the house when labor became strong. Narcis, a black midwife, had also agreed to come. The landlady, Mrs. Turek, would also be in attendance, and John would be there to do whatever he could.

The night of the twenty-sixth, the pains began in earnest. All through the night Clemmie lay awake, watching their only clock, and praying. She wished her mother were there. It was a time when a daughter needed her mother. She was terrified. All the "what-ifs" began to assault her. She tried to calm herself, thinking of all the millions of women before her who had safely delivered babies. At six o'clock she could bear the pain no more and shook John awake. He bounded out of bed with eyes big and fearful.

"Is it time fer me t' go get th' doctor, Clemmie?"

"I think so," groaned Clemmie, her eyes beginning to fill with tears.

John pulled on his clothes with record speed, brought Clemmie a glass of water, and was out the door, fairly running down the street. He had taken time to knock on Mrs. Turek's door, and she said she would get Narcis.

"Oh, Lord, please don't let her die," John prayed. "And let the baby be all right, too." It had been a hard few months for John, and he had no idea how they would continue to live on the little dab of money he made hauling water. He felt the crushing weight that men have always felt when they take a wife and have a child. And he really wished he could disappear for the day and just let the others take care of things.

By the time John and Dr. Sewall returned, they could hear screams coming from the little upstairs room. And there was some pretty loud praying in between the screams.

"Now, John, you make some coffee, and try not to worry. Everything will come out okay in the end." The doctor smiled wryly at his own humor.

"Oh, Lord. Oh, Lordy. Please. *Please.*" Clemmie felt the pressure, the unspeakable, untenable situation of a big baby being slowly pushed down the narrow passageway. She had the sensation that her body was going to burst and be scattered all over the room.

Well, so be it, she thought. *I will just die.* "Oh, Lord, receive me into Your kingdom!" she yelled aloud.

Doctor Sewall applied a little pressure to Clemmie's stomach and assured Clemmie that everything was just fine. Just when Clemmie knew she was dying, the baby's dark head emerged, followed by the little shoulder, then the other, and there was the dark red baby, taking her first breath.

"She's a fine girlie, Mrs. Briley. Yes, sir-re-sir." The doctor cut the cord and held the tiny girl upside down. The baby let out a loud cry, and John rushed up the stairs. It was ten minutes after ten o'clock in the morning, March 27, 1912.

Mrs. Turek seemed to know just what to do, taking away bloody sheets and towels and supplying clean ones in their place. The doctor was pleased that the afterbirth was intact, and the tearing of the vagina was not too severe. He cleaned up Clemmie the best he could and turned his attention to the baby girl. Checking her over and removing a little mucous from her mouth, he observed that the baby was unusually pretty for a newborn. And she seemed to be quite feisty, too. *Yes,* he thought, *this one is a survivor.*

Clemmie felt like she had been dragged for several miles by a wild horse. There were dark circles under her eyes, and her hair was disheveled and wet with perspiration. Mrs. Turek had wrapped the baby in a soft pink receiving blanket that she herself had made and placed the little girl in Clemmie's arms.

Clemmie remembered a Scripture from the book of John: "A woman when she is in travail hath sorrow, because her hour is come, but as soon as she is delivered of the child, she remembereth no more the anguish, for joy that a man is born into the world" (John 16:21).

Yes, thought Clemmie, *it was worth it all.* She gazed unbelievingly at the perfect little baby: full cheeks; dark, curly hair; little eyes, nearly black; and the prettiest little mouth. She looked at the tiny curled-up fingers and then uncovered the fat little legs and counted the ten perfect toes. John was standing above Clemmie.

"John, she is prettier than the Wilmeth babies. I believe she took after the Brileys. I think the name 'Ruth' fits her perfectly, don't you, John? And now we are perfectly blended…our little daughter, Ruth Wilmeth Briley."

John reached down and lifted the baby, ever so carefully, in his arms. His crystal blue eyes locked into Ruth's navy blue eyes, and he was never the same again.

THOUGH I PASSED
AWAY IN SILENCE

It took Clemmie several weeks to feel normal after Ruth's birth. John was so sweet to her and would rub her arms and legs. He even got up in the night and walked the floor when Baby Ruth seemed to have colic. On the eighth day after the birth, Clemmie sat up in bed. On the ninth day she began to get up and dress but felt so terribly weak that she had to lie down most of the day.

Spring arrived in all her glory, bringing joy to Clemmie's romantic heart. The spring meant rain, and that meant that John had to find other jobs besides carrying water. One day he unloaded a railroad car full of bricks.

Ruth had what most breastfed babies get, loose bowels. This concerned Clemmie to no end, and she was afraid something was wrong with Ruth. Clemmie knew that she needed to remain calm but simply could not help herself from feeling desperate and nearly in panic. John began to try to think of something to keep Clemmie from fretting so much about the baby. He went out and bought the

Sunday edition of the *Dallas Morning News* to help steer her thoughts elsewhere.

Clemmie fairly devoured the paper. A main piece of news was the maiden voyage of the *R.M.S. Titantic,* the most luxurious ship ever to set sail. Just a few months before, the *Olympic,* sister ship of the *Titantic,* had completed her maiden voyage and was heralded by multitudes in New York City. The two ships were equal in size, both being 882.5 feet, or about four city blocks long, and ten stories tall, costing over ten million dollars each. The well-known *White Star Line* in Europe had built both ships.

The claim was made that even God himself could not sink the *Titantic,* which boasted some sixteen watertight compartments that could be sealed off in case of a leak. As Clemmie read through the impressive list of passengers, she especially noted the famous name of Mr. and Mrs. John Jacob Astor.

"John, I wonder what it is like to be among the very rich and sail across the ocean in such luxury," Clemmie commented. Then she continued, "We've come a long way since my mother and grandmother sailed to Europe in 1857. It took three months, and they nearly drowned in a storm at sea. This *Titanic* is said to be unsinkable."

"Well, if this rain keeps up in Marlin, we're gonna have our own little ocean right here. It sure messes up the water-hauling business," John commented rather dryly.

The date on the paper was April 7, 1912. Just a few days later Clemmie read that on April 15, the unthinkable happened, and the unsinkable *Titanic* sank. There were 1,595 persons drowned of the 2,340 passengers and crew onboard. Only 745, mostly women and children, were saved. Clemmie had to go to bed for an hour after she read the tragic news. She asked God to forgive her notion that money would resolve all problems and asked the Lord to comfort the grieving relatives of those lost at sea. The paper said that the ship's little band played "Nearer My God to Thee" as the largest ocean liner ever built went under the cold, dark water.

The next afternoon, Clemmie put Ruth on the big bed beside her and nursed her. Both Clemmie and Ruth fell asleep, and the next thing Clemmie knew she was awakened to a most pitiful, loud crying of her little baby girl. She had fallen on the floor on her back. Clemmie began to shriek, cry, and pray all at the same time. Little Ruth's face was as red as pure blood, her little legs were kicking wildly, but one arm looked funny. Just then John arrived home, opened the door, and gazed with horror on his baby daughter, now in Clemmie's arms, but still screaming.

"What happened to Ruth?" John asked excitedly, trying to keep himself in control.

"She fell off the bed!" Clemmie fairly shouted.

"How could you let that happen?" questioned John.

"We both fell asleep, and the next thing I knew she was on the floor," explained Clemmie.

"You have done a very foolish thing and hurt our little girl. I am taking her to Dr. Sewell right now," John's voice was trembling as he made this statement.

It was the first time John had ever spoken harshly to Clemmie. Her cries were louder than Baby Ruth's. The three were soon in the borrowed buggy and trotting down the street to the doctor's house. Dr. Sewell put the baby on a table and examined her.

He said he thought her collarbone was broken and that there was not much to be done; it should heal just fine. They would need to be careful when lifting Ruth, and she should sleep on her back. He said it wasn't too uncommon for this to happen to babies, and Clemmie should not blame herself. To help Ruth sleep, Dr. Sewell gave them some paregoric in a green bottle with a dropper. Clemmie's feelings were hurt for a good while because she felt that John blamed her for the baby's fall.

As summer approached, the days and nights became hotter. One sweltering night Clemmie heard a humming sound in the bedroom. At first she thought it might be a fly, but alas, it was mosquitoes. Not just one—dozens of them! John and Clemmie began to discuss whether they should stay in Marlin or leave. They decided that Clemmie should take the baby and go home to Ebony for a visit. John would go to Dallas and see about getting a job as a motorman on the streetcar line where he had worked several years before.

So Clemmie made a train trip to Goldthwaite, and her papa met her in the buggy. Ruth was nearly three months old and weighed over fifteen pounds. Mamma, Callie, Grace, and little cousins Opal and Marie were enthralled with Baby Ruth. It turned out to be a wonderful rest for Clemmie. She was free from her domestic duties and had several women and two children ready to help with Ruth.

There was a big pile of lumber across the meadow that Papa had brought from town recently. Within the next year or two, Mamma would achieve her dream: a fine four-room home with a porch on two sides, cabinets in the kitchen, and a piano in the parlor, along with a finished attic with sleeping space for visitors. Clemmie wondered if her father would have many years left to enjoy the house. He would be seventy-seven before Christmas.

One evening, Clemmie took her baby up on Big Hill. It wasn't easy trying to push the old buggy of Callie's over the rocks. Once on top, Clemmie had a flashback of that day three years ago when she and Raleigh had met on the hill. How her life, and his too, she imagined, had changed since then. Clemmie wondered if he had ever regretted the choice he made. She wished only happiness for him and Lucy. She wondered if they had a baby yet, or if she and John were ahead in that department.

Clemmie lifted Ruth carefully out of the buggy and said, "Ruth, I hope you will love this land like your mother does." Ruth began to nuzzle Clemmie's breast, indicating that she was hungry. Clemmie spread the small blanket on the ground, sat down cross-legged, unbuttoned her dress, and positioned the breast in Ruth's eager mouth. Clemmie enjoyed seeing the child wrinkle her little nose and grab the nipple with gusto. Ruth put her little hand on her mother's breast, then looked up at Clemmie, smiled, and patted the breast.

The gold of the gloaming seemed nearly magical as Clemmie settled her little daughter back into the buggy and headed homeward. She felt a surge of thanksgiving to God and began to pray aloud. "Oh, God, I thank Thee for this quiet, precious time with Thee, and with my daughter. God, how I wish life could remain so calm, so peaceful, so beautiful. Please be with John as he tries to find work in the big city."

John found a job with the streetcar line in Dallas. He even had time to look around for a house to rent and found a small one on 8th Street in Oak Cliff. Clemmie and Ruth went home to Marlin on the train, then visited Ebony once more in September. John went on to Dallas to get things ready in the little house.

In mid-October of 1912, Clemmie and Ruth joined John in Dallas. Little did Clemmie realize how she would come to love that city…her schools, her parks, her libraries, her lovely homes, and streetcars to take one everywhere. Yet always, in the back of her mind, she would yearn for a little white house on her own land in Ebony.

John got hurt in a streetcar accident, and his foot was partially crushed. He had to hobble around on crutches for several weeks and then use a cane for several more weeks. The only good thing was that he received a settlement of $463, which included some pay for sick time. Clemmie was glad he decided to settle for the amount offered rather than going to court and trying to get more money. After this he was given another job at the interlocker. The pay was only two dollars per day, but there was opportunity to work overtime.

Ruth was growing like a little weed. Clemmie was proud that many people would comment about Ruth's beauty, even strangers on the street. Mrs. Summers from church said Ruth was the prettiest baby she had ever seen. Clemmie had begun teaching Ruth her ABCs, and by the time she was twenty-two months old she knew all of them. Often when Clemmie went shopping with Ruth in the buggy, the independent little girl would want to get out and walk, so Clemmie would end up pushing an empty buggy.

In early April of 1914, John told Clemmie about the war brewing in Europe.

"Well, John, I know war is terrible," Clemmie replied, sadly. "Thousands of young men will die. I hope the United States will stay out of it."

Clemmie began to feel the old melancholia return and confided to John that she felt like her spirits and her energy were going down again. John remembered how much the water treatments in Marlin had helped her before and insisted that Clemmie go back and take a few treatments. There was nothing to do with Ruth but to take her along since she was still nursing.

So Clemmie and Ruth left on the Frisco train and stayed with Mrs. Turek, where they had lived when Ruth was born. She was good to Clemmie and Ruth and charged very little. Clemmie had the same doctor as two years before, and he told her it was possible she had a type of melancholia that runs in families, or she was keeping some serious things locked up inside herself, making her feel sick.

Due to the doctor's questions, Clemmie began to try to think clearly about inner conflicts. Her thoughts ran like this: *John loves me, that I believe, and I know I love him. I think he does not understand me, and I am having trouble just accepting him. In a way he is a simple man who is content to have his meals on time and his job to go to.*

It seems to me that John has a great deal of temper that he tries to keep under control. But John is a good man and only wants to have a good home. He's such a good father and adores Ruth. There is a problem that I recognize, and I must ever strive to work out. It is about the fact that spiritual things, like going to church to worship God, are not important to John. I think that is why I lack respect for him.

John kept no diary, nor did he confide in a male friend. But he had his thoughts, too. He was scared that he had married a sick woman.

Clemmie was a woman with high ideals and good intentions, but she sure did have a lot of ailments. When it was that certain time of the month, she just had to stay in bed for a day or two. Then when she should be over that, she acted like she just felt too bad to show him any love. Now, he could understand if it was just once in a while, but it was all the time.

But here he was, still in his thirties, and without much hope in that area of his life. He believed Clemmie could change if she just wanted to. And yet the Clemmie he had loved in his mind and had dreamed of having always as his wife was gone; it was as if she had passed away in silence.

Another thing that bothered John was that Clemmie was very impractical. Why would a woman go buy flowers when they needed food so much more? *Women are really mysterious,* John thought. *Especially this woman of mine!* He didn't like the way she was always after him to go to church more.

The Lord knew he was working himself to death seven days a week. He would go when he could, but personally, he thought there was more to being a Christian than just showing up every time they opened the doors of the building. He wished most of all that marriage could be a little more fun and that he and Clemmie and Ruth could just have some good times and not be sick or sad or worried.

But he was afraid that the hope he had treasured of having a really good marriage this second time was dying. Yep, it was gone, like the Clementine who wrote those love letters seemed to be gone for good.

Ruth is sure a fine daughter, John thought. *A beautiful girl, too.* It made him feel real good when people said she looked like her dad. He wanted to be able to buy her everything she needed. He liked to take her to town and buy her a little bracelet or an ice cream cone. She was a smart girl, too. He didn't know it was possible to read when you were only three years old.

He figured she was smarter than either he or Clemmie, and it made him feel so good that Ruth was always happy and excited when her papa came home. She would let out a little happy cry and run to him with her arms outstretched, then she would hug his neck so tight as he lifted her up in his arms. Her dimples were so deep and her blue eyes and curls were enough to turn heads on the street.

John liked to sing to Ruth, and his favorite song was one that had come out in 1912, "When Irish Eyes Are Smiling." John Robert Briley was proud of his Irish heritage.

"Sure, she steals your heart a-way!" he would finish in booming voice, with full understanding and agreement. Ruth laughed gleefully, twisting her papa's moustache around her chubby finger.

"Sing it another—again, Papa!" Ruth squealed with delight.

LEFT YOU LONELY

"Ruth," Clemmie called, "come let Mother brush your hair. We want to go over to 10th Street for the nice man to take your picture. You're three years old today!"

"Kin I weah my wing Papa gave me? And kin I take Ma-we Kafween?"

"Of course you can take Mary Kathleen, and she can even be in the picture with you. Hurry and fix her hair pretty and put on her little hat. Then we need to find your shoes and stockings."

In no time at all Ruth came running with her doll in one hand

and her shoes in the other. Lately Clemmie was finding unexpected pleasure in her little daughter. Ruth was such a good companion. She was always cheerful and eager to please. She loved to go anywhere Clemmie suggested and never caused a moment's worry to her mother.

"Why, I never get that terrible lonesome feeling that I used to have. I believe I enjoy being with Ruth more than with John. Maybe that's because there's no disagreement between us."

Clemmie and John celebrated their fourth wedding anniversary by buying their first lawn mower. John took pleasure in cutting the grass in long, even rows. It reminded him a little of when he used to plow for his dad back in Mills County. Clemmie was delighted to look out her kitchen window and see her roses and geraniums in full bloom and the green carpet of freshly cut grass.

"I reckon we three are a real city family now," Clemmie stated aloud to herself. When they got the money from John's accident, he let Clemmie go to the dentist and have her teeth fixed and bought her a bathroom cabinet to keep her medicine in.

"Clemmie, I want us to get you where you feel good and don't have any worries. You're still a young woman, and I want you t' fix up an' look good," John said.

Clemmie was beginning to look some older than her thirty-four years, and John had noticed and wanted to rectify the matter.

Grace, Clemmie's youngest sister, would soon graduate from Gunter Bible College, a very conservative school established by friends of Papa Wilmeth. Since it was only a two-year college, Grace wanted to go on to Texas Christian University and complete her degree. The main reason Grace had chosen Gunter was because Papa's sister, Annie Davis, lived there. Grace begged Clemmie to come for her graduation, so Clemmie and Ruth went on the train. Clemmie spent the whole day of her own wedding anniversary making herself a white dress for the special occasion.

TCU was the same school that had begun as Add-Ran College

in Thorp Spring, Texas, where both Papa and Mamma Wilmeth had taught over twenty-five years before. Although TCU had conservative roots, the school was becoming liberal.

A few days later, the Brileys had a surprise visitor. It was Betty Burton, John's aunt from Kentucky. Clemmie thought John looked like her—his mother's sister.

John gave his aunt a big hug, and Clemmie saw a tear glisten in his eye.

"John, I've brought you a present. It's a rose bush grown from a cutting of your mother's, which came all the way from Ireland. I knew you'd enjoy having something alive that was loved so much by your mother. I want to help you plant it and tell you how to take care of it. Then I have to hurry over to meet some cousins for supper."

That same evening, Clemmie thought that John was happier than she had seen him since Ruth's birth, nearly like he had made contact with his mother, who had been gone for thirty-three years. He told Clemmie that he wanted to be the one to take care of the rose bush and for her not to bother it. Clemmie could not have been more amazed. He had all but made fun of her for the way she loved her flowers and had never seemed to be interested in them at all himself. She decided to take him at his word and not to water or feed the bush herself. She imagined that it would be dead by the time summer was over. John named it "Kentucky Rose."

The summer of 1915 was one that always remained alive and happy in Clemmie's memory. A memorable event had taken place on the Ebony farm. After twenty-five summers and winters in the little gray box house, Papa and Mama Wilmeth finally moved across the meadow into their new house. Papa had made his promise good, although the construction had taken much longer than planned. Mamma was like a queen in a castle.

Clemmie and Ruth had gone for their usual summer visit to Riverside Farm. This time they stayed in the attic of the new house with Grace. Their first morning there, Clemmie overheard her parents talking downstairs.

"Clara, you look mighty happy. It gives me great joy to fulfill my promise to you after all these years. I regret that it took so long. You deserve much, much more," Papa said.

"Oh, Mr. Wilmeth." Mamma rather enjoyed using the formal name she had first called J.R. "You are a man of your word. You have given me all I ever hoped and dreamed for. And waiting so long has made it all the sweeter."

Just that morning Clara had awakened on her big feather bed and blinked and pinched herself to be sure she wasn't dreaming. The bedroom seemed so large and spacious to her. It opened onto a long porch that wrapped around the east and south sides. Another bedroom door opened into the living room, which sported a new piano, a fireplace, a couch, and nice chairs.

Clemmie, upstairs in the large attic room on a cot, listened to this rare moment of intimacy between her parents. She was happy for them and realized how little of worldly goods Mamma had ever had since she'd married Papa. She fought her desire to feel a little envious when she was the one who had always dreamed of a home in Ebony, near her Big Hill. Mamma had never loved this land like she had, and something seemed a little unfair. But then Clemmie knew she had more of life ahead, and perhaps the day would come when she, too, would have a fine white home in Ebony. Or maybe Papa would will this one to her, or maybe she and John would strike oil.

"Clemmie!" Mamma's shrill voice broke Clemmie's reverie. "Are you coming down to breakfast or not?" Grace and Ruth had already been walking around the farm and arrived just as Mamma set the hot biscuits on the table.

Clemmie was enthralled by the food on the farm: blackberries, peaches, plums, and grapes, all fresh from the garden. Then there was fried chicken and milk and butter and all kinds of vegetables. Such feasting, and yet Clemmie was amazed that her family was complaining about something all the time. The conversation that morning was so pessimistic to Clemmie, considering that her parents were in a new home and had plenty to eat.

"It's sure good to have you three girls here with us in the new house. We miss our children a lot. Little Ruth and I need to get acquainted, don't we, girl?" Papa made a try at pleasant conversation.

"Yes, we are glad you have come, girls. I wish the countryside looked better than it does. Usually it is greener than this in mid-June," Mamma added to the topic. "Mr. Wilmeth, I don't see how we can make it if we don't get rain. I know that Jim is sick with the blues because his cotton is not looking good. It needs the moisture so bad."

"Well, Clara, at least our son has the cattle to sell and depend on. We are the ones who could suffer soon if the pecan trees fail to get any rain, not to mention the small crops we have planted. The grasshoppers are supposed to be extra bad since it is dry for June."

"Papa and Mamma, I cannot believe that my parents are showing such a lack of faith and no gratitude at all." Clemmie could hold herself back no longer. "Why, my eyes are big with amazement at how the good Lord has blessed you out here on the farm. In the first place, you have this wonderful new house. Why, if I had a house like this, I would think I had died and gone to heaven!

"Then you have an endless supply of milk, eggs, and butter, not to mention chicken and pork bacon. And just look at this bowl of fruit! In Dallas, if you could even find it, this would cost about five dollars. And there is no flavor in food in the city like out here on the farm. Oh, please be happy and just praise the Lord for blessing you so much!" Clemmie's smoky-blue eyes filled with tears as her voice rose and quivered.

Grace, who had just moved back home from Gunter, disliked discord and tried to change the subject. "Papa and Mamma, I wish you could have been there for my graduation from Gunter Bible College. I feel so happy to be out of school. I made some good grades this last semester, too. When I would get sick of studying, I pretended that I was out here on the farm, and I played like I was running up and down these hills. Later, I want to go back over to the old house and take an air bath."

"An air bath? What in the world is that, my child?" questioned Mamma.

"Oh, Mamma, it is the most healthful thing you can do! You take off all your clothes and run in a wide circle, with your arms outstretched like an eagle."

"Mercy, Grace! I forbid you to run around naked. I thought they would teach you some good sense at that college, but I believe you have lost what little you had."

Later that same day, in the early afternoon, Grace went over to the old house. There were a lot of memories for her there. She was conceived and born in the little bedroom and had always lived there except when she was with her sister, Clemmie, at another school or, more recently, at Gunter with Aunt Annie.

The June sun was beating down, and Grace remembered her intention to do the "air bath." There was such freedom in taking off your clothes and running. Grace thought it must relate to escaping the restrictions of dress and comportment that her strict parents had always imposed on her. Everyone else had settled down for an afternoon nap, so Grace felt sure there was no chance of anyone seeing her. She walked quietly past the house where Jim and Callie lived. Callie was expecting her fourth baby in mid-August. Marie was turning six, Ralph was four and a half, and Lillard was three. Grace wanted to visit with all of them a little later in the day.

Opening the back door of the little gray house, Grace smiled at the familiar creaking sound. A little mouse ran across the floor. The house was practically empty, except for a very old mattress in the corner where her parents' bed had been. Grace dropped down on the mattress and turned on her back.

"This is the very mattress where Papa and Mamma planted the

seed to get the triplets and me," Grace thought, half aloud. The triplets had been born in 1890 and had only lived a few days. They were buried right out in the yard.

"Oh, Lord, how could we all have lived in such a small little shack for so many years? I sure want something more out of life than my mamma and papa had. They are good people, but they have been so deprived of all the good things out there in the world."

Grace began to remove her clothes. First, the outer green cotton dress with a wide collar and large skirt. Then off came the petticoat with its ruffles of unbleached muslin, then the little corset with its many hooks and eyes, and last of all the drawers and stockings. Grace stood and looked down at herself. Her legs were well-shaped and long, her stomach was flat, her breasts were medium-sized. She decided to do some exercises. She bent over and touched her toes ten times. Then she tried running in place. Next, she lay down on the mattress and hoisted her hips up to do the "bicycle" exercise with her legs in the air. Finally, she ran outside.

She decided to run down the path that led to the bottomland and the river, making wide circles with her arms as she ran. After a few hundred feet she decided to return to the little house. Rushing in the back door, she headed for the mattress. Throwing herself down on her stomach, her rounded buttocks showed as pink and as bare as a newborn baby's.

At that moment Grace felt the presence of another person in the room. Before she could look and scream, a large calloused hand was spread over her mouth, then another big hand across her eyes. A hoarse male voice said, "Hi, Miz Grace. Guess yore prutty surprised! M' name's Rufus, and yore pa hired me to help him with stuff around here. It shore was fun watchin' you doin' them exercises with no clothes on. I ain't never seen nuthin' so prutty as yore naked body."

"*Please leave me alone!* Please go away! You have no right to be here, and my papa may show up and kill you!" Grace was terrified and hysterical.

"Well, I seen yore papa jes drivin' off in his buggy. Now you jes be nice and quiet and do what I says, and you won't git hurt. Matter o' fact, you may just like what I'm a-gonna do to you."

Just as Rufus grabbed for Grace, they heard the loud barking of a dog. Grace knew it was Ralph's big dog, Rusty, and she knew that Ralph was probably coming with his dog, since the two were inseparable.

"Oh thank you, God," whispered Grace.

"Enybody here?"

Rufus ran out the back door of the house in no time. Grace began to scramble to get her clothes on. Although Ralph was only four and a half, he was a sharp kid and knew people didn't go around naked.

"Hi, Ralph. Auntie Grace was taking an air and sun bath, but now I'm leaving. Are you and Rusty okay? I am *so* glad to see you!" Grace had never meant anything more in her life. She got the dress back on and began running for the new house.

"Ralph, go on back home now, please. I saw a snake in the house." She wanted to scare the little boy enough that he would get back home before Rufus could hurt him.

Grace raced up the attic stairs when she reached the house. She threw herself on her bed and tried to think what she should do. Her heart was racing fast, and she knew someone would ask her what had happened. Clemmie was gone, and so was Ruth, and that was answered prayer, Grace thought. She decided she would leave for Fort Worth in the morning, then stay with her Aunt Mattie until she could get into a dorm at TCU. Grace knew she had had a very close call and was nearly raped. She knew she could not tell anyone what had really happened. She would have to invent some reason for wanting to leave so soon. And she needed to ask Papa to get rid of Rufus. Now she could never come back to her beloved farm and feel completely safe again. He had ruined everything.

It wasn't easy for Grace to think of something to tell her Mamma and Papa and Clemmie, but she knew that if she told them the truth, they'd all say it was her own fault for being naked. She ended up with the story that she had recalculated the hours she needed to graduate from TCU in just two more years. She would need to take one course this summer, and enrollment was starting Monday. Maybe she could leave the next day.

When she approached Papa the next morning, he immediately wanted to know what had happened. He brought up the fact that she had been happy when she arrived, so why the sudden change in thinking? Finally, Grace told Papa that he needed to get rid of the young man, Rufus.

"Grace, are you saying that Rufus has hurt you in some way?"

"No, Papa, but he wanted to hurt me. I just cannot stay here any longer, knowing he could try something with me."

"I'm so very sorry, daughter. I will send him away immediately."

Grace kissed her papa on the cheek, and he took her to town to catch the Frisco to Fort Worth the next day. Everyone was sad to see her go since she brought a lot of fun and life with her. She liked to play the piano, sing, and make wonderful cookies and candy. Marie, Ruth, and Ralph said they felt lonely with Aunt Grace gone.

Late that night Clemmie wrote these words in her diary: "I want to come back among these country people and do everything I can to teach them to be happy and to get the best out of life."

John came and spent a week at the farm and seemed to really have a good time. Clemmie decided that when she got back to Dallas, she would continue to study and be ready to stand examination in December.

Yes, I am seized again with the idea of teaching, and I will save money so we can come back to this farm. We'll have a fine white house, and I'll invite people from all over the world to come and visit and exchange ideas with us. Having enough money is like being set free to live your dreams, thought Clemmie.

Like Raleigh used to say, "Our one regret will be if we do not get enough education." Oh, what a smart and kind man he is. Help us, Lord, this I pray. Good night.

SET YOU FREE

As fall of 1915 ripped the leaves from the trees, war raged all over Europe, and President Wilson tried to keep the United States out of it. In fact, he had run for his second term with this campaign slogan: "He kept us out of war." Americans seemed to generally respect Wilson. He looked like a president and was a friendly man, but he was never as beloved by the people as Teddy Roosevelt.

The Texas State Fair came to Dallas every October, and it was about as much fun as Christmas to Clemmie. This year Clemmie's favorite guest in the whole world came for a few days—her dear papa. Ruth seemed to really like her grandfather, and that pleased Clemmie.

"Papa, tell me a story about when you were in th' big wa-ah,"

Ruth would say as she climbed up in Papa's lap, and he would happily launch into one of his Civil War tales or one of the true adventures from his own life. He told her about how he had walked from Texas to Virginia to go to school, walked to Mexico two different times, and swam across the San Marcos River.

The day before Papa left Dallas, the three Brileys took him to the Fair. They went by streetcar, and Ruth was so excited as they got near enough to see the lights and the Ferris wheel, to hear the barkers selling their wares and touting sideshow freaks, and to smell the popcorn and cotton candy. Ruth squealed with glee, and her papa wanted to buy her something. He bought her a little monkey on a stick. Clemmie really wished he had not spent the dollar, sorely needed for carfare.

A few days later, John took Clemmie completely off guard with an idea.

"Clemmie, I know you're worried about your exam fer that teacher thing, so I wantcha t' hire a woman t' do the washin' for you for two months."

"Oh, John, I believe that is the best present anyone ever gave me." She planted a big kiss on his lips.

The exam was to be held on December third and fourth. Clemmie wanted to do well on the exam, get her certificate, and go back to teaching school.

Now that will be like a dream coming true, to never be poor again, imagined Clemmie.

— — — — — — —

Mid-November always made Clemmie think of the death of John's little brother, Homer. He had died of diphtheria on November 17, 1905. *Ten years ago this very evening,* Clemmie reminisced. *How could ten years have gone by,* she wondered, *since it is still engraved so clearly in my mind?* She opened her treasure trunk and took out her old scrapbook where she had pasted the obituary about Homer Briley, John's little half brother.

Homer was twelve years old and was in Clemmie's class at school that year. School had started late; in fact, it began on Monday, November 13. Homer Briley was an excellent student, and the kids and teachers liked him a lot. His mother, Brother Briley's second wife, Fannie, had died when he was very young. Clemmie had always felt sympathy for him. She wished she could take him home with her and take care of him.

Homer missed school that Monday because he had a sore throat. As the week went on, Clemmie heard that Homer was worse and that it was "membranous croup," or diphtheria. After a few days of illness, a doctor could look in the throat of a patient and see a gray membrane covering the throat and tonsils. If an antitoxin could be given in time, the person could recover; otherwise, it might be fatal within a week's time.

Clemmie decided she and Grace would go by the Briley place after school on Friday. It was about two miles from the schoolhouse, and that day Clemmie had her father's hack, pulled by a big horse. It was four o'clock when they arrived at the Brileys'. Clemmie asked Grace to wait in the hack. Brother Briley had made a trip back to Kentucky and didn't even know that his young son was sick. John was taking care of Homer, and Clemmie could tell that he was plenty scared. John's brother, Fowler, and his wife, Biddie, lived close by and were also helping with Homer.

"Hello, Miss Clemmie," Homer said in a small, hoarse voice, his cheeks rosy with fever. His eyes looked dark and slightly sunken. "How is school going? I wanna come back soon."

"Oh, Homer, we have missed you so much. Things are going all right so far, but we do need you there. You are my best pupil, you know. Everyone loves you, Homer, so you just get well and try not to worry about anything." As Clemmie left the room, she stopped to speak to John in the dimly lit front room.

"How do things look to you, John?"

"We sent Frank Dyer t' Brownwood for the antitoxin. I'm so scared we waited too long. It'll be two hours afore he's back. Clemmie, pray fer Homer, would you? If he dies, Pa may just die hisself."

"Of course I'll pray, John. Surely Homer will make it. I've heard of several people around here who recovered from this dreaded disease."

Clemmie decided to go on home. She pulled the rein forcefully and turned the hack back up the dusty little road toward the post office. Then she and Grace started for home. They got as far as the Hosea place, and Clemmie felt a strong urge to go back to the Briley place. She asked Grace if she would go on home without her. Grace said that she didn't mind at all and got down to walk home.

Clemmie got back to the Briley place just a few minutes before the little boy died. John was so distraught, and his body racked with loud sobs. There were several close friends and relatives in the little house. Another hour passed before Frank Dyer returned exhausted with the antitoxin. When he heard the news, he cursed himself for not making the trip faster. It had taken four hours and fifteen minutes to cover the rough twenty-five miles each way on horseback, find the doctor, and get him to issue the antitoxin. Then he had to go to the pharmacy and pick up the medicine and then ride hard, praying all the way.

Clemmie put her arm around John and tried to think of words of comfort.

"John, now little Homer is with his mother again."

"Oh, Clemmie, think how poor Papa's gonna be when he gits the news. And I loved Homer so much." John sat down in a rough chair, put his head in his hands, and sobbed for several minutes. "I shoulda saved him, Clemmie. I wish I'd died in his place."

After a while, Clemmie and Mrs. Griffin walked to Mrs. Kelley's house and prepared the funeral clothing for Homer. There was a nice new suit that Homer had bought for himself with his cotton money and never had a chance to wear. They washed Homer's little body, now stiff, and dressed him in the new underwear and his new suit. Clemmie sat up all night with John, Fowler, and Biddie. Their brother Bert was notified and was on his way. Clemmie's heart ached so much for John. She could tell that it nearly killed him to give up Homer.

The next day, Clemmie slept a little at Mrs. Kelley's and then helped the Brileys clean house and serve food that the neighbors brought in. The funeral was the next day at Elkins, where Homer's mother, and little brother, Leander, nicknamed "Runt," were buried under a spreading scrub oak tree. Brother Briley's mother, Elizabeth, was also buried there, since she had made the journey to Texas with her son.

A large crowd gathered for the funeral. The casket was white and covered with mums that friends picked from their gardens and brought by armloads. It was one of the saddest occasions that Clemmie ever witnessed. To think that a child so lovely would have a life so short. Clemmie wrote a long obituary that was published in the *Brownwood Banner Bulletin.*

Sweet little Homer, we sadly wept when we laid thee away, wept because of our own aching hearts, and wept again because of the father who left thee well and strong and should return to find thy face no more. Yet why should we grieve that in thy innocence and youth God saw fit to call thee home? We know not what temptations and what sorrow thou hast missed, we only know that now thou art in the arms of a loving Father, surrounded by beauty which will never decay, and flowers that fade not away;

And there in that beautiful place
Sometime we cannot tell when
But it will be when we look on His face
We shall see thee and know thee again.

Oddly, it was the day Homer died that Clemmie first felt that she was beginning to love John Briley. She had seen such deep love and compassion in only one other person, and that was Papa.

And so Clemmie wrote in her diary, ten years later, "There's a sacred memory in my heart tonight."

— — — — — — — — —

On November 18, 1915, the Liberty Bell passed through Dallas, en route to its home in Philadelphia from the Exposition at San Francisco. Clemmie caught a glimpse of it on the back of the train as it stopped just two blocks from the house. However, there was a line so long already formed that Clemmie felt she could not waste the time it would take to view the famous bell.

Thanksgiving Day arrived, and the Brileys had a good meal: pork roast and beef ribs, pumpkin pie, peaches and cream, and other dishes. Clemmie was aware that there were so very many things to be thankful for. John had the evening off, and the three Brileys went downtown to see the store windows.

In the windows of Kress and Woolworth there were Christmas trees displayed and lots of pretties to see. Ruth was so excited and began to clap her hands and jump up and down. Just then, an attractive woman who looked to be around fifty passed close to Clemmie and John on the sidewalk. Suddenly, she put her hand on Ruth's curly head and said, "What a pretty little girl." She was dressed in the latest fashion, and her perfume smelled expensive. She looked like she knew John.

"John, who is that woman? Do you know her?" Clemmie inquired.

John cleared his throat several times. "Yeah, that woman's Nancy Harris. An' I don't like to say it, but she's my first wife."

"Oh no! That is *Nancy Harris?* She seems very brash to me. How dare she touch Ruth's head! John, I hope you haven't seen her before this...have you?" Clemmie felt a rush of mixed emotions.

"I swear to you, Clemmie, this is the first time I've seen her since she left my house t' file for divorce, and that was over thirteen years ago. I hope to heaven I never see her again!" he added emphatically.

Clemmie later decided that it was good to have seen her rival. She was glad that Nancy looked older than John, but Clemmie decided she would ask no more questions. Still, it was quite a shock to finally see the woman who had slept with John for nearly three years, the woman who had hurt him so deeply.

But the woman who had also pleasured him, probably more than I, raced Clemmie's thoughts. *Now what was it that Sallie used to say? 'Jealousy can destroy the very thing it tries to protect.'*

— — — — — — — —

Christmas Day dawned bright and beautiful that year. Clemmie felt real bad with "grippe," or flu, and had for seven days. But, she told herself, she just had to get up and try to get ready for Christmas.

"There is no one but me to make Christmas for Ruth."

John bought a Kodak camera for Clemmie. She was more excited than she had ever been over a gift, and John knew he had really chosen the perfect gift this time. When little Ruth awoke on Christmas morning, she was so happy to find her new doll, little dishes, and a table with chairs. Then there were lots of nuts, candy, and fruit, including apples and oranges. Clemmie served delicious roast, dressing, potato salad, pineapple cake, and peaches and cream. She felt proud that she had made everything herself.

On a Wednesday near the end of February, Ruth developed a sore throat. Clemmie postponed a trip to the superintendent's office and devoted herself to Ruth. As the day went on, the little girl became as limp as a rag doll, lost interest in everything, and just slept or lay on the bed. Clemmie had heard of several cases of diphtheria. Feeling her heart begin to race, Clemmie rushed next door to her neighbor's house and called the doctor's office. She was surprised that Dr. White answered the phone. He said he would come by the Brileys' on his way home. After examining Ruth, he told Clemmie that she had a probable case of diphtheria, and that it was good that Clemmie had called him early.

Dr. White said he would return the next day and would see if he thought she should have the antitoxin. He saw the fear in Clemmie's eyes and tried to calm her and reassure her that even if it was diphtheria, she would be completely cured with the use of the antitoxin.

"Oh, Dr. White! John had a little brother who died of diphtheria ten years ago. He was so smart and sweet, and he was my pupil at school. Oh, Doctor, if my little Ruth should die, I could not bear it. Please, please, give her the medicine soon."

"Don't let yourself go, Miss Clemmie. I understand what you are saying, and let's just give this till tomorrow. I promise you that it will not be too late to stop it. The antitoxin is expensive and very limited, and once in a while a child will react adversely to it. But I believe God will take care of Ruth, and you will be surprised at the speed of the recovery she will make. So I will see you tomorrow, Miss Clemmie. Now try to get some rest."

Clemmie held back the full force of her panic until the door closed. Then she raced to the kitchen and fell to her knees.

Clemmie began to pray aloud: "God of my fathers, and my Father, too, I come to Thee on bended knee, begging Thee to spare the life of my little daughter.

"Oh, Father, how well I remember little Homer and the way he got sick, and no one thought it was serious. And the medicine came all too late to save him. Dear God, we know that you are the great Physician. Thou canst heal and make well again. Please, Father, I beg Thee, *please* make Ruth well!

"She is so smart, so pretty, so loving, and she is my only child, Lord. Please, if someone must die, let it be me instead of Ruth. Father, she has her whole life in front of her, and it seems so unfair. God, I thank Thee for healing her, for I know Thou wilt do that miracle for me. If Ruth could be well, Father, I promise that I will keep my life pure and clean, that I will be a much better wife to John, and that I will love him so deeply and never entertain thoughts of anyone else.

"And I will be a better mother to little Ruth, dear Father. I will pray more with her and help her all I can, and I will be a better daughter to my mother, and I will never argue with Mamma again. I will refrain from any criticism of other human beings and will keep myself only unto Thee, Dear God. I will let Thee use me in any way Thou seest fit and in any town or state. Please, Father, hear my pleas. In love and gratitude and thanksgiving for all blessings, I am Thy humble servant, Clemmie. In Jesus' name, amen."

John was equally as distraught as Clemmie, if not more so. With his haunting memories of loss of loved ones, especially little Homer with diphtheria, he would have gone anywhere at any hour to get the medicine for Ruth. He believed Clemmie should have insisted more that the doctor begin it that day. He planted himself in a straight-back chair by Ruth's bed and refused to sleep that night.

Clemmie lay in bed, stiff as a poker, never closing her eyes all night. She would get up to check on Ruth—to take her a drink, to be sure she was still breathing, to ask her if she needed or wanted anything. Once she hugged John for a long time, knowing they both were remembering that night a decade ago in Ebony.

Dr. White kept his word and was back the next day. He thought it best to administer the antitoxin and did. He reassured Clemmie that she was about to see a tremendous improvement in Ruth and that she would be nearly normal again by Sunday.

After the doctor left, Clemmie was so nervous and frightened she could hardly live, much less get any work done. She just hovered around Ruth's bed, watching her for any change. Ruth had slept so much and had hardly talked at all.

The antitoxin worked like a charm, and by Saturday of that week, Ruth was up and playing again, as if she had never been sick! How Clemmie praised God and renewed all the vows she had made, seriously considering how she would be a better person than she had been before.

Clemmie wanted to have a party for Ruth's fourth birthday. She invited all the neighborhood children. She felt so grateful to God for saving Ruth from death.

God set Ruth free from physical death, just as Jesus set us all free from spiritual death. Thank you, God and Jesus, for your marvelous gifts, Clemmie prayed.

John and Clemmie had their fifth wedding anniversary without much fanfare. Clemmie recorded in her diary that she sometimes felt very lonely, and she realized that their married life would be much happier if she and John could agree on some vital things—the main one being worshipping God together on Sundays. Clemmie confided her concerns to her friend, her diary, trying to focus on her blessings and her hope.

Dear Diary,

Not withstanding it all, there is much happiness for me, and there is hope in my heart that things which should not be, may yet be as they should. Yes, Father, keep on freeing us from everything that is of this world. Oh, Father, fulfill that promise in Isaiah Chapter 40: "We will mount up with wings, like eagles. We will run, and not be weary. We will walk, and not faint." And let us find true companionship with each other, and most of all, let us know Thee, as Thou art. Let us walk and talk with Thee, O God. Then we shall be free indeed. In Jesus' name, amen."

FOR MY HEART WAS
CRUSHED WITH LONGING

Clemmie made a habit of remembering one main event from every year that she lived: 1909 would be the good-bye to Raleigh; 1910 would be the beginning of her courtship with John via mail in Ochiltree; 1911 was her marriage; 1912 was Ruth's birth; 1913 would be the move to Dallas; 1914 was the beginning of the Great War; 1915 was her decision to get her certificate and go back to teaching; 1916 was the year God had saved Ruth from diphtheria; 1917 was the year the U.S. entered World War I; 1918 was the year of the killer flu and when the war was over; and 1919…well, she'd never forget that year!

It all began with the annual trip to Ebony on the train. Ruth had begun to love Ebony as much as Clemmie did and was as excited as a seven-year-old could be.

"Mother, it's just like being in heaven…all those cousins to play with, and horses to ride, the river to swim in…and we don't even have to work—just play all day long!" Ruth's face would just glow while she described it to her mother.

Clemmie thought about it this way: *I hope Ruth will never lose her love for our land. It seems to me that love for land is in our blood, that it is a gift from God to have a place under the sun that is always in your heart. And you are pulled to go back there, and one day you know you will live there.*

Ebony became a kind of Utopia for Clemmie, and she dreamed of coming back there to live. They would always have milk, eggs, and butter, vegetables fresh in season, pork, beef, chicken…*Why, for someone who had been hungry and seen her child hungry, it would truly be like heaven on earth.*

Jim Wilmeth, Clemmie's brother, met Clemmie and Ruth at the train in Brownwood. He was driving the first Wilmeth car. It was a Model T Ford, and all the adult family members at Ebony had decided to pool their resources and buy the car with joint ownership. Jim looked healthy and suntanned. His hair was beginning to recede, and he usually had chewing tobacco in his cheek, causing it to puff out like a chipmunk.

Jim was nearly always in a good humor and loved to joke. Clemmie really loved her only full brother, but she was amazed that he was nothing like her papa. He never really liked school nor books like Papa. He just didn't seem to be ambitious, but maybe that was an unfair judgment, Clemmie reasoned. He sure was optimistic, siring all those children! And he managed to give his big family all the necessities of life.

Jim and Callie had five children already: Marie, ten, the little mother; Ralph, eight, very confident and self-assured; Lillard, six, a sweet, quiet child who didn't talk quite plain, and Jim nicknamed him "Dutch," explaining to others that he was speaking Dutch. Then there was Bernice, nearly four, who was cute as a bug—a real showstopper; and baby Lucille, only eighteen months old, and as cuddly as a little lamb. Clemmie really felt sorry for Callie with all those children to feed and clothe, and there was no telling how many more she might have. Ruth adored her cousins and was so envious of the big family. She prayed every night for God to give her a baby brother or sister.

Clemmie knew that her papa was not feeling well. He would turn eighty-four years old that year. He tired easily, often felt nauseated, had lost weight, and had a pain in his side. The doctor said that he couldn't be sure, but he suspected cancer of the stomach or gallbladder.

In July, Papa decided to have a final reunion with his children. He called them all together, and everyone came. It was a grand time, and Papa felt gratified to have all his and Clara's children united with the children of his first marriage to Maria. Clemmie thoroughly enjoyed being with her half brothers and sisters that she didn't see often but always remembered in prayers and letters.

The Ebony trustees were at a loss to find a teacher for that school year. Someone suggested that Miss Clemmie always wanted to teach and could not get a school job in Dallas. All three went calling on Clemmie in mid-August and invited her to stay in Ebony and teach at the Ebony school. Clemmie felt so flattered…but what about her home in Dallas? And what about John…would he let her stay in Ebony for several months while he was alone in their Dallas home?

"Mother! Mother! Is it true that you might teach here this fall and you would be my teacher? Oh, Mama, please, please say yes! I'd be so happy, and Papa could come see us sometimes on the Frisco train." Ruth had heard the rumor and came bounding up the attic stairs and jumped up on her mother, arms and legs locked around her.

"Yes, Ruth, they have asked me to teach the Ebony school. It would be worth it just to know you are so happy! But first I need to talk to your papa and see if he will let us be so far away from him."

Clemmie knew the money would help them so much. Her greatest fear was living with Mamma and having disagreements. She knew she always managed to displease Mamma when what she wanted was to get along. Perhaps this was a God-given opportunity for the two women to work out their differences and learn to be friends, she reasoned.

Clemmie wrote to John and explained the situation. She suggested that John could come visit often, and she promised him it would be like when they were sweethearts again. When John wrote back, he gave his approval and stated that Clemmie should remember to keep her promise that they would be like sweethearts again.

Not long after she told the trustees that she would accept the job, Papa took a turn for the worse. He appeared to have had a light stroke, and the doctor thought that death was imminent. Clemmie spent a lot of time at his bedside, talking to him, reading to him, praying with him and for him. His hearing was very poor, and Clemmie had to practically shout.

Papa realized he was nearing the end of his life. He had hoped to live even longer, but lately he had been in so much pain that he had lost his fear of death. Besides, he had preached so many funerals and consoled so many grieving families that he had to believe his own message of hope. He often preached to his people that death was comparable to dropping an ugly seed into the earth, then seeing the beauty of the plant and the flower that resulted from the dried and wrinkled seed; and so would be the beauty of the resurrected souls in heaven. He drew that example from 1 Corinthians 15.

It was late in the day of Thursday, October 30, 1919. As Clemmie approached the house, having walked home the five miles from school, she heard the most awful wailing sound. She immediately knew that it was Mamma's cry, and that it could mean only one thing…Papa was dying.

Breaking into a run, she purposely dropped the book bag and lifted her long skirt. Rounding the corner field, she saw Jim, Callie, Marie, and Ralph running toward the house. They reached the porch at the same time, just as Mamma screamed loudly, "He's gone! Mr. Wilmeth is gone! Oh, James, please don't leave me! What will I do, what will I do?"

With that, Mamma threw herself onto Papa's body and convulsed in sobs. Clemmie and Callie both began to cry loudly, and the grandchildren ran to hide in the attic.

"He was a good man," Jim offered. "I'll go and fetch Dr. Hutchins in San Saba. I'll take the wagon and bring back a coffin." Jim pulled the sheet over his papa's dark face and helped his mother get to her room. Papa had died on a cot in the front room, where he had wanted to be during his last days.

"Now, Mamma, you know that the Good Book says, 'Blessed are the dead who die in the Lord.' Now we need to have strong faith." Jim felt unnerved around intense emotion. He had loved his dad, but it was easy for him to accept the fact that his father's time had come to die, and so he had. Addressing Clemmie and Callie, he said, "Now you girls need to rest in bed for about an hour. This is a lot for us to take, but he taught us to be strong, so let's be that way."

When Jim was alone in the wagon, he gave full vent to his pent-up emotions. Sobs racked his body, and he felt some regret about his relationship with his dad, thinking he had not been the type of son that his father had needed. Maybe he could make that up by taking care of his mother and the land and pecan trees that his father loved so dearly.

Clemmie was devastated. She made her way to her attic room and flung herself facedown on the bed. She felt like a little girl whose papa was very much like God, and now he was dead; and she was left to muddle through the rest of life with no life support. She felt like her heart would always be crushed with longing for her dear papa.

"Oh, God, my Father," she cried out from the depths of her soul.

"Why, oh, Lord, why did Thou leave me here alone? Couldn't I just die also with my dear papa? There is no one here on earth to take his place. Father, I needed him so. He was everything to me, dear Lord. I know it was time for him to come home and be with Thee. I admired him more than anyone I have ever known. In fact, besides Raleigh Ely, he was in a class apart from other humans. He was a man destined for greatness."

The next day, Clemmie managed to pull herself together enough to help get meals and make arrangements for her father's burial. Her brother brought home a simple wooden casket that was the proper length for Papa's body. Mamma had washed and ironed Papa's best white shirt, and Clemmie pressed his suit, which was worn nearly threadbare. Women of the community came in to wash and dress Papa's body, and he was lifted into the casket. Mums from Mamma's flowerbed were placed all around the body. His long white beard was combed neatly. He looked dignified and peaceful as he lay in state in the front room of the house he had built for Mamma.

The service was held under the arbor. All the Wilmeth children, eight of them, and their families, returned to Ebony for the funeral. Brother White preached his best funeral text taken from Revelation chapter 14, verse 13: "And I heard a voice from heaven saying, Write this: Blessed are the dead who die in the Lord henceforth. Blessed indeed, says the Spirit, that they may rest from their labors, for their deeds follow them.'"

As soon as the last prayer ended, the mourners began to line up and each extended their condolences to the widow and children. Suddenly, to Clemmie's extreme surprise, there was Raleigh Ely standing in front of her.

Clemmie had not seen him in ten years, since that day on Big Hill, and he had changed some, as had she. He gave her a big hug and whispered in her ear that her father had meant a lot to him and his mother.

"He would come by our little house late in the day and see if we needed anything to eat and to check on us. We will never forget that."

"Raleigh, how are you and your wife? Do you have children?"

"Yes, a boy who is six, named after me, and a little girl, Eloise, who is just three. We have just bought a house and made a move to Abilene. I think I saw your daughter, Clemmie. She favors you a great deal. She is beautiful."

Later, when Clemmie looked around to find Raleigh, he was gone.

Oh no, please, God, don't let him be gone already. My crushed soul is so in need of him, Lord, I am longing to talk with him. Oh, what unexpected pleasure to see Raleigh after all these years. Oh, if I could have had just five minutes of time alone to talk to him in a more personal way. Now I will probably never see him again. Oh, Lord, in your wisdom and providence, maybe Thou wilt let me again see that handsome face some sweet day. I know I need to turn to my own husband for comfort. Help me to be able to do that is my prayer, in Jesus' name and for His sake, amen, Lord.

John had come by train for his father-in-law's funeral. The two men, Papa and John, had gotten along fine, and John knew he would really miss the friendship that Clemmie's papa had extended to him, even helping him with loans or with bank business. It scared John a little to see Clemmie so distraught.

On the night of the burial, John and Clemmie were in the attic room alone. Ruth was sleeping at her Aunt Callie's with all the cousins. John was so kind to Clemmie and wanted to rub her back and legs. He couldn't have been more surprised that Clemmie seemed responsive to his tenderness. Clemmie kept trying to ward off the vision of Raleigh's face during the lovemaking.

The next day, Clemmie was very motivated to write a suitable tribute to her father and have it published in *The Firm Foundation*. More than anything else, it helped her work through her grief.

An Old Soldier Called Home

Brother J.R. Wilmeth, well-beloved preacher and teacher of Texas, fell asleep at his home near Ebony, Texas, October 30, 1919. Surviving him are his wife, Mrs. Clara Antonia Wilmeth, and eight children.

James Ransom Wilmeth was born in Lawrence County, Arkansas, October 17, 1835. The family moved to Texas and settled near where McKinney now stands in 1846. J.R. had 12 brothers and sisters.

At the age of 22, he walked to Bethany, Virginia, to study. One of his teachers was Alexander Campbell. After a year or so, he returned home and married his sweetheart, Miss Maria Florence Lowry, near his home at McKinney, Texas, on August 26, 1858.

He was very much opposed to war, but he did much good as chaplain during the Civil War and did much good preaching to the soldiers.

On July 20, 1868, his wife died, leaving him with five small children. After this he traveled in Mexico, studying their language and customs, teaching and preaching among them. Also in company with his brother, C.M. Wilmeth, he attended college at Lexington, Kentucky, where he finished his school days. While there he was a pupil of J.W. McGarvey.

On June 15, 1875, at Bryan, Texas, he married Miss Clara Antonia Schulz. Of the ten children born to this marriage, four lived to adulthood.

He taught and preached in many places, and it seems that everyone loved him. We are constantly meeting those who knew him and loved him years and years ago.

He taught in Add-Ran College at Thorp Spring. He taught at McKinney, at San Marcos, and many smaller places. His last teaching was at Corinth, Arkansas, where he assisted his brother, C.M. Wilmeth, in beginning a college. Since then he has lived on his farm near Ebony, in Mills County, a quiet little nook on the Colorado River, about twenty-five miles south of Brownwood. But he was always actively involved in preaching, teaching, and encouraging his fellow man.

He sleeps in the little country cemetery at Ebony. A man who was modestly great; whose life was rich and ripe; a Christian faithful unto death, who loved his God with all his heart, his soul, his mind, and loved his neighbor as himself.

His daughter,
Clementine Wilmeth Briley

Clemmie had to put her grief aside and return to her classroom the following Monday. It was a struggle for her to get back into everyday school life.

One day in December, Clemmie was walking home with Ruth and her cousins were running on ahead. A wave of nausea came over Clemmie. She sat down on a fallen tree and got so sick that she vomited up her lunch.

The rest of the way home she tried to think what could be wrong with her. In the afternoons it had been so hard lately to keep her eyes open.

"Oh no!" Clemmie said aloud. *I must be pregnant! And here I am thirty-nine years old. The child may not even be right. But perhaps this will be the son I have always wanted. And I had always thought a family should contain more than one child. Ruth is acting so grown-up that I needed another baby…but not now while I am teaching! It is all I can do to get up at five a.m. and get everything done to help Mamma, then get Ruth and myself ready, and walk to school. It is all so exhausting.*

All through the long winter Clemmie kept the secret to herself until she felt that the shape of her body was betraying her. By then it was mid-March, and once spring began it always brought life and strength and hope to Clemmie. She told Ruth first, and she screamed with delight. One of Ruth's real heartaches had been to be an only child.

"Mother, God answered my prayer for a baby sister or brother. And I hope it's a sister, my own little sister. But a boy is okay. I like boys, too."

John was due to arrive on March 15 for a short visit, and Clemmie wanted to break the news to him in a special way. She and her brother Jim went in the Model T to Brownwood, and John was so happy to see Clemmie as he stepped down from the train.

His kiss and hug were so ardent, and he lifted Clemmie high into the air. She felt the baby stir in her womb.

Late in the evening that day, Clemmie told John she would like to take him up on Big Hill. He was amazed at the change in Clemmie. Her face seemed fuller, her cheeks rosier, and even her breasts were larger under her white blouse. They walked through the field in the gloaming, reminiscing about the old days when John came to court Clemmie in the little gray house, now so empty and tacky-looking. They climbed the hill, stopping to let Clemmie rest when they were halfway. Reaching the top, Clemmie spread out the same green coverlet she had carried up there in 1909 when she and Raleigh had met.

Settled in the center of the cover, Clemmie motioned for John to come close. Then she wanted him to kiss her. John began to feel young once more. He could smell her perfume and feel her warm, full body. She could wait no longer to tell him the news.

"John, we're going to have a baby. Yes, I am...uh, in the family way!"

John was practically speechless. "But Clemmie...we didn't have much chance."

"Well, sometimes it only takes one chance. It was that night in the attic, after Papa's funeral."

"Why, that was…let's see…more'n four months ago, Clemmie. I wish you'd told me afore now."

"I know, John, but I was so afraid you would make me quit teaching and go home, and I wanted to complete the year and put aside some money."

"Here, let me feel my baby." John smoothed her skirt around her tummy, and sure enough, there was a little hump.

"Tonight, I want you to feel the baby move," offered Clemmie. "Are you happy about this, John?"

"Clemmie, you know I always wanted more young'uns. I'm as happy as a man can be. Boy or girl, we're gonna love this baby to pieces."

Mamma had been very quiet and more mellow since Papa had died. Her daughters, Clemmie, Edna, and Grace, began to realize that she was drifting into a depression. Each one would try to cheer her up by discussing the things she had interest in: her garden, the flowers, canning, cooking, the piano. But there was no spark. She would stay in bed until very late in the morning, then take a long nap after lunch.

Within her soul, Mamma felt a lot of regret. She thought that she had not been the sort of wife that Papa needed. She had been too stern and critical and just not any fun and not very happy. Sometimes contented, maybe, but not happy. She had even come to doubt the very God that Papa lived for. If God were there, He would no doubt see that she burned in hell for all her sins, she feared.

When Grace came home from school at Christmas and saw how bad her mother seemed, she made arrangements to take her to Fort Worth for treatment of depression. They stayed with Mamma's sister, Mattie.

With time Mamma was able to accept the reality of her husband's death and began to invest in life again. She was glad to get back to her home and to see that her roses were again in bloom, and the hills were covered with bluebonnets. She could again enjoy the sunrise over the river, and she asked forgiveness from the God that she knew was really there, watching over her as she tried to maintain her "Riverside Farm" that Papa had loved so well.

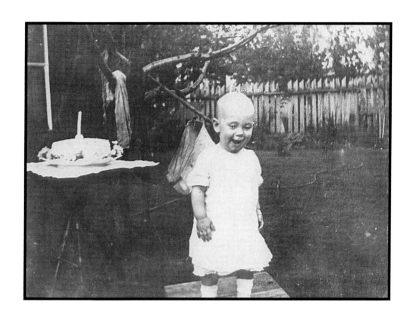

WHAT HAD BEEN

The "Roaring Twenties" nearly went undetected by the poor in Dallas, Texas. However, many people across America flocked to the new motion picture houses and dance halls. A new dance, the "Charleston," was popular, and young women were bobbing their hair and exchanging their corsets and long gabardine skirts for flimsy dresses with long waists and high hemlines.

There was celebration that the war was over and freedom was being manifested in many ways. Women won the right to vote after fighting for many decades. Prohibition laws had forced drinkers into "speakeasies," or drinking clubs. In the south the Ku Klux Klan was revived. However, there were many serious family people who only wanted to find a job and were walking the streets of Dallas.

John Brilcy found himself among them. Being motorman on a

streetcar finally became something he just couldn't face another day, and so he quit. That was the beginning of real troubles for the Briley family. Lack of money was the source of many arguments between John and Clemmie, and the blossom they had known in the early years of their marriage began to wither like a cotton plant covered with boll weevils.

John met Clemmie and Ruth at the train station in mid-May of 1920 as they returned home from their year in Ebony. Clemmie was nearly seven months pregnant and looked pale and exhausted from the train ride. Ruth was glowing and full of energy as she jumped into her papa's arms.

"Papa, I missed you so much! Can you believe that Mother is gonna have a baby for us, and we'll have a big family like Aunt Callie and Unnie! And I'm gonna take care of the baby, and Mother can teach school and make a lot of money."

"Ruth, you are as brown as an Indian girl. I missed my princess so much." John swept Ruth, now eight years old, into his arms, and then he extended his arm to hug Clemmie. Putting Ruth down, he took the hand luggage that Clemmie was carrying.

"Oh, John, I'm so glad to get home. I love Ebony, but that was much too long to be gone from my home. And too long to be with my mother. She has been so depressed ever since Papa died, and Sister Grace finally took her to Fort Worth for treatment."

"Oh, my darlin' girl! How I've missed you!" John bent over and kissed Clemmie on the lips.

"Now you lovebirds, let's go home," Ruth chimed in.

John so hoped things could return to normal after his year of celibacy, but how he dreaded to tell Clemmie that he had quit his job as motorman and had been unable to find another one.

Later that evening, after Ruth had gone to bed, John got up his courage and told Clemmie that he now had no job. At first she just stared at him, hoping against hope that John was teasing her and trying to get a rise from her.

But no! It is true. We now have no income. Oh, Lord, something must be awry in John's head. Why on earth would he have quit his job when jobs are very hard to get? And nearly time for the baby to come and there'll be the hospital to pay. Oh, what will we do? We'll have to go to the poor house!

After that Clemmie felt like her happy homecoming was ruined. John tried to console her by saying he would probably get another job the next day, and he thought she had more faith than that.

Clemmie saw the doctor one time, and he assured her that everything seemed in order for a normal birth. He wanted her to go to the hospital because conditions would be much more sterile.

Although John would go out looking every day, it was several weeks before he found part-time work with an ice house. A job connected with ice and its delivery was usually confined to the hot months, but some people were beginning to use big blocks of ice in ice boxes to keep food cooled year-round.

It was late Saturday night, July 10, when Clemmie's contractions began. The contractions got stronger and closer, and John went next door to call the doctor. Dr. Henderson offered to come by and get Clemmie and John in his car. John took Ruth to their best neighbors, and Clemmie hurriedly packed a few things for herself and the baby.

By the time Dr. Henderson arrived, Clemmie was getting worried that the baby might come too soon. She and John got into the Model T, Clemmie in the middle between the doctor and John.

"Oh, Doctor, I think we need to hurry. I think it is already to the push stage."

The doctor drove as fast as possible through the empty streets to St. Paul's Sanitarium. A nurse was waiting with a wheelchair, and Clemmie was whisked to a labor room and prepared for delivery. By this time she had started to scream.

They were in the delivery room about two minutes when the baby began to emerge, perfectly formed and filled out. A nurse took the baby and held her up by her feet. Tiny Grace cried lustily.

"It's a fine girl, Clemmie," the doctor reported.

"I knew she would be a girl. And her name is Grace," Clemmie responded weakly. "Grace Wilmeth Briley."

"Well, it is Sunday, and you know the poem, 'Sunday's child is full of grace...or is it Sunday's child is fair of face?' Either way, this one will fit the poem." The doctor felt good about this birth—there were no complications and a good, healthy child.

"Well, I hadn't thought of that, but I do think this child is a gift from God, God's grace being poured on me. She was conceived the same night my papa died. You know what the Bible says in the Book of Job: 'The Lord giveth, and the Lord taketh away; Blessed be the name of the Lord.'"

The doctor later sent a bill for twenty-five dollars, and the sanitarium did the same. John asked Clemmie to write letters saying they would pay the bills as soon as possible. When Clemmie finally got home, John, Ruth, and several neighbors all pitched in to help do the work and provide some food. Finally, John found a job selling real estate. His income was based totally on sales, and Clemmie wondered if they were any better off than before, since he rarely closed a deal.

One day John came home with a *Popular Mechanics* magazine.

"Clemmie, just look here on the front of this magazine. Whadaya think this is?"

"Why, John, it looks like buildings are being pulled by train engines. How ridiculous! What is this?"

"Clemmie, this is the town of Ochiltree, in the Panhandle. The article says that since the railroad bypassed it by eight or so miles, it had no hope of a future. The bigwigs of the railroad offered to move the whole town north, free of charge. They put wheels under the buildings and connected train engines in front, and by George, they moved the whole town! It goes on to say that they did the same thing for Gray, Oklahoma, moving it a few miles south, and they are naming the new town 'Perry Town' after that fella that has done a lot for Ochiltree."

"Why, I'll be switched! I wonder if they will move the school building where I taught. And the courthouse and all the homes I knew. It makes me kind of sad to think that Ochiltree will be gone the next time we go to visit. Surely they will leave the cemetery!

"John, it was in Ochiltree that I really fell in love with you. All those good letters you wrote me. It was a town with good people, but lots of wind."

"Well, Clemmie, you know that song, 'Time is filled with swift transmission…Naughty earth unmoved can stand…' Change is usually a good thing. But women are *so* sentimental. They don't want anything to change."

"Oh, John, in the first place, it is *transition,* not *transmission,* and then the song says, 'Naught of earth,' and that means *nothing on earth* remains unchanged. And it is certainly not just women who are sentimental. Do you remember how sad you can get about your old home in Kentucky? I don't think it is any more women than men who feel sentiment for a place. Women just show their feelings more."

As bad as things had become money-wise, somehow the little family always had something to eat. There were lots of suppers that consisted of only doughnuts and a glass of milk or a bowl of beans and a piece of cornbread.

In early 1921, John got word that his papa, "Brother" Harris Briley, was dying. Before John could get to Ebony, his dad was gone at the age of seventy-two. John Harris Briley would be laid to rest between his second wife, Fannie, and his mother, Elizabeth Briley, in Elkins Cemetery near Brownwood.

John, Clemmie, and the girls went on the Frisco to Brownwood. John took it really hard, and it scared Clemmie to see his shoulders shaking with sobs as the dirt was dropped on the casket. Ruth held her papa's hand tightly, and Baby Grace got cold and began to cry. One lovely surprise came from the sad death. Brother Briley had left an estate of nearly five thousand dollars. After a few months passed, John received a check in the mail for $950.

What a gift from the Lord's hand, thought Clemmie. She went straight to her bedroom, fell on her face, and cried out her thanks and praise to God. He had answered her prayers, and there was no doubt about it. That was more money than John or Clemmie had ever seen. It was more than he would make in two years of earnings, and there was still more land in Kentucky that was in escrow. John had hopes that they would never again have to depend on anyone's charity.

John and Clemmie both decided they should buy a car, and so they did. Not a new one, since that would have taken quite a bit of the money, but one that was in good shape. They paid one hundred dollars for a Model T Ford that was six years old. Clemmie knew she would never get over the good feeling of having their own car to go to church or wherever they needed to go. Gas cost eighteen cents a gallon, so they didn't go everywhere by auto.

One day John came home singing a new song. He had heard it that day on the first radio broadcast he'd ever heard, at his insurance office. The name of the song was "Ain't We Got Fun."

Every morning, every evening,
Ain't we got fun!
Not much money, oh but honey,
Ain't we got fun;
The rent's unpaid, dear,
We haven't a car,
But anyway, dear,
We'll stay as we are;
Even if we owe the grocer,
Don't we have fun?
Tax collector getting closer,
Still we have fun.

"Clemmie, that sounds just like us, 'cept we don't have any fun! Everbody's havin' hard times, and someday things'll be a lot better. Just you wait and see."

"Maybe so, John, but I always understood that we all make our own lives, and if we don't prepare ourselves for some trade or profession or learn a skill, then we have to work long hours for very little pay."

"Well, Clemmie, you're highly educated, and seems like you can't get work either. Now I don't say that it's your fault—but we're in hard times."

"There's truth in what you say, John. I'll try to not be so fussy and hard on you." They kissed and tried to be nicer to each other. Clemmie would hear John whistling the new tune early in the morning and sometimes when he came home in the evening.

Clemmie's little sister, Grace, had an exciting year in 1921. She had graduated some time before and had landed a teaching job in Fort Worth at Paschal. Now it happened that the principal, John Bateman, was a good-looking, tall single man. Grace was successful in captivating him with her charms, and they had a June wedding in the home of friends.

The John Briley family felt happy to arrive at the wedding in their own car, sporting new outfits, thanks to the inheritance of John's. Clemmie was happy for Grace, and perhaps a tiny bit envious, knowing that her sister would be "well-heeled" married to a school principal. Principals were generally well paid in the cities and could always find another job if things went wrong. Mr. Bateman even owned a nice home on Orange Street and a fine automobile.

Little Grace Briley kept nursing longer than most children. She bonded totally with her mother, and Clemmie was not one to cross her child. Finally, when Grace was way past two and her papa heard her say, "I want ditty, I do, I do," he laid down the law.

"Clemmie, it's disgraceful fer a child to talk so good and still be nursin' from its mother. Why, she can nearly reach your bosom by standin' on the floor. Now you be the boss and not Grace." Clemmie did not appreciate John's interference, but she knew it was high time that Grace drank from a cup. Within the week, Grace was weaned.

By the following summer, little Grace fell in love with Ebony, like all the Wilmeth women. And so the tradition of visiting Ebony in the summer continued on. As soon as school ended in Dallas, Clemmie and her daughters would head for the hills of Mills County. John put them on the train in Fort Worth, and Jim met them in Brownwood and took them to Ebony.

Finally arriving at the farm, there was Mamma and most of Callie's children giving them a welcome from the porch and then running out to the car. Ruth, Marie, and Bernice wrapped their arms around each other and did a little dance. Grace and Lucille hugged each other, while the boys just stared and grinned. Callie's youngest, Gene, two and a half, sat down on a big rock and began to turn around and around, as fast as he could go. Everyone started laughing at him, and he liked that. He had on a little sailor suit with short pants and looked really cute.

The next day, Clemmie and Callie took all the children for a swim in the river. This was what Ruth most loved about Ebony, besides all her cousins, and she would start begging her mother to take them swimming early every morning. It would usually happen only after all the chores were done, around four p.m.

Callie seldom had anyone with whom to talk on a deep level, and she unburdened her soul to Clemmie. "Clemmie, remember when we were girls and couldn't wait to be married! Oh, little did we know that the good times would practically end when we had families to take care of. And times are so hard, too. I don't mean that I'm sorry. It's just real good to have someone like you to talk to."

"For me, too, Callie. You are the best friend I have. I have more in common with you than I do with my sisters. Living in Dallas I sometimes envy all of you out here on the farm. I'll think that you at least have milk and eggs, fruits and vegetables, and beef and pork. But then I have running water and an opportunity to make some money, if I could only get a job teaching. You know, John really has trouble getting a good job. I hope we can come back to the farm some day."

Clemmie and the girls stayed a full month. Clemmie started to feel like her visit was over, and she was worried about a few odd symptoms that she called "female troubles." When she discovered that Jim needed to go to town early the next morning, she asked him if she and Ruth and Grace could ride with him to the train station. He said he would gladly take them.

They were at the train station at 8:20, and that's when they discovered that the suitcase had fallen off the running board of the car. Jim offered to take them back to look for the lost bag, but they knew they would miss the train. Clemmie asked Jim to just mail it to them. Besides the lost clothes, two of Clemmie's precious diaries, covering the years of 1917 through 1922, had been in the lost suitcase.

A few days later, Clemmie went to see her doctor. After the exam, he informed her that she had a tumor in her womb. The news made her despondent. In fact, she felt lower than she remembered feeling at any point in her life.

The next day, John took Clemmie to a second doctor.

"Mrs. Briley, you have two large fibroid tumors. It is not uncommon for these to begin growing in the womb of a woman who is coming into her forties and nearing the change of life. I think it is important for us to get you to the sanitarium very quickly and cut these tumors out. Although they are a benign type of tumor, they will keep growing and can cause the uterus to enlarge to the point that it might burst. I think it would be good if you could go on over there this afternoon and we can do the operation tomorrow."

"Oh, but Dr. Harder, I cannot possibly go to the hospital today!" Clemmie felt suddenly light-headed and sick at her stomach. Dr. Harder then suggested Sunday evening. John, little Grace, and Sister Grace went with Clemmie to the hospital.

She prayed, "Oh, Lord, I know I may die, and then who will raise little Grace? Thou knowest that John cannot make enough money to support our family. Oh, Lord, please, *please do not let me die!* I promise I will never say another unkind word to John, nor to my mother. I will try harder to teach Thy Word to people who know not the true way of salvation. Father, I will be content to live in my home and not try to find work in the schools. In Jesus' name, amen."

The next morning Clemmie felt resigned to her fate. If she died, she died. But she would probably come through it, she thought, and she prayed for that result. Her preacher, Brother Pulias, led a prayer. Clemmie was wheeled off to surgery. Her arms were strapped down, and something clapped over her face.

Pretty soon she was dead to the world. She had a vivid dream in color. She was the moon, traveling down a rather narrow canal. Coming to the end of the water, she attempted to turn around and go the other way. Although she tried and tried, it was hopeless. Her doctor was startled when he thought he heard her say, "Life is so hard for the moon."

COULD NEVER BE

The first thing Clemmie remembered as she regained consciousness was Sister James saying, "Mrs. Briley! Mrs. Briley!" She was trying to keep Clemmie wrapped up, and Clemmie persisted in pulling her hands out from the sheet. Next, Clemmie saw John, Ruth, and Grace, and she felt so relieved but a little confused.

"So I haven't died," Clemmie stated matter-of-factly. "I am so glad, or are we all in heaven?"

They all laughed heartily. "No, Mother, we are all still on earth!" Ruth answered. Then they told Clemmie she would have a special nurse for the night. Later, a group of house doctors gathered around the bed and seemed to be having a lesson in administering the hypodermic. Clemmie could remember her neighbor, Mrs. Milam, telling about this procedure being done when she was ill, and not long after she came home, she had died.

Clemmic was pretty sick all week, but the next Monday she went home in an ambulance. The church women and neighbors were so good to her.

Grace was so happy to have her mother home. She crawled in bed beside her and held her mother's face in her little hands and said, "Mowie, I sure was poor when you like to have died out at the hospital." Clemmie thought that was so precious that she treasured it the rest of her life.

John took Clemmie back to the doctor the last part of September. She weighed only 101 pounds. Soon her appetite returned with a vengeance. She began to eat like a horse and gained ten pounds. She felt stronger than she had in a long, long time and wanted to start doing housework again. However, many women had warned her not to do too much too soon, so she held herself back and had Ruth help her wash clothes after school for a few weeks.

John had a big shock. He had understood Dr. Harder to say that he would only charge two hundred dollars for the operation. The doctor had first said two hundred dollars if it were only to remove the tumor, but later added it might be necessary to remove the womb, and he never charged less than three hundred dollars for an operation like that. Since he had taken the womb out, the Brileys owed him three hundred dollars. So far John had paid only one hundred dollars down and had borrowed that from Clemmie's mamma. That night John seemed so discouraged that it made Clemmie's heart ache. The hospital bill was usually nearly as much as the doctor's charges.

John was having no luck selling real estate. Clemmie had to give him what little she had in the bank. They were down to $5.37 and were behind one month with the payment on the house. It was the last week of November when the last of the money was gone, and some out-of-town guests had contacted Clemmie to see if they could come for Thanksgiving dinner.

When she told John her plight, he managed to help, as he always did, and he brought home a pork roast, some pumpkin for a pie, and some peas. (Clemmie wondered if John kept a little money hidden back for emergencies.) Clemmie and Ruth added some cranberries and some celery, and it seemed pretty respectable to Clemmie. She thought it was a pleasure to be blessed with company. She never complained about unexpected guests and remembered the Scripture that said:

> Show hospitality without murmuring, and be not forgetful to entertain strangers, for thereby some have entertained angels unaware.
>
> Hebrews 13:1

John had to mortgage the Ford in early December in order to pay the semiannual interest on their home. The stores and streets were thronged with Christmas shoppers, but the Brileys bought nothing, except ten cents worth of candy and postage to mail in the seventh lesson of Clemmie's correspondence course that she was taking from Southern Methodist University toward a second degree, this one in the field of education.

John sold a lot in Trinity Heights in mid-December. His commission was twenty-four dollars. Clemmie remembered to thank the Lord since she had specifically asked God to provide dolls for the girls for Christmas. They went to town and bought two dolls and a Christmas tree for one dollar at Hunt's Department Store. Clemmie's heart nearly burst with gladness, and she made herself not think of the bills that they could not pay immediately.

Christmas Eve arrived, and little Grace was all broken out with a rash. Dr. Greer came to the house, pronounced that the rash was scarlet fever, and put the Brileys in quarantine. Ruth worked so hard to make it seem like Christmas that Clemmie felt sorry for her. She decorated the tree all by herself. All Clemmie had for Ruth was a small doll and doll chair. Nothing was prepared for Christmas dinner. The house was so quiet that it didn't seem one bit like Christmas.

When Grace was carried in on Christmas morning, she made no showing of joy. Because of germs, she was not allowed to touch her doll. Ruth was decidedly proud of her doll and carried her everywhere. Grace seemed to think that Santa had really come. Clemmie had always told the girls the truth about "that mysterious person," not wanting to trick them. But Grace preferred to believe in "Old Saint Nick." Within three days, Grace was as good as new.

"Health is better than money," Clemmie stated, "but to have both would be like heaven on earth to me. Maybe God knows some of us will be more faithful to Him if we don't have much of worldly goods."

Sister Grace wrote that their mother was having good days and bad days, and Clemmie gathered that Grace sure wanted to get Mamma back to her Ebony home. It was hard to have Mamma in the house with you for a long time. Grace said that the doctor had diagnosed their mamma with "involutional melancholia." Clemmie wondered if she had inherited the tendency to feel sad and melancholy from Mamma. Depression was such an awful disease and had a way of hanging on longer than scarlet fever or any other illness.

John made a big sale. It was a nice home bought by a Mr. Shaw for eleven thousand dollars. John's part of the commission was $250. Besides the other lot, this was the only sale John had made since Clemmie's operation four months ago. The little family owed quite a bit in payments on the place and back taxes, yet Clemmie determined to rejoice over the sale. She also began to imagine what she might be able to buy for her garden now—flower seed, daffodil bulbs, some chrysanthemums, and perhaps a Los Angeles Rose.

Clemmie decided to write a book about her own life, changing the names of the characters. The title she chose was "My Bluebonnet Hills." It seemed cozy to Clemmie to sit by the fire at night and write her book. She read quite a bit of her manuscript to Ruth, who said she thought it was good. Later, Clemmie read a chapter to John and had to stop two or three times when she cried so much she couldn't read. It was a surprise to Clemmie herself that it stirred up such emotion in her—feelings of self-pity and longings for the way things used to be, she decided. *Ah, but it could never be that way again, I know.* Clemmie could accept changes, but to give up all her dreams seemed impossible.

Although John sold life insurance, he had never owned a policy on his own life. Clemmie felt so pleased one day when he came home and showed her a policy for three thousand dollars on his life.

Now if he should die, I won't be destitute like so many widows.

It seemed like every time the Brileys came into extra money, something would become urgent that they had to pay, and soon the nest egg would be gone again. For a long time John had wanted Clemmie to borrow money on her Ebony land. Mamma had always warned her not to borrow on your land, because you could lose the land. Finally, Clemmie gave into John and consented to their borrowing six hundred dollars on her land. After Clemmie agreed to the loan, John was so sweet and kind to her. Clemmie could see right through John and the way the money had changed his attitude. Anytime John could see a way to survive the present crisis it made him very happy.

In late July the Brileys started on their first car trip to Ebony. It was noon when they got away, and they spent the night in Fort Worth at Sister Grace's. Grace was glowing with good news, which she whispered to her sister. She was expecting her first baby! Clemmie rejoiced with Grace and thought to herself: *And they have the money to afford a baby, unlike most of us poor people.*

The next morning the Brileys were up at four a.m. and on the road before breakfast. By noon they were at Brownwood. They did a few things there, mainly went by the bank and set the wheels in motion to borrow the money on the farmland. They reached the Riverside Farm at 4:30. All the folks seemed very happy to see them.

Sleeping up in the attic room at night brought back vivid memories of five years ago when Papa had died and Raleigh Ely had been at the funeral. Oh, how Clemmie would like to see Raleigh.

Just to see him and talk to him for five or ten minutes, why I could run another five years just on the memory of that, Clemmie thought.

On their way back home, they stopped by the bank in Brownwood, and John was given a check for six hundred dollars.

Clemmie tried to ward off the negative thoughts: *We are back to the same old thing, not knowing where our next meal will come from. There is nothing I can do but to work and wait and pray. Surely God will take care of us.*

A month later Clemmie still felt like she was in the dark as far as what was going to happen about the house. John really wanted to sell it or trade it for another one. She loved the house so much and had worked for years on the yard, and now it was looking like they would just up and trade it for another one. She prayed that God would deliver them and put them in a place of service to Him, and also where John could make a living.

By September they were still on Hollywood Street, and Clemmie felt grateful for that. However, John kept telling her that they had to make a change in order to keep afloat financially. John had written a Mr. Singleton about buying his farm in Ebony. Ruth and Grace were so excited about the prospect of living on the farm near their cousins.

One evening John said, "I'm wondering when you are going to say it's okay to trade in this house. There's no way we can pay what we owe, and if we try to keep it, we're liable to lose all the money we put into it. Now how'd you like that?"

"John, I have poured out my life's blood into this house, and I believe the good Lord wants us to stay here. I would hate to know how many hours and days and years I have worked with the yard and the garden and flowers. Now we have pretty flowers blooming for twelve months of the year. How can you even talk about trading it for some little tacky house out of town that doesn't even have a toilet?" That said, Clemmie burst into tears and left for the bedroom.

John had been trying to sell insurance, and that was the hardest job he knew of. People did not want insurance and had no money to pay the premiums. In spite of the recent loan on the land, the Brileys still owed back taxes, the hospital bill, and several other bills.

John thought that if Clemmie could be like other women and decide to stay at home and be economical, they could do better financially. But instead she enrolled in more courses, paid carfare, bought flower seed and stamps. But John knew he could not reason with Clemmie.

On November 4, 1924, Clemmie voted for the first time in her life. Actually, Texas had allowed women to vote since 1918, but it was only with the adoption of the 19th Amendment to the Constitution in August of 1920 that all women in America had full voting privileges. She hoped to exercise that privilege this election. After all, women had waged a battle for over sixty years for this privilege. Clemmie thought it was ridiculous that such a difference had been made in men and women and voting.

Clemmie got dressed up and left Grace playing with Virginia and went to vote. She saw a deaf man and asked him where the election was being held. After shouting her question a few times, he finally understood and told her where to go. Clemmie felt compelled to vote for "Ma" Ferguson, who had replaced her notorious husband as Governor of Texas after he had been impeached. Mrs. Ferguson's campaign slogan, "Me for Ma," had won her the nickname of "Ma." After all, this would be the first woman governor in Texas, or in any state. And Clemmie believed women were just as smart as men. Ma Ferguson was a real foe of the Ku Klux Klan, and that was a good thing, thought Clemmie.

That night the red light was burning on top of the Magnolia Building in Dallas for Calvin Coolidge. Clemmie had thought it likely that he would be voted in as president. He had assumed presidency after Warren Harding died from a stroke the year before.

John continued to try to sell the Hollywood Street house, much to Clemmie's dismay. She felt that her heart would break. She threw herself facedown on her bed and tried to figure it all out. Clemmie knew that the way she felt about her flowers could not be understood by John or anyone. She decided to put her feelings into a poem.

MY GARDEN

In the dim misty morn of creation,
God planted a garden for man;
Made for his favor a helpmate,
And earth's happy Eden began.

From the ground of this wonderful garden,
Grew everything pleasant and good,
Trees of rare knowledge and beauty,
Among which the Tree of Life stood.

But evil befell this garden,
And God in His anger did vow,
That man should pass from its borders,
And eat by the sweat of his brow.

I weep at the beauty of flowers,
They thrill me and lift me from pain;
They fill my soul with a longing,
Its lost happy Eden to gain.

I turn for comfort to digging,
And hope rises new in my heart;
And I work with gladness preparing,
For beauty spring soon will impart.

Each flower that follows cheers me,
But grief quite suddenly goes;
When I see through the pane of my window
The first pink bud of the rose.

By Clementine W. Briley

IT WAS BEST

Christmas was coming. Clemmie wanted to buy presents for all her folks, but alas, they would be lucky to have something for the children. Some of the people at church were concerned about the Brileys, since Clemmie had let them know how poor they were. One Sunday, Sister Vann told Clemmie that the church at Center and Llewellyn would like to give them a shower, if it wouldn't offend John. Clemmie said she would ask him.

However, after Clemmie thought about it for a while, she was really afraid that John would say no. The whole idea of receiving several sacks of groceries from fellow Christians was very appealing to Clemmie. She thought that sounded like what Christians did for each other in the Bible.

And all that believed were together and had all things in common. And sold their possessions and goods and parted them to all men, as every man had need.

Acts 2:44

Clemmie appreciated more and more the spirit of it, and she made up her mind that she would let them go ahead and do it and not say anything to John. So the next Sunday night, she indicated to Sister Vann that it would be okay, so the good lady told Clemmie that they would come to their house Tuesday night.

When the people began to come bringing their gifts, John was as surprised as anybody could be. It didn't take him long to figure out how this had come about. He knew that Clemmie had been going around telling the church people how bad things were for them— that her husband was unable to make a living, that they were hungry, that the children had nothing to wear, and only the Lord knew what else she had told. It was all John could do not to yell at everyone to take their gifts and go home. But he knew that the people meant well and simply wanted to help. He couldn't believe that no one had asked him, nor told him, that this was going to happen. He certainly would have put a stop to it! He was boiling inside.

John never did enter into the spirit of it heartily, Clemmie thought later in the night. *It was a great party for me. I wonder if I went too far when I read some of my poems to our guests. After they were gone, John seemed mad as could be. Well, it seems like one of the best things that has happened to us in a long time.*

The next day, the joy of it was gone because Clemmie saw plainly that John did not like it. When she opened the pantry and showed him how much they had brought, he said: "I appreciate their attitude, but it sure does make a fellow feel cramped. How do you suppose they ever got the idea?" Clemmie spent most of the day in tears, hurt that John should hold such an attitude, wondering if she had been too happy the night before.

On Friday, December 19, the thermometer in Dallas set a record of eleven degrees above zero. That was the lowest recorded temperature in the history of the weather bureau, established in Dallas in 1913. Even the flowers Clemmie had put in a fruit jar on the mantle froze, and the glass bottom dropped out of the jar.

On Christmas Eve, Clemmie bought two small fir trees, and the girls decorated them. They cut red disks out of cardboard, then pasted cute magazine pictures on the disks. Clemmie went with Ruth to the Christmas play at Center and Llewellyn. They had just gotten home and taken off their coats when they heard knocking at the door. Opening the door, Clemmie was a little startled to see Mr. Sharber, one of the neighbors, with his two children, Jack and Emma, clinging tightly to his hands. Clemmie asked them to come in.

John got up from his chair and walked over, extending his hand to Mr. Sharber. The man began to explain that he needed to be gone from home for about an hour, helping a friend repair his car. He had no one to leave the children with since his wife was out of town.

"I should be back in an hour or two. Would it put you folks out too much to let the kids stay with you? I really hate to bother you, but I couldn't think what to do, since I didn't want the kids to stand out in the cold."

"Why, of course, Mr. Sharber. We'll be more than glad to have Jack and Emma here with us. I want to read them a story. Now you just go on and help your friend, and don't worry at all about the children."

"Thanks a lot. In case you need to contact me, here's my brother's phone number."

Clemmie read *The Christmas Carol* to the children. Grace was tickled to death to have her playmates come over at night. When the story was finished, Grace took Jack and Emma to her room to play. Ruth went in the kitchen to bake some sugar cookies.

Time passed, and finally it was midnight. Mr. Sharber had been gone for four hours. John and Clemmie both began to wonder if something odd was going on. Just then there was a loud knock at the door. Opening the door, John's eyes fell on two uniformed Dallas policemen.

"Pardon the intrusion, sir, but do you happen to know a Mr. Bob Sharber?"

"Why, yes we do. He came by around eight tonight and left his two children with us. He said he needed to help a friend fix his car." John knew already that something terrible had happened.

"Is something wrong, sirs?" inquired Clemmie.

"Yes, very wrong. We recovered Mr. Sharber's body from the Trinity River around nine p.m. An apparent suicide. Also a Mrs. Sharber and a Mr. Thomas Mason have been found dead in Mr. Mason's car parked in Trinity Park."

"Oh my Lord!" Clemmie exclaimed and began to cry aloud. "Oh, these poor children."

"Do you know any relatives of Mr. Sharber's who might live in Dallas?" the officer asked.

"Yes." Clemmie's voice was tremulous. "Mrs. Sharber has a sister who lives down the block, and Mr. Sharber has a brother, and we have his phone number."

"Could you bring me the Dallas phone directory?" inquired the officer named Pat. "And what is the sister's name?"

"It is Mrs. Jimmy Smith," Clemmie replied. "And that would be on Hollywood Street, in the eight hundred block."

"We will ask this sister to come and get the children. Better still, we'll take them to her house. Mr. Sharber must have planned this and knew his wife's sister would ask too many questions. I will ask you not to say anything about this tragedy to the children. Their aunt should probably be the one to tell them. Poor little tykes."

"Officer, are there any more details as to why Mr. Sharber would have ended three lives?" Clemmie felt that she must know why this awful killing had occurred.

"I'm sorry, Mrs. Briley. We're not allowed to discuss anything at this time. There'll be a story in the paper by tomorrow afternoon."

Clemmie went into the bedroom to get the children, who had all three fallen asleep on Grace's bed. She gently wakened them and helped them put on their coats and mittens. She explained that they were going to their auntie's house in a nice police car. She asked Ruth to pack some of the fresh-baked cookies into a small box for the children to take with them. Both officers carried a child to the waiting car, and they drove down the street. John embraced Clemmie as she sobbed.

"Well, this is awful," John stated. "Sounds t' me like Mrs. Sharber had a fella that she was meetin,' and her husband came back t' town early and found out 'bout it, and jus' went and found 'em and ended it fer all of 'em. I can understand that. I believe th' courts would've let him off, too, or at least given him 'bout four years."

"Oh, John, you know that murder is never right. The Bible says, 'Thou shalt not kill.'"

"Well, it also says, 'Thou shalt not commit adultery.'"

"Well, I knew Leah Sharber, and she was as nice a lady as you've ever known. A good Baptist, too. I believe there is another explanation as to why she was with that gentleman. And those poor little children. So smart and cute…and now they are orphans." Clemmie started to cry again.

"This is one Christmas Eve we'll all remember," John concluded.

"Ruth, you've worked enough in the kitchen. Santa must be 'bout to Dallas. Best go t' bed."

"Okay, Papa. I'm sad about the Sharbers. And I don't understand what happened. It sounds like what's called a 'love triangle' to me."

Ruth is really quick at putting puzzle pieces together, John thought. *Quicker than her mother,* he concluded.

Clemmie thanked God that at least the Brileys still had their family together. And it came home to her that a love outside the marriage, even a fantasy love, was very dangerous business. She resolved to try harder to be a good wife to John.

When the story of the killings appeared in the *Dallas Morning News* the day after Christmas, there were more facts that came to light. It seemed that Mr. Sharber, a traveling salesman, had expected to get home on Christmas Day but had arrived the evening before. Finding no one at home, he had phoned his sister-in-law. She said the children were with her, and that Leah and a girlfriend had gone out for supper and to a movie. Before Bob could leave the house to get the children, the phone rang. It was the girlfriend who was supposedly with his wife, but she was calling to wish Leah a Merry Christmas, saying she would be out of town on Christmas Day.

At that point Bob knew that Leah had lied to her own sister about her whereabouts. *Now why would she do that?* he had wondered. She was a very honest woman. He had become suspicious of her beau of many years ago; in fact, he had been a good friend of Bob's back in their hometown of Midlothian.

Leah had been Thomas's girlfriend for four years of high school. Then things had gone wrong, and they had broken it off. A few months later, Leah and Bob got together. That had all happened twelve years ago. But Leah had gone back for the high school reunion last summer and had come in contact with Thomas. He was also married and had three children. Seemingly, a phone call had been made, and the two had agreed to meet Christmas Eve. Thomas must have picked up Leah at her house after she took the children to her sister's just down the street.

The reporter who wrote the story had discovered that the Sharbers had been up against a hard time lately, and one person thought that Bob may have been a wife-beater. Thomas's wife back in Midlothian had gotten very large and was depressed most of the time. No doubt when Thomas and Leah had seen each other in the summer, an old flame was rekindled. Both were religious and probably had no plans to leave their mates. In fact, Mr. Mason was a deacon at First Baptist

Church in Midlothian. Clemmie heard later that Leah's sister and husband had been granted legal custody of the children. The four Brileys and the whole neighborhood were deeply affected by the tragedy.

On Sunday, January 11, a very happy event occurred. Ruth, who would soon be thirteen, was baptized into Christ at the Center and Llewellyn Church of Christ. Clemmie knew that her daughter's becoming a Christian was one of the greatest blessings God could bestow upon her. Baptism in the Church of Christ was for the remission of sins and the salvation of your soul. Ruth had always had a keen interest in the spiritual side of life and had developed a great faith in Jesus and his power to save.

Lately she had been afraid she could die without having obeyed the teaching of Mark 16:16: "He that believeth and is baptized shall be saved."

John also seemed affected by Ruth's decision. Late that night he told Clemmie and Ruth that he wanted to be the kind of father who set a good example. He wanted to try to at least attend the services of the church as often as he could.

John kept asking Clemmie to let him trade in their home to help them financially.

"No, John. I will not give up my home. I came to Dallas against my will, and I have stayed here against my will. This is the second home we have had here, and one we own outright, except for a few payments. I cannot give up my home."

"Clemmie, today is my last chance to trade this place for another one out in the country, and I could farm there. You are contrary and low-down mean." That said, John bolted out the door without kissing Clemmie good-bye.

As Clemmie went to her class, she looked from the streetcar window and saw him standing forlorn and dejected-looking in front of his office. She wanted to get off the car and tell him to go ahead and trade, but she went on. Later, at the supper table, he told her the house was sold. She did not know whether he really meant it or was just trying to make her feel bad. The next morning she found out that it really was gone, and he reprimanded her severely for missing that opportunity.

Later that night, Clemmie defended her position to John. She felt that it was unfair of him to ask her to live in a house that had a dry toilet and no bathroom and was so far out of town. After a little he took her in his arms and said he was sorry for the way he talked to her yesterday, which lifted a load from her heart for the time being.

By the last part of May, Clemmie's Hollyhock Cottage on Hollywood Street was sold. Her tears splashed on the document as she signed it. John made the trade for a house in Trinity Heights, the neighborhood where the first house was. Clemmie wondered if John got any money out of their dear Hollyhock home.

Not long after the move, Clemmie made an entry in her diary: "We moved here last Saturday a week ago. We got here sometime after dinner and I was very much displeased with the change, but I am getting used to it now and I have discovered many pleasant things about this place.

For instance, the edge of the woods and the view from the east is beautiful. Marie wrote us about taking a summer course here in Dallas and staying with us. Ruth and Marie both started to summer school, but Marie was disappointed in it and quit. Then we decided it was best for Ruth to quit too, and we would all go home to Mills County for the summer. I believe this is what will make me feel whole again. Yes, this will be the very best thing for us.

TO LEAVE YOU THUS, DEAR

"You know, John, this living room is larger than the one on Hollywood Street. And besides that, I think I can put a narrow bed in this dining room. I may be able to fix this up where it looks decent." Clemmie surveyed the new house, trying in her own way to make amends for having been so negative about the move to Alabama Street.

"Well, no need to get your hopes up, Clemmie. If I get a good chance, I may jus trade this'n off before long," John said, not ready to totally overlook the way Clemmie had protested the move, but mainly bluffing.

"You know what I like the most, Mowie?" Grace always liked to enter the conversation, eager to derail an argument between her parents. "We have our very own woods across the street. I will be

Little Red Riding Hood. Ruth, you can be the grandmother, or maybe the wolf."

Ruth, now a lanky thirteen-year-old, made a horrible face, bared her teeth, and made her hands look like claws. Then she chased Grace out in the yard amid loud shrieks and growls.

Before Clemmie could get things organized at the new place, her sister Grace sent word that she wanted to go to Ebony the following week. Ruth and Grace were so excited that they worked hard unloading boxes and trying to make the rooms look livable.

John had mixed emotions about the annual imposed solitude he would experience.

I'll be lonesome, but maybe I can figure out something about our money problem. That would sure please Clemmie, if I could make a little money, John thought to himself. *Yep, women sure do get happy if they know you've got money.*

The little group of four was soon on their way south: Sister Grace at the wheel of the big Dodge car, Clemmie in the front, and Ruth and Grace in the back. Clemmie began to feel her troubles blow away with the warm June breezes whipping in the car windows.

In Comanche, Grace stopped the car to get gas, and Clemmie took the girls to the restroom. Back on the road, Clemmie was startled when Grace started to cry. Her younger sister never cried.

"Why, Grace, what's wrong?" Clemmie asked in fright.

"It was exactly two years ago today that we buried my little Daniel. Since then, Clemmie, we haven't tried to keep from it, but nothing has happened. Do you think the stillbirth may have ruined me, left me sterile?"

"I've never even heard of such a thing, Grace. It's common for a woman to go a year or two, even a little more, between births. Seems like nature helps our bodies get ready for the next little one. You know Callie's babies came with two or three years between them. Why, there's nearly four years between Lucille and Gene."

"That's right. If I already had a child, I wouldn't be so scared,

Clemmie. You had Ruth your first year of marriage, and I've been married four years now with no baby."

"Why, Grace, I've been so envious of you, having a good husband who makes you a good living. And being a school principal is so respected. I just never even thought of how much you're wanting and needing a child.

"Oh, my heart just ached for you when little Daniel was stillborn, but I knew you would have several children. I've known quite a few women who buried the first one and then had other babies. I know you will, too. I'm going to start praying every day for God to open up your womb."

"Thank you, dear sister." Grace reached over and patted Clemmie's knee. "Having a steady income is wonderful, but having babies is much, much more gratifying to a woman, I think."

The little group arrived in Ebony right before dark.

"Oh, girls, just look at our home in the gloaming! Some day, Lord willing, we Brileys will have a home here on this land. I know we will," Clemmie stated emphatically as the big car rounded the last rough curve and the rolling hill of home came into view. There was Mamma on the porch, waving her apron. A breeze was blowing, and the dryness of summer had set in.

Mamma did her best to make everyone feel at home. The beds were set up on the porch, and Callie had some of hers out in the yard. There was no danger of rain in Mills County, and if that happened, no one minded getting wet.

Jim always reflected the weather in his face: drought showed up in Jim's face as a frowning, worried look; rain made him as happy as a child on the last day of school.

The cousins began to run over to embrace Ruth, Grace, and Marie. Clemmie embraced Callie and rested her left hand on Callie's tummy, which was beginning to show the new little life within.

"Oh, Callie, another baby for you! Now you will be the mother of seven! And for me it seems like two is nearly too many! Well, you'll make it just fine, and this baby will be the joy of your older years. You and Brother have produced such beautiful, healthy children. God knew what good parents you would be."

Clemmie was surprised to see big tears sliding down Callie's cheeks. "Oh, Callie, I didn't mean to make you cry."

"Your words meant a great deal to me, Clemmie. And besides, I'm getting where I cry easily in my old age," Callie explained, laughing.

"Callie, you'll never be old. You and I will get to have some good visiting," Clemmie comforted.

"Now, Clemmie, while you're here in Ebony, we're planning to free you up from work so you can finish that degree you need in education. Then you'll be able to get a teaching job in Dallas." Mamma wanted Clemmie to understand her plan for the summer. Mamma was all for getting more education if it would help you get a job. She knew how hard her daughter had tried to get into the school system without any luck.

Clemmie began to feel like a new person. She began paying more attention to the sounds of Ebony: the cooing of the doves, the locust and grasshoppers making their loud, sizzling sounds, the mockingbird high up in its tree, singing sweetly. As the moon climbed high in the night sky and the millions of stars converged into the Milky Way, Clemmie would lie there on the porch and think.

Oh, Lord, prayed Clemmie that night in July 1925, *please help me to get over the past, to not live the rest of my life with regrets. Please help me and John to get along and to have enough income that every step of life doesn't have to be wrapped up in a dollar bill. God, I know John is basically a good man. Father, I need more humility. I need to learn to be like Jesus was...lowly in heart...*

▬ ▬ ▬ ▬ ▬ ▬ ▬ ▬

"Aunt Clemmie, breakfast is nearly ready down at our place. We want you and Grandma to come on down, and try to hurry." Marie, oldest child of Callie and Jim, was standing over Clemmie on her porch bed.

The sun was just coming up. Clemmie sat up in her white nightshirt, trying to remember where she was.

"Why good morning, Marie! Do you mean you have made breakfast for all of us at this early hour of the day? What time is it?"

"It's nearly 6:30. Ruth helped me a lot. Come on down as soon as possible."

Marie had always been serious and highly motivated. She was not beautiful, but when she fixed herself up, she looked attractive. Being the oldest of six kids, she seemed to truly enjoy responsibility, and she loved to cook.

She had made a deal with her family during cotton-picking season. She would stay home and fix lunch while the rest of them picked cotton. Everyone was happy with that deal. She had all the ambition that her dad seemed to lack when it came to getting education. Long ago she had formulated a plan for her life, and furthermore she had plans for all her siblings to get a college education also. She thought it was ridiculous to spend your life in poverty when there were doors of opportunity swinging wide.

She was really embarrassed that her parents kept having babies. After all, they were in their early forties and old enough to be grandparents. Why, she had been so mad at her father when she discovered that her mother was pregnant with this baby that she went a month without speaking to him. Everyone knew that she would be wild over the new baby and would carry him around on her hip for several months, as if she were the mother.

Clemmie was amazed that a long table was ready out under the trees, and plates and silverware were set as if for a banquet. There was a big platter of sausage and one of scrambled eggs, and a huge basket of biscuits, light and golden brown on top. There was plenty of butter, jelly, molasses, and fruit jars full of fresh milk for the children and steaming cups of good coffee for the adults.

"My goodness, Marie! What a manager and cook you are, and only sixteen years old. This is the best breakfast I have ever seen,"

Clemmie commented, truly amazed. Everyone pulled up a chair or a wooden box and ate heartily. Marie took over the cleanup after the meal and didn't mind giving orders to the whole bunch. In no time at all the table was cleared off, and the dishes were clean in spite of the fact that there was no running water.

Callie's youngest son, Gene, was cute as a bug's ear. He was four years old, and he and little Grace could have a big time playing together. Both could get emotional if things didn't go their way, and Marie would usually intervene and tell them either to straighten up or go to their rooms for the rest of the day. You could tell that Gene would really be a boy that girls would like when he grew up. He was handsome, funny, smart, and quick.

Clemmie thought it was so loving that Callie and Jim had named him after Mamma's little boy who had died at age three, before Clemmie was born. One thing Mamma had told Clemmie about her Eugene was what a beautiful voice he had, and his favorite song was "In the Sweet Bye and Bye." And to the present day Mamma could not sing that song without crying, even if forty-eight years had passed since she lost her little boy.

Later in the day, there was a small uproar. Grace, Gene, and Lucille came running toward the house, all out of breath.

"There is a mountain lion coming after us!" screamed little Grace.

"I really think it is a panther, or maybe a jaguar," added Gene, proud of his knowledge of the wild animal kingdom.

"I think that was Dad, but I'm still not sure," explained Lucille, who was the oldest of the three, and knew her Dad was capable of playing tricks. Clemmie's brother would often show a playful side of his personality. He could get down and play with the kids, often being the "horse." Sometimes he would tell them about seeing a mountain lion in the hills. More than once he hid along the pathway when the children were approaching, then made a terrible roaring noise like a lion. Then he would jump out and laugh so hard at the running, screaming children that his sides nearly split. Seemingly, he had done that today, but without showing them that it was really him instead of an animal.

The greatest excitement of the day happened about ten that night. Clemmie had gone out to use the outdoor toilet, then came back to the porch, taking off her shoes and placing them inside the screen door of the bedroom. She was walking barefoot to her porch cot.

Standing by the cot, she turned back the bed and checked it for spiders. Just at that moment she heard the unmistakable rattle of the Texas diamondback rattlesnake and felt something like a sharp knife strike the big toe on her right foot. She immediately screamed as loud as she could, lifted the quilt, and caught a glimpse of the big snake slithering away toward the house.

"Oh my Lord! Oh come and help me! I've been bitten by a rattlesnake! *Help! Help!*"

Mamma was there immediately with a big wooden box that she put over the snake.

"Clemmie, you lie down! No! Rather sit up so your heart is higher than your leg. We don't want to rush the poison to your heart. Ruth, run and get Jim and tell him to bring the car and his gun and his sharp knife." Ruth ran as fast as the wind to get her Uncle Jim.

"Oh, I'm going to die!" Clemmie screamed. "Oh, Mamma, my toe burns like fire! Oh, will I die, Mamma? Look how it's swelling!"

The big toe was already twice its normal size, and her ankle was turning red.

There is no time to lose, Mamma thought. Jim arrived, and Mamma pointed to the box.

"Jim, the snake is under there, so be careful."

Jim raised the box, took careful aim, and shot the snake in the head with his .22 rifle. He put the box back over the snake as it writhed in misery.

"Hey, sis, so you got bit. Try not to be excited. They say that sends the poison around faster. Let me see the place on your foot. I've been bit before and am alive to tell it. The main thing is this first aid and then the antivenom."

Jim saw that her big toe was swelling fast. He made a clean, medium deep cut in her toe and then another cut that crisscrossed the first. Then he sucked the poison from the bite. He spat it in the flower bushes. Mamma had water for him to rinse out his mouth. Then he repeated the sucking and spitting and rinsing. They wrapped Clemmie in a quilt, and Jim carried her to the Ford. Mamma grabbed a pillow and said she wanted to go, too. All the children were trailing along, eyes popping out of their heads.

Jim began to give quick orders: "Ruth, you stay here and watch after Grace. Well, on second thought, we might need you. Ralph, you take all the kids back to your mamma, and tell her we're takin' Clemmie to the doctor. Tell her not to worry, that everythin'll be okay. We may have to go to Brownwood."

They got Clemmie settled in the backseat with her head on a pillow. Then Mamma and Ruth climbed in the front. Jim cranked the car from the front, then got in and they started off.

Jim yelled back out the window, "Ralph, don't let anyone else dare bother that wooden box. Snakes can still be poisonous when they're dead."

They took off for Dr. Hutchinson's home, just two or three miles away. Arriving there, Mamma ran to the door and began pounding on it. Mrs. Hutchinson appeared immediately. "Oh, Mrs. Wilmeth! What's happened?" inquired Gladys Hutchinson.

"A snake bit Clemmie on the toe. A big rattler. Is the doctor in?"

Just then Dr. Hutchinson, a rather portly man who was six feet tall, appeared. Dressed in his nightshirt, he was quick to size up the situation. He told Jim to carry Clemmie inside and put her on the couch.

"Clemmie, I have some rattler antitoxin right here, and this will be so much faster than waiting till Brownwood." He began to prepare an injection. Clemmie's whole foot had turned bluish red, and her ankle and calf were red and swelling. There were bright red spots curving up her leg to her groin.

"How are you doin,' Miss Clemmie?" Dr. Hutchinson inquired. "Now don't worry, I have treated lots of snakebites here in Mills County, and most of the folks are still alive. Ruth, you talk to your mother and try to keep her awake."

Within an hour after the injection, Clemmie was much better. The doctor suggested that they leave Clemmie at his house the rest of the night so he could check on her. Then they could come back and get her in the morning. Ruth insisted that she wanted to stay with her mama.

The Hutchinsons stayed in the front room another hour and told stories of snakebites. Clemmie seemed to be improving all along. They fixed Ruth a bed on a cot right by the couch. Off and on all night Ruth had short dreams about rattlesnakes being in her bed. She hoped this wouldn't put an end to their trips to Ebony, but she knew that they all needed to be very careful and wear boots when they were in the grass.

"Mother, I wonder why the most wonderful place on earth has to have these awful rattlesnakes."

"I don't know, Ruth, except that even the Garden of Eden had a snake in it."

Jim came for Clemmie and Ruth about ten the next morning. The swelling had gone down in Clemmie's leg and foot, and you could see two fang marks that the children found fascinating. Clemmie stayed off her foot for three days and managed to get a lot of work done toward finishing her course and that degree in education.

Clemmie felt so grateful to God that she wasn't dying. She had personally known three women who had died of rattlesnake bites. All her life she had tried to be careful where she put her feet down, but it never entered her mind that a snake would come up on the porch. The sad part was that she would be afraid to ever sleep outdoors again, and that had been one of the greatest delights of coming to Ebony.

The next day, it became cloudy and windy, and finally, on the last day of July, the rains came! Clemmie and Sister Grace went to Brownwood for the purpose of Clemmie taking her final examination in the course. The car left the road once and went into a ditch. A nice man, Mr. Perkins, got them back on the road.

When they finally got to Daniel Baker College, Mr. Chandler asked Clemmie if she would stay on for the graduating exercises on the night of August 25. She said she would. Then Clemmie and Grace went shopping, and Clemmie splurged and bought herself a lavender hat for four dollars. Then she got a pattern, fabric, and thread and buttons so she could make a new dress of lavender linen. She knew that John would want her to look nice for the final exercises.

The rain kept on coming down, a slow, gentle rain. Brother Jim came up to his mother's house, singing in full voice, to fetch his rain barrel. The next day, when Clemmie was at the store, she noticed that all the men who were hanging around there looked so pleased.

Clemmie read in the *Dallas Morning News* that William Jennings Bryan had died suddenly the Sunday before. His death had come on July 26, right after he had helped prosecute John Scopes. Scopes was a teacher in Tennessee who had taught evolution, contrary to the State law.

Bryan was well-known as a politician who had run for president three times and had been secretary of state. As a noted orator and a fundamentalist, he strongly favored a literal interpretation of the Bible. He had won the case and died right before it ended, bringing everything to a dramatic close.

Sister Grace took Clemmie back to Brownwood the night before graduation and attended a party. Mrs. Chandler served the graduates delicious cherry sherbet and angel food and devil's food cakes. Clemmie was asked to recite her poem "Down on the Farm." Everyone liked it so much, they begged Clemmie to recite it the next night at graduation. Since those in charge also asked her, she consented.

The next day, it began to rain. It was a slow, cold fall rain. Clemmie knew that meant her family might not get to come in from the farm for her graduation exercises. That night, as the graduates began to file in, Clemmie was near the first part of the line, with the "Bs." Her eyes darted around to see if she knew many in the audience.

There was a noise and commotion near the back of the auditorium. Clemmie turned her head slightly, making sure her cap did not fall. *Oh, hallelujah!* she shouted in her head. There came Jim and Callie, Marie, Ralph, Dutch, Lucille, Bernice, and Gene. Then she saw Edna and Oll and Opal sitting with Grace. And there were Ruth and little Grace, who was waving her whole arm proudly, and Mamma, wearing a stylish hat! There was Aunt Nell and even Ernest, and there were Dr. and Mrs. Hutchison. Last of all, in came a beautiful couple with two children. Clemmie could hardly believe her eyes! It was Samuel and Lettie Mae Smith with son Luther, now thirteen, and daughter Clementine, age nine. They had driven up from Austin where Sam was a respected lawyer. Clemmie was overjoyed.

Her heart raced and tears came to her eyes when her name was called to accept her diploma. All twenty-three of her friends and relatives stood together and clapped. It was one of the happiest moments of Clemmie's life. When it was time to recite her poem, she stood like a queen and recited it without a bobble. Everyone stayed for the reception afterward, and it was a grand celebration for Clemmie.

Not long afterward, Sister Grace and Clemmie loaded up the big Dodge car of Grace's and started for home. When they finally got to Alabama Street, John was so happy to have his girls back and gave them big hugs. It was discouraging to Clemmie that her home was bare and dusty. There were no rugs, and the curtain rods were still on the floor. John had not changed the sheets or pillowslips the whole time his family was gone. There was no money to get anything with.

I have just come back to the miserable life that I left. But maybe I was wrong to leave John thus…We hadn't finished moving in when I took off for the summer…and I very nearly died. I will make our little home beautiful, and perhaps I can help with our income now that I have this new degree in education. I am taking new courage tonight that I will yet be allowed to break into the Dallas school system, and Lord, this will be done by Thy grace alone. Please watch over us, dear Lord.

BEST FOR YOU

On a Monday in mid-October, John left Dallas early headed for Haskell County and his new job—selling the Colt Carbide Farm Lighting System. Clemmie doubted that he would make any sales. Clemmie also had a new job. A friend from Daniel Baker, now at SMU, had lined her up to teach at a school for troubled girls. There was no pay, but Clemmie would get college credit. Grace went with her mother to school. At night the house seemed lonely with John gone.

On Thursday, Clemmie got a postcard in her mother's familiar handwriting. It told of the birth of Callie and Jim's seventh child, a boy, named Howard Clayton Wilmeth. The baby had been born the day before.

"So, Callie has a fourth son to go with the three daughters. I am happy for them, but I am not envious. How could you feed and clothe seven children?" Clemmie said to Ruth that evening.

"Mother, I think that is the most wonderful thing a family can do, to produce many children. Just think, all of my cousins will grow up and have children, and all the families will probably be Christians. That is what makes it so much fun for me to go to Ebony, all my cousins that live there. Mother, are you too old to have another baby? We need to have a boy around here for Daddy. And I would really like a little brother."

"I'm not only too old, my dear daughter, but I no longer have my womb. And without that, it would be a miracle. Besides, I will be forty-five next month. That is way too old."

"How old is Aunt Callie?"

"Let's see…she was born in 1883, like Brother, so she is forty-one and will be forty-two in April. That is pretty old to be having a baby. I hope this will be the last one for her, and that the child will be all right. Sometimes, if the mother gets too old, the baby is not right in the head."

"Oh, maybe that's what happened to Grace, then," quipped Ruth.

"Why, Ruth. I'd be ashamed of myself. Grace is plenty smart, and you know it."

"I was trying to make you laugh, Mother. I declare, you are always so serious and tragic. Don't you even have a sense of humor?"

"Well, a joke told at the expense of another person is not funny to me."

Fall began to turn into winter. Finally, on the second of November, John drove his car up in front of the house.

Clemmie, Ruth, and Grace ran out to greet him. Unhappily, he had not made even one sale. He had done odd jobs in order to support himself. That day he got a new job selling real estate with Mr. Smith on Tyler Street.

Clemmie was so happily surprised when the director of the girls' school called her in and paid her five dollars for all her hard work. She told Clemmie that she had inspired the girls to get into their work in an unusual way. Clemmie took the five-dollar bill to the Oak Cliff State Bank and opened an account.

In early November, Clemmie got the long-awaited envelope in the mail—her teaching certificate! She squealed with delight.

"Mowie, why are you happy?" inquired little Grace.

"Oh, Grace, I got my permanent teaching certificate from Austin."

"Oh, Mowie, let's make a jubilee celebration. My Sunday school teacher said the Israelites would do that every fifty years, and nobody would owe anybody money."

"What a good idea, Grace! I'll make hot chocolate, and you pop us some corn. We'll say a prayer of thanksgiving to God."

In mid-November, the Brileys went over to the home of Annie, Clemmie's cousin, for a very special event. First, they ate dinner, then they all went in the parlor and gathered around a strange oval wooden thing called a "radio." It was amazing to Clemmie. Voices would come out of it just as clear as you please. It was the first radio broadcast Clemmie had ever heard, although John had heard one before. The station was WFAA.

They heard the music "Eighth of January" played over the radio, and also "Turkey in the Straw." Then there was more music that Clemmie recognized as some of the tunes she had played on the organ or guitar, and the boys had played the melody on the French harp or violin. The last song played seemed to Clemmie to be a sign, because it was "In the Gloaming," her all-time favorite song.

The haunting melody lingered in her mind, especially: *Left you lonely, set you free...It was best to leave you thus, dear; Best for you and best for me.*

It set Clemmie to thinking that perhaps her best course, since things were getting so bad—was to just leave John. There was no money for anything, and now she saw no love to speak of, from John to her. (She brought her wandering mind back to the radio subject with a start.)

"So this *radio* is the invention that is changing our world," said Clemmie aloud. "I just hope people will not stop reading altogether."

That night Clemmie decided she must take some kind of action about the horrible depression she felt herself falling into. If she were no longer a married woman, at least she would be hired for a job and could support herself and the children. It seemed like John didn't care how anguished she was over their constant poverty. Who could advise her? How she wished for her wise, sweet papa. And who would be most like Papa of all the people she knew? Why, her half brother Campbell, of course.

That night she sat down and wrote Alexander Campbell Wilmeth. She poured out her heart and also related all the specifics, how much they owed, how her daily life was, and everything she could think of to make her case and give him a true picture.

One day John was driving Clemmie to a school to substitute for the day.

"John, I wonder if you know just what you have done to me and the girls," ventured Clemmie.

"Done to you? What are you talkin' 'bout, woman?"

"Ever since you quit the streetcar you have been in awful shape financially. You have caused your family to suffer unthinkable poverty, worry, and shame."

John knew he hadn't made a lot of money, but these were hard times, and he had always been able to get some kind of work. Clemmie thought he should never have quit the streetcar line, but she didn't have any idea about what all was going on there. Why, there was a lot of pressure to be part of the Ku Klux Klan, and he refused to have anything to do with that bunch of murderers. Better to starve than to burn houses of innocent people, and even hang some of them, mostly because of racial hatred.

"Clemmie, you don't always know ever'thing like you think you do. But I plan to try to get work in an oil field. I'll have to be away from home, but then I kin send you money ever' week." He knew he had to get Clemmie some money so she wouldn't leave him. *Women sure do like money, all o' them do. I reckon men had druther have sex and a littl' fun any day,* surmised John.

Clemmie and the girls visited sister Grace for New Year's Day. Grace pulled Clemmie into the bedroom to tell her the good news. "Clemmie, guess what! Yes! I am finally pregnant! Isn't it wonderful, except that I am so sick. I am just throwing up my socks!"

"Oh, dear little sister! I am so happy for you, and I praise God, for we have all prayed that you would conceive a child." They embraced each other very tightly.

On January 26, Clemmie received the long-awaited letter from her brother, Campbell. Her hands trembled as she took the letter from the box and headed up the front steps of the house. She put the other mail on the kitchen table and went out the back door to her garden area. Somehow she needed to be outdoors when she read this. She settled in the only yard chair and never felt the biting cold of the winter wind. This would help her know which road to travel for the rest of her life.

Snyder, Tex

Dear Sister:

I received your letter several days ago, but one doesn't write on cold days. The cold depresses. Sorry indeed to hear of your struggles. I presume we all have them, some more, some less. It would take a volume to explain mine.

I think your financial struggles were part of the cause of the physical ills. Disease, like the Devil, takes advantage of our weakest places. While your mind was worrying over your financial affairs, disease took up its abode in the weak and worn places of the nerves and grew excessive. I find the ability to throw off and temporarily forget my woes has kept my body active and healthy.

Authorship is what you should follow. You are a born storyteller. You used to gather the children around you and tell them pretty tales. Well, now utilize that power.

Don't tell stories that would make a child want to become a prince or princess, but stories that would make them want to be good private citizens. We need more good common people than we need big fine display notorieties. Can't you weave a story with a hero like our father? He was one of God's heroes. Weave through it heartthrobs of failure, love, success. Don't fear to take in the mob that was there, and mix it with law enforcement, the supremacy of law and last and greatest have them to become Christians, saving the heroine in the last chapter. I cannot do this but you can. Do it, Girl, and become a benefactor and great!

Now do not think any more of breaking up home. Live in a dugout first. Home is all there is to existence on this earth. A child can miss school and still get its heritage, but a child who has no home is ruined. There is nothing to look back to, no sweet remembrance, no brother and sister ties. You cannot imagine how broken my life has been. And you cannot know how I have suffered for my children who have had no home and now no ties to a home and sweet remembrance. They do not care for my isolation, they were isolated all of their life, they know no other. Don't leave your home to teach.

I am stretched out very much financially but where there is a will a way can be found, so write me how many dollars you need and I will try to help you.

With love,
Your brother,

Campbell

So, there it was. Campbell himself was in his second marriage, and his second wife had been through a divorce. Clemmie had thought he might support the idea. He was now married to his first cousin, Mary Wilmeth Gano, daughter of his Uncle C.M. (Mac) Wilmeth.

Clemmie put her face in her hands and sobbed loudly for ten minutes. Then she thanked God for this answer and made her vow: *Dear Almighty God, I know it is Thou who hath spoken to me through my blood brother. I want to keep my home together, and beyond that I want to love John like Jesus loved the church, and even laid down his life for His bride. I will remain true to my husband and my home. I thank Thee, Father. In Jesus' precious name I ask this, amen.*

On January 29, Ruth graduated from Lida Hooe Grammar School. Clemmie got up early and re-hemmed Ruth's rosewood dress that she had gotten for Christmas just for the occasion. Grace was wearing her blue crepe, a last year's present from her Aunt Grace. Clemmie thought both Ruth and Grace looked beautiful.

Ruth had been asked to write and read the class prophecy. She was the star, Clemmie thought, as she read her part exceedingly well. When Mr. Peeler, the principal, got up to deliver the diplomas, he said that he would like to say many things, inasmuch as he knew some of the students personally. Clemmie just knew he was thinking of Ruth. He went to church with them, and even before Ruth started to school and would bring her doll to church, Mr. Peeler told her that she was prettier than her doll.

Later, Mr. Peeler told Clemmie she should really be proud of Ruth.

"I am," Clemmie replied.

"Mrs. Briley, would you be interested in teaching?" Mr. Peeler ventured to ask Clemmie.

"I surely would!" Clemmie's smile spread all across her face.

"Well, get your knitting together. We will be notifying you in a few days."

Clemmie could not believe it! After all these years, would she really have a place in the Dallas schools? *Oh, God, I pray for strength and courage and wisdom,* Clemmie said silently.

Mr. Peeler explained it would be in the Alamo School.

Clemmie went home and set her house in order. Daily she waited for the phone to ring with the hoped-for news. She was about to give up when finally the call came. Ruth answered the phone as Clemmie was out burning grass. It was Miss St. John from the Board of Education Building.

She said, "Mr. Cauthorn has asked you to report at the Alamo school in the morning."

"Yes, I can be there. What time should I arrive?" Clemmie could barely catch her breath.

"About eight o'clock."

"Thank you very much."

Clemmie felt a thrill of delight she had not felt in many a year. In fact, she was so energized that she went into action like a West Texas tornado. She washed her hair, set out a lot of rose cuttings, made a dress out of the two parts of old black dresses, and made a slip out of an old black satin skirt. Then she cooked biscuits and sausage for supper, washed the dishes, ironed several pieces, and worked the buttonholes in Grace's crepe pants.

Clemmie began to phone around to try to find a private kindergarten where she could send Grace. Finally, she got Miss Mosely and found out that she would take Grace and keep her busy for monthly fees of five dollars tuition and hot lunches for three dollars extra. She felt right pleased that she had found a good place. At eleven p.m. Clemmie bathed and went to bed. She prayed that God would keep her and give her wisdom and courage.

On Wednesday, February 3, 1926, the three Briley women got off to three different schools. Ruth began high school at Sunset High. John and Grace took Clemmie to the Alamo School, letting her out at 7:53 a.m. Then John took Grace to Miss Mosely's kindergarten.

When Clemmie presented herself in the school office, one lady said they were so glad to have her, for she was going to take some undesirable children off their hands. That sounded a little alarming, but Clemmie knew she could handle things.

Clemmie found herself with eighteen children in the Domestic Science room. Even though their dismissal was early, at 1:30 p.m., it was the longest day of Clemmie's life!

Leaving Alamo, Clemmie walked to Miss Mosely's to get Grace and found her delighted to be going to real school. Back at home, Clemmie fell on the couch and went to sleep immediately.

She dreamed that she was back in Mills County, on the first day of school, and seated at each desk was a different type of wild animal. There was a skunk, a red fox, an o'possum, and a raccoon on the first row, all staring intently at Clemmie. On the second row were a rattlesnake, coiled and ready to strike, an armadillo, a wild turkey, and a coyote. On the last row was a growling mountain lion, a bobcat, a tiger, and an anteater. When she awoke, she stated aloud, "I think I have quite a job!"

AND BEST FOR ME

Clemmie had been teaching about five weeks when one of the older girls brought her a message. "Mr. Ogier want to see you in duh office, Miz Briley."

Clemmie went immediately, preparing herself for any outcome.

Mr. Ogier did not make eye contact and busied himself with a stack of papers. Finally, he asked Clemmie to have a seat.

"Mrs. Briley, uh…uh…we have had so many transfers away from the school, that we find we…uh, uh…no longer need this special room of students, so…uh, it will be absorbed into the two other rooms. We will no longer…uh, uh…need you as a teacher."

Clemmie stared at him, a short, balding man in his mid-forties. He was overweight, and his suit was tight. His white shirt appeared to be on its second day of wear. Clemmie thought of so many things to say, either about the children, or about how hard she had tried, or how much she needed the money, but she knew it was a lost cause.

Suddenly, her heart grew light! *Oh, hallelujah, she wanted to shout! I will not be returning anymore to this forsaken school.* She decided to defend herself to the principal.

"Mr. Ogier, I am not too surprised that you have to let me go, but I doubt if you can find a teacher, male or female, who will be able to teach this group of horrible misfits. I tried very earnestly, but most of them seem to lack the capacity to learn and have not been taught to respect the authority of the teacher. I challenge you to spend one day in that classroom. I believe there must be an easier way to earn five dollars per day. I shall clean out my things and check in the books. And I wish you well. Good-bye."

With that, Clemmie held her head and shoulders high as she made her exit. She was never so glad to leave anywhere in her life. The children went totally wild as she checked in their books. Then she shed a few tears as each one told her good-bye.

"Oh, Mowie, I'm so *glad* you will not go back there! Those were very naughty children. I didn't like any of them. I'm so glad for *you* and for *me*." Grace smothered her mother with kisses and hugs.

After supper Grace said, "Sometimes I'm so happy. I'm happy now." And her crystal blue eyes were shining with joy.

Thursday afternoon, Mr. Cauthorn, who worked with teacher placement for the Dallas school system, called Clemmie. He said she could go to work at Colonial Hill Monday morning. Clemmie felt glad, like God was taking care of her after all.

On Friday, Clemmie felt energized with the promise of another job. She got up, dressed, made biscuits for the family, then went to Oak Cliff State Bank and got out the five dollars she had deposited there last fall. Then she went to the education building and waited for her check. It was for ninety-five dollars. That was for nineteen days of teaching at five dollars per day. It was the biggest check that

Clemmie had ever received, and she hoped to make the money last a long time.

Clemmie taught eight days, and on Wednesday, March 23, she received a note asking her to stop by Mr. Glasgow's office before she went home. She knew in her heart that something was wrong. She sat down across from the well-dressed man in his late forties, who reminded her slightly of Mr. Smith from Bowser days.

"Mrs. Briley, I am very sorry to have to tell you that we will not be needing you anymore." With that statement, Clemmie felt like her beautiful playhouse, made of exquisite glass, had shattered into a million little pieces. *So, it really had been too good to be true,* she thought. Like so many of the truly beautiful things of life, it could not last. The next day, at home, Clemmie found herself in a daze. She would just walk around and try to figure out what she should do next. She prayed for God to give her faith and courage.

The only happy thought she could entertain was that spring had come to Texas. The narcissus, the redbud trees, and the roses were all budding. It never failed to renew Clemmie's faith in God and His power of creation and His promise of renewal of the seasons.

By the same token, I, too, will rise again out of the ashes of John's lack of love and inability to support our family, of school principals who failed to see my worth, of school boards who discriminate against married women, of children who are not taught to behave and respect my authority, out of not having a dime to buy groceries, clothes, or make payments. Yes, I will show them all that Clementine Wilmeth Briley is a survivor and, not only that, is a success at teaching, as a wife and mother, and as a daughter of the King of the universe. Yes, I will show them all, vowed Clemmie.

John took Clemmie in the Ford to pick up her check of forty dollars for teaching the eight days. She then went to the bank and deposited it, withdrawing ten dollars. John had been without money for three weeks. Clemmie felt that it was now up to her to foot the bills. She prayed that God would help her find a job.

Clemmie began to assess her situation and any positive action she could take to better herself. She remembered one of the recent lecturers, a Mr. Dorsey, say that the first thing noticed about a prospective teacher was her appearance. Ruth had mentioned several times that Clemmie should wear some make-up. So she got dressed and went downtown.

She purchased face cream, powder, and rouge, which cost $3.35. She felt really bad to spend so much but thought it would be better economy to get the larger sizes and avoid having to buy more in the near future. When she got home and applied the face paint, she felt pleased. Ruth was so happy, too. For a long time Ruth had been embarrassed that her mother looked older than her forty-five years. Clemmie dedicated the month of May to trying to get a teaching job in Dallas or in a small town nearby.

Ruth and Grace got a chance to ride to Ebony with another family, and Clemmie let them go on ahead of her. The house was so quiet. Ruth would write clever letters back to Dallas, telling of happenings out on the farm. In one letter, Ruth gave some interesting insight into Mamma's thinking.

By the end of June, John had decided to join his brother, Fowler, who was working in Best, Texas, west of San Angelo. Oil had been discovered there, and they needed men to help drill and maintain the wells. The pay was very good, Fowler said.

John and Clemmie found a renter for their home on Alabama Street. Mrs. L.E. Moore and her four daughters seemed to be the ideal renters. They seemed sweet and like the type of people who would take care of the house and yard.

It was decided that John could take Clemmie to Ebony since it wasn't out of his way on the trip to Best. Clemmie couldn't resist singing the last phrase of her favorite song, "Best for you and Best for me." Arriving in Fort Worth, they found the Batemans feeling well, although Grace looked huge pregnant. The baby was due the first part of August. John Bateman had just mowed the lawn, and it really looked nice. They slept there and left at 4:30 a.m. for Ebony.

Finally arriving at Ebony, in the gloaming, the children came running to the car and stepped up on the running board. John stopped, and Grace and Ruth covered them with kisses. That night Clemmie and John slept on the porch of Mamma's house, and Clemmie again proclaimed the beds the best in the world. Clemmie wore her shoes on the porch and checked very carefully under the bed and everywhere to be sure there were no snakes.

John left early the next morning for Best, Texas. Clemmie wondered when they would all be back together as a family, or *if* they would. She said a prayer for God to watch over John and herself until they could be together again—and hopefully have some income.

Jim and Callie's baby, Howard, was nine months old and getting so big. He had the sweetest disposition and just laughed nearly all the time. They made a birthday party for little Grace on July 11. Ruth fixed six geraniums with toothpicks and stuck them on the cake in lieu of candles. Then she made a garland of sweet peas all around the edge. Clemmie thought it was beautiful. There was lemonade to drink, and the children had made up a little play that was quite creative. The kids played some games: hopscotch, hide-and-go-seek, and rig-a-ma-jig. Afterward Ralph and Dutch went to Zephyr to see some girls. They got back home after midnight.

Lucille was nearly over her appendectomy, but was still not supposed to lift anything, especially Howard. It was so hard on her not to pick up her baby brother, since she adored him. She just couldn't wait to be well. She liked to pretend that Howard was her baby and she was a grown-up lady.

On August 27, Jim and Marie had gone to town to see about getting a row binder. There was just too much feed to cut it all by hand. Another election was coming up—a runoff for the governor's race. Jim had said there was talk of sending Moody to the penitentiary because of his having accepted illegal money. Jim enjoyed talking with the men around the square.

That evening Clemmie was reading on her bed. She was caught

up in the story of *Adam Bede*, and as it began to grow dark, she read this startling sentence: "Hester Sorrek, you shall be hanged by the neck until you are dead," and Hester had screamed and fell in a faint. Clemmie made herself put up the book, put on her papa's old overcoat and a boy's cap, and started out to milk the cow. As she approached Callie's house, she saw her run out the door with Howard in her arms, screaming, "Oh, he's choking to death! I don't know what to do! I think it's cornbread."

Howard was screaming and looked scared. "Why, Callie, he is not choking, or he couldn't be crying at the same time!" Clemmie screamed as she took Howard from Callie.

Then Clemmie remembered that she had seen him earlier that day in the kitchen, and then he had seemed to be choking or strangling or something. Clemmie stuck her finger down his throat and felt something that felt like a lot of soft bread. Then they turned him upside down, beat him some on the back, then dashed some water on him. He was in a really bad condition, and once both women thought he was gone.

"Oh, he's gone!" Callie cried.

They could see that he was turning blue. Clemmie ran and got castor oil, and they got some down him. He vomited some. Still, he was so distressed and seemed about to die. As they went through the south room of the house with him, Clemmie began to pray aloud: "Oh, God! Please help our Baby Howard. We cannot help him, but Thou canst."

Howard seemed better immediately, Clemmie thought. "Let's get him to the doctor as quick as we can!" Clemmie cried.

The children had gathered round, and Ralph ran to his grandmother's house to call Dr. Hutcherson. Then, since they had no car there, he phoned Hubert McMullin to come and get them. Too impatient to wait for the car, they wrapped Howard up and started out walking with him. The children were frightened to death. Dutch looked like he was going to die. The little girls and Ruth all ran to the back of the house to the bushes, not knowing what to do. Ruth told them to start praying.

Ralph and Dutch started out walking with them, but Callie begged Ralph to stay there at the house, and he turned back. Soon Hubert arrived in the car and took them to the Crowders,' where they met the headlights of the doctor's Model T coming toward them. They were welcomed into the Crowders' home and frantically explained what had happened. Dr. Hutchison hurried in and washed his hands. He took the baby and stuck his finger down Howard's throat until it looked like it would choke him to death. Howard vomited twice.

Pretty soon he went to sleep. He had a rattling sound that made them uneasy. However, pretty soon he seemed to breathe easy, and the rattling ceased. He slept for some time until the doctor decided he was safe, and then Dr. Hutchison went home. The rest stayed on a while longer, then wrapped up the baby and started home. Hubert's car lights were bad, and he suggested they all spend the rest of the night with him and Kate.

Kate got up and lit a lamp and welcomed them in. They put Howard on a little white bed, and he slept peacefully for a long time. Finally, they decided to go to bed. Before they could lie down, Howard woke up and had a strangling, screaming spell. Soon he fell asleep again. This pattern kept repeating itself into the night.

Callie felt uneasy about the baby and wanted to take him to Brownwood by daylight. At three a.m. Ralph and Clemmie decided to walk to Ernest Malone's, hoping he could take them home in his car and then take Callie and Howard on to Brownwood. It began to rain. Ernest could not get his car to start. When the rain let up some, Clemmie and Ralph walked on home, got Bernice up, and decided to milk and get ready to go to town.

Bernice was only eleven, but she knew how to wash and scald the milk things. There was Howard's bottle still on the stove where Callie had put it to warm just before he got choked the evening before. Bernice got the bottles all ready. Ralph milked two of their cows, and

Clemmie milked her cow. (Jim kept a very few cattle for Clemmie.) Bernice got clothes for Callie and for Howard. They were about to send Ralph back with the clothes and milk when Callie phoned. She wanted someone to bring her clothes so they could take Howard back to Dr. Hutchison's.

As dawn was breaking, they arrived at the doctor's house. He examined Howard again and said he did not see anything wrong, except that his throat was badly irritated, probably from all the gouging. He gave Callie a throat wash to use. Hubert took them back home, but Baby Howard didn't seem well at all. Finally, about ten a.m., Jim arrived home from Brownwood. He was very upset to see his baby in this shape and agreed with Callie that they needed to get him to Brownwood. They left immediately.

They got Howard to Dr. Locker's office by early afternoon. Upon examining the baby, he thought that Howard's stomach and intestines were in bad shape but did not think it necessary for them to stay in town. They went to the pharmacy and got the medicines that the doctor had prescribed. By the time they got home to Ebony, it was the gloaming. They gave Howard castor oil and some powder that Dr. Locker had mixed, besides a spoonful of another medicine.

When Clemmie saw them return with Howard, she thought that meant he was going to be okay. She started down to their house from Mamma's and heard Howard screaming again. Her heart sank.

She stayed with Callie that Saturday night to help care for Howard. He would go to sleep, seeming to breathe easy, then he would wake up and that awful rattling would set in and he would seem so sick. His bowels moved often, and that seemed to relieve him some. He wanted water all night. He would turn his eyes until he saw Clemmie, then she would get the glass of water and he would reach out both his little hands for it and drink like he was famished.

Callie wanted to send for the doctor before day, but Clemmie thought it was not necessary. She said it was probably the medicine that had made him seem so sick, and she thought he would soon be better.

Several times Callie said she believed that was the "death rattle" that he had. As Sunday, August 29, was dawning, Jim went to his mother's house to phone the doctor, and Callie went with him to help explain how Howard was. Clemmie stayed with Howard. Soon he began to choke. Clemmie lifted him to try to relieve him, but it didn't help. Clemmie got scared that the baby might die before his parents returned from the phone call. Clemmie called out for Ralph to go tell them to have the doctor come immediately. Soon Callie and Jim returned.

"Oh, he's dying! Oh, little blue lips!" Callie cried.

Howard choked and lost his breath and died in Clemmie's arms. They fixed a tub of water and put him in it but could not bring him back. They lifted his lifeless body from the water, wrapped him in a blanket, and Clemmie sat on the bed and rocked his little dead body, hoping the doctor would come. Then Howard began to get cold and stiff, and they had to lay out his little dead body. They put a little clean dress on him and laid him on a large box lid on the bed.

A car drove up soon, and it was Jenny and Wood Roberts.

"Oh, Jennie!" exclaimed Clemmie, hugging her tight. "You are always there to help when people are in trouble."

In a little while cars were arriving from every direction. The dear country people with one loving heart were closing ranks around their good neighbors who had lost a child.

The six children, Callie and Jim, Grandma Clara, who adored the baby, Clemmie and Ruth and Grace, Edna, Oll, Opal, Nell, Ernest, and many more from the community gathered on the porch, held hands, and prayed. It was the only time the Jim Wilmeth children had seen their papa cry. It was the first death experience for most of the children. Suddenly, Callie said, "Oh, we have to take his measurement and send for the casket." The awful thought had struck her like a blow. They measured little Howard's body, and it was thirty-three inches long. Reide Haynes offered to go for the casket. The women asked him to bring new material for a white dress to bury Howard in.

Lucille went out in the field and picked the prettiest flowers she could find to put in her little brother's hand. Clemmie and Kate gathered flowers to put around the little body. When Reide returned with the fabric, Clemmie, Kate, and Belle began to cut out and sew a little dress for Howard. They had it done in less than an hour and dressed the little stiff body in it.

The undertaker arrived with the white casket, which was thirty-six inches long, and placed the baby in it. Clemmie placed the flowers Lucille had picked in his little hand. Clemmie thought he looked so sweet. She went to get Callie to come and see him. The whole family left soon for the Ebony Cemetery. When they arrived, it looked like the whole countryside was there. Brother Allen from Dublin conducted the service under the tabernacle. There was a beautiful bouquet of fern and tuberoses lying on the casket.

The six siblings and the cousins all sat together on the second row, and all the little shoulders were shaking with sobs. After the service the funeral coach brought the casket around through the gate to the grave. They took down the fence so the crowd could just walk straight over to the grave. A few songs were sung as the grave was covered, including "In the Sweet By and By."

> *There's a land that is fairer than day,*
> *And by faith we can see it afar;*
> *For the Father waits over the way,*
> *To prepare us a dwelling place there.*
> *In the sweet by and by;*
> *We shall meet on that beautiful shore,*
> *(By and by)*
> *In the sweet by and by,*
> *We shall meet on that beautiful shore.*

Clemmie stood with her arm around her mamma, knowing her mother was grieving not only for little Howard, whom she adored, but also for her own little Eugene, who had sung that very song so sweetly before he had died at the tender age of three. Although fifty years had passed, the memory was as fresh as the present tragedy.

"Now I have lived too long," Mamma whispered as tears followed the wrinkles in her face and dripped from her chin. Clemmie felt more sympathy for her in that moment than she could remember feeling previously. Her own baby's death and now her only living son's baby. It was too much to bear, and Clemmie feared that either Callie, Mamma, or she might faint.

The thermometer registered ninety-five degrees, and they were in the full Texas sun.

The tiny white casket with its precious cargo was buried in the red and rocky Mills County dirt. The children threw their wildflowers into the deep hole and whispered their good-byes to the happy and playful Baby Howard.

Two of Callie's sisters went home with her and stayed a day or two. They helped Ruth and Marie with the washing and ironing.

Monday morning the Wilmeths had to resume their hard life on the farm. Jim went to Bangs and bought a row binder for twenty-five dollars. On Tuesday Stanley Reeves and Jim brought it home in a truck. Marie began sewing herself some clothes for college, expecting to leave for CIA in Denton the following Monday. Clemmie and the girls would leave for Dallas when Marie left.

Sunday after church the family was all invited to Stanley and Willie Reeves' home after church for dinner. Clemmie had an awful sinking feeling as she approached the house, like she might just drop dead. As they gathered around the heavily laden round oak dinner table, Clemmie announced to the crowd that she was dying. Willie seemed to know that she was having an attack of nerves, took her out on the porch, and gave her some brandy.

BABY HOWARD

He came in bright October,
When harvest time was here;
When hills were bright with autumn leaves
And autumn skies were clear.

O how the children loved him,
As they watched him kick his feet;
And wave his tiny hands above,
And smile and coo so sweet.

How dear to Grandma's heart,
His unfeigned love for her;
No other joy concerned her now,
Since he did her prefer.

But ere the autumn time,
Her fruits of harvest bore,
He flitted back from whence he came,
His sweet, brief life was o'er.

Strange, how empty are our arms;
How idle seem our hands,
Since he no longer now
Our loving care demands

Oh, how we miss the little life,
And with what comfort fraught;
Those dear remembered words
The children's Savior taught.

When in His arms He blessed them,
And suffered Him to touch,
Rebuking men's displeasure

Saying heaven is of such.

Ah, there's a brighter day;
Though, now, in grief we bow,
For in those pearly portals,
We have a treasure now.

O Little Life, so short and sweet
To us in blessing given,
Will not thy pleading love
Draw us near to heaven?

By Clementine Wilmeth, in memory of her nephew:

Howard Clayton Wilmeth.
October 21, 1925 - August 29, 1926

PART THREE

IN THE GLOAMING

It always seemed sad to the Briley women when they had to leave Ebony, but it had been a full three months for the girls, and two and a half for Clemmie. The sadness of Howard's death had left everyone depressed. It was time to go home to Dallas and get back in school. So Jim took Clemmie and the girls to the train station on the second Thursday in September, and they left Brownwood on the nine-o'clock Frisco for Fort Worth. No one was at the depot to meet them in Fort Worth because Clemmie's sister Grace was now a mother. Little Joe Wayne Bateman had a faithful servant in his mom. Grace wouldn't even come to the door to meet the Brileys for fear of waking the little man.

Sister Grace supplied the train fare for the Brileys from Fort Worth to Dallas. Arriving at home, Clemmie had another shock. The Moores had vacated the house the night before, but they left things in a big mess. They had paid no rent, left a twelve-dollar phone bill, a four-dollar light bill, stole the tubs, left the house filthy, broke two of the beds, broke some of the dishes, tore up some pillow slips, let the grass grow a foot high, and let the weeds take over the flowerbeds. Clemmie was mad and wanted to find Mrs. Moore and make her pay for the destruction.

"How ironic," Clemmie thought aloud. "I left people in my house to help a little with income, and it ends up costing me a lot of money and a lot of work." In the end, Clemmie decided to forgive the Moore family since she realized that they would have no money to repay her if she did find them.

Clemmie's doctor put her on a milk diet to try to build her up. John began sending ten- and twenty-dollar bills in the mail! One night Clemmie drank three quarts of milk and felt as gaseous as a hot air balloon.

Meanwhile, in the little town of Best, just west of San Angelo, Texas, John's life had changed drastically. In one of his letters John described his new town this way: "Best is a disolute cow town clear out of civilisashun and no one to love…and anyone that can stand this can stand anything…" A year or so earlier, oil had been discovered beneath the dry Texas dirt. A deal was made, and a newly formed oil company took over the sleepy town.

There were twenty-nine men staying together in a long, cheaply built bunkhouse. They had a Mexican man and wife who took care of all the cooking. Each man had a bunk bed and two light blankets. There was one bathroom with several urinals and three cold-water showers. John's brother, Fowler Briley, was there and was responsible for John getting the job. The pay was seven dollars per day, and the workday ran from sunup to sundown. The men had Saturdays after lunch and Sundays as free time.

Most of them would crowd into a truck and go into San Angelo for the weekend. John and Fowler, being married men with convictions, would avoid the low life and would usually see a movie, eat a real good meal at the best café, and maybe go to a cantina afterwards. John knew better than to mention the last event to Clemmie, but he didn't see anything wrong with hearing a pretty Mexican girl sing or watch her dance on a tabletop.

Whenever John was away from Clemmie, she would become dearer to him in his mind. He wondered why that was, and why he couldn't feel this love toward her when he went home. Maybe it had something to do with the saying "Absence makes the heart grow fonder." But he knew that there was another side to that saying, and sometimes the men would joke and say, "Yeah, fonder of somebody else."

John paid fifty dollars a month for room and board and three dollars per week for washing his shirts and overalls. By the time he sent about twenty dollars home to Clemmie each week, there wasn't a lot left for small pleasures; in fact, there was nothing left.

The work was hard, tedious, sometimes boring, hot, and dirty. But when a wildcat well would come in and the rich black oil would spike thirty to forty feet into the air, and all the men would shout, "Yahoo!" it was pretty exciting.

One day a letter came from Mamma with a check for fifty dollars. Clemmie's brother, Jim, had sold two of her yearlings. Her heart began to sing since God was taking such good care of her. In mid-November John sent a package to Clemmie for her birthday. It contained a beautiful brown eiderdown jacket.

One morning in November, Clemmie was reading the Dallas paper, and suddenly her heart skipped a beat. There was a short article about Raleigh Ely!

Abilene Judge Offered Place on Appeals Board

Austin, Texas, Nov. 18. Judge W.R. Ely, Forty-Second Judicial District, who resides at Abilene, has been tendered appointment by Gov. Ferguson as a member of the Commission of Appeals aiding the Court of Criminal appeals to fill the vacancy caused by Judge E.A. Berry's resignation, it was unofficially reported here today. The appointment had previously been tendered to District Judge Lewis Jones of Belton and James R. Hamilton of Austin, both declining.[3]

Clemmie reread the little article three times. Then she got the scissors and clipped it out and glued it in her diary. *So,* she thought, *Raleigh is coming into his own; another honor has come his way.* She wondered if his wife, Lucy, knew how fortunate she was to have a husband like Raleigh who could support her in fine style. She had heard that judges were making over four thousand dollars a year, and that would be around eighty dollars per week, and that was living in "high cotton."

John arrived in time for Christmas, and Clemmie and the girls were so happy to see him. New Year's Eve, 1926, Clemmie wrote the following in her diary:

The Old Year is passing. So many hard things came this year: Howard's death, my breakdown, and many other things, yet there have been so many blessings. John's visit has been both mostly good and some distressful, but tonight he was his sweet, fascinating self. I'm happy just for that. Welcome, 1927! What will you bring us? Dear Father, take care of us all.

OH, MY DARLING

Clemmie liked to personify the New Year—even to speak to it. She thought of it as a beautiful young girl, and in her hands the girl was holding a white book with 365 pristine pages, one for each day of the new year. She liked to think of a new year as a chance to begin again—to live in a new way and have better relationships; a chance to accomplish new things and improve oneself in various ways. John got in Clemmie's good graces by bringing her a rose cutting. It was an American Pillar rose and had been given to him by a nice neighbor lady as he walked around the block.

The time came for John to return to his oil field job in Best, Texas. This meant that Clemmie and the girls wouldn't see him again until the summer. They helped him pack his bag and load his car. All three cried as he backed out of the driveway and drove off down the street.

After a week, the first letter from John arrived in the mailbox.

1/7/1927

Best, Tx

Dear Sweetheart,

Things are going OK for me. The trip out went goode. Best, Texas is probably Not the Best that Texas has! It's very small, of course. Say, I wish we could live at San Angelo. The climat is better than Dallas, I hear. The oil business isnt' bad. There's a lot to learn but when a well blows in, it's fun. Everyone shouts and throws there hat up in it. Then you have to git another hat. Write me. Good bye Dear and kiss Ruth and Grace.

John

As soon as Clemmie finished reading the letter aloud, little Grace popped up with another of her funny statements. "I want to live in San Angelo because it has a pretty name. It sounds like Jell-O!"

Clemmie, Ruth, and Grace got along well together. Clemmie enjoyed receiving money in the mail from John, and she liked the lack of conflict. But nights were lonely.

More letters came from John, always with cash inside.

You Said you didn't understand how I Stood those long Seiges of hard work I tell you I am tough and I have decided I am a pretty good man physically.

Say Dear you mentioned a little love feast and maby you think I am not anxious and longing for one and I can draw on my emagination some Still that dosnt quite Satisfy and I want it in reality with you in my arms Dear. I expect I will Soon have to quit the oil field for it is playing out most ever where on account of too much oil and a fall-off in prices I wish I could get money a head So I could be able to try Something else for I aim to keepe up Some way when the oil work is over I would like to keepe making as much or more. And I must do it Someway.

> Kiss Ruth and Grace for me. Good bye Dear,
> John

Clemmie bought a newspaper and read about a twenty-five-year-old man leaving New York City in a single-engine monoplane, *Spirit of St. Louis.* He took only four sandwiches, two canteens of water, a few army rations, and 451 gallons of gasoline in his small plane. Only thirty-three hours later, Charles Lindbergh landed in Paris, France, and collected a prize of twenty-five thousand dollars as the first man to fly the Atlantic alone.

Even though no one knew who Charles Lindbergh was before that day, his name was immediately a household word. Clemmie began to follow his career and carefully clipped articles and pictures from that day on. She thought the story was remarkable.

She especially liked his first words uttered in Paris: "Well, here we are. I am very happy." He seemed to use "we" to speak of the airplane and himself, like it was his companion.

Now, that's a man with fortitude, thought Clemmie.

May 24 marked the sixteenth wedding anniversary for Clemmie and John. In the mail that day Clemmie received a very sweet letter, a twenty-dollar bill, and a poem that John had written himself. Clemmie had no idea that he could write a poem, and it was so beautiful and unexpected that it made her cry. Later, John admitted that one of his new friends in Best had helped him with the rhyming of the poem and the spelling.

FOR MY DARLING CLEMENTINE

By John Briley
5/20/27

When I was a lad I knew a girl
Her name was Clementine
Her papa was a preacher
My papa was a preacher
I wanted the girl for mine
But the girl had another
And I was like a brother
So in Dallas I cast my lot
But things went bad
And I was sad
But Clemmie I never forgot
When I was a man
I asked for her hand
She loved me and said Yes
We married in Eleven
It was like heaven
She made her own wedding Dress
Then God sent a child
A pretty little girl
We named the baby Ruth
Then God sent another
It was not a brother
Our own little Grace full of truth
Now I'm getting older
But I still can hold her
16 years of laughter and tears
It's hard to find work

But since I'm no jerk
I've lived in Best Texas 2 years
Our papas were preachers,
And mighty good teachers,
The Good Book was what they did heed
Not clothes and food makes us feel good
But God who supplies all our need

John finally came home for a visit near the end of June. Clemmie, Ruth, and Grace were delighted. They made a little "Welcome Home" party. That night, Clemmie wore the new gown that she had made for herself. It was off-white satin with some lace. She tried to be a good lover and made a point not to complain or fuss or ask any questions. Two weeks later, John returned to the oil field.

It was mid-August before Clemmie and the girls got to Mills County. Ruth and Grace nearly gave up on the trip. Once there, Clemmie wondered if she should have stayed in Dallas. Mamma was so hard to get along with. If Clemmie left anything out of place, if she even left a little piece of lemon on a plate, her mother wanted an explanation. There was no way to please her, and she and Clemmie had words several times.

John wrote discouraging letters from Best. He said the work there was about to play out, and they had that note due on the farmland.

Well, times will just have to get better, Clemmie thought. The good Lord had brought them this far, and He would never leave them, nor forsake them. He had promised.

The Wilmeths and Brileys worshipped at Brookesmith one Sunday. Clemmie got to meet Brother Vaughn. He encouraged Clemmie to teach at Abilene Christian College. Clemmie thought that would be grand, to teach in a Christian college, and in the city where Raleigh lived.

The next day was when the cotton picking began in earnest. Ruth picked seventy pounds, Grace picked eighteen pounds, and Clemmie picked fifty-three pounds, only joining the group after lunch. All together the group picked 548 pounds. When they went home in the evening, Marie had a hot supper ready. She had two tubs of warm water for the children to have their baths. Then they would put on their nightclothes, eat, and go straight to bed. At sunrise, the whole process would begin again.

Clemmie made a notation in her diary about the cotton picking:

It has been thrilling, this cotton picking experience. It is backbreaking, it makes you sore and stiff, it blisters you, but still there is lots of joy to be had out of it. When the evening shadows steal across the field, making the sunset on the horizon and all the hills about such a lovely scene, in the gloaming, joy wells up in my heart. And when we weigh up for the last time and gather up the things and start for home, there is a satisfying joy of rest well earned, a rich reward of honest toil.

Clemmie and the girls left for Dallas in mid-September. The letters containing money from John stopped coming, and Clemmie began to feel desperate.

There was nothing to eat in the house, so she took forty-three cents she found, her checkbook, and went to the closest store. She wanted some butter really bad and asked the man if she could write a check on a Brownwood bank for two dollars. He did not want to cash a check. He said he could cut the butter in half.

In the end Clemmie got a dime's worth of eggs, which were three eggs, and two bottles of milk. It came to thirty cents. She went out into the rain, which mingled with tears streaming down her face. She didn't feel so hurt at the storekeeper since she knew he had to protect his business, but to be in such a humiliating situation was horrible.

"How long, my God, oh, how long must this continue?" she prayed.

The next day, John arrived home at nine a.m. He was in good

spirits, and Clemmie thought he looked very young for a man fifty-one years old. Later, Clemmie found out that John had only seven dollars to his name. She awoke in the night, troubled about what she should do. John was sleeping like a log, not seeming to be at all worried about the poverty that was eating them alive. Something hard and fast held Clemmie.

What does John expect to do, I wonder? Home with seven dollars in his pocket and no job, and me with only ten dollars in the bank after I pay the bills.

The next morning Clemmie felt more relaxed and wrote checks for the bills. John slept on. The light bill arrived that day. It was $1.32.

When John got up that morning, he hinted that he would like some hot biscuits.

"John, I have no flour to make biscuits for you. The girls and I ate oatmeal, and you will have to also."

"Well, Clemmie, a man needs a cup of coffee to get hisself going. I'll go next door and borrow a little coffee from Mrs. McDuff."

Later, Clemmie wanted John to sit down and make some plans about how they could survive and not end up in the poor house. But as soon as Ruth left for school, John got up immediately and said he was going to see about a job

"John, I am down to my last few dollars in the bank. What can we do?"

"I don't know. I have to try to get some money some way," John replied.

"You are going to borrow some?" Clemmie asked.

"And make some too," John replied. Then he walked out the door.

"Grace, your daddy only has seven dollars to his name," Clemmie reported to her young daughter as Grace dressed for school. Grace made a frown.

"It's not seven dollars, it is seven hundred dollars, no, eight hundred dollars that my daddy has. You are the biggest worry cat I ever heard of."

Later, as Grace left for school in her pongee dress and red sweater and green hat, she kissed her mother, then turned back as she skipped down the walk. "Bye- bye! Have a good time. Don't worry about seven dollars."

Clemmie laughed loudly.

Things would seem like they could not get worse, then they would. John hocked his watch for fifteen dollars. Clemmie found a note in his pocket from Uncle Bill saying he would have to be repaid the four hundred he had loaned John by the first of November.

Clemmie experienced a kind of quiet, steady, resigned mood settling over her. She had survived so many months of very sparse income that she came to a point of knowing somehow, they would survive.

"I guess this is the 'peace that passeth understanding,'" Clemmie stated aloud.

Ruth had fallen in love for the first time. The tall, lean boy was Lynn Henderson, who was a neighbor and also a member of the church. Ruth had known him a long time, but suddenly she reached that age where she looked at him with new eyes. They began walking home together from school and from church. So far, Anita, Ruth's girlfriend, had always been with them.

Clemmie kept following every lead for a place to teach school. Finally, she was put in contact with the principal from Whitewright, Texas, a Mr. Smith. He told Clemmie that he was a distant cousin of Luther Smith, and Luther had told him to get in contact with Clementine Briley. They needed a teacher for the high school study hall. Clemmie had to decide quickly if she would really leave their home and John.

"Yes, Mr. Smith, I will take that job."

They located a family who wanted to rent their house, and that would at least help them pay the taxes and a few bills. John could continue to live in one bedroom. The girls would go with Clemmie. Everything had to move quickly, and by Saturday, December 10, Clemmie, Ruth, and Grace were on a train to Whitewright.

There was a silent gray mist that perfectly fit the occasion, Clemmie thought. *Why, this is exactly like the day Papa took me to Lane's Chapel in the wagon to begin teaching my first school. It was 1898, and I was eighteen years old. And now I am forty-seven, but I feel the same way.*

I wonder where this separation will all end, thought Clemmie as the train whistle blew and the huge wheels began to turn. There were tears in the eyes of Clemmie, Grace, and Ruth on the train and John and Lynn waving from the platform.

"Good-bye, my darling," Clemmie managed to say as the train rolled out of the station.

WHEN THE NIGHT

The train from Dallas to Whitewright took only one hour and forty minutes, and that included several stops. Two teachers met Clemmie, Ruth, and Grace at the depot and took them to Mrs. Gillet's for dinner. However, they discovered they could not stay there overnight. Clemmie, Ruth, and Grace got out and began to hunt rooms and places to stay. There was a fine mist falling, adding to the sadness.

Mrs. Smith, who ran a boardinghouse, offered to keep all three for fifty dollars per month. Her place looked and smelled awful. Ruth's raised eyebrow and Grace's turned-up nose were all Clemmie needed to make an excuse. "We need to see some other places on our list. Thank you very much."

Once outside Ruth and Grace fell into a fit of laughter.

"Mother, what was that awful smell?" asked Grace. "It smelled like one hundred-year-old underpants!"

"Why, Grace, what a terrible thing to say!" Then Clemmie started to laugh too.

Arriving at Mrs. Hampton's with their things, they all three thought her place was a paradise. The price would be sixty dollars a month for the three of them with all meals furnished. Grace seemed much happier, still she cried for her home and her daddy that night. Clemmie felt like she could not dare think about the way things were. She also shed tears. Ruth didn't say much, but she was suffering the loss of Lynn, Anita, her senior year at school, and much more. And Ruth was good at math and could see her mother would not make anything above the bare necessities.

On Monday morning Mr. Smith came and delivered the three Briley girls to the correct places. By the end of the week, Clemmie thought the study hall assignment wasn't too bad, although it was a real challenge to keep order. She felt happy to know she had made twenty-five dollars when school dismissed on Friday.

Mamma wrote and sent Clemmie a check for fifty dollars with which to buy a typewriter. Clemmie had asked her to do this, not knowing if she would or not. Clemmie's heart leaped with joy when she saw the check. Now she would be able to really write and put to use some of the things she was learning in her authorship course. Clara wrote that Jim and Callie and the children had moved into the house with her. That made Clemmie very happy. She hoped they could all get along and be happy.

The second week of school finished on December 23. The girls were wild to go back to Dallas for Christmas. Clemmie wondered if they should spend the money but had never been able to disappoint her girls. So they would go.

"What a peculiar position I am in," wrote Clemmie that night in her diary. "Here with two children, a home in Dallas with a husband in it. A husband without a job. I have hoped that he would land something, but it seems that hard luck just camps on his trail. The school children were noisy today, and just a few things have been said which made me think I might be failing. Nothing hurts me worse than that. I am so eager to succeed. By God's help, I *will* succeed." Teardrops fell on the diary here, making blurry blotches.

Clemmie's mother and brother sent her a check for $11.73 for a Christmas present. It seemed like an odd amount, but Clemmie assumed that there was some reason. Sister Grace sent a box of really nice things, including a dress she had made for Grace.

Mr. Smith gave out the checks at noon Friday. The amount was for one hundred dollars. Clemmie was sad that sixty dollars of that would go to Mrs. Hampton. The three caught a ride with a nice truck driver who didn't charge them anything. He let them out at Lamar and Elm in Dallas. They bought a small Christmas tree for one dollar and caught a streetcar home. Ruth, Grace, and Clemmie all three had tears in their eyes. John was not at home, but he phoned and said he was on his way.

The house seemed forlorn and lacked the touch of the female hand. Still it seemed glorious to be home, and it was Christmas Eve. Ruth sat down at the piano and played "Jingle Bells." Grace did a happy little dance around the living room carrying Kitty. Soon John arrived, and there were big hugs all around. Then Clemmie and John went to the nearest grocery store. They bought a chicken, oranges, nuts, lemons, cranberries, and a few other things. Clemmie was surprised that John had $2.55 to put on the bill.

Clemmie was tired to the bone but wanted to fix the chicken and bake the cakes. John got unhappy that she would not come to bed. Finally, he got out of bed and dried the dishes for her, then went back to bed. Clemmie felt sorry for herself as she fixed the stockings, straightened up the house, finished the food, and cleaned the kitchen. When she finally crawled into bed, John seemed to be sound asleep. She snuggled up close and thanked God that she was home.

Grace was up at five a.m., yelling and rejoicing over her Christmas doll. Clemmie got up and started the fire. Ruth had spent the night at Anita's. Then Clemmie went back to bed. John awakened and told her how much he had missed her and said he really needed her and the girls to come back home. And then he cried. Clemmie felt frightened, because he had never cried before. The three went to Sunday school and church.

On Tuesday, the twenty-seventh, Clemmie went to town and bought a beautiful green and white Remington portable typewriter. She thought it was a beauty and was the fulfillment of a dream she had had for a long time.

By sleeping at Anita's, Ruth was able to go out with Lynn without fear of her parents' disapproval. As he walked her home from church on Christmas Day, they stopped in front of a vacant lot. Lynn took her in his arms and kissed her long on the lips. He told her how much he had missed her and that he loved her. Ruth was nearly sure she loved him too, but she wondered how you could know for sure if it was really love.

Later, in Anita's bedroom the girls were talking.

"Ruth, how can you bear to be separated from Lynn for four more months?"

"Well, you know we are writing a lot of letters to each other."

"But it's not nearly as nice to write to a boy as to talk to him in person, is it?"

"Yes, I think it is. They will put nicer things on paper than they will say to you."

John went with his girls to the bus station for the return trip on New Year's Eve. The bus cost only seventy-five cents each for Ruth and Clemmie. Grace could ride for free. Clemmie sat near a couple who had actually lived in her Uncle Manse's house at one time. They passed right in front of Clemmie's grandpa's old place. As they came into Sherman, Clemmie thought the town looked beautiful. Arriving at the station, they were told that they could go by car to Whitewright. It was a Ford sedan, and they had lap robes to cover up with. They were taken right to Mrs. Hampton's door in Whitewright.

They found their room all cleaned up and a warm rug on the floor. Clemmie thought it was very cozy. The temperature outside was near zero, and it was the coldest norther of the winter. They ate a good supper of Irish stew and cornbread, then lay out their clothes for Sunday and retired early. Clemmie had been happy to find a letter from Brother Phillips, recommending them to their new church home. She put it in her purse.

Mr. Smith called Clemmie about 9:30 p.m. and asked her to please be ready to teach fourth grade the next day, since that teacher had gotten married. Clemmie said she would be glad to. She was secretly disappointed, preferring the high school students.

Soon Clemmie ran into her principal at the post office. She decided to wait for him to come out.

"Oh, Mr. Smith, could I talk with you a minute about my teaching the fourth grade? I have been pleased to do that but wonder if I will be getting my high school students back soon."

"Well, Mrs. Briley, I believe you have found an excellent place with these younger students. You know it takes a lot more skill to teach those fourth-graders than it does to sit with a study hall."

"Well, I want to do what seems best for all concerned," Clemmie concluded. "I will do my best with the room while I have it."

About a week later, Clemmie saw in the paper that they had elected another teacher to be in the study hall at the high school. She knew that Mr. Smith was avoiding her.

John would write at least once a week and sometimes two or three times. He got a job collecting for Prudential Life Insurance Company. Although he admitted he wasn't making a lot, he had been able to send some money toward the semi-annual interest on their place. He mentioned that he would not be able to wear his suit much longer. Clemmie took hope that perhaps God would help them keep their home on Alabama Street after all. She noted that the daffodils had begun to bloom in Whitewright.

One evening Grace pestered her mother to take her to a musical program. It was a quarter, and Clemmie hated to spend it. When they were nearly ready to go, Grace looked up at her mother and said in her most fetching way: "You look so pretty. The wrinkles are nearly all out of your face, and you look so young. And Mother, I like to hear you read because your voice is so soft and silent-like."

Both Grace and Ruth had found new girlfriends, and that made a lot of difference to a girl. Anita wrote Ruth that she had "busted" up with her boyfriend, Paul. The next day, Ruth told her mother that perhaps she and Anita would be old maids and go live in Alaska. She was reading *Snowbound* and was enamored with it.

"But what I had rather do is marry Lynn if he wants me."

Poor girls, thought Clemmie. *I hope love will let them off light.*

Ruth went to Dallas the last Saturday in February, mainly to see Lynn, but also to see her daddy. She got a ride on Saturday morning on the Mangram truck. The driver was very courteous and respectful to her. He was a young married man and seemed to enjoy her company. Arriving in Dallas, Ruth knew which streetcar to catch that would take her to Trinity Heights. She got home about noon. Her papa was not there, and the house was in pretty bad shape. Ruth phoned Lynn, and he was so glad she had made it home. He asked her when he could come by for her, and she suggested he give her about two hours. She wanted to clean up the house some for her papa and needed some time to fix herself up for her beau.

Ruth worked like a Turk and cleaned up the house for her papa. She hung up clothes and put dirty ones in a pillow slip to take back with her, stuffing the dirty sheets in too. When she had things pretty much in shape, she had only forty minutes left to transform herself into a "vision of loveliness" for Lynn.

First, she fixed a bath for herself, then dressed up in her favorite dress that Aunt Grace had given her at Christmas. She pulled on stockings and cleaned up her shoes. She put on a little powder and rouge and worked with her naturally curly hair, resolving to let her hair grow out some more. She put on some earbobs and surveyed herself in the mirror. *Not too bad,* she thought. She felt her heartbeat increase as she anticipated the knock at the door and seeing Lynn again.

It was after two when the *rap rap* came. She felt shy as Lynn looked her over, then stepped inside and took her in his arms.

"Oh, Ruth, I have nearly died here in Dallas without you. Couldn't you come home and stay with your dad and go back to Sunset?"

"Lynn, I have missed you so much, but school will soon be out, and I'll be back home. In some ways it has been a good experience for me. Mother really needs me. She hasn't had an easy time of it. I know Papa needs us to all get back together. If he could only find a job."

"Your dad is not the only one having job problems these days. Things are not real good for a lot of people in Dallas. Ruth, let's go over to the park and maybe swing and talk, okay? I sure do like that dress. Most of all I like you in that dress."

"Okay, Lynn. Let's go."

It was a warm and beautiful day with the flowers and trees in their new spring colors. Arriving at the park, Ruth and Lynn settled on a bench near a little brook. There was no one else around. Lynn decided to take a chance and see if Ruth would allow him to kiss her. Her lips were full and warm, and she seemed very willing. The kisses became more ardent.

"Ruth, my parents have gone to Greeneville to see my aunt and will be home after dark. What do you say we walk over to my place and I'll make us some lemonade?"

"Okay, Lynn. We can listen to the radio and make some popcorn."

They arrived at the Henderson home in no time. Ruth liked their house, and Lynn's mom kept it really neat. They turned on the radio and went in the kitchen to make the lemonade. Lynn found a lemon and started to cut it. Suddenly, he put it down, grabbed Ruth by the hand, and pulled her into his bedroom.

"Oh, Lynn, we better not go in here."

"I just want to show you my model car, Ruth."

Lynn grabbed Ruth's arms and began kissing her.

"Lynn, you know I really like you, but I am not even sixteen years old. Maybe you and I will get married some day, but it will be a long time from now. So we'd better not get carried away with passion."

"Ruth, you are right, but I sure do love you."

That evening Ruth was at home with her papa. She fixed him some sausage and eggs with toast and asked him if she could talk to him about boys.

"Papa, Mother isn't the type who can talk to me about love and all, so could I ask you some things?" The two sat across from each other at the simple kitchen table.

"Well, 'course you kin, and I hope I know th' answers, Ruth."

"Well, Lynn is wanting to hug and kiss a lot, and he says that he can't explain how he feels. I can tell that something is about to go out of control. I just wanted to get you to help me understand how boys can get to feeling and what should girls do about it."

"Ruth, I'm glad that you know you kin talk t' me. A father wishes he could always protect his daughters from young boys, but probably knowing more 'bout boys would be the best thing to tell you. I know that Lynn is a pretty nice boy, but any boy can get too…uh, sort of carried away, well, too lovey, and then one thing leads to another. And what can happen is that things can go too far.

"It seems like the good Lord made girls and women where they have more gumption, and more…uh…control over these things than boys or men do. Ruth, you are a real pretty girl, and a good girl. And I want you to stay that way. And when you're a lot older, around twenty-one or more, you'll find the right boy an' git married and that's the way God wants us to do."

"Papa, you are saying that boys and girls are different, and girls can be the ones to keep things from getting too…out of hand?"

"Yeah, that's it. Someday when you're older, I'll tell you 'bout a mistake I made…afore your mother came into my life. "

"Thank you, Papa. It's not easy to talk about this kind of stuff, but it helps me a lot. You are a mighty sweet papa to me." Ruth went around the table and kissed her daddy on the cheek.

When Ruth got back to Whitewright Sunday night, she reported that things seemed a little sad in Dallas. Their dog, Jack, had no home now and no one to feed him. Ruth said he wasn't even barking at everyone the way he used to. Clemmie surmised that things had not gone well between Lynn and Ruth.

The next day, Clemmie gave out report cards. She wondered how many heartaches they caused. She always hated giving grades. She doubted if human beings were capable of giving fair grades.

By the end of the day, Grace delivered another blow to Clemmie: "Lula Lee said about all the children but her just hate you. They were crazy about you at first, but they hate you now."

For Clemmie it was like a stab right through the heart and a sad reminder of past wounds to her heart in days gone by. She decided to compose the following poem:

I know not why such bitter tears should fill my eyes,
I know not why such depths of sorrow I should bear
I asked such an humble little cot to be my paradise
I know not why I cannot be there.
I only know my heart doth love,
And is with deep emotion filled.
Sorrow I sometimes rise above
And with peace sublime my aching heart is filled.

The month of March began to go by rather quickly. One day Mr. Smith saw Clemmie in the hall and asked her not to let a child help her grade papers anymore. Clemmie kept from crying, but it gave her an unpleasant feeling every time she thought about it.

One Sunday in March, Grace, Ruth, and Clemmie were invited to eat Sunday dinner with the Yowells. They lived just outside of Whitewright, west of town in a little white house. They had two fine Jersey cows and chickens outside and a cozy fire in the front room. The meal was magnificent, Clemmie thought. There was tender baked chicken, gravy, dressing, cranberry jelly, lettuce, stuffed eggs, salmon and potato croquettes, pickles, relish, pimento and cheese salad, sweet potatoes with marshmallows, Jell-O with fruit, and whipped cream. Later, there was homemade candy passed around. The Yowells had a son, Guy, who was seventeen, and a daughter, Anna Lee, just a year older than Grace. Guy and Ruth made a connection that day, putting an end to Ruth's first love, Lynn Henderson, back in Dallas.

On March 27, Ruth had her sixteenth birthday. Clemmie couldn't believe that sixteen years had gone by since Ruth's birth. Her Aunt Grace sent her a pretty white cotton-print dress. Mrs. Hampton baked a birthday cake, and then that night a school friend gave Ruth a surprise birthday party. With the end of school Ruth would lack only two credits to graduate. Clemmie and her sister had figured out a way that Ruth could live in Fort Worth with Grace and get the two courses at summer school where her Uncle John was principal. Then she would be ready to start to Central Industrial Arts (CIA) in Denton in the fall.

April seemed to bring fresh hope to the Briley three. John wrote that he had worked some at a filling station. He said that if he had a car, he could sell ads for the *Dallas News.*

Clemmie was shocked to hear that Tommie Browning, the cute teacher who stole Luther Smith's heart in Bowser, had died.

One day at recess the children were playing on the ocean wave, a type of merry-go-round. One of the children shouted out, "All who love Miss Sallie get off and push." Nearly every pupil got off and pushed vigorously.

Next someone said, "All who love Mrs. Briley get off and push." Only two little girls got off, looking sheepish like they were ashamed, and pushed weakly.

Clemmie had been near enough to observe the whole episode. Her heart sank. *Why should something so silly take all the joy out of life?* Clemmie wondered.

A discouraging letter arrived from John. He had lost fifty-three dollars out of his pocket two days before and was flat broke. He also said the renters were not paying rent. Clemmie surprised herself and stated: "I know not why such fate befalls me, but the strength God gives me is marvelous."

Clemmie was devastated to not be re-elected for the following year. There was just a crushing silence when time for the vote came up at the school board meeting. Mrs. Yowell told Clemmie that was what had happened to other teachers. Just silence.

Finally, when school ended and Clemmie was back in her own home, she felt like a queen in a castle. She resolved in her heart to be at peace and to trust that God would take care of them. John seemed so glad to have them back and was trying hard to make a go of his job with the ice company. He even went to church some with Clemmie and Grace.

Ruth lived with her Aunt Grace that summer and finished high school at Central in Fort Worth, as they had planned. Graduation was set for August 30, and Clemmie made Ruth a lovely white silk dress with tiny cap sleeves and a nice slip. She wore white stockings with her "Mary Jane" shoes and had a rose corsage. Grace and Joe went after Clemmie and Grace in Dallas. Clemmie thought that Ruth looked as nice as any of the 113 graduates. Her teacher gave her some lovely beads that matched her dress. She got several other nice presents.

Sister Grace insisted that Clemmie wear a nice pink dress of hers that had just come from the cleaners. Grace also furnished her white kid shoes and a hat. Clemmie thought to herself that it was nearly strange that clothes should change one's looks so. Little Grace was delighted with the way her mother looked.

The following day the women all went to Denton and looked over CIA and got Ruth enrolled. They also went to see the larger Texas Teachers College. Then Grace took the Brileys home to Dallas.

The next day, Ruth and Grace had a chance to ride to Mills County, and they were off for a twelve-day holiday at their dear Ebony. Clemmie was relieved to have a few days alone. She went shopping for shoes one day and found some she really liked. They were brown oxfords in the window at Volk's. Clemmie went in, tried them on, and decided to purchase them. The price was $8.50. She opened up an account there. That same day she bought stockings, pen points, and a writing tablet. Then she decided to do something she hadn't done but maybe once before in her life: she took herself to a movie showing at the Capital. It was *Uncle Tom's Cabin*. The cost was twenty-five cents, and she felt nearly wicked to spend that much on pure pleasure. Later, she felt that it was a quarter well spent, and the movie was *grand*.

Ruth wrote that they were having a "scrumptious" time in Ebony, and the house was all dressed up like it was going to church. Clemmie smiled broadly when she read that. Another of her minor dreams fulfilled. The next letter from Ruth contained a check for $115.00. *Oh, thank you Lord!* Clemmie exclaimed. Her brother had sold a cow, a calf, and a yearling of hers. Clemmie knew this money was a direct answer to the fervent prayer she had prayed.

John came in late on a Saturday and said he was going to be laid off from the ice company. Clemmie went in her room, got on her knees, and cried, then prayed for God to see after them and give John another job. He soon landed another job in a paper mill.

On Sunday Clemmie visited the Oak Cliff church, wanting to

see the new church building. It thrilled Clemmie's heart to see the church growing. She thought the new building was magnificent.

John went to Trinity Heights Church with Clemmie Sunday night, the first time he had been in two months. He said his shoes were not good enough to go to church.

Ruth and Grace arrived home Wednesday. They rode to Fort Worth with their Aunt Grace, then caught the interurban home. Clemmie was so excited to see them and had them sit down and tell her everything. It was like a feast for Clemmie.

On October 2, 1928, John had his fifty-second birthday and received the best present of his whole life. The rest of the Briley Estate had finally come through probate court, and each of the living children received $1,165. John had to pinch himself to be sure it wasn't a happy dream! Clemmie and John decided to buy a good car.

Clemmie made this entry in her diary:

Dear Father,

I thank Thee for Thy Blessings. My cup runneth over. It seems like the night of separation is turning into the dawning of a new day.

Judge Is Named on Highway Commission

W. R. ELY.

Ely Appointed To Road Board By Governor

MEETS GOLD OF DAY

January 1, 1929, dawned clear and cold. The four Brileys, along with Ruth's friend, Lynn, got in their large new Chevrolet in their new clothes with their self-esteem at an all-time high. Little did they know what the year held for them and for the rest of the country.

Clemmie sat up proudly in the front, Lynn and the girls in the back. Lynn held Ruth's hand under the folds of her coat, so little sister couldn't see and perhaps broadcast the news. For Ruth the romance was waning, but Lynn hadn't given up yet.

Lynn read some headlines from the *Dallas Morning News* as they traveled the forty miles due west to Grace and John Bateman's nice home in Fort Worth. The Brileys were invited to spend New Year's Day there.

"*Hoover Lines Up His Cabinet*, it says right here in the paper. Mr. Briley, were you surprised that President Coolidge didn't want to run again for the office?" inquired Lynn.

"Oh, I think Mr. Coolidge was gettin' tired of bein' blamed fer all this poverty and stuff. After all, six years of bein' th' big cheese is enough fer any man."

"Mr. Hoover sure came up with a good slogan, didn't he?" Ruth wanted to show that she knew about politics, too. "'A chicken in every pot, a car in every garage.'" I sure hope that comes true."

"Well, it already did for us!" piped up little Grace.

"Well, it's not *every* day our pot has a chicken," Clemmie put in, "but I can be happy with beans. And I'd sure be just as happy with a Model T Ford. This big car is embarrassing to me, like we've outdone ourselves." Clemmie couldn't resist criticizing John's buying an oversized, expensive car. He had paid four hundred dollars and still owed that much more, to be paid at the rate of thirty dollars a month. That was six days of teaching school, and they didn't call Clemmie very often. She felt really skeptical about John's sales ability.

"Clemmie, you know I plan to make our livin' usin' this vehicle, and t' haul stuff t' sell you've gotta have a big car."

"Look, Mama and Daddy, there's an old gray mare. Let's see who can spot the most of them." Grace wanted to be a peacemaker.

When they arrived at the Batemans on Orange Street in Fort Worth, Mamma and Marie were there, and also Mamma's sister, Mattie. The meal itself was a real feast for the Brileys, consisting of turkey and dressing and all the trimmings. After a full day the Briley bunch loaded into the big, closed car and headed home. After so many years of poverty, the Brileys felt like they were in a dream. Ruth started singing and everyone joined in: "*Come away with me, Lucille, in the merry Oldsmobile…*"

About the third week in January, Clemmie was reading the morning paper and saw a picture that caused her to gasp. It was none other than Raleigh Ely! Memories that had been stuffed away for years immediately leaped to life for Clemmie. Her hands began to tremble, and she felt suddenly light-headed. She started reading the article with her heart in her throat.

It told that Governor Dan Moody had reappointed Judge Ely for a six-year term as one of three Texas Highway Commissioners. Clemmie immediately wanted to compare the only picture Raleigh had given her of himself, at age twenty-five, with this present one at around age fifty-one. She had an old candy box that served as storage for her special keepsakes. She ran to her trunk and found the picture.

Age has changed the looks of my youthful Apollo, but I think he is still handsome. And he's certainly coming into his own in this world.

Clemmie carefully clipped out the picture of Raleigh along with the article and pasted it on the inside cover of her present diary. What an unexpected pleasure—to open the morning paper and find a picture of the one man she cherished.

Clemmie went to SMU to rejoin the teacher's agency. Dr. Nichols told her that four years of education and a thesis would give her an M.A. degree. Clemmie figured she already had one year of credit and was aflame with the desire to go for her master's in education.

Surely that will open the door to my teaching career in Dallas, she reasoned.

Little Women was being presented by Oak Cliff Little Theater at the high school, and Clemmie was smitten with the desire to see her all-time favorite story, just as a treat for herself. Clemmie understood the price was twenty-five cents, and she wondered if she dared spend her last bit of money in that way. Arriving at the ticket table that evening, the lady told her it was seventy-five cents. Fishing around in her purse, she found exactly that amount. She shed many a tear over what she considered a touching masterpiece of ideal American home life.

I would not have missed it for anything! declared Clemmie to herself on her way home. *Oh, how I identify with the character Jo March,* thought Clemmie.

John kept trying to find other jobs after he gave up the sale of cottonseed, which had been unsuccessful. He talked with Mr. Barnes about getting another ice station for the summer. He felt very discouraged. He knew Clemmie was down on him, and he was down on himself.

I'm just no good at making steady money like people have to have in the city, became John's obsessive thought. One whole afternoon he thought about killing himself. He tried to plan how he would do it and what everyone would say. He envisioned his own funeral service out at Ebony or Elkins Cemetery. He went so far as to ask Lynn what he thought about suicide.

"Mr. Briley, that would be a sin. God doesn't want us to try to be God."

Then John made the decision that he would not put his family through such a disgrace. He would just do the best he could, and one day the whole situation would be better. Good times would come. He would be back on the farm, making money hand over fist in the cattle business. He felt the black night of his depression begin to lift. It was like the glinting of sunlight across the shadow of his soul.

Yes, John determined. *Clemmie and the girls and I will come through this horrible time in our lives, by George! What I need to do is to start prayin' like Clemmie does.*

Dear God, this is John Briley. I need Thou to help me and my family right now. I know I need to do my part, and I aim to do it. This is my prayer, and it's prayed in the name of Jesus. Amen.

The next Monday, John came home and asked Clemmie if she

wanted him to take her around in the car to see some principals about a teaching job. Although Clemmie was nursing a headache, she could not pass up such an opportunity. She fixed herself up the best she could, and they set out. She couldn't believe John was helping her like this.

First, John took her to Sunset High, and she visited with Mr. Wilson. He treated her with courtesy and promised she would be on their substitute list for the coming school year. They went to Mills, Bowie, John F. Peeler, Lida Hooe, Irwindell, and Rosemont. Finally, she visited Mr. Cauthorne, the superintendent, at the administration building, and she asked him if he had anything for her.

"No, not at this time. However, I have a notice that a teacher is needed for a junior college at Terrell, Texas." So John took Clemmie there, but the place was filled.

"Clemmie, I think I may have t' sell this car, because I can't make the payments. I wanted t' use it in ever' good way I could, so I've tried to take you 'round to schools. But no luck there. That door's closed now. But there'll be somethin' good come up. I know it. Now all we've gotta do is hang in here and wait and not break down."

John announced that he was advertising his big car for sale in the paper the next day. Grace was just killed about it. Her daddy said he would get another car some day. Clemmie wondered how that would ever happen. The next day, the car was sold for ninety dollars, and the new party would take up payments. The Brileys had invested over four hundred dollars in it. John paid fifty-three dollars to Mr. Huvelle as interest on the house. Clemmie wanted him to pay seventy-eight dollars, which would have made a payment on the principle, but John refused because it would leave him with so little money.

"Mowie," Grace began with her pet name for Clemmie, "can I have a new hat and shoes for Easter? If we're too poor, that's okay."

That night Clemmie prayed. "Oh, Lord, what wilt Thou do about it? I have tried my best and failed. Wilt Thou let my little girl do without, when Thou dost clothe the lilies of the field? O Father, I beseech Thee that Thou hear my prayer for help. Bless these little children dependent on me, O God. For their sakes, give us work, I pray, in the name of Him who was ever a friend to the distressed. Amen."

On April first, the first rose of the season bloomed in Clemmie's yard, and Clemmie and Grace went shopping for an Easter hat. After walking all over town, they bought one for $2.95. That left Clemmie four dollars to her name, and a gas bill in that amount would arrive very soon. But she decided to rely on her faith in God's promises to clothe her family like the lilies of the field.

That night at Clemmie's journalism class, Mr. Ellis of the circulation department of the *Dallas Morning News* talked to the students. He offered a prize of five dollars to the one who could write the best rewrite of a certain story. Clemmie thought to herself that there was nothing in the world that could help her as much as winning that little prize. Two days later, the announcement was made in class by Mr. Ellis.

"This wasn't an easy choice, but we do have a winner for the best rewrite of the story. It is Clementine Briley."

Clemmie nearly shouted. In her head she said over and over, *I thank Thee, Lord! What a direct answer from Thee, just when my hope was low and wavering.* Clemmie rose from her desk and made her way to the front of the class.

"Thank you very much, Mr. Ellis. I enjoyed rewriting the story. This five dollars will be used to buy a new pair of Easter shoes for my little daughter." The other students clapped and thereafter seemed to have more respect for Clemmie.

That very afternoon, Clemmie and Grace went shopping. They found just exactly the kind of shoes Grace wanted, and the price was $4.95. Back outside, Clemmie looked up at the blue sky and the pretty clouds and she smiled.

"Grace, let's always remember that God answers our prayers. Even the prayers for five dollars for my little girl to get some new Easter shoes."

"I know, Mowie. That's why you and Daddy don't ever need to worry about anything."

Ruth had really done herself proud at CIA and hoped to continue on there the coming year. Her grades had been straight A's, and her conduct and participation were outstanding. The Round Table Club of Fort Worth, due to Aunt Grace's influence, had taken Ruth on as a student whom they wanted to sponsor. They gave her a scholarship of two hundred dollars for her first year and now wanted to award her the same amount for her second year. Ruth also had the promise of an on-campus job, serving in the dining room. This was direct answer to prayer, Clemmie thought, and the goodness of her sister Grace.

The man who held the mortgage on the Alabama Street house was threatening to foreclose unless he received a payment. Clemmie went and talked to him. He agreed to hold up if the Brileys could pay him a little before July 2.

Later that day, Clemmie heard music and marching on nearby Elm Street. She went out in the yard and watched the parade. It was quite a few Negroes, marching in formation.

There is something very majestic about seeing them marching this way, Clemmie thought. Her eyes filled with tears. *Why, just a few years ago, they were brought as slaves to our country and sold like cattle. Now they march through the streets of this great Southern city, to the music of their own making, looking straight ahead as though they saw a vision.* To Clemmie it was prophetic.

John was given a night job at the ice station. He made as much as twenty-four dollars a week. He worked all night, getting home at seven a.m. Clemmie would have a hot breakfast ready, then he would go to bed. The strain of the heavy blocks of ice really hurt his back, and sometimes he had to hire a man to help him.

The next day, John cut his working hours back to only five p.m. to ten p.m. For Clemmie, all hope of paying anything on the house was gone. She prayed fervently that she would not lose heart and have a breakdown.

Ruth came home from CIA for the summer. She was eager to try to find a job and make some money. She and Clemmie went all over downtown Dallas submitting applications. Finally, she was hired to work a few days at Grant's. She was paid $1.75 per day.

Sister Grace wrote that she wanted to make a trip to Mills County soon. Clemmie could let her know which day she would like to go, and Grace's husband, John Bateman, would come and get her and the girls.

Clemmie decided she must do the interview with Aunt Martha, nearly ninety-eight, before she left Dallas. She wanted to write a full-page article, with pictures, for the *Dallas Morning News.* With a huge effort of will, Clemmie rode the interurban to Van Alstyne, borrowing the money from Ruth. Clemmie got all the facts, the right pictures, and spent hours getting the story just perfect, then turned it into the paper.

Grace came with little Joe to get the Brileys and took them to Ebony on July 13. They had a good time as always, with just one big serious discussion on dancing. It was Clemmie against everyone else.

"Yes, Mother, it was Bernice and Letty and I trying to learn to dance. Do you think three girls just practicing together is a sin?" Ruth defended herself.

"No, I don't think that is wrong, Ruth. However, what is the point of learning to dance except to go to these clubs where you dance? Then you will have partners who you don't even know, possibly men who have been drinking. It's a good way to get into some bad trouble if you ask me. No good can come from girls going around the countryside, just looking for places to go dancing."

"Well, Mother, in the Bible we can read that David danced before the Lord. And he wasn't considered worldly," Ruth answered.

"I think you will find that David was praising God with his dancing. Now is that what you girls are wanting to do, to praise God?"

Just then Mamma heard the loud voices in heated argument and said, "Please hush, please hush!" Mamma could not abide a religious discussion.

Ruth stayed through August in Ebony after the others returned home. As soon as Clemmie got back, she saw the huge article she had written on Aunt Martha in the *Dallas News,* big as life!

So I have burst into print, Clemmie thought. *Finally!* Later, she received a check for $17.50 for contributing the news article.

Ruth wrote that on Wednesday, August 14, Jim tore down the little old house that had been the original homestead in Ebony. He said he needed the lumber for a henhouse. Ruth said they took several pictures of the house. The "little gray house in the west" had stood for forty-nine years. Clemmie felt unspeakably sad that the little house was gone.

My brother doesn't have one bone of sentimentality in his body, she thought.

Guy Yowell, Ruth's friend from Whitewright, was going to school at SMU in Dallas. Ruth called him one day and invited him to supper, also inviting her best friend, Anita Bownds, and her boyfriend, Paul. Ruth warned Clemmie not to bring up the subject of money and how bad off they were. Ruth fixed most of the meal by herself and had the house spotless. However, not long after that evening, Clemmie noticed that Ruth didn't talk much about Guy. She seemed to have lost interest.

"Ruth, are you thinking about the Yowell boy these days?" Clemmie inquired.

"He's very nice, Mother, but I don't think I want to spend my life with him. He just doesn't give me a 'buzz,' if you know what I mean. He likes poetry and nature, and I can't explain why, but there is no 'chemistry' at work for me. But I know there will be someone. I am thinking that I may need to go to a college where there are boys. Maybe the one in Denton called North Texas State Teachers College. But this year I want to stay at CIA. Then maybe I can teach for a year and save money for school."

Clemmie was called to substitute only eighteen days in the fall of 1929. She made around one hundred dollars in all. She enrolled for Spanish and Short Story and continued on her path toward an M.A.

One night in Clemmie's Short Story class, Mr. Barrington was returning papers and chose one to read aloud. Clemmie was so tired that she was slumped in her desk, about to go to sleep. Suddenly, she recognized her own writing, a short, thirty-five-word description of the neighbor, Mr. McDuff:

> Careless, tousled, noisy, and squirmy, he presented a constant problem; unintelligible, ink-be-spattered hieroglyphics for writing, quick at figures; but oh, how he tugged at my heart with that wistful, stoic look behind his clear blue eyes.

Mr. Barrington walked straight to Clemmie's desk and handed her the paper, smiling at her. On the outside of the paper this comment was written: "Human, every word of it—so an entire success." Then Mr. Barrington began to read Clemmie's other description.

> Fine physique, smooth white skin, large dark blue eyes, hair as black as a raven. Smiling adorably, his blue eyes sparkling, my raven-haired, white-browed Apollo pushed through the crowd to me.

On the outside of the folded paper was written Mr. Barrington's comment: "Oh, if he only knew how well you remembered him."

Of course Clemmie had Raleigh Ely in mind for this description, and Mr. Barrington's comment was all too appropriate to the situation. It was one of the high points of several years of night classes for Clemmie. She carefully placed the two papers inside her diary that night, and there they remained for the rest of her life.

That night Clemmie wrote these words in her diary:

> It was more significant than he thought. Joy welled up in

my heart immediately. I was no longer tired. Strange how a mere little comment of written words could change things so for me.

The entire United States was cast into mourning on the weekend following October 24. It was called "Black Thursday," and it was the crash of the stock market. The common people had little understanding of the workings of higher finance, but they understood the meaning of not being able to find work or of having their regular pay cut in half. The people understood that it was not the fault of President Hoover, but they wondered if he would know what to do to help make everything better.

There were many cases of reported suicides that weekend and scores of other cases that went unreported. As Clemmie read the *Dallas Morning News* that Saturday, she did not see how things could be any worse for their particular situation. Maybe it meant there would be a lot more families in the same awful predicament they were in.

During the months of November and December, John was without work. They received notice that unless a sizeable amount could be paid on the house by January 1, the Brileys' property on Alabama Street would enter foreclosure. Clemmie took her last five dollars and bought groceries. She had nothing else in sight, but she had faith that God would take care of their family.

Ruth came home for Christmas and got three days of work at McCrory's, a five-and-dime store. She would work from eleven a.m. until nine p.m. and get paid $1.75. A Mrs. Fender came over from the Round Tree Club in Fort Worth and brought Ruth her Christmas presents. There was a five-dollar gold piece, sixteen one-dollar bills, and many other lovely gifts.

Clemmie received a letter from Aunt Mattie with a check for five dollars. In the end, the last dollar bought Christmas dinner for the Brileys—pork chops for thirty cents, mashed potatoes, lettuce, whipped cream, and Jell-O. A neighbor sent over sweet potatoes with marshmallows, chicken, and candy. Ruth furnished most of Christmas that year, being the only family member with any money at all.

With the threat of foreclosure, the whole season had a huge dark cloud over it for Clemmie. A good friend, Mrs. White, told Clemmie the following: "Remember that possession is nine points of the law. Do not leave your home as long as there is any hope of keeping it." Mr. Huvelle wanted four monthly payments plus the delinquent taxes and insurance by January 1, 1930. The total amount in dollars was about $166. It might as well have been $166,000 since there was not even one dollar available to the Brileys.

The last day of 1929, John got up at dawn and dressed. He paced through the house, making quite a bit of noise. Finally, he threw himself down on the bed and put his arm around Clemmie. He cried out, "Oh, Mother! What will become of us?" Then he sobbed loudly for two or three minutes.

Clemmie wanted to say that God would take care of them and offer some comfort to John. However, she could not make the words come out of her mouth. She knew that she was terrified that they really were going to lose the house and have to go to the poor house. She lay frozen, facing the wall, and prayed for God to save them and the house. John got up from the bed, and Clemmie heard him in the next room, lying down by little Grace.

"Don't worry, Daddy. All you have to do is to be good and trust in God."

"Grace, that is the sweetest thing I ever heard."

January 1, 1930, dawned clear and cold. Clemmie cried before she got out of bed due to her level of distress. This could be the day of the foreclosure. At breakfast, Clemmie thought something needed to be said.

"John, Ruth, and Grace, we do not know what is going to happen, but we have been warned that our home may be taken from us today. If that happens, it may mean that our family will have to be broken up—separated. That is the most disgraceful thing I can think of.

Please pray with me that God will provide another way for us to make it through this terrible time in our lives."

Ruth and Grace remained silent with sad looks on their faces. John did not get angry. He looked at each of his three women and simply stated, "I do not plan to give you up."

AND THEY SAY GOD
SHOWS HIS FACE, LOVE

Today is the first day of the New Year, and the day that we could lose our home in Dallas. Mr. Huvelle expects to foreclose at any time. I have prayed continually for God to save this house for me, if that is His will. If it is not, it is well.

If I were allowed to keep this home, I would fix it up so pretty, inside and out. Oh, people would gasp when they saw the beauty of it. Instead, it is a poor, run-down home, about to be foreclosed.

Seemingly in answer to prayer, Clemmie was called to teach school the very next day and ended up making ninety dollars by the first part of February. The foreclosure was forestalled. Clemmie paid the taxes, insurance, the utility bills, and got a few groceries.

One day the phone rang, and it was Sister Grace. "Clemmie, I have an idea to help you get a good income. What if you, Ruth, and I go on a little trip through some Texas towns, talk to some school trustees, and try to find teaching jobs for you and Ruth? I bet we could find jobs for both of you."

"Oh, Grace, that is the best idea I've heard in a long time."

"We'll take little Joe and your little Grace with us, and I'll furnish my car and all the gas. We'll have a good time, and I think something will come of it. What if I show up there next week, let's say on Thursday, March twenty-seventh?"

"Wonderful! You know that is Ruth's eighteenth birthday? What a present that will be!"

"Well, we'll just take the bull by the horns and see that you don't lose your home." And so it happened as Grace planned. They had angel food cake and grape juice and sang "Happy Birthday" to Ruth, who had come home from Denton on the interurban that morning.

They slept at Grace's house the first night. Uncle John Bateman, her pleasant and somewhat rigid husband, announced the weather report. "Girls, it says here in the *Star Telegram* that there is snow and sleet all over West Texas. Don't you think you'd better wait up on this trip?"

"John, we need to do this to find some jobs, and I think our good car will make it fine," replied Grace.

"Oh, you Wilmeth women have such strong wills. I guess even the Lord couldn't stop you. Well, good luck on the ice and snow!" Uncle John retired for the night.

At six a.m. the little group started out on the Weatherford road. Although there was some blowing snow, the road was still good for travel. It was 10:25 a.m. when they got to Abilene, and they went straight to Abilene Christian College. Once there they found the president of the college. President Baxter did not offer Clemmie any encouragement about getting a job teaching there, since so many were on the waiting list.

It had crossed Clemmie's mind more than once that they were in Raleigh's hometown, but she couldn't think of any real reason to ask Grace to drive by his house or to try and find him.

The road had been paved all the way to Abilene and on to Ballinger. Then the pavement ended as they headed toward Norton, Texas, where Marie Wilmeth was teaching, and Bernice, her younger sister, was a student. Marie had encouraged them to apply for a job there, and Ruth thought it would be delightful to teach with her cousin.

Marie was out in the yard for recess and was very happily surprised to see her relatives drive up. They soon had the addresses of the three trustees, and Clemmie and Ruth managed to find them, talk to them, and fill out applications.

From there the entourage went to Carlsbad, Texas, and visited Opal and Austin Cawyer. Aus was teaching high school, and Opal taught first grade. Opal was cleaning the kitchen of the school when they arrived. She let out a squeal of delight and was so kind and sweet to her guests. Opal had the best laugh of anyone in the family, Clemmie thought. Austin Cawyer was so capable and confident. He assured Clemmie he would be on the lookout for a job for her and Ruth. The town looked desolate. They could see the smoke of the TB Sanitarium but didn't have time to go by.

They met with some of the trustees there, slept, then went to San Angelo the next day and saw the county superintendent, Mr. Parker. Leaving Little Grace and Joe with their half sister, Clara, Grace, Ruth, and Clemmie went to Christoval and then to Averitt. That night they went on to Water Valley. Early Sunday they went back to San Angelo and got the children and then went on to Norton.

They reached Ebony by Sunday afternoon. Everyone was so glad to see them. Clemmie thought her mother looked older and depressed. As the two women hugged, Clemmie felt the slightly wooden reserve that she had always felt with Mamma. That night other relatives joined them, and they had a good time. Clemmie and Ruth talked to the trustees. Clemmie figured they already knew who the next teachers would be.

By Monday afternoon they were back in Dallas, having stopped at Grace's home so she could put a roast on to cook for supper. Clemmie marveled at the way Grace could plan her life, then make her plans work.

"Grace, you're just good at everything. And here you have given us so much of your time to help us find jobs! I believe something good will come of it."

"Well, it was the least I could do, and besides, I've had a big time. Even little Joe had fun." Ruth rested about an hour, then started back to Denton on the interurban.

Five weeks later Clemmie received a letter from Stanley Reeves, John's cousin and an Ebony trustee. He said their present teachers would stay on, but they wanted to hire a third teacher, and Ruth could have the job if she wanted it.

Clemmie was so excited and called Ruth immediately and told her she had better go ahead and accept the job. Stanley had said in the letter that a lot of other teachers were "rearing" for the job.

Soon a letter came from Mamma saying that Ruth had indeed been elected as the third teacher of the Ebony school! Clemmie felt so happy for her daughter. It meant that Ruth's first real teaching job would be at the place she and Ruth most loved. On the other hand, it was a slap in the face for Clemmie, that with all her experience and degrees, they preferred her eighteen-year-old daughter. Of course *all* schools preferred the young, single women to the older married ones. And for her firstborn, conceived near that very school, to be teaching...that was very gratifying.

On Easter Sunday, April 20, 1930, Grace Briley was fixed up like a little doll. Almost ten years old, Grace had a hint of womanly curves. She wore a new pink voile dress that Clemmie had made the night before out of an old dress of Ruth's, new blonde kid pumps, new anklets, and a new pink hat. She was very happy until she overheard Sister Burns say to Clemmie at church, "Miss McCollum said you're hoping to get Grace's teeth fixed soon. Oh, that makes such a difference in our little girls, don't it? I'm glad you plan to do that for little Grace."

Grace's happiness was over. She was so mad at her mother for ever discussing her teeth with those old ladies. All during the church service she kept pinching her mother's arm and rear. As they started home from church, Grace exploded.

"Ding-bust-it, Mother! Why did you have to talk to those old mean ladies at church about my teeth? It's none of their business, and that makes me so mad!"

When they got in the door of their house, Grace had a big tantrum fit.

"Mother, you ruined Easter, and you have ruined my whole life. I wish I'd never been born, and I wish you weren't my mother! I hope I'll never see you again!" Then she went to bed with her Easter regalia still on, and covered up her head.

"I sure agree with Grace," John joined in the argument. "Clemmie, you had no business on earth tellin' that church woman anything 'bout little Grace's teeth. And I think her teeth are beautiful anyhow! She never has t' have her teeth fixed if she don't want to."

Then Clemmie's nerves gave way, having sat up all night sewing and having to get lunch, clean the house, and be talked to in this way.

"Why, you two are just alike, both just as selfish as can be and so ready to hurl the blame at me. I never said anything bad about Grace to that woman. We were just talking about dentists one day, and she asked about Grace's teeth." Then Clemmie cried out loud. Grace felt remorseful.

"I'll be real good the rest of the day, Mowie." And she was.

Something good happened for Clemmie on May 3. She was called on to make an impromptu speech during a meeting of the Writers Club. At first she felt frantic, searching her mind for what she should say. Then it was like words were given to her.

"I am Clementine Briley. I substitute teach in Dallas, and I am a night student. I attend four classes every Monday, Wednesday, and Friday, from four till nine p.m.

"Mrs. Viligria, when you are elected to the Senate, I hope you can do something about all this opposition to married women working and the discrimination against them. My husband has joined the army of the unemployed, and I assume that all of you are aware of the attitude that Dallas holds against married teachers. Why, it's enough to make us consider breaking up our homes so we can feed our children!

"I want to commend my night school teacher, Mr. Barrington. He is very respectful of women and is helping us feel worthy of the talent and the special places that we are capable of filling in modern society and out there in the marketplace."

Several distinguished people complimented her speech, and that made Clemmie's spirits soar. Dr. Young later dismissed the meeting with prayer. That night Clemmie made this entry in her diary:

> My bathwater is heating, and my spirits are singing. The reason for my elation is that I have been with people who think about some things as I do, and because I have made a speech in Dallas. Not that I am such an egotist, but for a long time I have walked through the streets of Dallas, a tired and troubled little girl, alone and unnoticed, in want and in distress, that it is heart-gratifying to be placed on a level with the others and be called on for a speech.

A letter came to the Brileys from Leon Huvelle about the house, demanding a monthly payment. It angered Clemmie since it had been less than a month since she had made a payment of forty dollars on the interest.

One day Grace and Virginia came in from playing in the yard. "Mother, Ginny and I want to get our teeth fixed right now!"

Clemmie wanted to move while the iron was hot. She called several dentists and found one who could take the girls. Virginia's mother was disabled, and she was so happy for Clemmie to take her daughter to the dentist with Grace.

Later, the girls were excited to think that now they would get a tube of the coveted toothpaste from the school nurse, which was the real motivating factor in the dental hygiene. Unfortunately, because Grace still had some unfilled cavities, she was not awarded membership in the Health Club and got no toothpaste. Clemmie couldn't understand how some people had no feeling and no mercy.

They simply cannot understand the heart of a child, thought Clemmie.

Clemmie saw in the Dallas paper that R.S. Sterling had announced his candidacy for Governor of Texas. He was Chairman of the Highway Commission of which Raleigh was also a member.

I wonder if this will mean that Raleigh will move up to be the Chairman if Mr. Sterling becomes the Governor. Then one day, why Raleigh may even be the Governor of Texas!

Ruth came home for the summer looking very stylish. She had learned to put waves in her naturally curly hair. Boys and clothes were both very interesting to her, now that she was eighteen. Clemmie helped her get some new outfits. They shopped all over Dallas and found a white crepe sport dress at the New York Dress Shop for $5.95. Then they went to Titche's and got fabric to make a matching coat. Ruth knew how to sew for herself but still needed Clemmie's help for complicated things. By the next Monday, Ruth was dressed up in the white dress and short summer coat and had her hair fixed pretty in waves.

"Mother, I've met a boy at church in Denton who is staying on my mind. I can't believe I did this, Mother, but I had to trick him a little bit to get his attention. We were on a church picnic, and I sort of faked a fall and acted like my ankle was hurt. O.R. came running over, helped me get up, and was so nice to me the rest of the afternoon."

"Ruth, I'm surprised at you…that you would be dishonest in that way."

"Oh, Mother, you know what they say, 'All's fair in love and war. And love *is* war!' His name is O.R. Mitchell, and he's *really* cute. I think he wants to be a teacher. That's good, isn't it, Mother? I mean, I know you respect teaching as a profession."

Sister Grace wrote that she could come to get the Briley girls for their trip to Ebony the next week. It would be another first, since Ruth would be staying there all year to teach at her first school.

John gave Clemmie five dollars for them to finish up Ruth's wardrobe for the school year. Clemmie and Ruth went shopping and got dress material for Ruth. It was brown printed rayon crepe from Sanger's, and they bought some solid contrasting material for trim. They hurried home and got the dress cut out. Clemmie felt that old excitement as she began to sew the dress together. By the time Sister Grace arrived they had Ruth decked out like a movie actress, ready to take on the children of Mills County.

One week from the day they arrived in Ebony, they made the return trip, leaving Ruth there. As they drove away, Ruth stood at the door and waved. Clemmie fought back the tears and made herself think of all the blessings.

Back home in Dallas, little Grace was drying the dishes when she said, "I don't know what makes me cry, but I don't see how I can do without Ruth until Christmas." At that point, mother and daughter embraced each other and both cried aloud for a few minutes. Then they both started laughing. Clemmie said, "If Ruth could see us now, she would call us both sissies."

Aunt Martha, sister to Clemmie's papa, passed away on October 7, 1930, at three in the afternoon. A little piece came out in the paper.

Funeral services for Mrs. Martha Wilmeth McKinney, 99 years old, one of the last of the pioneers of the Peters Colony, west of where Dallas was built later, were held Friday afternoon at 2:30 o'clock at the Van Alstyne Christian church. Burial was in McLarry Cemetery. In 1849 Mrs. McKinney was married to David Leek McKinney, grandson of Collin McKinney, for whom the town of McKinney is named, and also Collin County. She also is survived by fifty-two grandchildren, seventy-six great-grandchildren, and fifteen great-great-grandchildren.[4]

Clemmie was gratified that the entire piece in the paper was taken from the big story she had written just two years before, and she was so glad she had gotten that published.

One evening Clemmie and Grace had gone to town on the streetcar to get Grace some new shoes. As the car passed through a lower-class part of the city, suddenly Grace said, "There's Daddy!"

Clemmie looked, and sure enough, there was John, and he was smoking a pipe! Later, Clemmie hoped it had just been someone who resembled John. Late that night Clemmie searched his pants pocket for the pipe. There was none, but she found smoking tobacco.

At the breakfast table the next morning Clemmie broached the subject.

"John, Grace and I saw you smoking a pipe yesterday. We were going on the car to get Grace some shoes. Was that really you?"

John said nothing.

"Well, your silence confirms it. How long have you been smoking in secret?"

Still no comment, but John looked down at the floor and made circles with his right toe, as if very ashamed.

Later, Grace told her mother how sad she felt about her Daddy's smoking. "I feel like someone died. Now I wonder if he does other things we don't know about. I feel like my daddy is dead."

Clemmie was afraid John had broken something fine and sweet within Grace, a faith that could never be repaired.

The first Saturday in December, Clemmie went to the Teacher's Institute. One of the honored speakers was Mr. Turrentine from CIA. Later, Clemmie was determined to speak to him and mention Ruth's name. Since Ruth was an excellent student, Clemmie thought it might help her case if Mr. Turrentine would put in a good word with Mr. Stockard, the Superintendent of Schools in Dallas. It was hard to get to him, since Mr. Stockard, Mr. Wilson, and other "great ones," as Clemmie called them, were engaging him in conversation. Finally, Clemmie got her chance.

"Mr. Turrentine, my daughter Ruth Briley was a student at CIA for the past two years."

"We had a Miss Briley at CIA two years ago."

"That was she," Clemmie responded happily.

"Are you connected with the schools here?" Mr. Turrentine asked Clemmie.

"I am a substitute teacher," Clemmie replied.

Turning to Mr. Stockard, Mr. Turrentine stated, "This woman is the mother of the brightest student we ever had at CIA."

Clemmie hoped Mr. Stockard would later ask her to teach, but no such luck.

On Christmas Eve Clemmie sat in front of the fire and stared into the burning logs for a long time. They had put little Grace on a bus to Brownwood so she could spend Christmas with Ruth and the others. She tried to picture the fun going on at Ebony. She thought of other Christmases when she was a girl in Mills County and when she was a single teacher.

Then she thought of all the Christmases in Dallas. This would be the nineteenth. She wondered if this would be the last. It certainly looked that way, but then she had thought that for several years. Perhaps they would keep hanging on and things would get better. She made herself go to the store and get three pork chops, a pound of bacon, and a little box of mincemeat for ten cents. As Clemmie returned with her purchases, she heard John singing in the front room in front of the fire:

I am a man of constant sorrow,
I've seen trouble all my days;
I left my home in old Kentucky
Where I was born and raised.

Clemmie stood with her hand on the door, tears streaming down her face, and prayed that God would help her and John to be able to be close to each other without criticizing. *We really do need each other,* she thought. That night Clemmie was kinder to John than she had been in a long time.

There were roses blooming in December. Clemmie fixed a vase of them on the table with a white tablecloth for their Christmas dinner the next day.

"Clemmie, this is our first Christmas without the children. The house is sure quiet. Don't you think, if it comes down to it, we could make a go of it on the farm?"

"Well, all my life I have wanted to live in Ebony, John. I came to Dallas against my will. But after these nineteen years, I have come to love this big city, and I know I will miss it. Yes, I know that if we do leave, we can make it. But just as I came here against my will, I will leave here against my will."

That started Clemmie to thinking that she would like to write a poem about Dallas—a tribute to the city that she loved, even if she had been mistreated by it many times…even if its superintendents, principals, and other teachers had deemed her unworthy to join their ranks.

On Christmas Day Clemmie got up early and went down to watch Mr. Rude give away clothes to the needy. It was estimated that there were ten thousand people in line waiting to receive their free clothing. Clemmie hoped the newspaper would publish the article she was writing about the spectacular event and its extraordinary man.

That night in bed, as John took Clemmie into his arms, it seemed sweeter than it had in a long, long time. Clemmie thought to herself that she had been somewhat like the person in the fairy tale who cut off her own nose to spite her face. When she was unforgiving to John, she was the one who suffered. Tears ran in her ears as she lay on her back and prayed.

Oh, God, help me to love and respect this man that Thou gavest me. Help me to learn how to love like Thou lovest me, even when I was undeserving and in my sin. Dear Father, watch over our little girls tonight and keep them safe. And Father, in the midst of our present fears and troubles, please show us Thy Face. In Jesus' name, amen.

WALKS WITH US

DALLAS

by Clementine W. Briley

Ho! Dallas, Centennial City!
Born of Texas' rich, black prairie land,
City of majestic skyline
Towering high against smokeless sky.
Splendid City!
With miles and miles of smooth paved streets;
With parked creek ways and homes magnificent
Future city!

With wide expanse of cottages
Where children play
Beautiful City!
With winding creeks and sylvan hills
Where golden elm and crimson oak flaunt autumn glory
Midst the cedars evergreen
Where spring breaks through
In redbud blossoming
Where mockingbird and cardinal sing
And dog-toothed violets grow
Ah! City fair and blest!
Within the memory of some who live
The red man roamed thy prairie
And camped upon thy streams
Blood was shed upon thy soil
And then thy virgin sod was turned
And structures built upon thy base
Men and women who labored with their hands
And walked humbly with their God
Is there more lovely heritage than this?

Nineteen hundred and thirty-one dawned cool, still, and partly cloudy. Bowie School needed Clemmie to substitute early in January, and she got to teach for three weeks, but then it ended. The check for eighty dollars was really a blessing straight from heaven.

Ruth wrote the first part of March that her Aunt Edna had received a very interesting letter from Raleigh Ely. It was in response to a letter concerning a request for a donation for a fence around the cemetery. He said that in flying from Austin to Abilene in his airplane, he had flown low enough over Ebony that he thought he located his mother's grave. And Raleigh was now the head of the Texas Highway Commissioners, just as Clemmie had envisioned!

Why is Raleigh's name always coming up? Clemmie wondered.

Oh, Raleigh, I am so happy for you, that you have lived well, have accomplished much, have had a good family life, a fine home to live in, a table loaded with good food, possibly servants to help your wife, have become well known in Abilene, Austin, and in the State of Texas. But my lot has been so different. Here I am in a small home in Dallas, practically penniless, often knowing hunger, humiliated by my poverty, and now about to be thrown out of the little home. I am beautifully happy for you, Raleigh.

A letter came from Mr. Huvelle saying that May 1 would be the day of foreclosure. The day came and went in peaceful quiet. Foreclosures were generally delayed for months, but Clemmie knew that one day soon action would be taken.

Ruth came home from her year of teaching at Ebony and had many a tale to tell! Incidents from school and from home life that made Clemmie and Grace nearly die laughing. Ruth had to use some of her precious savings to support her parents.

The first part of June, Clemmie saw a notice in the *Dallas Morning News* under marriages that caught her eye.

"Oh, Ruth, come see the paper! Look here under 'Marriages: Lynn Henderson and Beulah Potter, May 31, 1931." How old is Lynn, Ruth?"

"He's twenty-three, Mother. Yes, when I saw Lynn with Beulah one day it looked like he was in love with her. There's something different about Lynn, but maybe he'll be happy. I hope so. I think Beulah is only twelve or thirteen years old."

Ruth left for Denton and summer school at North Texas. And more than that, she left to be with the man she was hoping to marry. She left her parents two dollars.

Mr. Slay sent a letter saying that if no payment was made on the insurance on the house, it would be cancelled on Wednesday, June 10. In answer to fervent prayers sent up by Clemmie and Grace, a letter came from Clemmie's brother on June ninth. When little Grace saw the brown envelope, she began to jump up and down with excitement.

Sure enough, there was a check for seventy dollars. Clemmie and Grace fell on their knees and praised God.

Clemmie went immediately down to Titches Department Store, cashed the check, and paid off the insurance and taxes due on the house. She decided to take the tithe that she always set aside from any income for church and use it to buy John some clothes. She thought the Lord would want her to do that. John looked so ragged, and that made it more difficult to get a job.

Sister Grace, who was pregnant again, sent word that she was going to Ebony on August 8. Clemmie began to try to clean things up the best she could. She told Lynn and Beulah they could live in the house for a while, hoping they would pay some rent.

Clemmie thoroughly enjoyed seeing all her beloved people and places.

Even though living in Ebony is my dream, to go home to the farm to live as defeated, pitiful charity cases makes me feel sick, thought Clemmie. Both Mamma and Callie talked to Clemmie about the possibility of the Brileys moving back to Ebony.

The only house available would be Jim's old house, and the Sheltons were renting it now. It would not win a prize for beauty either, but at least it was structurally sound, large, and in a good location. With some paint and a little fixing up, it could be quite handsome. Yes, that would have to be their back-up plan if the foreclosure actually happened. A letter arrived from John.

Dear Sweetheart–

I Saw Mr. Leon Huvelle to day. And I can get him to waite awhile yet. his Father is in New York. Now-and he Said by the 10th of Sept–we could let him know if we could go on with the place And if not. to move by the 10 or 15th of Oct now I Still do not know what can be done, I know things look bad there for us to move out there and it is quite a problem either way. I am eating one or two meals with Lynn & wife. We failed to get The light bill paid

I don't know what is going to be done people out there cant understand Just how Serious this depression is. If I could make $25 per week–we could make it. with lots of love to you & Sweet Grace: goodby Dear

John

That fall Clemmie got word that her beloved half brother, Alexander Campbell Wilmeth, had died. Clemmie cried, knowing she would miss Campbell and his sage advice. Also the youngest of Papa's first family, Jo Brice Wilmeth had died earlier in the year. Jo was only one year old when his mother, Maria, had died in childbirth.

November 3, 1931, Clemmie made a diary entry:

It seems that we have come to the end of our days at Edge of the Woods. John went this morning out to Bessie's to see about getting them to move us out home. They have offered to move us free, or to pay the man themselves.

John had come back from Bessie and Theo's, his cousins who lived in Garland, about dark on Wednesday, November 4. Clemmie was anxious to know what he had done but was also fearful. She decided that she would wait until he got ready to tell her. They went to prayer meeting, got back, read the paper some, and then John went to his room. Immediately, he came back into the living room, pulling off his shirt. All of a sudden he said, "Mother, could you get ready to go by Saturday?"

To Clemmie, John might as well have said, *"Mother, can you get ready to be hung Saturday?"* considering the effect it had on her. All her being revolted at the thought of being so suddenly and violently ejected from her home, so dear to her heart, and from the city in which she had lived for nineteen years.

"No, I can't!" she answered with vim. Finally, John agreed to give

Clemmie until the following Saturday, November 14. She went to bed with a heavy load upon her heart.

On November 6, the notice of the sale of the house was listed with others in the paper, and the Brileys received a registered letter. Clemmie had expected to write to Mr. Huvelle and tell him they were giving the place up.

She got pen and paper and wrote the letter right then.

2211 Alabama
Dallas, Texas

Mr. Leon Huvelle
7025 Fidelity Union Bldg.
Dallas, Texas

Dear Sir:

I have received your notice this morning , but I had planned to write this letter before receiving it.

I give up the struggle, the place is yours. If ever a poor mortal tried to hold on to her home I did, but it must be best as it is, or else it could not be.

Not one day's work have I had, after all my asking, nor has Mr. Briley had but fifteen days work since May. For some time my neighbors have been supplying us with food. Mr. Briley went out to Reinhart Tuesday to see his people and they have agreed to hire a man with a truck to move us to my brother's farm in Mills County, twenty-five miles south of Brownwood. We are scheduled to leave Dallas Saturday, November 14.

So the place is yours.
Very sincerely,
Clementine Wilmeth Briley

On Saturday, November 7, little Grace burst into the house holding a bouquet of rosebuds and yellow cosmos, fresh from their yard, tied with a pink ribbon. It had not crossed Clemmie's mind that today was her fifty-first birthday.

"Happy Birthday, Mowie!" said Grace with a beaming face as she presented the flowers to her mother. "Mother, here's what you need to write in your diary: 'We have one week left in our home, and we don't know how this will all turn out.' And Mother, I just want to say that I love you from the earth to the sun and back again!"

Clemmie laughed till her side hurt and thought, *Oh, how wonderful to have a little daughter who will go to any extreme to please you.*

Since it appeared that nothing could save the Brileys from losing their home now, Clemmie felt reconciled and calmer and began to think of all the things she wanted to do before she left Dallas. One of the persons Clemmie really wanted to see was the daughter of General Gano, Mrs. McLaurin. She was on the list of famous persons Clemmie had wanted to interview for her journalism class. So a week before they left, she went to 5019 Ross Street and paid a call.

Mrs. McLaurin was in bed, and a polite maid took Clemmie upstairs to her room. She was able to tell Clemmie some wonderful things about her great-great-grandfather. His picture was hanging in the dining room, a beautiful portrait in oil. He was a Baptist preacher in Guernsey, France, when the Catholics began an awful persecution of Protestants.

He had befriended a little Catholic boy, and this boy found out that the Catholics were going to behead Gano that night. The boy begged Gano to give up his religion, to save his own life. Gano refused. Then the boy told him to get in a barrel that was there, and he would nail him up and have a dray wagon come and haul it to a boat that was leaving in the morning for that new country, America.

So they did this, and the boy got on the boat as a stowaway, and when they got well out into the water, he opened up the barrel. They landed at New Rachelle, then went on to New York. There he met

General George Washington. When the war came, Washington chose Gano to be his chaplain. Later, General Gano baptized General Washington.

Mrs. McLaurin's brother went to New York and went to church. It happened to be the one his ancestor founded, and there he found General Gano's picture hanging. He had an artist to come to the church and paint it. That was the very picture that Clemmie saw that day in the dining room.

On Wednesday Clemmie went out in her yard and dug up most of the rose bushes to take to Ebony with her. Thursday and Friday she got all their clothes washed and did nearly all of the packing. John brought boxes from the store.

There was so much to do at the last. The neighbors were very kind. Bessie and Theo, John's cousins, came Friday evening.

"Clemmie, here is twenty dollars for you to pay the truck men. Bessie and I want to help you pack up. We're gonna really miss you." A big tear slid down Theo's cheek. Clemmie believed that God had sent John's cousins to walk with them and to supply their need in this dark hour.

It was close to one p.m. Saturday, November 14, when the loaded truck, the driver and a helper, and the Brileys left Dallas. Clemmie and Grace rode in the cab with the driver. John and the other man rode on the truck bed on top of the piano. It was twenty minutes till four when they arrived at sister Grace's in Fort Worth.

Sister Grace had waited as long as she could and was gone. They loaded the linoleum that was for Mamma's house on the truck and got directions to get out of town from Mr. Ross next door. They ate just before sundown, just before they got out of Fort Worth.

Grace hated the fact that they had to ride in the truck. It was nearly dark when they got to Cresson and very dark at Granbury. The truck driver wanted to sleep there in Granbury. John found out that it would be $1.50 per bed at the hotel. Clemmie asked the bus station man about a boardinghouse, and he called and found a place in the home of a widow where they could all three stay for one dollar.

They drove on to Brownwood the next morning. Clemmie tried to tell the driver about the bad road conditions ahead and lack of gas stations, but he didn't seem to understand. As they got close to Ebony, the truck ran out of gas.

Luckily, Ralph, Clemmie's nephew, came along and let them get gas out of his car. Then the truck stalled on the steep hill, then broke down completely. Everyone had to get out and walk. Jim brought the team of horses but to no avail. During the next two or three days they had to transfer everything from the truck to the wagon, except the piano and the kitchen cabinet. It took two trips to Brownwood to get the parts for the truck. Finally, the truck was able to leave for home on Wednesday afternoon, in the gloaming.

The renters were still in the house that the Brileys would occupy, so they had to put all of their furniture in one bedroom of the house. It had rained hard while the things were still in the truck, but John had borrowed a wagon sheet from Oll and covered everything tightly, so nothing got wet.

Clemmie felt like she was in a daze. She would awake in the night, in the attic of Mamma's house, and think about the view of the woods back in Dallas and cry. She ran across a poem that her friend Whitney Montgomery had written, and it seemed to speak to her condition.

DEAD DREAMS

by Whitney Montgomery

He soothed his dreams to sleep.
Then sadly, went his way,
He sighed, "I'll wake you, darlings,
A more convenient day—
A more convenient day,
When I have gathered gold
To shield me from the storms of life
When I am weak and old."
He plunged into the fight
And won as courage can.
Then to his sleeping dreams
He called, but called in vain,
And wept because he could not wake
His darlings up again.

IN COOL OF DAY

Winter was threatening to arrive in Mills County. Clemmie and Callie found themselves alone in the house since the men and children had gone to Brownwood. The sisters-in-law usually got along well, but they had a few areas of disagreement. One of those concerned the fact that the boys, Ralph and his cousin Bebe, liked to smoke. The subject came up.

"Callie, I don't know how you can be agreeable to the boys smoking cigarettes in this house that Papa built. Why, he must be turning over in his grave. That is so bad for the boys, and then it will lead them into other vile habits, like smoking pipes and chewing tobacco and drinking beer and whiskey."

"Now, Clemmie, I am glad that you have high standards and want our children to do the right thing. But I wonder if you are trying to give advice when it is not really your concern. You don't have any boys to raise, and they are very different from girls, I guarantee you. If I told Ralph he could never smoke in his own house again, then he might up and leave. And it is not my place to tell Bebe what he can do."

"Callie, please forgive me for overstepping my boundaries. I am a guest in your home, and I am trying to give you advice!"

"Clemmie, you are forgiven. It's a hard situation for all of us to be together so long. Your family needs to have your own home again, and maybe it won't be long."

Everyone's nerves were getting frayed with thirteen people and three generations living together in one relatively small house.

On Christmas Eve there was a family gathering and a program put on by the children. Then they sat around the fire and the piano and sang carols. Marie and Lucille made popcorn, and Ruth and Bernice made fudge. Some of the boys played carrom and cards.

Clemmie felt sad to think that modernism was creeping into the family. In her father's own home, where there used to be talk of the Bible and sacred music, there were now dominoes and vile tobacco and talk of dancing.

Christmas Day was close to ideal. Marie moved a long extra table into the dining room, and everyone could eat at the same time. Edna furnished beautiful roses for the centerpiece. Baked chicken, dressing, cranberry sauce, buttered beets, green beans, fruit, celery and nut salad, gravy, bread, butter, coconut cake, fruit cake, whipped cream and bananas made up the menu. The Briley family couldn't help but compare the meal with the meager fare they had had the last few years in Dallas. It was a feast fit for royalty. The living room had a special cleaning the night before by Ruth and Marie, and it was lovely. Everyone got nice presents.

Monday a letter came from John Bateman. Sister Grace had given birth the day after Christmas. It was another fine boy named John Robert. His hair had a reddish look, and he was a long baby, his dad reported. Sister Grace was missed at the farm for Christmas. She always added a lot of life to all the activities.

New Year's Eve held more excitement at the table. Gene was eating his coconut pie with a spoon.

"Gene, you should always eat pie with a fork and never with a spoon," Marie said, and at the same time she swooped down on Gene like a big bird and grabbed his spoon, giving him a fork.

"Then I just won't eat my pie," Gene stated, then clamped his mouth shut.

"Dad, will you let Gene act that way after I worked so hard to make us a nice meal?" Marie chided.

Jim pushed back his chair, grabbed Gene by his arm, and dragged the poor little chap out on the porch where he was properly paddled. The injustice of it all just made Clemmie boil inside.

"Marie, I don't think that was very kind of you to cause Gene to suffer," Clemmie said.

All the girls, including Ruth, nearly fell out of their chairs laughing. Clemmie saw nothing funny about it. Grace began to cry. Then the big girls laughed at Grace. Clemmie felt very disgusted and very alone.

The next day, which was New Year's Day, Ruth and Marie said they were going to tell the Sheltons to move out of the old house so the Brileys could move in.

"Girls, please don't do it. It will hurt them bad. They will move out as soon as they find a place," Clemmie pleaded.

Later, Marie and Ruth came walking kind of prissy-like back from the Sheltons.

"We told them that they needed to move out because there were too many people in this house and everyone was getting fussy," Ruth reported. Then she said they were just kidding; they had only asked them *when* they would be moving out. The Sheltons actually moved out the next day, on Saturday, so Clemmie figured the girls had said something pretty rude.

Even though it was raining pretty hard on Monday, John went down to the house and began scrubbing the floors. He felt the need for some action to happen to get his family situated. Clemmie had many ideas and suggestions, and John was *not* favorable to most of them.

As soon as school was out every day, Ruth helped her parents with the house. She could do almost anything she set her mind to, and usually much faster than Clemmie. She swept off the porch, moving the pile of wood to the back of the house. When the mail came there was something that cheered Clemmie—a letter from the *Brownwood Banner* saying that Clemmie could be their correspondent for the Ebony Community. They would furnish stationary and stamps and would pay twenty-five cents a week. Clemmie was elated and sent her first article that very day.

Clemmie and Ruth got the bedroom and the living room ready for occupancy. Both looked quite nice by the time they got the bed up and the furniture placed, complete with rugs and curtains. Mamma and Callie and Edna helped Clemmie get a start of chickens. Clemmie was overjoyed that Edna gave her a dozen and Mamma and Callie gave her six each. Later, Sister Nell sent seven more little hens over. Jennie Roberts came over with hollyhocks, phlox, petunias, and pomegranates. Tears of joy sprang to Clemmie's eyes as she envisioned the burst of color in her new garden.

Oh yes, another little home is going to happen, Clemmie thought happily.

On January 7, 1932, the Brileys set up housekeeping again. The first meal Clemmie made consisted of sausage, hot biscuits, and tomato soup. It was fun for the family to be alone at last. Of course it wasn't perfect. Now that Ruth was a schoolteacher she had become accustomed to being bossy, and therefore was constantly telling little Grace what to do and correcting her mistakes. Grace would run crying to Clemmie, who would defend her, and John would side with Ruth.

Ruth had a mountaintop mood swing when she opened a brown package addressed to her in O.R.'s now-familiar handwriting. It was an eight-by-ten photograph of O.R. in a simple wooden frame, mailed from Telephone, Texas. Ruth squealed with delight, then immediately began planning to have her picture made in Brownwood to send to O.R.

Yes, and I will have it tinted, Ruth thought to herself. *Oh, Lord, thank you! Thank you for my wonderful man who loves me, and thank you for deliverance from my childhood home that I have outgrown. I hope I will never fuss with my husband and go around crying and feeling sorry for myself. And Lord, may I never know the degree of poverty that has haunted our family for a long, long time. In Jesus' name, amen.*

In mid-January, Clemmie walked over to the original house site. All that remained was the chimney. Crawling through the fence for a closer look, Clemmie saw the hearthstone, washed clean and white by the rains. The memories, and the poignancy of the scene, the chimney rising high above the hearth in the gloaming of the day made Clemmie cry.

John and Jim, Clemmie's husband and brother, were very compatible and fell into a pattern of helping each other with farm chores that had to be done. They terraced the land, trying to prevent soil erosion. One day they brought in dirt and put it all around the house, like Clemmie had wanted. She was delighted!

Jim killed his huge hog the last of January, and everyone helped. The women ground the sausage and rendered the lard, then made soap. Every part of the pig had a use—nothing was wasted. Callie gave Clemmie a shoulder, some tenderloin, sausage, and liver. The slaughtering of a hog was bloody and gruesome to see. The smaller children were sent to the far side of the house so they couldn't see all that was going on. They would sneak around and look at everything. They knew a way to get under the house, and it was one of the high points of the year for the kids. The next morning the Brileys had some fried ham with red gravy and hot biscuits. It tasted so good.

A jersey cow was purchased by the Brileys. She was a beauty: light fawn in color with soft brown eyes. Clemmie named her Rosemary. It was soon discovered that Rosemary gave lots of milk, up to three gallons a day. Mamma gave Clemmie a nice churn with a lid and a dasher. Soon there was plenty of butter and cream. Ah, what luxury that would have been in the Dallas days. How vividly Clemmie remembered the storekeeper saying he would not take a check for butter, but he would cut a pound in half for her. Clemmie never wanted to take butter, milk, and eggs for granted.

In early March, Clemmie read in the Dallas paper that the little Lindbergh boy had been kidnapped from his own bed in their home in New Jersey. The police had no clues, and a massive manhunt was underway. *How tragic!* thought Clemmie. *This is another proof that having money is not necessarily the door to happiness. Look what it has cost the Lindberghs.* The kidnapper had left a note pinned to the window, demanding fifty thousand dollars in ransom for the safe return of the child.

Something wonderful happened for Clemmie—another gift from God, she counted it. Della, one of the two other teachers at the Ebony school besides Ruth, was expecting her first baby and was forced to resign her job. Clemmie was quick to apply, and the trustees soon told her that she had been chosen to finish out the year in Della's place.

Oh, I thank Thee, Lord, for watching over us. Eighty dollars a month will be wonderful income. There were only about two months left in the school year, but Clemmie might keep the job in the fall. The dream of building her house took on new life.

Sure enough, before long Wood Roberts, the main trustee, came to tell Clemmie that they wanted her to keep teaching school for the next year. Just then great big snowflakes began to fall, and it was nearly spring! *Another sign from the Lord, another gift for me,* thought Clemmie. She felt like she would burst with joy. *Oh, God, Thou art blessing us so bountifully, after the hard, cold winter.* Clemmie was the happiest girl in Mills County.

Two days later, Clemmie began teaching school in Ebony. She and Gene, Callie's youngest son, now eleven, walked together through the woods and fields along a path the cattle and children used. It ran directly across the land that Clemmie had inherited from her papa and then across the creek as the crow flies. It took an hour. There were quite a few red birds and other kinds of birds singing and flying, and the earth was white with frost. To Clemmie, it was a very happy walk, and she didn't even feel tired. She and Gene arrived before Ruth and Grace, who rode double on Sceeter, the horse. In mid-May Callie brought down a Dallas paper to show Clemmie that the body of little Charles Lindberg had been found, decomposed. The two women cried at the pathos of the situation and in sympathy for Anne and Charles Lindbergh. Callie thought of her own little Howard, and Clemmie remembered the deaths of so many little ones in the community, including John's little brother, Homer.

Summer arrived in all its suffocating glory. The wildflowers wilted, and the peaches and plums ripened. John dug up potatoes for the first time from his own land. It was a good feeling to him. He liked to smell the warm earth as the shovel pushed down into it and brought up several brown spuds.

The truth was, John was enjoying his farming more than any job he ever had in Dallas. There were roasting ears of corn to be had for the plucking, both green and yellow squash, okra, beans, and black-eyed peas, not to mention great big juicy tomatoes. It was nearly strange how the semi-dry rocky ground could produce a garden rich in vegetables and fruits. The land nearer the river seemed to be much more fertile than land off to the north.

"Mowie, sometimes I miss Dallas, don't you?"

"Yes, Grace, I do. I miss the libraries, and the streetcar, the corner store, the neighbors, the churches, the streets and white houses with flowers outside and water and toilets inside, and children playing on the sidewalks. I miss the State Fair, the night school, the chance to know famous people—lots of things I miss. But there are lots of things here we didn't used to have…a job, a cow, a house with low rent, cousins and my sisters and brother, fresh fruits and vegetables, eggs, cream and butter, Big Hill, the river, the sunrise and sunset, the horses, your daddy has work and likes it…so many things to enjoy."

"But I miss it when the kids would get together with sparklers for the Fourth of July, and the parents would sit out on the porches to be sure we didn't start a fire. And we would all catch lightning bugs in quart jars and they would be like lanterns on the porch."

"Grace, the next time we go to Fort Worth, how would you like to go and visit your friend Virginia? I think we can arrange that."

"Oh yes, Mother, I would love it! Isn't it funny that we always want what we don't have, or what we used to have, and when we had it, we didn't want it! I have always wanted to live out here in Ebony. Now that I *have* to, I miss Dallas a lot."

"Ah, my little daughter, now you are getting wise."

On July 11, Grace turned eleven years old. Clemmie actually forgot it at first, just like Callie had forgotten Gene's birthday, but Grace reminded her mother early on.

"Mother, I call this my 'golden birthday' because I am the same age as the date I was born. I am eleven on the eleventh. People only have one golden birthday."

"Bless your little heart, honey! We are going to make you a party. You make an angel food cake, and I'll make some grape juice with the grapes I picked yesterday. We'll invite Gene and Lucille to come.

And Grandma and Aunt Callie and Unnie and Aunt Edna and Uncle Oll."

When the mail came there was a package for Grace from Ruth containing cute pajamas. Mamma gave Grace seventy-five cents, and Aunt Mattie sent one dollar. Clemmie ordered new shoes and stockings and bloomers from the Sears catalog for her little daughter.

John's cousins from Dallas, Bessie and Theo Jennings, came to visit. Theo asked John if he would like to buy his car. He wanted two hundred dollars for it, and it was a nice Ford sedan, gray and reconditioned like new. That night Clemmie and John talked it over and decided that they would buy the car. It would be wonderful to have a good car of their own again. The "Whoopie" they had been using was the old 1916 car the Wilmeths had bought, and it was worn out. Ruth had said she would put in sixty dollars on the new one. Clemmie had seventy-five dollars saved from her first voucher. Then they could pay the rest when her second voucher came. Later, Mamma agreed to pay fifteen dollars on the car.

Some of the family got to meet Ruth's beau the next week. Sister Grace had a meal in Fort Worth for Bernice's graduation, and Ruth and O.R. were there. Grace reported to her sister that he was certainly a well-mannered young man, and she said he seemed to really like Ruth. He even kept his arm around her chair while he ate! And Ruth wore her organdy dress and looked very pretty.

Rumor had it that cotton was going up. Even eggs were up to fifteen cents a dozen, and cattle were up. Farmers in Mills County were beginning to smile. However, Clemmie read in the Dallas paper that over 11 million people were without work. Franklin Delano Roosevelt was campaigning with this promise "to restore this country to prosperity." Previously, he had made a statement about war against four horsemen.

"I am waging a war in this campaign, a frontal attack, an onset, against the Four Horsemen of the present Republican leadership:

the Horsemen of Destruction, Delay, Deceit, and Despair." Clemmie hoped he could defeat those horsemen, for she had seen their faces and knew them well.

Most of Callie's children were leaving home for college. Little Grace went up to her Aunt Callie's and reported to her mother: "Aunt Callie seems so lonesome. Everything's so quiet. Usually Aunt Callie and Bernice are rattling just as hard as they can rattle, and Lucille is making bright remarks in between."

John sold the spring calves to a Mr. Durham. Five steers brought thirteen dollars each, and one heifer was sold at fourteen dollars. John bought a full-blooded heifer from Jim with sixteen dollars of the money.

Mr. and Mrs. Burkett visited the Wilmeths in October. He gave Clemmie a copy of a long paper he had written called "Pecan Development in Texas." Clemmie found it fascinating to know such an important man in person. She only wished her papa were still living to converse with Mr. Burkett. He had been in Ebony once before, while Papa was still alive. Mr. Burkett was complimentary of all the pecan grafting that Papa had done.

School started again on October 17. The car was wonderful for the trips to school, and Clemmie and Ruth didn't have to leave home nearly so early and were back home much sooner. The kids seemed better behaved this year, too.

On November 7, Clemmie had her fifty-second birthday. She decided it was the "least celebrated" of any birthday she had ever had. She wrote in her diary: "Swiftly pass the sands of time."

November 8, 1932, was Election Day. The little community turned out to vote, with every single vote being cast for Franklin Roosevelt. The next day, they heard that he had won by a landslide. In fact, he had carried all but six states. It was a time of deep depression, of long bread and soup lines in the cities, of bank failures and farm foreclosures, and tremendous unemployment. So much hope was pinned on Roosevelt, whose wife was the niece of the beloved Teddy

Roosevelt. FDR had promised to revive prosperity on farms, to renew the railroads, to regulate banks, and to develop public works. He promised he would see to it that no American would starve.

On the evening of November 23, after a full day at school, the three Briley women started for Fort Worth in their gray Ford. Little Grace was plenty scared of having either her mother or her sister at the wheel. With only minor problems, they arrived safely in Fort Worth. Ruth went on to Denton, where she met O.R., and they went on to Telephone to be with the Mitchell family. Ruth was appalled to see every love letter she had written to O.R. on display in the hall tree as she entered the big house with gingerbread trim. Other than that, Ruth said she had the time of her life.

It worked out for little Grace to spend time with her friend Virginia. Early Sunday morning, the little family group began the trip home, stopping for church in Granbury. They reached home before dark with no car trouble. No one was as relieved as John when he saw that gray car rolling around the bend. He had been very worried about Clemmie's lack of experience as a driver. Besides, he had been lonesome.

Clemmie's sister Edna came over with her face beaming. Her daughter, Opal, oldest grandchild of Mamma and Papa, along with her husband, Austin Cawyer, were proud to announce the arrival of Edna Beth Cawyer, born on December 7. Opal was the only child of Edna and Oll. Opal and Aus were both teachers. Often Austin would be the principal of the school with Opal as a primary teacher. Clemmie thought they made such a wonderful pair—both being so dedicated to Christ and His church as well as to children.

The Wilmeths and Brileys ate together on Christmas Day. Marie was in charge of the meal, since that was her gift. They had turkey, dressing, and all the good things that go with it.

O.R. sent Ruth a pretty cameo necklace and matching long ear screws. Clemmie hoped that Ruth would not wear the ear screws, but she did. Ruth got to fulfill her yearlong dream to send O.R. a good picture of herself, tinted and in a beautiful easel frame.

Beautiful dawn! Beautiful day! John went to town with Brother to take Marie. Ruth cleaned house and cooked. Grace ironed, I worked all day on mattress ticking. Got only one finished. And so our first year ends in the shanty on Sunrise Hill. Good night, Old Year, you have not been unpleasant. There have been many rich blessings along with the difficult things. This coming year will be even better. I want to walk with Thee, God, in the cool of the day, on my Big Hill.

THROUGH THE WINTER
HARD AND CRUEL

Ruth and Clemmie finished the third month of teaching at Ebony School with only three and a half months to go. Ruth felt ecstatic with her wedding date approaching. It was hard to keep her mind on Spanish and mathematics and English literature, knowing she would be Mrs. O.R. Mitchell within five months. She had several garments she was sewing at home and was more interested in cooking than ever before.

The lovemaking part of marriage was something Ruth was anticipating with pleasure, unlike her Victorian mother. She wanted to buy some pretty undergarments and gowns.

Ruth's co-teacher and good friend Mirla had been married for nearly a year. Ruth loved to hear what Mirla would tell her about being married, especially the lovemaking. The two young women had some time at noon to take their lunches and go off together, away from the kids, and make a picnic under a tree.

February brought the coldest spell on record, with the temperature in the classroom down as low as five degrees before the big potbellied stove was started. Some days there would only be one or two pupils. Surprisingly, church attendance went up some, and John conducted the Bible school lesson for the first time. Grace told him that her Aunt Callie said he was a good teacher.

"I guess I ought t' have been a preacher, though there was a long time when I didn't go to church," John responded to his thirteen-year-old daughter. Grace looked surprised.

Clemmie overheard John's statement and nearly passed out. It was the first time John had ever expressed any thought like that—"should have been a preacher." *Why, whoever heard of a preacher who stayed home on Sundays! But I do feel real proud of him that he taught a good class. Perhaps there shall be compensation yet for me,* thought Clemmie.

On the fourth day of March, Clemmie saw that ty-tys were leafing and tears came to her eyes.

Oh, spring has broken through again! And my firstborn child will be married before summer. It doesn't seem so long ago that I was at Ochiltree planning my own wedding. Oh, Lord, let Ruth find happiness with her Mitchell man.

And surely it was the most magnificent spring in memory. Clemmie knew that there were people who didn't believe in God. Maybe not many in this part of Texas, but she read a lot and knew all about Darwin and his theories.

They must not even see what is happening, or they would be forced to believe. Why, trees that you would have sworn were dead long ago begin to sprout little green leaves, right out of the dried-up bark. Birds that disappeared when the first cold norther came all return the same day. The very same fat robin that nested in your yard returns to inspect her nest and see if it needs patching for the new little ones, soon to be hatched from blue-speckled eggs that she will lay.

Spring flew by, but something happened that really made May 10 unforgettable—a devastating tornado. All day the wind had blown hard, and things looked smoky and strange. In the gloaming, the whole sky looked cloudy and threatening, and lightning flashed everywhere. The wind blew hard against the clouds from the northwest.

John wanted to go up to Callie's to the storm cellar. Clemmie kept thinking they might go eventually, but maybe it wasn't necessary, and there were already a lot of people up there. There were clouds in every direction. Suddenly, the wind changed to the north and a mist of rain came with it. Clemmie thought the worst had passed. Just then it struck with such a fury that it seemed it would wreck the house, and fear gripped the four Brileys.

They hovered near the front door in case they needed to make a run for the cellar. Hail, lightning, thunder, and torrential downpour of rain all happened at once. The wind blew something awful for a long, long time. Finally, it quieted down, and Grace and Ruth went to bed. After a half hour had passed, John decided to retire, and after a few more minutes, Clemmie also turned in. The next morning the news began to come that many buildings in the community were destroyed, including the schoolhouse, all the church buildings, and many homes and barns. The good neighbors all pitched in and helped each other restore their buildings.

Ruth talked to Brother Hoover about coming out to Ebony on June 3 to perform her wedding. He agreed to do it.

Finally, the gala event of Ruth's wedding began, and the guests all arrived. June 3 dawned clear and bright. Clemmie was up before dawn, thinking of all she needed to do on her daughter's wedding day. She began working on the net sleeves for Ruth's dress, condemning herself for putting that off until the last minute. Ruth got breakfast for O.R., Grace, her daddy, and herself. She wanted so much for O.R. and her daddy to get to know each other and to get along well. They had a little trouble finding a subject of mutual interest but ended up talking about cars and baseball and President Roosevelt.

Ruth made lunch, and then O.R.'s sister, Maude, made Ruth and O.R. go for a drive in the car while she washed the dishes. Clemmie was very impressed with this jolly, industrious, and generous sister of O.R.'s.

Ruth and O.R. went up to Callie's around two p.m. and practiced walking in for the ceremony and decided where they would stand. Then they drove up to Aunt Nell's, who had invited the couple to spend their wedding night in her house. She and son Ernest would sleep at Edna's, so the newlyweds could be alone. Sister Grace decorated Callie's house with wild daisies and mountain pinks. She put them everywhere, helped by all the girls, and the effect was stunning.

About four p.m. Brother Hoover arrived from Brownwood. O.R. talked to him about the charges for a wedding. He assured him there was no set charge, just anything that O.R. thought his bride was worth, he said jokingly. O.R. paid him two dollars.

The punch was put together by Bernice and Dutch. At 4:30 Sister Grace began singing "At Dawning." Then she sat at the piano and played "The Wedding March." The groom stood by the fireplace in the front room with Brother Hoover. Ruth entered on her papa's arm, looking radiant in her white dress with the new net sleeves. She carried a bouquet of roses the girls had made. John looked handsome in his new gray suit. Brother Hoover tied the knot, and everyone had punch and cake. About seven thirty the bride and groom drove over to Aunt Nell's. It was right before the gloaming.

The house was small with a low roof. There was a bedroom, a living room, a small kitchen, and a screened-in porch. Aunt Nell had fixed everything nice, with several food items and a turned-down bed with pretty sheets. Ruth and O.R. felt very happy but very nervous. It was the first sexual experience for both of them, and they had anticipated it for a long time. They began with long kisses and hugs, then undressed each other and got in bed. Ruth felt so strange to be doing this, like it was wrong somehow; but she knew it was right and wanted very much to be all that O.R. needed and wanted her to be, and she thought her sex drive was strong for a woman.

Unfortunately, Ruth had the same problem on her bridal night that her mother had, but she handled it more graciously, explaining to O.R that she should have seen a doctor. One or two of her married friends had warned her that virgins did not always have an easy time of it. O.R. said he was very glad she was a virgin, and he was also, but that men were not "sealed for safety" like women. He said they would have the rest of their lives to make love. He went on to say that they would keep trying, and before long they would be experts at the event the Lord had planned. It was not something that Ruth could talk to her mother about, unfortunately, or she would have heard a similar story. They both knew that the problem would be solved in a few days. Ruth did some extra praying, and it wasn't long until she knew she was normal.

Before many days passed, Ruth became quite a lover and found that "wifely duty" was very enjoyable for her. Later, Ruth would entertain the female relatives, telling them how much she enjoyed being married and that O.R. was a "hot number."

Not long after the wedding, Clemmie received a letter from Dr. Harry Locker. He wanted her to start a petition to get the new Brownwood-San Saba Highway through the Ebony community. He knew that Judge Ely was a childhood friend of Clemmie's and thought perhaps a letter from her to Ely would carry some weight.

How odd and how stimulating, thought Clemmie, *to be asked to write to Raleigh after all these years!* It was a request she could not refuse. Yet she knew better than to ask John if he thought it was a good idea.

She waited until John and Grace were asleep and then stayed up until three a.m. carefully composing the letter, thinking long and hard about her wording. Early the next morning, Grace and Lucille took the letter to the little store and mailed it. They bought some fish and took it home for Clemmie to fry for breakfast.

As Clemmie dipped the clean fish in cornmeal and then into the hot oil, she felt so extraordinary. She had trouble realizing that she had actually written to Raleigh. What would he think when he got the letter? Would it stir up sweet memories, or would he answer it in a real business-like way, or maybe she would never hear from him at all. She hoped things would work out where John would not know about the letter. He would not understand that it was strictly business and would bring up stuff from the past.

Just as Clemmie and John arrived at church on September 3, before Clemmie could get out of the car, someone put two letters in her lap. One was from an old friend, and the other was from the State Highway Department. Clemmie's heart jumped when she saw the return address, knowing it was from Raleigh. It was the first time he had written to her in over twenty-four years. Of course it would be in answer to the letter she had written him concerning the paving of the highway from Brownwood to San Saba.

Clemmie kept the letter hidden until long after lunch, than stole away to her favorite spot on Big Hill. She withdrew it from inside her dress, carefully opened it, and unfolded the pages.

State Highway Commission

W.R. Ely, Chairman
D.K. Martin, Commissioner
Gibb Gilchrist, State Engineer
Mrs. Clementine Briley
Ebony, Texas

My dear Friend,

Your letter of August 24th addressed to me at Austin was forwarded to my home address, Abilene. I have had many appeals for highways but none quite so strong as this. If I consulted my judgment I would say no, but if I listened to sentiment I think I would favor the designation. Your beautiful letter brings back vivid memories of the long ago, and I love that area quite as much, I am sure, as you do. I have not visited there for more than twenty-four years (with the exception of your papa's funeral) but I frequently fly over and recognize all the old familiar places.

It is such a secluded and "Happy Valley" sort of place that it looks like a shame to give it better connection with the outside world, but I am willing to give your request most careful and serious consideration and if I can bring myself to the point where I think it will be a wise expenditure for the State at large, I certainly will intercede with my associates in behalf of the project. I assure you that at any time a highway should be designated from Brownwood to San Saba, I will insist on making the location on the route you desire. That would be small recognition of the fine friendship I have enjoyed with you since our childhood.

I am happy that you have returned to your old home. It makes very little difference after all where one lives and your letter is evidence that you have found a lot of happiness and contentment in that particular spot. I note also that you are teaching, and the community is certainly fortunate in having you to guide its youth.

With very best wishes, I am,
Sincerely your Friend,

W.R. Ely

Clemmie read the letter over and over. To her it seemed like a dream that she really had this letter from Raleigh after all these years. Twenty-four years, to be exact, on this very hill, was her last contact with Raleigh (except for the two minutes at her papa's funeral). She sat nearly motionless in her special place, dreaming and living again sweet memories, enjoying a beautiful reality that lifted her up and made her better, for this was a once-in-a-lifetime letter.

As darkness approached, she put the letter inside the envelope and stuffed it inside her blouse. Clemmie was about to turn fifty-three, and suddenly she felt like a young girl again. She seemed to be walking on fluffy clouds as her feet hit the sandstone rocks and withered grass and stickers as she descended the hill. There was practically no light left, and Clemmie knew she would be in for a fuss with John when she reached the house. But what did it matter? Did anything else in the world matter now that Raleigh had written to her, and such a complimentary and sweet letter?

Oh, Lord, I do not understand all this, but I feel that Thou hast given me a little sweetness to lighten the burden of my heart as I go from one weary day to another. Lord, I am reminded of Abigail in Bible times whose own husband had grown surly, yet she remained with him, and Thou intervened and gave her the handsome King of Israel to be her bridegroom.

John was in a good humor that evening and didn't ask Clemmie about her whereabouts. She breathed a prayer of thanksgiving into her pillow that night. It was a full week before Clemmie wrote back to Raleigh.

My dear Friend:

Your letter reached me and left a kind of a happy, exultant feeling in my heart. I see that success has not spoiled you. I am glad that childhood memories are still dear to your heart. It pleased me very much that you should think of our quiet abiding place as a "Happy Valley."

After your letter I almost felt, too, that it might be a shame to give it better connection with the outside world. But I was in Dr. Locker's office Friday, and he asked me to write you again and state some more facts to you concerning why some of us think we should have this highway.

It is this way with us, Raleigh. We are in the extreme west corner of Mills County. We do all of our trading at

Brownwood, hence Mills County sees no inducement to work our roads. Our roads here are never worked unless some private individual fixes some place that becomes impassable.

To get a state highway seems our only chance to get a road. If you don't remember how bad these roads are you just ought to come down here and ride over them in an auto. I am always afraid that some rainy morning I'll be unable to reach the schoolhouse. If I cross at the wide rock-bottomed crossing at the Hosea field, I bog down. If I go to the other crossing, the water is too deep and the banks too steep and slick.

And then we get tired of everlastingly bumping over rocks and gullies and going up and down steep sliding hills. We hardly need a road so wide and big as a state highway must be. But don't you think our "Happy Valley" would be happier if we had a good road? And do you see any other way than the highway route for us to get one?

Most sincerely your friend,
Clementine Wilmeth Briley

That same day John and Clemmie went into Brownwood. John let Clemmie out at Daniel Baker College. Mrs. Craig, the registrar, told her she had two majors: one in English and one in education. She had twenty-four semester hours in English, and thirty hours in education. She had minors in math, Latin, and Greek. In all she had 150 hours of professional training.

Clemmie happily reported all the information about her college hours to John.

"Clemmie, I'm so proud of you. I'm a-shamed of myself for not gettin' more ejucation, but it just seemed like I always needed to work hard so I couldn't be studyin' an all. But I'm sure proud of you an Ruth an Grace for gettin' your studies an all."

Clemmie got busy and started the petition around in favor of the new highway like Dr. Locker had suggested. Everything came into place for Clemmie to ride to Brownwood, then on to Abilene with the men to see Judge Ely about the highway the first week in October. Clemmie's heart was beating in her throat. John was not the least bit happy.

"The very idea of neglectin' your home and going off with a bunch of stags on account of that silly highway!" was John's reaction. Finally, he reluctantly relented.

"I guess you can go then, but I think it's awful silly."

Clemmie's heart leaped for joy quietly inside her body.

Clemmie worked on her clothes until midnight. Then she took her bath in the tub in the kitchen. It was two a.m. when she lay down on her bed, and she was up at four thirty. John let her drive the car to Reide Hayne's house. She wrote the following account of the trip in her diary.

I nearly froze it was so cold. We picked up Dr. Locker in Brownwood and went on to Abilene, arriving about 10 a.m.

I went into the Grace Hotel and freshened myself in the fancy ladies' room. I sat down in one of the soft, fancy chairs in the hotel lobby, to wait for Reide. I felt somewhat shaky and afraid. I wanted to see Raleigh, yet I was afraid to.

We were soon at the Alexander Bldg. Judge Courtney Gray was outside to welcome me. Others of the Brownwood Chamber of Commerce were waiting there. We all went up and Reide piloted me to Raleigh's office.

Then suddenly, there he was! He did not look old and stout as I expected, but he was still an Apollo, though slightly gray. To me he is still my ideal of a man as to looks. And there is something so sweet about Raleigh. The years have not taken it away from him. Enemies may falsely accuse him, but to me the Raleigh I know has one of the loveliest personalities I have ever known in a man. I cannot have a harsh thought toward Raleigh.

I wish I could have talked to him more. He seemed to want to talk to me and he asked me to go home with him. I wanted to go, but he had another bunch to meet right after us and I didn't know whether or not he meant it. Just about this time the door opened and Dallas Scarborough, who had been my pupil back in Indian Creek long ago, came in. He held my hand as though he were extremely glad to see me. He asked me why I was there.

Raleigh said, "She wants a road."

"Well, if she wants a road you give it to her," said Dallas with vim.

Raleigh said, "I would come much nearer giving her a road than any of these men who were in here."

Then Dallas said, "Miss Clemmie, I am on the way to the Lion's Club. Come and go with me." I did and the meal and fellowship were wonderful.

It seems like a happy dream that I have again seen Raleigh, felt his warm handclasp, and looked again into his eyes. Dear Father, I do not understand it but I thank Thee for this privilege, and for this glorious day.

A week later, a short letter from Raleigh arrived. The letter stated that he would like to come down to Ebony soon to see if he thought they needed a road beginning at Brownwood. Clemmie thought long and hard about whether she should answer the letter, when all along she knew that she would write that very night.

She tried to be very careful with her selection of words, not wanting to say anything that could bring any regret. She put it in her purse with another letter she had written to Ruth and wanted to get them both in the mail the following day.

Fairly early Saturday morning, John was looking in Clemmie's purse and saw the letter. Without letting Clemmie know that he had seen the letter, he tested her.

"Who were you writing to last night, Clemmie?"

"To Ruth," Clemmie replied innocently.

It was noon when John exploded. He was furious. He told Clemmie that he had asked her that question to see if she would answer truthfully or lie. "Now I've caught you, and I will never have confidence in you as long as I live."

Clemmie wanted to melt into the wooden plank floor. The worst part of all, Clemmie thought, was the fact that Grace was there to witness the battle royal.

"It's not enough that you wanna be the boss and even have our farm land in your name only, but now you're sneakin' around, writin' love letters to a married man an' chasing after him like a wanton woman."

"Well, you can go and put the land in your name. Just get the papers fixed up, and I will sign them," Clemmie conceded in her misery, starting to cry.

Later, at the supper table, Grace tried to defend her mother.

"Daddy, you should not talk so mean to Mother. She is only trying to be a good wife and a good mother."

"Honey, you're too young to know now, but when you're older, you'll understand how your mother has disgraced all o' us...you, me, herself—all th' family." His words cut Clemmie like a knife, and she cried and moaned aloud for a long time.

Clemmie and John barely had time to recover from the event before there was another invitation for yet another trip to see Judge Ely. Clemmie first heard of the second invitation to meet with the Highway Commission by way of Dr. Locker telling John and then through her brother, Jim. She decided to get John to go talk to Dr. Locker about it. The word was they would go to Austin with the meeting being at three p.m. on Monday, November 20.

Clemmie thought she should not go in view of the fact that

school had begun and the larger fact that John would again end up enraged. John, Clemmie, and Grace went to town to take care of their business. Clemmie had become aware of the fact that she had no coat to wear if she should get to go to Austin. Grace wanted her mother to get herself a pretty new coat and began to urge Clemmie to go to the dry goods store. They found a lovely dark blue cloth coat for $19.95. Clemmie didn't dream that they could spend that much for a coat. John wanted to be a man who dressed his family nicely.

"Clemmie, I want you to buy that blue coat for yourself," John stated emphatically.

Later, John and Clemmie saw Chester Harrison concerning the trip to Austin. He said he thought Clemmie's being along might help influence the Highway Commission in favor of the paved road. Clemmie quietly thanked God for Mr. Harrison and thought he was a prince among men. John began to be willing to let Clemmie make the trip.

The next morning, Sunday, Grace discovered that the beautiful new coat had been chewed by rats! It had been hung in the only closet that was open in places to the outside. One corner of the collar was almost riddled in two. Clemmie cried and then determined to darn it the very best that she could.

The little family hustled on to church. Brother Green preached that morning. Clemmie sat tense in her desk chair, her mind racing with thoughts of trying to repair the coat. Her stomach began to churn. Gas bubbled through her intestines. Cold sweat popped out all over her, and she felt deathly sick. She made her way outside to the outdoor toilet. The smells increased her sick feeling. She knew she would not even be able to teach school the next day, much less make the trip to Austin and get to see Raleigh. She had been living in a dream world.

After sitting about ten minutes on the toilet seat in the outhouse, she began to feel better again. Yes, she would live through this. But wasn't this some type of warning that she could not stand much more?

"John is killing me!" she said aloud.

By midafternoon Clemmie had repaired the coat and thought it looked fairly good. She had packed her little valise with clean underwear, another blouse, a gown, her comb, toothbrush, powder, and the lip-rouge.

Clemmie kissed John on the lips and asked him if he would not be mad at her.

"No, I am not mad at you," John replied. "I have buried the hatchet."

Clemmie rode into Brownwood with Lucille, who was finishing high school there. She let Clemmie have her bed in the little house where she boarded, and she slept on the floor. Clemmie awoke at 1:30 a.m. and could not get back to sleep. She got up at 3:15. At four a.m. Mr. Pierce and Reide came for her.

It was exciting to Clemmie to be on the highway so early in the morning, heading to the capital city of Texas, where she would again see Raleigh for the second time in the last six weeks. The little group stopped for breakfast in Lampasas. Clemmie was aware that she had only a dollar in her purse and only got a cup of hot tea, saying she had eaten a little before she left. Mr. Pierce insisted he wanted to pay the whole amount.

Back on the road, Clemmie had a feeling of exuberance, like she was a carefree girl again. *I haven't felt like this in a long time,* she thought to herself.

The hearing was set for three p.m. Clemmie and Reide got to see Raleigh for about three minutes before the session began. Clemmie felt her heart speed up as those sincere eyes met hers. His hand felt soft and warm as he squeezed hers. She so hoped they would have time later to talk, but it didn't turn out that way.

The little group couldn't even wait to hear the report. They left Austin at eighteen minutes till four. They stopped again at Lampases for supper. At nine p.m. they were back at Brownwood and were back home in Ebony by ten thirty p.m.

That same afternoon back in Brownwood, John had gone to town to get some feed for his cows. When he walked into the store, his friend Jim was holding a white short-haired puppy that looked to be about 4 months old.

"John, I bet you need a good dog on your own farm. I'm trying to get rid of this one, part Boxer, but undesirable because he is white. I know he's smart and will make a good farm animal. What say?"

"Well, Jim, I do need a good dog. How much will ya take for him?

"He's free, John. I know he'll have a good master in you."

When Clemmie came in that night, she told John all about the trip. Then she heard the yelps of the pup on the back porch. "What is that, John?"

"Clemmie, I've been needin' me another dog since we gave away Jack in Dallas. Today Jim at the feed store offered to give me this'n. He's still just a pup, and I reckon he'll make a fine farm dog. I call him 'Sport.' He needs a little training and he'll do fine."

Clemmie went to the porch and looked at Sport. He cocked his head to the side and wagged his sleek tail. "He doesn't look like much, John, but we did need a dog. I hope you'll look after him, John. I've already got more than I can handle."

"I plan to, wifey. I'm gonna take good care of Sport. He'll be fine. You'll see."

— — — — — — — —

Thanksgiving and Christmas came and went. Clemmie finished the year with this diary entry:

Day after Christmas, 1933

Diary, there are many things I would like to say to you since there is no one else ready to receive them or to advise with me concerning them. Many things trouble me. Things that I should act upon if I knew which way to act. The future of the church, my house I want to build, where Grace shall go to school, how to get along with John in a gracious manner and yet cling to my own ideals of honesty and right living. Dear Father, help me, I pray, for the long winter is hard and cruel, and I long for Thy Spring.

WE WERE
BEATEN DOWN AND BLUE

On a Sunday afternoon in January, Clemmie walked with John and Sport over to their own land to feed the cows. Sport stuck to his master like glue. They took advantage of the time and place to plan just where their future house would be. They couldn't reach a decision. Clemmie felt the excitement of thinking they might spend Christmas of 1934 in their very own little white house on their own land. It would be one of her dearest dreams coming true.

On Friday of that week, a letter arrived from Raleigh. Fortunately, it reached Clemmie without John's knowledge. With racing heart she followed her usual course and took the letter to the top of Big Hill, in the gloaming. It was about the highway and a follow-up on Raleigh's mention that he needed to come down and actually see the road they were discussing. Raleigh suggested that the best time might be in the spring, when the possibility of bad weather was past. Would Sunday, April 15, be a date that Clemmie could reserve to meet an old friend?

Clemmie's heart jumped for joy at the thought of such a meeting, and she resolved that the little problems of her life would be as nothing given the great anticipation of that day. She knew she couldn't afford to let John know, yet neither could she tell him a lie.

Ah, two dreams during this one weary week of January: my home to be built in Ebony, and my first love to meet me in Ebony. It was enough to get Clemmie through the darkness of winter and the pettiness of her life. Yes, she certainly could keep that date clear to meet with a friend she so admired and had not talked to privately in the last twenty-five years!

Winter went slowly by, and things were starting to happen. John had onions, potatoes, and peas planted. Several of the cows had their calves; in fact, there were six little calves, two of them half Jersey. And on the last day of March, Clemmie and John went to Goldthwaite and saw Mr. Horton about building a house on their land

Finally, April arrived. Clemmie felt a surge of new life flowing into her veins just as the Ebony countryside turned into a perfect fairyland of beauty. In another week the bluebonnets would color the Ebony hills, reminding Clemmie of that spring so long ago when the family had first moved to their desolate acreage. That was 1888… forty-six years ago…and although so much had changed, the hills were still exactly the same.

There had hardly been an hour in the day since Clemmie got the letter from Raleigh that she had not thought of him and their meeting that was now so near. Clemmie had the day all planned out in her mind.

Sunday, April 15, arrived. The world was still turning that morning. Clemmie awoke before dawn and did the chores, and John marveled at how sweet she was, how good the breakfast seemed. They got off for church earlier than usual and avoided any disagreements. Clemmie had trouble keeping her mind fixed on Brother Green's lesson; in fact, she later wondered what the subject had been.

They got back home earlier than usual, and Clemmie served John some canned roast, cabbage, green beans, and new potatoes. She had even made his favorite lemon jelly cake. John was pleasantly surprised. She told John she wanted to check on one of the new calves and perhaps make the final decision on where the house should be.

Clemmie went upstairs to her bedroom and got out the dress that she liked best. It reminded her of the way she had dressed as a girl. It was a blue-checked jumper with a white organdy blouse. It showed off her small waist. She had some white "Mary Jane"-type shoes with rounded toes and a strap across the top of the foot.

Clemmie worked a good while with her hair, pulling a little toward the front. She backcombed the crown to give a little height there. She applied just a hint of pink lipstick and a tiny poof of "Evening in Paris" perfume. She packed the faded green coverlet in her cloth bag, along with two slices of the lemon jelly cake. Thankfully, John had wandered off to the back lot when she quietly let herself out the front door. She walked as fast as she could until she was out of sight of both their house and Jim and Callie's, hoping her mother was not looking out the window and that Sport would not bark at her. Her heart felt as happy and light as when she had been a girl. Within ten minutes she arrived at her own little acreage. She looked to the left at the spot where Indians had lived so long ago. Coming to a clearing, she could just visualize her pretty white house, facing east toward the rising sun, with a beautiful view toward the west. The barn would be on the north side of the house. She could even see a windmill across the creek at the Griffin place. *Yes,* Clemmie decided that moment, *this is the place we will build our home!*

The time was marching on. She headed for the cemetery and schoolhouse, walking so fast her shins ached. Back on the little rocky road she descended the steep hill and could see Buffalo Creek ahead.

Clemmie's father had baptized many a person near this crossing in years gone by.

She began to run to try to get to her destination before Raleigh arrived. Finally, she reached the end of the lane on the east of the Griffin property, crossed the road to Goldthwaite, and ascended the hill toward the cemetery. The sandstone rocks bruised her feet, and grass burrs caught in her stockings. Finally, she could see the school and thought she saw a new-looking black car. Sure enough, Raleigh had beaten her there.

He had spotted her and began to walk fast to meet her. Clemmie felt her knees going weak when she saw that still thick hair blowing slightly, those sincere blue eyes gazing at her, that wonderful mouth smiling broadly, and that large hand waving a happy "hello."

"Raleigh! I'm so sorry I'm late! I wanted to be here before you!"

"Clemmie, you're right on time. Besides, I had the advantage of a car under me!"

As they met, they instinctively embraced, and Clemmie surprised herself by starting to cry. Raleigh immediately felt embarrassed at this show of emotion and took a nicely ironed white handkerchief from the pocket of his tweed coat.

He kept his arm around Clemmie for support as her small body shook with sobs. It was two or three minutes before she could be sure of her voice.

"Oh, Raleigh, please forgive me. It's just that it has been so long since I've had this chance to be with you, alone like this, and I am really happy to see you. Seeing you takes me back to the way things used to be."

"Well, I hope those are tears of joy, Clementine. Let's go sit under that tree and talk about the old days."

"So this is where you are teaching school?" Raleigh began. "Now, this building was built around 1913, wasn't it?"

"That's right. You and I went to the old Reeves' school together… when we still called our community 'Buffalo.'"

"I see an old pump there…ah, what memories. How many times I walked to school during those four years we lived out here. And as soon as school let out, in the warm weather, we'd head for the old swimming hole right down the road."

"Yes, that land is now the Thompson place. If you like we could go up there in your car in a little while, so you can see it."

"Let's do, Clemmie. First, tell me a little about your life. I know you have the two girls, Ruth and Grace. Ruth got married last year, didn't she? And your young one must be about thirteen years old… about the age you were when we had so much fun in these hills!"

"You are good with dates and ages, Raleigh! I know you have two grown children, W.R. Junior and your daughter, Eloise. When my niece, Opal, was in Austin at a teachers meeting, she told me she saw the name 'Eloise Ely' on a dorm door. Your son is following in your footsteps, I hear. I know you are proud of your children."

"Yes, Clemmie, they are two fine young people. Clemmie, let me get personal. Have you been happy in your marriage? Are things going well for you and John?"

"Well, Raleigh, I know that John and I love each other, but we argue quite a bit, and he says things that are very hurtful to me. We were in love when we married, and for the first four or five years we treated each other with kindness. I tried to overlook things that might have been hurtful to me. John has had trouble making a living. He is not lazy, just did not have a chance to get an education like you did, and, of course, times have been hard for a lot of people the last few years. Have you and Lucy been compatible, and have your years together been good?"

"I would say that my life with Lucy has been very gratifying. She keeps our home in fine order and enjoys being involved in many clubs and charities. She is just what I needed, and we seem to work together well. We do not argue much at all, although we do not always agree on everything."

"I really wish John and I could be best friends. I would give nearly anything if we could get along with each other and even have a good time together. I am afraid our disagreements are nearly every day, and often in front of Grace. I fear it may mark her for life."

"Clemmie, I do not profess to know a lot about this subject, but there is something I have discovered over the years. I try real hard to make a study of Lucy...I mean, to really know what she likes and dislikes. When she says or does something that I would not say or do, I try real hard to imagine just what made her do that. I try to think like she does. I guess this could be called developing sympathy, or perhaps empathy, for her. She and I have both learned to say, 'I am sorry I hurt you. I did not mean to. Will you forgive me?' And although it is hard to do, we try to forgive each other quickly. Once I read that 'slow forgiveness is about the same as no forgiveness.'"

"Raleigh, perhaps the highway business is not what you should be doing. I think you could make a great counselor or minister. I want to remember what you said and think about this and put it into practice. I'm ashamed that I have not been very obedient as a wife, and the Bible says that wives should be submissive and should respect their husbands. That is hard to do if you are not treated with love and respect."

"Well, I agree with you there. Love and respect are both reciprocal, and someone has to be the one to swallow pride and return the soft answer. I believe that is from Proverbs: 'A soft answer turneth away wrath.' Clemmie, anger just cuts love like a knife."

"I know that's right. You've helped me, Raleigh. I believe I could talk to you forever and never run out of a subject. Why is it that way, and then sometimes with John I can think of nothing to say?"

"I think that is because love has different faces, like the moon. There is new love, and then there is full-blown love. Clemmie, would you help me find my mother's grave over there? And I want to see the stones that mark your father's grave."

"Oh yes, Raleigh. I know exactly where your sweet mother lies buried. I can't count the times I've brought flowers and laid them on her grave and thought of her and of you. All those years I taught school before I married I would come here, especially in April, and place some bluebonnets on her grave. Here it is, right here."

"Yes, here it is! I'd like to replace this tombstone with a new one—this one is barely legible. Ah, she was a fine woman, Clemmie. Raised us ten children with so little of the world's goods. We always lived in tiny houses and were so poor. I wish she could have lived a long time and I could have given her all the things she did without."

"Raleigh, you gave her what all mothers desire. A son like you means more than fine clothes and a big house. *You* are your mother's legacy."

"I appreciate your compliment, but I know there's room for improvement with me. Clemmie, would you be willing to take a little drive with me down to the old swimming hole? I still remember how to go…right down the little road up there on the ridge, past the Reeves' place, then on a little piece."

"Of course I want to go with you, Raleigh. I doubt if anyone will see us. We won't need to get out of the car, will we?"

Clemmie got into the front seat of Raleigh's new-smelling car. It had a pretty dashboard and large dials and gauges. The seats were upholstered in real leather. Clemmie felt like a real lady. She wondered how it would be to be Raleigh's wife…to live in a fine two-story home in Abilene and never have a single worry about money, but more than that, to have a husband who was well-educated and respected by all, and who would not dream of talking ugly to the wife whom he adored.

The car rides as smooth as glass, Clemmie thought. *Why, one would think all the roads of Ebony had already been paved!* They went past several old houses. They passed in front of the Briley place where Burt and Hattie Briley lived. There was the very porch where Clemmie had lain on a cot, so sick the summer of 1911. It crossed her mind that it had been very loving of John to take her to Marlin for the water cure.

Wasn't it stupid that neither of us knew I was pregnant? her thoughts rambled on.

It seemed like no time at all until they were near the swimming hole. The grass had grown up around it, and it looked like no one had been swimming there in a very long time. Raleigh stopped the car on the little dirt road. There was no house, nor any sign of life anywhere around, just those familiar country noises of a dove cooing and katydids making their sizzling noise.

"I remember this as much larger…Do you think they have filled some of it in, maybe had dirt hauled in?"

"Oh, I doubt it, Raleigh. I find that everything appears smaller when I go back to visit after many years. After all, that was about forty years ago."

"It just doesn't seem possible, Clemmie. Let's get out and walk right over there to get a better view."

Raleigh hurried around to open the car door for Clemmie. As she stepped onto the running board of the car and the sunlight glinted on her brown-gray hair, Raleigh felt transported back in time. He yielded to an impulse to hold her very briefly in his arms as she stepped onto the dirt road, her small face aglow with the adoration of a lifetime, her eyes shining with love light. She nestled her head on his chest, then he held her face with both his hands, kissing her cheek.

"Forgive me, Clemmie. I couldn't resist. You are beautiful, and you represent my past to me, my roots."

"Raleigh, you probably know that you are my ideal man, and I have fantasized about you far more than I should. When things seem so hard for me in my everyday life, I seem to draw some joy from the memory of you."

They walked over closer to the muddy water. They stood together, not touching, tears gleaming in their eyes, and watched the memory of carefree kids in old play clothes and homemade haircuts jumping delightedly into the murky water. Then, without another word, Raleigh walked Clemmie around to the passenger side of the car, opened the door, and helped her into the car. They drove back to the cemetery, and Clemmie explained who now lived in the few farmhouses along the way. She told him about her dream of building her own home by Christmastime. Raleigh insisted he drive her partway back to her house, so he took her as far as the creek. He pulled over, stopped the car, and opened the door for her. With his hands on her shoulders, he looked deeply into her eyes, now brimming with tears.

"Clemmie, you have a good husband who loves you. Remember that poem you liked so long ago, 'Maud Mueller?'"

"Of all sad words, of tongue or pen, the saddest are these, it might have been," quoted Clemmie. "Yes, Raleigh, I have thought of that poem often."

"Clemmie, I feel inspired to write a poem about today. Is it okay if I send a letter to your address? Are you the one who usually gets the mail?"

"Yes, I usually manage to go by the little store on my way home from school. I will really cherish a poem from you. Being with you and the words you have said to me today have really lifted me, more than I can express. Perhaps it is not too late for another dream of mine to come true. I guess I'd better start back now, Raleigh. I hope I will see you again one of these days."

"Yes, and I hope I can manage to get that road paved for you, Clemmie. There are so many demands on us that it may not be possible for a long time, but I will give it my best effort. When I leave you, I plan to drive on south to Richland Springs and then return to Brownwood. I want to have firsthand information for our commission. "

"So good-bye for now, my sweet girl. I will think of you and pray that the good Lord will bless you in every way."

"Good-bye, Raleigh. May God bless *you* in every way."

Clemmie stood and watched the big black car as Raleigh turned it and drove cautiously down the rocky, dusty road. Then she set her face toward her own land and toward her own man and arrived at her home. A Bible verse came to her mind.

"I will lift up mine eyes unto the hills, from whence cometh my strength."

A few days later another envelope from the Texas Highway Commission was awaiting Clemmie as she checked at the little store after school. She tucked it safely inside her blouse, waiting until the gloaming on her Big Hill to read it.

POEM FOR CLEMMIE, 1934

A cameo of Paradise,
Silent city of the dead,
Bluebonnet time in Texas,
Let's meet at two, I'd said.

And there she was, that darling,
That old sweetheart of mine;
I must admit I felt a rush
As our arms intertwined;

I felt I was that boy of yore
As I clasped her to my breast;
The years of care all rolled away,
Hearts pounding in our chests;

We studied the changes
Time had wrought,
Yes, years had etched their mark;
Thank God, the eyes don't wrinkle,
And neither does the heart;

For childhood days, and first love,
We hold suspended in the mind,
That morning of our lifetime
Lies apart from ties that bind.

We went to see the old haunts,
The swimming hole…Can it be,
The same one I remembered,
Or is the change in me?

The old schoolhouse
Still standing quiet;

Listing slightly to the west;
The pump where many a barefoot lad
Showed his girl he pumped best!

My mother's grave, so silent,
Her name carved evenly in stone,
What would I give to hear her laugh
See her welcome us kids home;

But I know that part of Mother
Lives daily in my heart,
And I can hear her say to me
"Son, only do your part;

"Keep your life as sweet and pure
As when you were a boy,
Don't let the cynics jade you
Nor Satan work his ploy."

Suspended in time those two hours;
Then honor, and truth, and shoulds;
The dust of the wheels has settled...
The cows still chew their cuds.

The spring of the year and daydreams,
Fear of illness and growing old.
The pent-up desires of a lifetime,
Yet family and God and soul.

The rest of April and May would later seem to blur into a dreamy maze for Clemmie. She had committed to memory the poem Raleigh wrote for her. Was there a deeper meaning, pondered Clemmie? Did he really consider leaving his family for her? She knew the answer to that was, "No, not for a minute." It was just his way of stating what he considered most important in life. Not "feelings" at all, but one's family and one's soul, and above all, *God.*

He and I at least share the same philosophy, as far as what really matters in life. He told me some very wise things about dealing with your spouse…to try to see things from John's point of view instead of from my own. Perhaps I should keep more to myself when I disagree with John. In a sense, maybe I win a battle but lose the war.

Clemmie determined to let Raleigh's words make a difference for the good in her day-to-day life. She wanted with all her heart to write an answer of sorts to the poem Raleigh wrote her. So she spent several hours up on Big Hill composing her poem, then mailed it to Raleigh's office in Abilene.

FOR RALEIGH

A score and ten…a lifetime
Of longing for that embrace;
The spring of the year, the beauty
Of land and music and place.

No fear of interruption,
The quiet of field and cows:
Two hearts in tandem racing,
Toward edges of their vows.

Two score and four a lifetime,
Of commitment and love and mate;
So good-bye, Dear Heart, I love you,
It's God who holds our fate.

The spring of the year and daydreams—
Fear of illness and growing old;
The pent-up desires of a lifetime,
Yet Family and God and Soul.

Clemmie included a brief note with the poem.

Dear Raleigh,

I realize that I have probably enlarged the affection that you felt that day for me, but you will have to consider it my "poetic license." You will notice that I stole the last verse from your poem, purposefully, because you stated the truth of the matter better than I ever could. I wish this poem to be a final "good-bye," so please do not answer. God bless you, Raleigh, and thank you for helping me toward my largest lifetime goal—to have John as my best friend.

Your friend until time shall end,
Clementine Wilmeth Briley

The last few days of school were hard to get through, since the children were so excited as school neared its end. Jim Wilmeth's sheep were sheared in two days with three machines. It was amazing for the girls to watch. All the boys and men wanted to be involved. They all learned the technique of holding the sheep in the crook of the left arm while shearing with the right hand.

They even had a little contest to see who could shear a sheep in the shortest time. Ralph won by several seconds. Dutch came in second. Gene was really sad to be last and determined he would come out ahead the next day. He suffered a lot because he was the third son and always younger and less experienced than his brothers.

Both Clemmie and Dutch, her nephew, got their contracts signed for the next school year. What a relief that was to Clemmie. She went into high gear over plans for her house. She bargained with Jack Williams about the drilling of a well. The matter of water was always the first item when any kind of building was done in the country. Clemmie and John were in agreement over a simple four-room plan for the house.

However, several of Clemmie's relatives were discouraging her about having to go in debt for the house. To put the land in a loan was the only possible way Clemmie could see to pay for the house. Her hope was to be able to pay off the loan in a few years. There was always fear that one would not be able to make the payments and would lose the land. Clemmie prayed nightly that God would see them through.

But tomorrow will be a new beginning, a world made new. God, help me, I pray.

Mr. McCullock, the lumberman and builder, came out from Brownwood to look over the land where the house would be built, so he would be ready with his estimate. Jack Williams began to drill the Briley well on June 28, 1934. By a stroke of divine providence, President Roosevelt signed into being the Federal Housing Administration (FHA) that very same day! The purpose of this act was to insure loans made by banks and lending institutions for the construction and improvement of homes and farms. Within thirty days there would be a strong possibility of getting the much-needed loan for the house.

"Thank you, Lord," praised Clemmie.

Within two days the well was drilled down to 142 feet. It was an exciting thing to watch the drilling. There was a piece of immense equipment out there on Clemmie's land, and a little group of men, and it gave her a feeling of power.

Just think, even though I may not be worth much, I have caused this to happen right here on my land, ran Clemmie's thoughts. The drilling kept on, even after dark. Clemmie paid Jack seventy-five dollars, and he said he would drill another five feet for free. They tasted the water from the new well. It was crystal clear and delicious!

Brother Whit came out from Goldthwaite to talk with Clemmie about house plans. He seemed very efficient, very knowledgeable, and was aware of the latest happenings in Washington, including the recent FHA loans. He thought it would be wise to wait thirty more days for the new bill to go into effect. He wanted to go over with Clemmie to see the land. Once there, he said that was a beautiful place to build.

John and Clemmie made a trip to Goldthwaite to see what could be done about getting a loan to build the house. Mr. Dickerson said he would have more information for them very soon. Mr. Whit had a house plan drawn that they liked. It was a simple two-bedroom home. It had a living room with a fireplace, a kitchen with a window that would face the windmill and the barn, and a screened-in sleeping porch on the south side, with windows on the east that would catch the good night breezes, those sweet zephyrs of Mills County. There would be a bathroom between the kitchen and back bedroom, but it would not have plumbing facilities in it at first, and no electricity, of course.

Ruth and O.R. came for a short visit right before school started.

Ruth knew she must be pregnant and was very happy about it. However, she knew her mother would not see things as she did and decided to keep her happy news to herself for the time being. Of course O.R. knew and was nearly as glad as Ruth. He had faith that their money problems would work out.

Ruth blamed the fact that she did not feel well on the extreme heat of Texas in August. When they left for Bailey and O.R.'s new job, they took Grace as far as Fort Worth and Aunt Grace's home, where she would attend high school.

When everyone left Ebony, the silence closed in around Clemmie. Callie and Jim had rented a house in Brownwood so the children could finish high school there. Mamma liked to stay there some and help with the work. Even John was gone, doing jury duty in Goldthwaite. It was about the first time Clemmie had ever been alone in her house that she could remember. And she didn't like it at all.

On the ninth of October, the Ebony School began. The teachers were Miss Clemmie and Dutch Wilmeth. Clemmie felt a lot of respect for Dutch. He was like the son she wished she had had. He was nice-looking with a calm and polite manner about him, yet able to control the schoolchildren in a way that Clemmie never could.

Things were sounding more hopeful about building the house. Mr. Anderson sent the house plan and a history of the project to the Federal Land Bank at Houston, and it was approved. The next step was for Clemmie and John to sign a Mechanics Lien so the builders would be paid even before the loan came through. John got cold feet and wanted them to wait till spring. Clemmie begged and pleaded and told John that she knew God would take care of them and that they had to be in their own place by Christmas. So on October 20 they went to Goldthwaite and signed the lien. Mr. Pleas Caraway was to be their builder.

On October 26 the first load of lumber arrived on the Briley land in Ebony. It was the happiest day Clemmie could remember living through in a long, long time, perhaps with the exception of April 15.

The building began on Monday, October 29, 1934. In just a week Mr. Caraway and Mr. Clements had all the framework up. Most of the weatherboarding was on the roof.

On Friday, November 9, Clemmie was teaching and heard a strange noise on the road outside. The shades were down, so no one could see out. One of the boys ran to a window and looked out.

"Miss Clemmie, that is your windmill!"

Suddenly, the whole class was at the windows, watching the unusual scene of a windmill lying on a truck, slowly traveling to its new home on the Briley place. Clemmie felt too excited to do much more teaching that day. As she went by to see the house in the evening, they were just putting the finishing touches on the windmill. It began to pump water at once, and the water was as clear as crystal.

The next day, John and Clemmie went to Goldthwaite and then on to Brownwood. They bought their wallpaper for the kitchen and little bathroom. It was a morning glory flower design, with blue flowers and green vines. Clemmie thought it was beautiful. Then they went over to Weakley Watson's and bought the kitchen sink for $6.85.

November 14 marked the third anniversary of the Brileys arrival in Ebony. It was also the day the drought, which had begun in May, was broken. Rain fell copiously. The day before, the painter had put the first coat of paint on the new home. Clemmie had decided on a name for her new white house. She would call it "Avalon." She knew that was the name of a legendary British Isle where King Arthur was buried, and the Celtic meaning of Avalon was "Land of Apples." It also meant "Land of the Blessed" and "Rest for the Soul." Yes, this paradise on earth would be her "Avalon."

Ruth and O.R. wrote that they would be arriving for Christmas and would bring little Grace.

Oh, my cup runneth over! Thank you, Lord! So the Lord is giving me another gift—we are moving into the house on Christmas Eve!

— — — — — — — —

Christmas Eve, 1934

My dream came true! We moved into our Avalon on
Christmas Eve! All of us together—Ruth and O.R., Grace
and John and I. Marie invited us to Sunday dinner at Callie's
tomorrow so we could use today for moving and not have
to cook. Now that was very cordial of her! Ernest came this
evening and helped us put down the linoleum. We lack only
one joint of pipe having the stove put up.

The kitchen is lovely with the green and ivory linoleum
and the little breakfast nook and the green and ivory stove
and the beautiful cabinetwork. The Christmas tree is all fixed.
The living room is warm and so cozy and lovely. We bathed
in the front room in front of the fireplace with a fire going.
John and I are sleeping in the bathroom. I am so happy and
thankful. Dear God, thank you for the beautiful gift of our
own new lovely home. May we use it to your glory. Amen.

New Year's Eve, 1934

My bubble has burst. Tonight the letter came from the
Federal Land Bank saying they would *not* give us a loan on
our house. How my heart has ached since Sister Nell brought
the letter in out of the dark, cold night while we were eating
supper. John read it to me in the living room where I had
gone to light the lamp. Oh, we are beaten down and blue!

I tried to keep from showing my grief to Grace and Sister
Nell. I don't know if I succeeded. This is Grace's last night
at home. Tomorrow she has to go back to Fort Worth. Dear
Father, I look to Thee to relieve me from this burden and to
provide a way for us. In the name of Thy precious Son, Jesus,
I pray. Amen.

IN THE MORNING, WHEN THE DOVES COO

A New Year has dawned, and the sun is shining outside. Within my heart there is a terrible thunderstorm in progress—all because of the awful calamity about our loan on the house not being approved. Although my heart is full of tears, this house is so pretty that I know God is going to take care of us and open some door.

The next day, John and Clemmie went to Goldthwaite. Their first stop was at McCulloch's Builders & Lumber Yard. Clemmie beat John into the office.

"Paul, we got a letter saying our loan was not approved after all," Clemmie blurted out to the second in command.

"Well, Miz Briley, we'll just call up the appraiser and see what needs to be done, and then we'll meet the requirements," drawled Paul. About that time, Mr. McCulloch came in.

"Now, you folks need not worry. This happens all the time. It will work out just fine. We may need to include a few more acres of land in the deal. Mr. Briley, I don't want you to worry, and don't let Mrs. Briley worry either. We may have to get the appraiser out there again, but I *know* we can get approval for the loan."

Late that evening, John took one of the wooden kitchen chairs out in the front yard and turned the chair toward the house. Then he sat down and tilted it back with his feet resting on the porch steps.

"John, what are you doing out here?" Clemmie opened the front screen door, puzzled at this new behavior.

"Clemmie, for twenty-four years we've been talkin' 'bout *someday* when we have our own place on the farm, and now this is it, Clemmie. This is that *someday* we talked about. Get a chair for yerself and come on out here. Those stars are here for us t' enjoy, and there's no charge from the good Lord. Why, I kin see the Milky Way and the Big Dipper."

"Oh, look, John. The moon is on its back with a ring around it," commented Clemmie as she dragged a chair over to sit near her husband.

Several huge tarantulas appeared as if on parade. Sport had a spasm of barking at the gigantic black fuzzy spiders, then he finally gave up and settled down by his beloved master.

"John, let's try to come out here every night. It's so beautiful to sit under this huge sky in front of our own home. And to know it's really going to be ours to keep."

"Clemmie, do you like this dog o' mine, Sport?"

"I've been wanting to talk to you about him, John. Yesterday he pulled one of your best shirts off the clothesline and now it has a tear in it. I think we need to get rid of Sport. He's been digging in the rose beds, too."

"Clemmie, now you have overstepped. That shirt, the blue one, is the one I had on the day Sport took the rattlesnake bite in my place. He loves me so much that he tries to show it in ever' way. He come bringin' that shirt to me, like he wanted us to not forgit what we did for each other that day. Clemmie, this may sound goofy, but Sport is teachin' me stuff."

"Teaching you stuff?" Clemmie laughed really loud. "What kind of stuff, John?"

"Stuff like how he loves me, and how he'll always obey me, 'cause I'm his master. An' how he chose me…He didn't have t' like me…he could've run away into th' woods. But he knew that I'm the one who cares, who feeds him and watches out fer him. All he has t' do is foller me. He knows he kin trust me all the time. I won't let him down."

Clemmie was speechless. John made some good points about how an animal comes to life in a person…perhaps just the way humans come to life in Christ.

John may not use the best English, but he is quite a thinker. That is very profound, what he just said, Clemmie thought.

On Tuesday, April 2, a card arrived from O.R. Mitchell. Ruth's baby had been born—a fine girl named Marilyn, born on March 31. They had gone into the hospital in Bonham. Since Marilyn was the first baby born in the new facility, they named the nursery "Maryland" after her. Ruth had done fine and would stay a few days in the hospital. Later, a detailed letter arrived from Ruth.

Dear Mother and Papa,

Little Marilyn is really a pretty baby. She is kind of reddish, and her hair—the little that she has—is black. She has a cute pug nose and her ears are small and close to her head. She has a dimple in her chin and a roll of fat around her neck. Her feet look large for her size. She cries some when I put her in her bed. Do you think she is spoiled already?

The letter continued on with details of the birth.

Later that day there was sad news for Clemmie. She recorded it this way:

Heartbreak and tears for me tonight. Two of the trustees refused to sign my contract to hire me as a teacher, so I'm out. I saw in the *Fort Worth Star Telegram* at Brownwood today where Harry T. Hines, Wichita Falls oil operator, had been appointed by Gov. Allred to succeed Raleigh as Highway Commissioner. I wonder if it hurt Raleigh to be put out of his job as much as it did me to be put out of mine.

It was one year ago that we met in the cemetery and twenty-six years since we met on Big Hill. Ah, how the years have gone by. And the present burdens seem almost too great for me to bear. Help me, God, this I pray.

A few months later, Clemmie received a great blessing. On Wednesday night, July 3, during the summer gospel meeting, Grace Briley went forward to be baptized. Clemmie's eyes began to smart with tears to see her baby daughter make her way down to the front of the tabernacle. Another dream of Clemmie's was being realized: Her second and last child was expressing her obedience to the Lord.

Hadn't this been one of the main goals of my life, to deliver my children to the Lord and to His church?

Several others joined Grace at the front, including her first cousin, Gene Wilmeth. Brother Clark asked all seven to stand, and he asked them one question: "Do each one of you believe that Jesus is the Christ, the Son of the living God?"

"I do!" answered the seven in unison.

"The baptismal service will take place immediately following this service, in the tank just south of the building," explained Brother Clark. There was an urgency about baptism according to the belief that salvation was granted in obedience to the instruction found in Scripture.

He that believeth and is baptized shall be saved.

Mark 16:16

Two of the men went on ahead to take lanterns and to be sure there were no snakes around. The candidates for baptism waded out in the water in the clothes they had on. Heated by the July sun, the tank water was relatively warm. The people began to sing as they made their way to the tank, startling a few of the cows standing nearby. The moon was bright that night, and the strains of "Shall We Gather at the River" formed an unforgettable mental picture for Clemmie.

Grace was the first one lowered into the water, her hands clasped over her chest. Clemmie knew her child was very afraid of the process but was determined to endure it so she would be saved.

"I now baptize you into the name of the Father, the Son, and the Holy Ghost, for the remission of your sins," Brother Clark's voice boomed out in confidence.

As Grace was lowered into the murky tank water, her white dress floated to the top. As she carefully made her way back to the shore, her feet sinking into the muddy bottom, her dress clung to her slender body. She was shivering but ecstatic that she had been saved. Her face was glowing.

After the seventh baptism the congregation began to sing loudly in unison.

Oh, Happy Day, that fixed my choice,
On Thee my Savior, and my God;
Well may this glowing heart rejoice
And tell its raptures all abroad.

Happy Day! Happy Day!
When Jesus washed my sins away!
He taught me how to watch and pray,
And live rejoicing every day:
Happy Day! Happy Day!
When Jesus washed my sins away!

It was way on into the summer, on July 26, when Clemmie and John received a letter from Mr. Dew and from the Federal Land Bank telling them that the Land Bank Commissioner would loan them the $1,200 on the farm that they desperately needed to finance the house.

"Oh, John!" squealed Clemmie in delight. "It has finally happened! Avalon is really ours to keep forever and ever!" Relief and joy flooded Clemmie's soul. She ran to John and gave him her biggest "movie star hug." Oh, this was happiness, this was joy!

"Well, Clemmie, I have t' hand it to ya. I was 'bout as skeptical as your mamma, and figur'd we might lose the house and maybe the farm."

Arriving in Goldthwaite early the next morning, they went first to the First National Bank and met with Mr. Dew, their loan officer. Mr. McCullough, their builder, was already there. Both were extremely courteous. John and Clemmie signed the papers for the $1,200 loan. The total bill for the house, barn, garage, and tank came to $1,420. Mr. McCullough explained that he could take a second lien for $280. That would include the six months of interest on the whole note, which figured out to be $56.86. Then they were required to pay $28.20 for a three-year insurance policy on the place.

As they shook hands with the two men and told them good-bye, Clemmie felt such happiness well up in her heart. After all those sleepless nights and weeks and months and even years of worry, everything had worked out so well.

As John headed the car toward home, raindrops began to fall on the hot windshield. It rained on the car most of the way home, and they could see that a good rain had fallen on their land. The smell of rain on the dry, warm earth filled Clemmie with thanksgiving. God had given them two huge blessings in one day—money for their home and rain for their land.

O.R. and Ruth and Baby Marilyn arrived from Denton on Friday, August 23. O.R. was carrying a green tube that held his diploma from North Texas State Teachers College. He had received his Bachelor of Science degree the evening before. He seemed very happy about that accomplishment. Ruth was beaming with joy, knowing how much her mother admired people who finished college. Clemmie and John were so happy to get to hold their first grandchild. The three generations enjoyed a long weekend together.

Clemmie had applied for a teaching position at a nearby small town, but the job went to a younger woman.

Well, maybe I can help John wrest a living from the soil, dry and rocky as it is. Maybe my chicken and turkey money can make a difference in days to come, Clemmie consoled herself.

At supper that night something out of the ordinary happened. Somehow the subject of the Sunday morning class came up.

"You ought to teach that Bible class, Clemmie. You know a lot more 'bout the Bible than anyone else in there," stated John, crystal blue eyes flashing.

"Why, John, thank you for saying that. You could knock me over with a feather. You just gave me a very fine compliment." Clemmie felt elated. She decided she would remember this, and it would help her not feel so angry toward John.

Clemmie had always admired families who had traditions. She wanted to begin a cookie tradition now that she was a grandmother. She determined to always have cookies ready for grandchildren. She made her best sugar cookie recipe, rolled out the dough, and cut the round cookies with a big tin cup. She sprinkled the tops with granulated sugar and was careful not to overcook them. After they cooled she put them in a pretty cloth sack that sugar had come in and placed them in the second drawer from the floor on the left side of the sink. In years to come, her seven grandchildren always found their cookies waiting.

O.R., Ruth, and Marilyn came back for Christmas, bringing Grace with them from Fort Worth. On Christmas Eve the little family gathered to sing carols in the front room. O.R. was supporting Marilyn while she stood in front of him. They were singing "Away in a Manger," and suddenly little Marilyn began to toddle, hesitating after each step, across the room to Clemmie's outstretched arms. She was nearly to her grandmother when she sat down hard on the floor. She was walking alone for the first time, and she was only nine months old! Everyone began to clap, and Marilyn laughed big and clapped her little hands.

"Mother, this is our best Christmas ever," Grace stated.

A week later, on New Year's Eve, Ruth's little family had gone home and Clemmie was finishing up the supper dishes. She heard a lovely sound. John and Grace were singing "The Old Rugged Cross," and Grace was playing it on the piano. Clemmie sat down and listened, tears gleaming in her eyes.

Perhaps things are beginning to change for the better for John and me, thought Clemmie. *Dear God, by next Christmas, help John and me get along better and learn to be good friends again.*

Spring was at the threshold. That very evening Clemmie vowed in her heart that something had to change.

John and I have been married twenty-five years, and we cannot get along. It seems like the others in our family—Callie and Jim, Edna and Oll, Grace and John Bateman, and people I know in the community, get along just swell. Before I face twenty more years of this kind of fussing, I'm going to make a last effort to get to the bottom of this trouble. We need someone to give us advice that we can follow, or we can't go on. Papa is dead, and so is my brother, Campbell, so who can help us?

Just then she remembered her great-nephew, Perry Wilmeth. He was a preacher for the church and had just begun pursuing a graduate degree at Columbia University in New York City, with a specialty in home and family.

Clemmie wrote to Perry, explaining her problems and how she had no one nearby to talk to or to ask for advice. Within a week, she had a letter back.

Dear Aunt Clementine,

I was happy to get the letter from you, but sorry there is conflict in your marriage. You are not alone, but most won't seek help, so congratulations! It so happens that I'm coming that way in 2 weeks, and if it's okay we could talk face to face.

Here are some questions for you to be thinking about:

1. Why did you and John marry in the first place?

2. Why did you and John get along so well during the first 3 or 4 years of your marriage?

3. Can you and John become compatible, and enjoy each other's company, feeling at rest and peace in your own home?

Here is one suggestion for you to work with until I arrive.

When John says something you do not agree with, try to just not say anything, instead of letting him know you think his idea is absurd. Clemmie, marriage sometimes needs only a slight adjustment to make things work right.

In Christ and in family love,
Perry Wilmeth

Clemmie wrote back to Perry and told him how happy she would be for him to spend a night with them. She was afraid to tell John the real purpose of the visit but did say that Perry was coming to spend a night at Avalon.

"Perry's area of study is about the home and family, and he knows how to help people get along," she ventured to say.

"Well, it'd be good if he could he'p us, but I doubt if enybody could," John said.

Perry arrived at the time expected, and Clemmie was amazed that he looked so young. Soon after supper, John went to milk and Perry and Clemmie had a chance to talk.

"Clemmie, have you had a chance to do what I suggested about keeping some things to yourself?"

"Yes, Perry, I've tried to do that several times lately. It sure does cut down on the disagreements. And usually it doesn't make so much difference, even if I thought my idea was better. I mean that it's worth it to just keep quiet about it. And I'm feeling more like I'm in submission. You know a lot, Perry.

"Perry, about those questions in your letter—I think John and I married because we were in love. He had a previous marriage that failed, so he was looking for somebody who was religious and would stay with him. He says he always had liked me."

"And what about you, Clemmie? Was there any other beau you loved more than John?"

"Honestly, Perry, there was another man in my heart. But he jilted me for another woman. I know he's stayed in my mind like the ideal husband."

"Clemmie, no man can compete with the perfection of one's imagination. That's very strong. Imagination is stronger than our willpower. You need to ask God to take away this imagination. That's a form of adultery. If you had married the other man, you might have had just as much trouble, but that's unknown, and it doesn't matter."

"Perry, one of the questions I'd like for you to answer is that third one. Can John and I ever feel good about the other one again? Can we get those romantic feelings like we felt in the beginning?"

"Clemmie, the answer is yes, thank the good Lord! But the secret is that you must change your behavior. The way you behave toward

John is what's causing him to act like he does toward you. We feel close to each other, or we despise each other according to our behavior and our decisions."

"But Perry, is that really true? I mean, what if I act sweet, but he acts mean?"

"Yes, it's true. In fact, I want to make a wager with you. If you will actually change yourself, saying nothing about it to John, he will change also. That's a sure thing. Now, it's very hard to change ourselves, and so it's very rare to see it done."

"Well, I want to do this like you've suggested. I'm very sincere about it. Can you think of anything else I should do, Perry?"

"Yes—there are two more things. You'll need to try to recreate some of the scenes of your initial romance. For example, you'll need to fix yourself up pretty, like in the beginning. Use make-up and pretty clothes whenever you can. Even perfume seems to mean a lot to a man. He knows when you're trying to impress him, and that makes him feel special."

"Well, after so many years together, it seems kind of silly to try and be young again. Can we really go back in time?"

"Strangely, Clementine, you nearly can go back, at least the same feelings you had in the beginning of the romance can be recaptured, if you'll repeat many of the same actions.

"And Clemmie, here's the other thing—use that active imagination of yours to pretend that *you* are John. Try to feel his feelings, and try to imagine what it is like to be John. For example, you have been out-of-doors in the heat or cold all day. Is it like a little heaven on earth when you arrive home at the end of a hard day, or is your spouse fussing and griping at you, and you just wish you could be out in the barn with the animals where there's at least peace and quiet?"

Perry and John talked alone for about two hours that night. Clemmie prayed that the talk would help John to change himself.

Weeks went by, and daily Clemmie would read over the questions and answers that her nephew had left with her and that she had written down. She began to try to put some of the ideas into practice.

Near the end of April, a letter came from Ruth. There was one outstanding bit of news—Ruth was pregnant again!

Clemmie had a short cry over the plight of her daughter.

Well, she will never have another minute to call her own now. Not to mention the poverty knocking at the door since she won't be able to teach and help with the income.

The womenfolk in Ebony began to hear about a new novel that was the story of the Civil War, written by a woman in Atlanta. Word had it that several thousand copies had been sold already. Clemmie wished so much that she could buy a copy, but they said it cost three dollars, and that was way too much to spend on a book. Perhaps for her birthday, if her Sister Grace happened to ask her what she wanted, she would tell her she wanted a copy of *Gone with the Wind.* Clemmie could hardly imagine how it could be better than her favorite book to date, *Little Women.* Sometimes Clemmie still pretended to be Jo March.

Before the summer ended, Ruth and Marilyn came to the farm for a visit. John was sweet and patient with Marilyn and seemed to really enjoy carrying her around. From the kitchen, Clemmie watched with a touch of envy to see how the little girl brought out the best in John.

Why, he seems like that slender, handsome boy I knew so long ago when he's alone with his granddaughter. Marilyn was holding out her little arm and directing John toward the barn.

Clemmie had a flashback to those early days in Dallas when Ruth was the age of Marilyn. She and John had been happy then. Thinking again of Perry's words, Clemmie resolved in her heart that she would change herself, even though it seemed to her that John was the one who needed changing. Nevertheless, if what her nephew told her was right, John would change in time if she could be different in what she said and did.

Clemmie walked outside and out the back gate into the wooded area behind the house. Looking up through the mesquites, into the blue of heaven she prayed.

Oh, God, give me a sign that my only remaining dream might come true. God, give me your blessing and some small sign that John and I can be loving friends and soul mates and even lovers again. Please God, grant me this, my heart's desire.

At that exact moment, Clemmie heard the soft, sad cooing of a male dove. She looked straight up, and there on the branch of the tallest mesquite was not one but a pair of mourning doves. She knew that only God could have made that happen at that exact moment. What a beautiful symbol and promise of true love. She immediately remembered that when Jesus was baptized, the heavens opened and God's own Spirit descended in the form of a dove and perched on Him. And then the voice from heaven spoke, *"This is my Beloved Son in whom I am well pleased."*

Thank you, God, prayed Clemmie, *for giving me such a beautiful sign. Now I know that the deepest desire of my heart will come true.*

WE'LL FIND LOVE WHEN
SPRING BREAKS THROUGH

Texas was having a birthday...one hundred years since she had won her independence from Mexico and had become the Republic of Texas. So much was spent on advertising and public relations that six and a half million people visited Texas Centennial Exposition and Fair Grounds in Dallas from June 6 until November 30 of 1936.

The Wilmeths were among those visitors. Clemmie's nephew Ralph and his bride, Blanche, offered to take their car. They left at daybreak with Ralph and Jim in the front, Edna, Clemmie, and Blanche in the rear. Clemmie felt nearly giddy with the prospect of such an occasion. For her, this was real happiness. John stayed home to work and take care of the animals, which was much more to his liking. Callie wanted to stay home and visit with her sisters.

The travelers arrived in Fort Worth in the early afternoon. Mamma was already at Grace's home, taking treatment for depression. That evening Mamma, now eighty-three, and her four children, Clemmie, Jim, Edna, and Grace, and her grandson and wife, Ralph and Blanche, sat on the porch at Sister Grace's home and talked about how it must have been when their grandparents had first arrived in Dallas only ninety years before. Ralph had an idea.

"Say, folks, what if we go to McKinney tomorrow and see the old home place of the Wilmeths? It won't be much out of the way and will be something to remember."

"Oh, Ralph," said Mamma, "that is something I would treasure! I can show you children some things you may not know."

It was late morning when the little group got to McKinney. Grace drove her car and took Mamma and Edna with her. Ralph got some help from Clemmie as he neared the home of the family settlement. Finally, he drove up, right off Highway 5, into the driveway of the two-story white house that had been the home place of Nancy and Jo Brice Wilmeth so long ago.

Mamma got out of the car and began walking north. She seemed to be in a trance. The four siblings and Ralph and Blanche followed a few yards behind Mamma. The land was green and rolling, and Mamma was headed toward a grove of trees.

"Our house was in there. Right in there." Mamma pointed to the center of the grove. "Clemmie, you and Jim would play right along here in the upper garden. I didn't like for you to get too close to that water."

"Mamma, where was the little cemetery where the babies and Eugene and your sister Clementine are buried?" Edna asked.

"Right over here." Mamma pointed where there was a grouping of large rocks.

"Oh, we had three funerals in such a short time." She began to cry out loud, and just then her foot seemed to slip and she fell. It happened so quickly that no one could catch her. She went down to the ground and began to scream out as if in great pain.

"*Oh*, my hip, my hip," she moaned. By then the others were around her, not sure of what to do first. "*Oh*, Eugene, little Gene." She seemed to begin to hallucinate, and then she passed out.

"Oh, Mamma! Is she dying?" Clemmie fell to her knees and began to cry, trying to cradle Mamma's head in her lap. Jim and Ralph thought they should carry Mamma toward the car, and Sister Grace said she would drive her to the doctor's office. Clemmie said she would go too, although she was very sad to miss the picnic on the Texas Centennial Grounds.

On the way to the doctor's office, Mamma, who was lying down in the backseat with her head on Clemmie's lap, had come to and began to talk to Clemmie.

"Daughter, I may be dying, and I need to say some things to you," Mamma began.

"Mamma, you're going to be okay. Just rest right now."

"No, I must say these things. Clemmie, when you were born, I had buried Eugene, baby Matilde, and my sister the year before. I was in such pain. I think I was angry with God because of my loss. You know my life had been very unusual to that point, being born in Brazil, returning to Germany, and finally arriving in the U.S.

"Why, my own mother asked me to keep a big secret. It was that my papa was not really lost at sea. The fact was he had taken another lover and had several children with her. My mother nearly died of shame. I felt a keen sense of the loss of my father.

"Then to lose our money, to lose my mother for one year when she came to America, and later to lose her in death when she was only forty-five left me feeling very insecure in my new country of America. Meeting and marrying your papa seemed to fill me again with all that was taken from me, Clemmie.

"I want you to know that I did truly love Mr. Wilmeth. And I always loved you, Clemmie, my first child to live past the age of three. But you and your papa began to grow close with time, and you seemed to share so much that my old insecurities returned, and I felt envious of you. I felt that you took Mr. Wilmeth away from me.

"I am ashamed to say it, but I wished I were more like you. You understood the Scriptures, you could talk to your papa about the things he loved, and you could go around the state with him when he traveled. Clemmie, I am afraid I treated you differently because of my own jealousy and not because of anything you did wrong. Can you find it in your heart to forgive me, my child?" Mamma began to sob loudly.

"Oh, Mamma, of course you're forgiven. I think I always knew you loved me and that you admired the qualities that I have. It's true that I wanted to get along with you better, like Edna and Grace and Jim, but I always knew that you loved me."

Grace wheeled the big car into the clinic parking area and went in to get a wheelchair for Mamma. It turned out that Mamma was not dying; her hip was badly bruised and not broken. But the confession that day lifted a weight from Clemmie's soul, since she had always felt responsible for the lack of warmth in her relationship with Mamma.

Grace and Clemmie found all the family at Centennial Park late that afternoon. And there was a big surprise for Clemmie, too. Hiding behind a large shrub, jumping out at the right moment, were Ruth, O.R., and little Marilyn! Clemmie screamed with joy. They had such a good visit, but it was too short. Clemmie was a little appalled that Ruth would have come to the State Fair being eight months pregnant and with a little one. But women had really changed from the old days, and they didn't seem to be suffering any with all the activity.

Clemmie hugged Ruth and told her she was coming for the baby's arrival in one month. Ralph told his bunch to get in the car for the trip home, and they left in the gloaming.

John seemed happier than usual to see Clemmie that night and listened patiently to all the details. He was glad that Mamma had said what she did to Clemmie. He knew that had troubled Clemmie most of her life. He couldn't believe that O.R. and Ruth and Marilyn were there. Clemmie sat up until the wee hours composing an article to run in the *Fort Worth Star Telegram,* telling about the Wilmeths' visit to the Texas Centennial.

News about King Edward of England and his ladylove, Wallis Simpson, was always in the papers, and Clemmie had a keen interest in the subject.

"John, would you have given up being king if it had meant we couldn't marry?"

"Well, I guess I woulda done somethin' to get outta being king. I wouldn't wanna always be in the spotlight like that royal fella."

"Oh, John. I was talking about the romantic part of it. I wonder what King Edward will do. I think he should find a virgin girl and not that Simpson lady who's been married twice already."

The days passed swiftly, and the time came for Clemmie to go on the bus to Henderson, Texas, to be with Ruth during the birth. Arriving there about ten p.m., Clemmie was met at the bus station by O.R. Mitchell, who said, "Mother Briley, we are so thankful that you made this trip to help us."

When they got to the house, Ruth and Marilyn were waiting up for them.

"Oh, Ruth, I believe this baby will be a boy. You are so large," Clemmie blurted out as she gave Ruth a sideways hug, then stooped to hug little Marilyn.

"Well, I think I was equally as large with Marilyn. Mother, I'm so happy you came. You're just saving my life."

"Well, there are times when a girl just needs her mother," answered Clemmie.

"Ruth, the only day you cannot have this baby is next Thursday, the nineteenth," Marie Wilmeth announced. Marie was home demonstration agent for Rusk County. "That is the day I have to be gone for a demonstration in Kilgore. Now I want to be in on this home delivery!" Marie was twenty-seven years old and still single, and she had a strong love for babies.

Sure enough, the baby was born on Thursday, November 19. By the time Dr. Boswell arrived, Ruth was so miserable that she was tossing her head from side to side, and the veins in her neck were protruding as she gripped the wooden slats at the head of the bed. She was thinking she might die, and it would be a blessed relief.

"Now it's time to push this baby out, Mrs. Mitchell. You just push as much as you can, and I'll help just a little by placing my hand right behind this little feller."

At exactly 2:35 on Thursday afternoon, the baby emerged, crying lustily. Dr. Boswell held her up by her feet and pronounced her large, female, and as strong as a baby horse.

"Why, this little gal weighs every bit of nine and a quarter pounds! And she's pretty long, too. Must be twenty-one inches. A fine little girl! Yes-sir-re-sir."

Just then O.R. arrived home from school, and he and "Mother Briley" could hear the happy sounds of the baby's safe arrival. Soon Mary Magdalene, a neighbor who babysat for Ruth and O.R., came to the front room holding the baby wrapped in a soft pink blanket.

"Mister Mitchell, you done got yoreself a'nuther dauter. She's a fine'n, she is."

O.R. hurried to Ruth's side. "Ruth, this is another pretty little girl."

"I had hoped she was a boy for you, O.R. Maybe next time! But I already love her! The name I like best is 'Carol Jean.' Do you like that?"

379

"I do, Ruth. That name fits her just fine."

After that Clemmie had her work cut out for her. She felt relieved when it was time to get back home. Marie took Clemmie as far as Waco where they visited Mamma's brother, Alfred Schulz, and then Clemmie caught a 5:45 p.m. bus for Goldthwaite.

The only other passenger got off right out of Waco, leaving Clemmie and the driver. The road was awful and all cut up from rains. Then there was a blowout and a broken spring, delaying the trip by about an hour. Clemmie took advantage of the time alone to think about her life and to try to make some plans to change things for the better as far as getting along with John.

While at Ruth's one afternoon, Clemmie had read a magazine story that involved a fine woman who felt she had married the wrong man. Her husband did not treat her right at all. An earlier beau reappeared in her life and was always in her mind. In the end she left her family, losing her precious daughter to her husband's custody. After she married the romantic beau, she became disillusioned in that he expected her to constantly wait on him and be at his beck and call.

He never took her out, nor was he a very good lover like she had thought he would be, and furthermore, he was the silent type and never talked to her. The poor woman ended up despising the second husband, crying herself to sleep every night, and wishing she had never left the first one. Because of her religious faith, she feared she might end up in hell with the devil and his angels. Oh, what regret! The last line of the story was: "So make a bouquet of the roses in your own garden. Never covet nor steal roses from the garden of a friend."

Dear Lord, prayed Clemmie as she bounced in the bus, rolling home toward her destiny, *please, please let me appreciate all the good things about my life and all the fine qualities that John has. Please take from my mind those fantasies and daydreams of Raleigh. Let me always realize that John's short temper does not mean he does not love me, nor that he wants to hurt me, but rather that he has been hurt and is just trying to defend himself from more disappointment.*

Without knowing why it happened, Clemmie began to hum and think of the words of that old song she had loved, "In the Gloaming."

It must be because it is *the gloaming,* she thought. *That song is too sad, like too many lives. I think I'll write a third verse and make it a happy ending. Songs and lives should end happily, I believe.*

She took a small notebook and a pencil from her purse. She first thought about the gloaming and what it meant to her and what she remembered reading that the Scots and Irish had to say about "gloaming." Then she thought about her life with John and how they had been through so many hard years with no money, and how it seemed they were losing their first love and all was blue. Then she thought of the ending of the magazine story…about making a bouquet from the roses in your own garden. She remembered the words Perry Wilmeth had written her. With many attempts and strikeouts, she finally had words that she felt were right.

In the gloaming, oh my darling,
When the night meets gold of day,
And they say God shows His face, love,
Walks with us in cool of day;
Through the winter hard and cruel,
We were beaten down and blue;
In the morning, when the doves coo,
We'll find love when spring breaks through.

Clemmie had worked with the words and rhyme scheme for nearly an hour, and the gloaming had turned into night. Tears slid down her cheeks as she read over the words she had written. Finally, she felt happy with the verse.

By now Clemmie could see the lights of Goldthwaite. As the brakes screeched at the little store that also served as the bus station, she spotted a lone car, an old Ford with an opaque windshield, and a slender man in overalls and a straw hat leaning against the car, bright moon overhead. And Sport had come and was running toward Clemmie to welcome her home.

Clemmie gathered up her belongings and nearly tripped in her haste to meet John. John embraced her almost like a movie star hug, Clemmie thought. The smell of Bay Rum aftershave and those smiling crystal blue eyes were the light of home to her.

They drove the twenty-three miles home with Clemmie talking most of the time about Ruth, the new fat baby, the pleasant little white cottage, the gentlemanliness of O.R., the way Marie had shown her around, the bus trip home, and everything Clemmie could think to tell.

"Was li'l Marilyn good to the new baby?" inquired John.

"Oh yes, she seems real proud. Once she stuck a candy cane in the baby's mouth and wanted us to come see how her baby likes candy!"

It was ten o'clock when they crossed the creek and drove up to their own little cottage in the country. The bright, full moon was directly over their house. John gathered up Clemmie's suitcase and purse and magazine. Sport was jumping up on Clemmie, wagging his tail as fast as he could. Stepping inside her own home, Clemmie seemed to feel like she was a whole person and was so glad to be back home.

John looked down at her face and saw that it was totally lit up with her smile.

"Home was not a home without a woman in it," he said with embarrassment. Leading her into the bedroom, she squealed with delight.

There were hundreds of red rose petals all over the clean white sheets! Looking closely at the huge petals and deep red color, Clemmie realized those were not just any old rose petals...those were petals from John's beloved Kentucky Rose, the one that had been grown from a cutting of his mother's rose.

Her eyes brimmed with tears. John scooped her up in his arms, lifting her until their eyes were at the same level.

"Julia Clementine Wilmeth Briley, I've loved you since you were fourteen years old. You and I've been through the wars together. I don't know why we've had to fuss an' fight like a cat and dog for all these years. For my part, this is gonna be a new time for me and you. By Jove, we're gonna get along and enjoy what life we've got left together!"

"Oh, John. You're saying just what I needed to hear! I've been thinking about us trying to make a new start, making some changes.

"John Robert Briley, I promise in my heart of hearts to stop fussing at you, to even begin to like it that you think different from me. Maybe it's not right and wrong…it's plain ol' *different*. Maybe it's man-and-woman-type differences."

"Now, Clemmie, let's go see what I put on the table."

"Hubby, my sweetheart, could we try out our rose-covered bower, our bed, first?"

"Clemmie, I've waited a mighty long time for it t' be *your* idea."

Clemmie lay awake for about an hour after John was lightly snoring. She began to formulate a plan.

What if John and I were to really try to get along with each other? Wasn't it a fact that God made people so they could change? Animals can't, but people can!

What if I could be as happy with John and love him as much as I've loved Raleigh in my imagination? What if John treated me with such kindness that I'd begin to long for his touch? Why live and die with such mental anguish if there's a way to change, a higher road to travel? Why have I missed out on the joy of having an understanding friend living with me instead of an angry enemy?

My own brother and my educated nephew both thought my behavior has an awful lot to do with my situation. To me it's seemed like John has a lot of character flaws. I guess he thinks that I'm more flawed—that I'm fussy and selfish and strong headed. So who's right? Can we fix ourselves if we really want to, or is it impossible?

The next morning after the milking and early chores were done, Clemmie was still pondering thoughts from the night before. She sat down at her library table in her bedroom and bowed her head in prayer, asking God to guide her to some Scripture that would give her more wisdom. Then she opened her Bible near the middle and let her eyes fall on a certain Scripture.

> Come unto me, all ye that labor and are heavy laden, and I will give you rest. Take my yoke upon you and learn of me; for I am meek and lowly in heart, and ye shall find rest unto your souls. For my yoke is easy and my burden is light.
>
> Matthew 11:28–30

Clemmie knew that the religious world called this "The Great Invitation" of Jesus. She read the passage again. She felt like a light was turning on in her head.

Jesus was saying that if we come to Him, and learn about him— namely that He is meek *and lowly in His heart, that we will find rest for our souls. It is implied that if I will become like Jesus, meek and lowly, I will find the rest I seek.*

Clemmie had studied the true meaning of *meek* in the past. She opened up the dictionary that she kept on the library table. She read that *meek* meant "gentle, kind to others, humbly patient or submissive, tame." She remembered her papa saying once in a sermon that "meek was like a powerful horse that had been broken and now was easily controlled with the bit in his mouth."

Learning to be like Jesus is like having a control in your mouth and in your spirit. That is what has been lacking in me, and that is why I have not found rest in my soul, nor true happiness in my marriage to John.

I can change this part of me. Through the power of Jesus living in me, I can learn to act in a way that would be meek. I can stop putting my own strong desires and feelings ahead of everything else and especially above whatever thoughts John has on the matter. I have always felt in my heart that I know more and that I know better how to do everything.

I have not been in submission to my husband, and the results have been disastrous for our marriage. This can change, and it can start right now. Something tells me this will not be easy, but I am going after the soul rest that Jesus will let me find.

Within the hour Clemmie's new resolve was put to the test. John came rushing into the house, calling her in his angry voice, "Clemmie! Clemmie! Didn't I tell you to pen up Rosemary and her calf early this morning? Now they have both disappeared and are probably dead somewhere. I wish you would do what I ask you to just one time."

Clemmie bit the end of her tongue gently before she answered. "John, I'm so sorry. Because I was on my way to milk, I actually forgot to do as you asked. Please forgive me, and let's go in opposite directions and find Rosemary. I know where she likes to go and rest."

For the first time in her life, Clemmie could see John's viewpoint and did not feel sorry for herself that he was so angry. Sure enough, Clemmie found the ailing cow with her calf and brought her into the lot so John could doctor her. John told Clemmie he was sorry he had been so "riled up" and thanked her for finding the cow. His blue eyes twinkled with wonder as he seemed to notice some difference in her. He even gave her a little "love pat" on her backside.

In the evening, Clemmie told John that she had a new understanding of a verse in the Bible, and she was going to try to change herself. She asked John if he would agree to something.

"John, what if we let the next three and a half months be like a trial for the new me. Then, in mid-April, when the bluebonnets are blooming, let's have a sort of date to go up on Big Hill. I'm going to have a surprise for you then."

"Well, if you want to. Sounds kinda mysterious, but that's something I like about you. Always a little bit of the quaint in you, ol' girl!"

The weeks went by, and Clemmie had plenty of chances to try out her newly found *meekness*. Sometimes she disappointed herself when her old nature returned and she answered John sharply and then cried loudly in self-pity. But other times she was pleased that she controlled her own spirit, answered softly, and a terrible argument was avoided. Maybe she had begun her journey to Avalon—"rest for the soul."

The miracle of spring began to happen once more in the hills of Mills County. The old, dead-looking branches sprouted little lime green leaves, and the rocky ground brought forth little wildflowers. The mockingbirds began to sing their varied songs, and the cooing of the doves could be heard in the land, reminding Clemmie of a certain verse in the Bible.

> For, lo, the winter is past, the rain is over and gone; the flowers appear on the earth; the time of the singing of birds is come, and the voice of the turtle dove is heard in our land.
>
> Song of Solomon 2:11,12

Clemmie had chosen the day for the date with John, and, of course, it was April seventeenth, the very day that she had arranged the date with Raleigh so long ago. In fact, it had been twenty-eight years ago to be exact, when she had been twenty-eight years old. And now she was fifty-six and John was sixty.

"John, today is our date. Do you remember?"

"Of course I do. What time d'ya wanna go, Clemmie?"

"Could we meet up on the hill instead of going together, John?"

"Well, okay, if you want to, but it seems kinda silly. So you wanna walk?"

"Yes, I need a little time to think and pray. So will you meet me in the gloaming on Big Hill?"

"I'll be there, li'l mystery girl."

She dressed carefully for the occasion, wearing a young-looking jumper that was blue-checked with a pretty white blouse. She fixed her hair in a becoming style and put on a little bit of make-up and perfume. She packed a picnic basket with fried chicken and biscuits and two slices of apple pie for dessert. She also fixed a bag containing the faded green coverlet and two of the letters John had written her when she was in Ochiltree.

Clemmie left Avalon in midafternoon, wanting to have plenty of time to think and pray as she walked the three miles to the hill. She thought carefully through all the things she had learned, all that Perry had told her, all of the Bible verses on the subject, and tried to plan how she wanted to be when she met John on Big Hill. Clemmie arrived first and climbed to the rocky top, watching the ground carefully. Her knees and hips hurt a little with the degenerative arthritis that she had inherited from Mamma.

Just as the sun was sinking in the west, Clemmie heard John's familiar Ford truck approaching. Looking down, she saw the top of a very familiar straw hat, and under it a slender man, suntanned and dressed in overalls. A short-haired white dog was right at his heels. Clemmie watched as John and Sport easily climbed the hill.

Arriving at the top, he spotted Clemmie, and she signaled for him to come where they could see the best view of the river. Taking Clemmie in his arms, John said simply, "Clemmie, do you love me?"

"Why, John, what a question! After all these years!"

"I've always felt jealous of that other guy…that Riley fella," John admitted.

"He was nothing more than a fantasy to me…a childhood friend who never loved me," Clemmie replied, knowing her statement was not entirely true. Then Clemmie decided to add, "And John, I have also been jealous of Nancy Harris and the way she knew how to love you in the beginning."

"Clemmie, you should never be jealous of that woman. She was a hellcat, and she done me wrong. She had no upright trainin' in the Bible and all like you, Clemmie. Do you think we could start over? I mean, stop all this fussin' and fightin' and try to understand why the other one acted that-a-way?"

"John, to be your best friend would be my most precious dream coming true." Her statement was the truth, Clemmie felt. "Don't you think I have done a lot better these past three or four months, John? I have tried hard to be meek and think how *you* must feel instead of just thinking of myself and feeling sorry for myself."

"Yes, there's been a big diff'ence, and I'm a-gonna make some changes, too."

He held out his arms to her, and Clemmie flew into his embrace. Pulling her closer, he squeezed her so tight it took her breath. She caught herself before she yelled at him. Instead, she tilted back her head, closed her eyes, and felt his warm lips on hers. As he slightly opened his mouth, she felt a sudden rush of the almost forgotten "liquid fire." It was only the second time in her life she had felt that way.

EPILOGUE

Easter Sunday, April 18, 1954
(Seventeen years later)

Dear Diary,

We are leasing our place and moving to El Paso to live with Grace and Bill. John just sold his beloved horse, Don, for $50. Everything has such a finality to it. I feel like my life is ebbing away. Yesterday the cattle were sold for $2,449. The place was leased for $576. I could have died last night

Today dawned beautiful and clear and God gave me a gift—a beautiful ray of sunshine. Raleigh came to church and sat by John and me! The reason was motivated by my efforts to get new stones on all the graves, including Raleigh's own mother's grave. I had told him in a letter that today would be a good time to come down and locate the grave. Sure enough, he arrived in a brand new black Cadillac with a friend.

He almost hugged me, and my heart skipped a beat. I would not have known him (age has changed him) except for the big black car. After worship I spread a lunch in the tabernacle for Raleigh, John and me, and Raleigh's friend from Abilene.

After we ate and found Elizabeth Ely's grave, we stood there with our memories. When I looked at Raleigh, I saw two tears sliding down his cheeks. He said to me, "This was one of the two greatest traumas of my life, losing my mother when I was only fourteen and giving up Lucy in her late fifties."

Raleigh wanted the four of us to go see the swimming hole. He asked me if I would sit in the front with him. I did, fearing the aftermath of John's anger. In the end, John did not act ugly at all. He seemed to enjoy it as much as I did! Raleigh had brought a beautiful pot of lavender chrysanthemums for his mother's grave, but he said he wanted me to have them. They are sitting here on the table by me.

This has been a great day. I have so wanted to see Raleigh again just to talk with him as friend to friend for old time's sake, and for it to be all right. It all happened just right. I have found my Avalon, my "rest for the soul." Even though John and I are leaving our beloved Avalon, I *know* we will come home again.

April 20, 1954

Dear Diary,

John was gone to town all day. He got home and found me watering the yard. He asked me if I had something to tell him.

I said, "No, why do you ask?"

"I saw Riley at the cemetery when I passed by. There was a truck and some men unloading the new monument for his mother's grave."

I said, "Well, he didn't come here." He continued being sweet.

"I bought you a car today. It is a 1949 Black Chevrolet. It cost me the pickup and $400. It sure looks nice. A man will bring it out tomorrow."

I could have fainted! I looked at the purple flowers and smiled to myself. Then I gave John a movie-star hug. Then I prayed a prayer of thanksgiving to God.

Dear Lord, Thank you for giving John Thy ability to forgive. Lord, forgive me for hurting John through the years. I thank Thee for making John my best friend at long last. Now my dearest dream has come true.

— — — — — — — — —

Clara Antonia Schulz Wilmeth: June 3, 1853- June 24, 1939. Clemmie's mother lived on three continents: born in Brazil on June 3, 1853, was taken back to Germany by her mother in 1861, came to the U.S. in 1870, married J.R. in 1875, and died in Ebony on June 24, 1939, at age eighty-six. She lies beside her beloved "Mr. Wilmeth." She was a teacher, a wife, and a grandmother.

Clementine Wilmeth Briley: November 7, 1880–May 23,1968. Clemmie and John had many happy years in Ebony on the farm at Avalon. Her seven grandchildren adored her, and there were always sugar cookies in that certain drawer in the kitchen. Grace and family invited Clemmie and John to move to their home in El Paso in mid-1954. John and Clemmie would drive home to Avalon from El Paso every summer when school was out as long as they were able. Clemmie received honors from the *Brownwood Banner* and the *Goldthwaite*

Eagle for faithfully writing a column called "The Ebony News" for twenty-seven years. *Progressive Farmer* honored her with a plaque for being the *Star Scribe of the South, 1952.* Clemmie was placed in a nursing home in El Paso for the last year of her life and died of renal failure on May 23, 1968. Her body was taken to her beloved Ebony Cemetery, where she rests in peace beside her true love, John.

John Robert Briley: October 2, 1876–January 20, 1967. John loved farming and raising cattle and was good at it. Money was always as scarce as rain in Mills County. I remember Grandad teaching Bible class on Sunday morning in freshly starched khakis in the same school building where Clemmie and Ruth taught school. He was the best as a grandfather. He took us to the field with him and let us drink cold water from his leather pouch. He rode his horse until he was nearly seventy eight years old. He died of a cerebral hemorrhage in El Paso on January 20, 1967, when he was ninety years old, and was buried in the Ebony Cemetery.

Walter Raleigh Ely: April 3, 1878–January 31, 1978. Ely practiced law in Abilene after our story ends. He is credited with helping transform the Texas Highway Department into a model of efficiency, integrity and service, and began the beautification of parks and roadsides in Texas. Abilene honored Judge Ely on his ninety-sixth birthday, April 3, 1974, with "Judge Ely Day." A principle street in Abilene was named "Judge Ely Boulevard, and a tall downtown building is named the Ely Building. Judge Ely's secretary for twenty-five years said he was the kindest and most honest man she ever knew. I talked to Judge Ely in 1974. I told him my grandmother held him in high honor all her life. He said she was a very good friend and a smart woman. He died two months before his one-hundredth birthday. The funeral procession traveled on Judge Ely Boulevard to the Elmwood Cemetery in a final gesture of honor to the beloved judge.[5]

Ruth Wilmeth Briley Mitchell: March 27, 1912–July 16, 1994. Clemmie and John's firstborn daughter, Ruth, had five children, including three more after the book ends—Marilyn, Carol Jean, Robert, Jill, and Jan. O.R. and Ruth moved to Beaumont, Texas, in 1941. O.R. worked for Mobil Oil as a chemist and was an elder in the Church of Christ for twenty-seven years. Ruth taught school a total of seventeen years and loved being a wife, mother, and grandmother of eighteen. She developed Alzheimer's disease at age sixty-eight and died on July 16, 1994, in a nursing home in Edmond, Oklahoma. She was buried at Ebony beside her beloved O.R., her "Mitchell Man."

Grace Wilmeth Briley Belich: July 11, 1920. Clemmie and John's second daughter, Grace, graduated from CIA, now TCU, with her degree in Music Education. She met William Anthony (Bill) Belich while he was in the army, stationed at Camp Bowie in Brownwood. They married December 24, 1943. Bill got his BBA from Texas Tech University in Management. They spent most of their working years in El Paso, Texas, where Bill managed a Western Auto Store and Grace taught music in public school. At retirement, Grace and Bill remodeled Clemmie's home in Ebony and moved to the farm. The Beliches have two sons and daughters-in-law, Bill and Charlotte, and John and Ruth, co-heirs of the Briley farm at Avalon. Bill and Charlotte have put the farm at Avalon back into operation. Grace lives in a nursing home in Brownwood and is eighty-eight years old. Grace has three grandsons and one great-grandson.

Riverside Farm: Purchased by Fred and Shirley Wendlant in 1981, they improved it as a game preserve and built a lovely rock home on the exact spot where the original Wilmeth home stood. Looking toward the west, the 1913 Wilmeth home can be seen, now used as a hunters' lodge in season, with a birdwatcher's paradise with marked trails for bird-watching.

ABOUT THE AUTHOR

Carol Vinzant graduated from Abilene Christian University with a B.S. in Home Economics in 1957. The main street of ACU is named for the man who jilted Clemmie, Judge Ely Blvd. Carol found the type of man she wanted...a tall preacher—Don Vinzant. They have been given fifty-two years of marriage, four grown kids, and eight nearly grown grandchildren. Carol and Don have been missionaries to Brazil and Don has preached in several churches in Oklahoma and Texas, as well as teaching Bible at OC in Oklahoma City. Carol wishes she lived on a farm like Clemmie did and that her grandchildren could know those types of pleasures, but times change. Thankfully, what really matters remains constant, and that is God and his Son, his Spirit, and his Word. Everything else is nothing. Clemmie knew this secret, and she would be happy to know that she helped even one person with her story.

ENDNOTES

1   Robertson, Mary L. "Judge." *Abilene Reporter News.* April 2, 1978, page 19A.

2   *Dallas Morning News.* October 31, 1909.

3   "Abilene Judge Offered Place on Appeals Board." *Dallas Morning News.* November 18, 1926.

4   *Dallas Morning News.* October 9, 1930.

5   "Hundreds Pay Tribute to Judge Ely." *Abilene Reporter News.* February 4, 1978.

LIVE

---

listen|imagine|view|experience

AUDIO BOOK DOWNLOAD INCLUDED WITH THIS BOOK!

In your hands you hold a complete digital entertainment package. Besides purchasing the paper version of this book, this book includes a free download of the audio version of this book. Simply use the code listed below when visiting our website. Once downloaded to your computer, you can listen to the book through your computer's speakers, burn it to an audio CD or save the file to your portable music device (such as Apple's popular iPod) and listen on the go!

How to get your free audio book digital download:

1. Visit www.tatepublishing.com and click on the e|LIVE logo on the home page.
2. Enter the following coupon code:
   5a4b-f7a2-7fe1-7b9f-6743-e6c4-3050-964c
3. Download the audio book from your e|LIVE digital locker and begin enjoying your new digital entertainment package today!